The Tall Tales of Tatiana Blue

Previous books by Mr Oh:

L & I

The Train

Seven Floors

Little Black Book Volume One

Little Black Book Volume Two

Little Black Book Volume Three

The Tall Tales of Tatiana Blue

Mr Oh

Mr Oh

2017

Copyright © 2017 by Mr Oh

All rights reserved. This book or any portion thereof may not be reproduced or used in any manner whatsoever without the express written permission of the publisher except for the use of brief quotations in a book review or scholarly journal.

First Printing: 2017

ISBN: 978-0-244-64039-2

www.mroh.co.uk

Ordering Information:
Special discounts are available on quantity purchases by corporations, associations, educators, and others. For details, contact the publisher.

U.K. trade bookstores and wholesalers: Please contact Mr Oh via email misterohyes@gmail.com

Dedication

This book is dedicated to all shoe lovers who feel they deserve all the shoes in the world!

The Tall Tales of Tatiana Blue

Acknowledgements

First of all: thank you so much for purchasing this book. This adventure has been six years in the making and I cannot convey how happy I am that you have it in your hands.

Thanks to anyone who has ever supported me in this journey of shoe-discovery or asked me 'when is Miss Blue coming out?'. This book was a lot of fun to write and Miss Blue is such an enthralling character to even think of so I hope you enjoyed her story as much as I did making it.

Big thank you to Nancy aka the real Maya for her inclusion and anyone who embraced the spirit of Tatiana Blue. Thanks to Mark for taking an amazing cover and my cousin Elizabeth for letting me use her shoes and her stairs. Massive, absolutely gigantic, gargantuan thanks to Natasha for being Miss Blue with those boots and Cocoa Brown (love this name) for facilitating.

Massive shout to the editors and of course, the biggest shout out has to go to Tatiana Blue herself for allowing me to write this story with only minor injuries.

Any questions you have about the story, please direct them to Tatiana Blue herself:

Twitter: Tatiana_bluey

Instagram: tatiana_bluey

Mr Oh

Final thanks goes out to you the reader. You are the reason I write these books and continue to do what I do. I hope you enjoy this book and the following books to come in the Chocolate Network.

Mr Oh

The Tall Tales of Tatiana Blue

Foreword

Kisses and sexy slippers to all of you who made the right decision in buying this book about me, the great Tatiana Blue.

Now before you dig in and learn a whole heap about me and my criminal life - as well as the sexiest shoes on the planet - I just wanted to say a little something to the shoe lovers out there. Each of every one of these shoes are real. Believe me, I know.

They exist. They are highly priced, beautiful, feel good on my feet (being free) and are out there for you shoe lovers who simply appreciate a damn good shoe.

If you love shoes as much as I do, you will love the fuck out this book. Oh, by the way, my language is the epitome of disgusting so, be warned... I swear a lot.

I don't want to say too much... I want you to fall in love with me all by yourself. And you will... I'm a lot to love. Maybe a few violent, taser-addicted tendencies but still, a lot to love.

Oh yeah, and fuck Marcus!

You'll see why!

And remember: a bitch ain't a hole for a man to feel, a bitch is a beauty in tremendously cute heels.

Mr Oh

Enjoy The Tall Tales of Tatiana Blue.

See you in there...

Tatiana Blue

The Tall Tales of Tatiana Blue

Disclaimer

All shoes stolen in this book are real.

Any crimes committed in this book may or may not have happened in real life.

Mr Oh

Moment of Blue

A tall woman in a three quarter length mac was looking through a throng of shoe shoppers, at a curly-haired female who was desperately trying to force a pair of shoes into her hand bag while shaking her head.

First timer, she thought.

Maya Delasouzé's eyes darted between the security guard walking amongst the crowd and the staff who were serving customers. She wasn't watching the public as customers passed her while she hurriedly stuffed the pair of black Charlotte Olympia heels into her giant handbag.

'Damn it,' she muttered. 'This is the first store that had them in my size. And both on display.'

Maya subtly pulled the heels out of her bag and put them back on the display, but, as she looked up, she noticed the wandering guard had walked off in another direction.

'Hmmm perhaps I could fit it under...' she said, picking up the shoes again. She nervously looked around and saw the nearest shop assistant was moving into the stockroom, before tucking the shoes under her jumper. Maya kept manoeuvring so they didn't protrude, but she couldn't make it work as people passed around her.

The Tall Tales of Tatiana Blue

Tatiana Blue looked on in disbelief at the poor soul struggling to conceal the shoes underneath her jumper and didn't know whether to laugh or help the young woman. Finally, she walked over.

The tall woman with the full head of short blue-tipped dreadlocks strolled over, passing staff, customers and displays upon displays of beautiful shoes. She walked behind the hunched over woman and turned until they were back to back.

'Put them down and leave, now!' Tatiana said in a hushed voice. Maya looked up in a panic and could only see the back of a woman who was taller than her.

'Put them back!' Tatiana said more assertively through gritted teeth. Maya slowly removed the heels from underneath her jumper and put them back on the display case whilst looking straight ahead. There was something about the way the woman was watching everyone in the shop at the same time while keeping an eye on Maya's antics. In her mind, she had just been caught by a store manager and was on her way to the police station; all for the love of shoes.

'Good. Now, close your bag and leave!' Tatiana ordered.

Maya was stuck in place as she looked at the floor, still in shock. She seemed to have lost the ability to move or speak and, even though she sent the order from her brain, her body refused to follow.

'I won't tell you again,' said Tatiana, walking around Maya with a steel look in her eyes.

Mr Oh

She stood so close; Maya could smell the perfume on her neck. Something about the air of the woman made Maya back away slowly before turning and running out of the shop.

Tatiana chuckled to herself. She knew she had scared the poor lady senseless but amateurs frustrated her. Besides, she'd make it up to her. After all, she did manage to slip her purse out of her bag before she ran.

'She looks like a five and a half,' Tatiana muttered as she ran a finger along the shoe before walking out.

Mr Oh

Tatiana's blue shoes

*T*atiana Blue was her.

Dreadlocks with blue tips reaching the back of her neck, sitting in a single leather chair naked in a pair of Charlotte Olympia heels, staring at the 50-inch TV she didn't turn on.

One leg was bouncing in anger and a large wine glass in her hand was swirling pink liquid while silence filled her living room.

She was looking at her distorted reflection in the screen, thinking about her life and what a piece of shit it had become. How all the happiness of her regular life seemingly washed away with the rain that was pounding the windows of her Stratford flat.

Her mind was switching like a TV from one channel to the next.

Marcus was on channel one.

The carcasses of her dead shoes were on channel two.

The colour red was on channel three.

Work was on channel four.

The corner of her mouth sneered as she sipped the rum and rosé she had in her glass. Tonight, she was drinking to forget.

The Tall Tales of Tatiana Blue

She was hoping the memories of the last few weeks would disappear and she could live for five minutes without wanting to lash out at the nearest person to her.

It was that moment, with her mind still flicking through the channels of her angry thoughts, that she looked down at her feet and everything stopped. Looking back at her was a pair of Charlotte Olympia all-black suede peep-toe heels that were curved around her feet like silk at a cost of £879.

The sky blue colour on her toes wiggled back at her and, for the second time in a long time, Tatiana felt good. And with the emotional war she had going on inside, it was a miracle to be able to find anything to smile about. Yet here she was, naked with a stinging combination of *Echo Falls* rosé and *Wray and Nephews* rum burning her chest, staring at the brand new pair of shoes on her feet that she did not pay for.

She brought her leg up and stroked the shoe, feeling goose bumps rise on her skin. Her nipples rose and she licked her lips at the first pair of shoes she had in her possession since the "incident".

The moment of adulation and fantasy was broken by the sound of her phone ringing. She jumped, watching a splash of drink rise out of her glass. Aiming the glass perfectly, she caught the liquid back in the glass and answered her phone with a tiny grin.

She instantly recognised the number.

'Hey,' she said, trying to mask the misery in her voice.

Mr Oh

'Hey, hi, look...' said a very excited Maya. 'Do you know how much I LOVE you right now? These shoes are absolutely amazing. I wore them out today for the first time and I'm telling you, I'm turning heads.'

Tatiana sat up, knowing it would be rude to cut Maya off in her excited state. Really she wanted to tell her she wasn't in the mood to talk, hang up and return to the staring competition she was having with her reflection in the TV screen.

Instead, she encouraged her excitement.

'I know,' Tatiana said, lifting her heeled foot. 'I'm wearing mine now and... they are just too sexy for words.'

Or clothes, she thought.

'I cannot thank you enough... I swear, you have no idea how much I love you right now,' Maya gushed.

'It was no problem at all. I imagine you didn't think you'd see them again.'

'Hell no, I thought when I left the place, that was it. And I didn't even notice my purse was gone... anyway, that's not why I called. What are you doing tonight?'

Maya caught her off-guard and Tatiana stumbled on herself, stuttering while making random noises.

'Erm... I er... well... tonight? I'm not... erm... doing anything.'

As the words left her mouth, she instantly regretted saying them. She wanted to stay naked in her shoes and stare at herself. Be alone with her

The Tall Tales of Tatiana Blue

thoughts and plans of what type of revenge to deliver to the most evil person she had ever known.

And drink her ass off while doing it.

'I'm having a house warming tonight and what better way to say thank you than to invite YOU! Please say yes, please please please...'

Socialising wasn't something Tatiana saw herself doing that night. She wasn't in the right frame of mind to converse and talk about society's this and the world's that, whilst her shoes were probably still smouldering somewhere.

Stealing another look at her feet, Tatiana sighed heavily, feeling the pressure of a rock and a hard place.

'It sounds like you won't take no for an answer will you?'

'What's no? You're coming. I'm gonna text you my address. Come around 8pm. And, AGAIN, thank you thank you thank youuuuuu...'

Tatiana blushed. 'It's alright; I just didn't wanna see you get arrested for some rookie shit. Pretty girls like you should be wearing shoes, not locked up for stealing them. Anyway, I'll... I'll come tonight, okay? You can turn your beg machine off, I'll be there.'

'Sweeeeeeeeeet,' Maya said. 'See you later then. Peace out.'

Tatiana hung up, looked at the time and suddenly felt under pressure. With under two hours until she had to be at Maya's, she had to find a way to snap out of her funk of anger and transform into Tatiana the socialite. First, she had to turn on her dress mode thinking.

Mr Oh

'For fuck sake...' she said to herself as she took her shoes off, held them with two fingers and walked to her bedroom while taking an extra large sip.

To have to interact with other people and seemingly take an interest in their lives when her own was in such disarray would need another glass of her wine and rum concoction.

By the time she reached her bedroom, her mind was in full-on, if not slightly tipsy, dress-up mode. She was mentally connecting skirts, jeans and trousers she owned to go with t-shirts, blouses and dresses. But if they ultimately didn't go with the Charlotte Olympia shoes, they were not an option.

By the time she opened her wardrobe, she had her choices narrowed down to one that would mirror her emotional state.

Reaching for a pair of her extremely fitted jeans, a Michael Jackson *Bad* t-shirt and her black trench coat, Tatiana laid them on the bed.

Another long sip of her drink while staring at her possible outfit brought a rush of calm over her that she hadn't felt since Marcus found that picture in her phone and her world unravelled from there.

'Thinking about that prick won't help me be sociable tonight.' Tatiana downed the half a drink left in her glass, burped then walked off to the shower, slapping herself on the backside, just to feel the sting and hear the sound.

She liked both.

The Tall Tales of Tatiana Blue

Tatiana took a long shower with jojoba and lime for her skin and linseed oil for her six-month old dreadlocks, which were starting to tickle the nape of her neck.

Although initially she didn't want to go out, now she was lost in the groove of Darrius Willrich's *Can't Get Enough* which was playing on her phone.

With hot water dropping down her back and between her cheeks, the idea of going out didn't seem so daunting. Though she knew who would be popping into her head periodically.

He had the power to do that.

He gave himself that power and Tatiana knew she let him.

The song was interrupted by a text message but it didn't stop the Tatiana Blue dance as she turned the shower off and swung her towel above her head while dipping and rising with the beat.

While she was throwing shapes and beginning to feel the remnants of happiness growing again, she gave no thought to her self-imposed work sabbatical, or her dead shoes.

Instead she was head nodding like a bass player lost in a neo-soul groove.

Astral for her skin, White Diamonds for her neck, wrists and behind her ears and she was dressed in her heels and ready to leave in 20 minutes. No make-up.

Mr Oh

She danced her thick thighs into her jeans, grunting and heaving to slide them over her hips.

At the door, she put her scarf on and picked up her house and car keys then she stopped.

The car keys.

For a moment she rolled them between her fingers, looking at how important they once were. And now, they were just keys.

'They don't FUCKING start shit do they?' Tatiana shouted then threw the keys down the corridor.

In an instant, Marcus was back in her mind. So were the flashbacks. The car. The shoes. Watching suede burn and not being able to do anything about it.

'You know what...'

Tatiana breathed heavily and closed her eyes tight. She could feel her blood boiling and her heart pumping quicker than she'd ever felt.

She needed to calm down.

'These Marcus-attacks are not going to be cool in front of strangers.'

Forcing her breathing to slow down, she turned off the light and locked the door behind her.

With her phone twirling between her fingers, she booked a cab and enjoyed the swish she felt as she walked towards the lift.

The Tall Tales of Tatiana Blue

25 minutes flew by and the Asian cab driver argued over £5 as Tatiana sat comfortably in the back seat refusing to leave until he gave her correct change.

Somewhere between Stratford and Mile End station, the price had gone from £10 to £15 and the cab driver refused to give Tatiana full change from her £20 note.

'Look, sir, seriously, the app said £10 so, GIVE ME, my change sir, thank you!'

'Listen madam...'

'I'm DONE with you now! I dunno why you wanna try add a lil' money on top but I'm not the one and now is NOT the time to be trying it. Now, we can do this cool and calm or, I swear, we can get into some other shit.'

Tatiana's legs were crossed and one foot was bouncing as she put her phone away.

'Madam, look, the traffic on the road...'

'Is nothing to do with me, so, last time, give me my change!?'

'I sorry madam, I can't...'

Tatiana sprung from the back seat with a low growl in her chest and managed to slide between the two front seats. Quickly, she grabbed a £5 note out of the man's hands before mushing him in the side of his head.

'I am NOT a victim ya know!' Tatiana said as she got out, slamming the door with a strong heel kick that dented the car as it pulled off.

'Fuck face.'

She checked herself to make sure she didn't leave anything in the car before scanning for Maya's door number.

Walking the pavement, she enjoyed the clean clip clop sound her heels made on the ground and began to walk with a touch of flash and flair. Each step made her inner model pour out and throw more attitude into her strut. To anyone watching, she must've looked like an over-excited model with a serious case of Tourettes the way she was talking to herself.

'That's it baby, work it out... shake it don't break it, watch me work it baby... uhhh... uhhh... Oh I slay... uhhh... yeaaaah...'

Making her trench coat flow behind her, Tatiana looked up and noticed she'd walked two houses too far and doubled back.

She found the house and took a slow, fully dramatic, hip swinging walk up the steps before ringing the doorbell.

The walk felt good.

She needed that.

A light turned on and a figure appeared through the glass door that was vibrating with a bass line. Maya opened it with wide eyes and a smile.

'YOU CAMMMME!'

The Tall Tales of Tatiana Blue

'I said I was coming...'

'You DO deliver don't you? Lemme see 'em!'

Maya dragged Tatiana in and closed the door before looking straight at her feet.

'They look GOOOOD on you. Oooooooooooh! Them jeans are nice... that t-shirt is nice.'

Maya's overload of excitement was a lot to take at once but, with her catwalk session outside, Tatiana embraced the onslaught with a smile.

'Thanks babe, how are you? How's the party?'

'Oh it's great, everyone is through there, lemme take your coat.'

Maya hooked Tatiana's trench coat over her arm while looking her up and down.

'What?' Tatiana said, catching Maya's confused look.

'You've got a very nice past behind you. Has anyone ever...'

'No one has EVER said THAT! Anyway, shallap ya face... come show me where the drinks are...'

Hanging Tatiana's coat, Maya watched as she walked towards the kitchen. 'Do you class yourself as thick or just dammmmn?'

'I prefer to class myself as blessed,' Tatiana said, looking back at Maya with bedroom eyes. 'At least get me tipsy before you cop a feel.'

Mr Oh

'Deal...' the host said as she pushed Tatiana into the lounge which was full of people standing, sitting, talking while Candi Staton's *Victim* was playing.

'Everyone this is my good GOOD and BRILLIANT friend Tatiana... Erm... what's your surname?'

'Blue. Tatiana Blue.'

'Oooooooooh... okay, I like that. This is Tatiana Blue.'

A big cheer went up and Tatiana blushed and offered a playful wave to the room before skulking off to the kitchen with Maya behind her.

'So what you drinking Miss Blessed?'

'What you got?'

'You know what, I'll MAKE you something and you tell me if you like it. Can you handle your rum?'

'I'm a niece of *Wray and Nephews* so I'll be fine.'

'Alright if you say so,' Maya said as she turned to a counter full of drinks.

From behind, Tatiana watched her reach for lemon, ice, nutmeg, cherries, lime and a straw. Maya spun on her heels with a colourful drink in her hand.

'What the fuck is that?'

'Reggae rum punch. See the colours...'

The Tall Tales of Tatiana Blue

'Looks like... okay, I get it... how'd you make that?' Tatiana was truly mystified by the way the colours of the drink held in place and with the lemon, lime and cherry on top, it looked like a bar-quality drink.

'I used to work in Juno Bar in Shoreditch and this used to be my favourite drink... taste it.'

Still amazed at how pretty the drink looked, Tatiana bent the straw and took a long sip.

Just as the first shot of rum hit her taste buds, the doorbell rang behind her.

Maya excused herself and dashed to the door as a short caramel man took her place, looking Tatiana up her down like he wanted to climb and conquer her.

'So, Miss Blue, what's up with you?' he asked, sipping a Stella.

'I'm sorry,' Tatiana replied, taking a long sip and looking down at him with a giggle. 'I wouldn't let you eat me out although you are the perfect height. Thanks though.'

She turned on her heels and walked into the living room, leaving the short man stunned in silence, as he watched her thighs switching out of the kitchen.

Tatiana could feel his eyes on her as she took her drink to the living room.

She sat down in an empty chair and sighed. 'Gonna be one of those nights is it?'

Mr Oh

From the maze of her Marcus thoughts, Tatiana was not in the mood for random guys with no game. Short ones at that. Maya walked into the lounge and was pulling a dread-locked man in a suit behind her.

'Everyone, THIS, is my good good friend from way back. The text book definition of a brother from another mother and guess who he works for?'

The man with the shoulder-length dreadlocks who was yet to turn Tatiana's way pulled Maya's hand and gave her the shush signal.

'Oh sorry... I can't tell you who he works for but, anyway, this is my long time bredrin, Quincy.'

On cue, the room reacted with cheers and whoops and a short round of applause. Tatiana followed suit by silently raising her glass. She couldn't see his face but she could smell his aftershave as he came and went.

'Nothing like dreadlocks in a suit,' Tatiana said to herself before taking another sip of her drink.

After a couple hours of random conversations with folks whose names she'd already forgotten, Tatiana felt intense tipsy creep over her. She was on her fifth reggae rum punch, she'd gotten herself into a puff puff pass circle between a pair of friends who went outside for a spliff and there were enough moments where she caught Quincy on the other side of the room, giving her weird looks.

The Tall Tales of Tatiana Blue

In between thinly veiled chat-up lines from random guys with varying levels of game, a large group rendition of the electric slide and two more large reggae rum punches, Tatiana found herself sitting alone again. Under the music and the conversations taking place around her, Tatiana felt good to just sit down and exhale by herself, especially as she felt a Marcus moment boiling in her stomach.

Looking at her shoes, fighting off the allure of negative thinking about her life, Tatiana didn't notice the man standing right in front of her.

She saw his shoes first, up to his trousers then the rest of his grey three-piece suit came into view.

Quincy looked down as Tatiana looked up.

'Hello?' Tatiana said with her eyebrows raised.

'I like your shoes,' Quincy replied, coldly. 'Where did you get them from?'

'Birthday gift from a flash friend,' she said, sticking to the pre-prepared script.

'That must be an extremely flash friend. Those are expensive shoes...'

'Yeah... she likes to think she's flash. That's why she bought me two pairs and I gave one to Maya.'

'Really?' Quincy asked with a frown across his brow.

'Yeah, ask her... MAYA...'

Mr Oh

Maya the hostess turned around with a drunk laugh and joined Quincy and Tatiana with hands on both their shoulders.

'What's up you two? I had a feeling you guys would end up talking. It's a dreadlock ting I guess.'

'I was just telling your friend about our "friend" that bought us the shoes.'

Maya caught on. 'Oh yeah, our "friend". She rules. Anyway, I gotta go and get some ice from the shop, we've run out.' Maya said, putting her coat on.

'We'll go.' Quincy said lightly, turning to Tatiana.

'WE will? Why would WE do that?'

'So the hostess can keep hosting. Come on, let's go for a walk.'

Turning to Maya, Tatiana waved a tipsy finger. 'This Quincy dude? He's not crazy or Nigerian is he?'

Maya laughed hysterically. 'No, don't worry, this is literally the safest guy in the entire world. And he IS Nigerian. Could you get me two bags please?'

Knocking back her drink, Tatiana chose not to give him the short, sharp response that was on the tip of her lips and decided the fresh air would do her good.

She put on her coat, hooked her handbag and met him at the door.

'Come on then suit man,' Tatiana whispered.

The Tall Tales of Tatiana Blue

They hit the street and passed another house party, where a group of men smoking weed gave Tatiana the deepest of stares.

Quincy watched the men and smiled. 'So... what's your story Miss... what's your name?'

'Tatiana Blue.'

Quincy stopped and looked at her. 'That's... a name!'

'I know right? And Italia Blue is my favourite porn star, go figure!'

She didn't know where the words came from but she was certain she heard herself tell a complete stranger who her favourite adult entertainer was.

Quincy laughed for the first time since he arrived at the house warming. A cute, handsome, Andre 3000 of a smile that took her by surprise.

'Okay, Tatiana Blue, what's the deal with you?'

'What's the deal with me?'

'You, yeah. What's the deal with you? You've had something on your mind all night. There is a whole world of shit going on behind that sexy façade you have up at the moment. I can smell it.'

'You can what?' Tatiana recoiled. 'You trying to say I smell!?'

'No, no, I'm just saying, whatever it is that's on your mind, you're not hiding it well.'

Mr Oh

'Ooooookay, I get you. You're one of those guys who likes to pretend he's the agony uncle that talks me through my problems until he talks me into bed. Haven't met one of you Slick Ricks in a while.'

'Wow,' Quincy recoiled. 'You either have a pretty woman complex or you've been asked for your number a LOT tonight.'

'Number two please Bruce.'

'Yeah thought so. Maya's got a few of her thirsty friends in there tonight.'

'Something about the tightness of my jeans and the MJ t-shirt draws them in.'

'And the thighs! I can see why,' Quincy stole a quick look. 'So, what's the smell in your mind Miss Blue?'

'Take a guess.'

'Erm, current or ex-boyfriend? I'd say ex.'

'You're two for two.'

Whatever was in the reggae rum punch had loosened her tongue, given her a woozy step in her heels and dropped the wall of protection that Marcus forced her to build.

The restraint she had on talking about the barrage of bullshit her ex put her through felt like it was unravelling the longer they walked.

'So, what did this ex of yours do?'

'Oh... don't worry about it. I can't even be bothered...'

The Tall Tales of Tatiana Blue

'Nah, nah nah... that's the answer you give to everyone else. That's what you say to someone who you don't wanna talk to. But I wanna know what he did to you that has you so lost in your own thoughts. I'm not trying to be slick but I can tell.'

She didn't answer. At that moment, Tatiana was more concerned with walking a straight line, which required all of her focus.

They arrived at the shop in silence, with her heels making a clean clip clop on the ground. Quincy paid for the ice and they were back to their slow stroll when he whipped out a cigarette box filled with pre-rolled spliffs.

'Want one?' he asked.

Tatiana thought about it, then a quick film played in her mind. In this blockbuster, she took a spliff, smoked it, then felt more woozy, realised it wasn't weed she was smoking, collapsed and woke up with her knickers around her ankles.

'No thanks, I don't...'

'Yes you do... but you don't trust me cuz you don't know me, I get it. Would you rather roll your own?'

Quincy pulled from his pocket a mini jar full of weed and a pack of RAW rizla.

Tatiana looked at his hand. 'I'm old school. I don't take pre-rolled tings from anyone. Need to see what goes into it.'

'Okay, well let's stop and...'

Mr Oh

'Nah, it's okay, I'm old school. I've been rolling standing up from the days of Chimes and Palace Pavilion.'

'So... tell me about your ex. What was his name?'

Tatiana couldn't help but sigh heavily as she brought the jar to her nose and inhaled deeply. The scent was stronger than she anticipated and she made a strong screw face.

'His name is Marcus.'

'Like Mr?'

'Yeah. Quite ironic that he's a REALLY big dick!'

Quincy laughed heartily, almost dropping the bags of ice cubes.

She pulled a sheet of Rizla and held it between her fingers and ripped off a piece of the packaging for a filter. Between quick glances in front of her to make sure she was still walking straight, she mixed tobacco and weed in her hand.

'So tell me about the big dick.'

'It's not that easy. This isn't some regular everyday bullshit problem. It was...' she trailed off.

'I wouldn't ask if I didn't wanna know.'

By the time Tatiana finished rolling, they made it back to Maya's, where the house was filling the whole street with sound. Dancers were dancing, talkers were talking and drinkers were taking shots and chanting loudly to Kanye West's *New Workout Plan*.

The Tall Tales of Tatiana Blue

Quincy slid into the house, put the ice in the freezer and fixed two Disaronno and Cranberry juices before going back outside where Tatiana was sitting on a step, tying the end of her spliff.

'So... Mr Marcus? What'd he do? Steal from you? Cheat on you? Cheat on you with your sister? Your mum? Cheat on you on a train? Sleep with a prostitute? Is he illegal in this country? Is he underage? Are you on a register? Did you come home and find him fucking a cat?' Quincy said excitedly, handing her a drink and sitting on the step above her.

She looked at him totally confused.com. 'What?!'

'Thought I'd take a few guesses. Was I right with any of 'em?'

'Fuck no. Waaaaay off I'm afraid.'

'Okay,' Quincy said lighting a brown roll up. 'So put me back on track.'

'He killed me.'

'No he didn't. You're sitting in front of me so you're not dead that's for sure.'

'He killed me. Not literally. But he killed me.'

'How did he kill you? You're sitting right here.'

'Not...' she sighed. 'Okay, this all started over the stupidest thing. I can't even believe it went this far. God, what a fucking idiot. Basically, me and Marcus were in a relationship. Nothing to really complain, things were going alright then one day he went and looked in my phone and saw a picture I took of myself.'

'And what were you doing in said picture?' Quincy asked, sarcasm raising the tone of his voice.

Tatiana looked up at him from her step, 'It wasn't that kind of picture. I bought a new skirt and shoes so I wanted to see how they looked...'

'Looked how?' Quincy asked, slightly more interested. 'What kind of skirt was it? What angle was it taken from? Were you naked except for the skirt and the shoes? Were your nipples–'

Tatiana turned around to face him. 'ERM, easy there... it was just me in a thigh length skirt and heels and a vest, okay? No nipples.'

'Awwww mayne, no nipples huh?! Okay, so anyway, he thought you sent such a picture to someone else I'll bet?'

Tatiana lit her spliff. 'Exactly. Now before he does the logical thing and ask me about it, he waits until I go out and...'

Quincy exhaled into the air as Cameo's *Candy* came on again behind them.

'Uh oh... this doesn't sound good.'

'While I was out shopping, he called me and was in full man-rant mode 'blah blah blah who are you taking pictures for blah blah blah'. I was like "huh? What'd you mean, what pictures?"'

'And he thought you were playing dumb?' Quincy added.

'Riiiiiiight. But I really didn't know what pictures he was talking about. I only took that one picture to see what I looked like and he made it into this big old bullshit.'

The Tall Tales of Tatiana Blue

'That's not just it is it?'

From the higher step, Quincy craned his neck and bent down until he was eye level with Tatiana, who took a long draw before closing her eyes and holding her breath.

She exhaled and spoke. 'No that's not it.'

The memory of the moment she came home after hanging up on Marcus and saw his sinister side at work was numbed by the weed and alcohol in her system. Had she been sober, her anger would've risen to the surface and Quincy, being the closest male representative, may have caught some violence his way. Such were her feelings towards Marcus at that moment.

'So what, he's found a dirty picture of you in your phone, thought you probably sent it some guy to turn him on and now he's pissed. So what did he do?'

'You know what he fucking did!? You wanna know? You know what I'll show you.'

Tatiana reached for her bag and searched for her royal blue Samsung S6. Unlocking it, while lighting her spliff, Tatiana drew a shaky finger across her phone screen until a video started to play.

'Watch that.'

Giving Quincy her phone, Tatiana dropped her head and took a long sip of her drink, recognising every sound from the video while running her fingers through her hair. She watched it enough times that she knew every sound, every scene, every colour of every moment and every nuance in Marcus's angry voice. The moment he whistled the *Twisted Nerve* theme tune as he recorded himself carrying bags of her beloved, fully paid for shoes and emptying them onto the back seat of her sky blue Mini Cooper. She could hear the wind blowing as Marcus drove her car with the windows down, all the while whistling the same song over and over again. He knew just how much she hated it.

Tatiana didn't need to watch to know what was coming next and she was expecting to hear Quincy's reaction any moment.

Marcus parked in a random open space, being careful not to film too much background. The scene cut to a close up shot of Tatiana's shoes that were piled so high, Marcus had to drop the back seat. He held up a bottle of bleach to the camera before emptying the industrial-sized bottle over her shoes. Still whistling.

To hear the liquid splashing over and ruining her shoes hurt Tatiana like the first time she saw the video.

In her mind, even if she did send the picture to another man, she'd hope they could talk about it like adults and if it didn't work out, they could go their separate ways and done. She liked Marcus but it was still well within their probation period and things were going well up to that point. That's what really confused her. Where did this come from?

THIS was Marcus being an "absolute wank face cunt hole". Tatiana's words.

The Tall Tales of Tatiana Blue

'Bleach. BLEACH! He put fucking...' she trailed off into a slightly maniacal laugh.

Quincy sucked in air through his teeth and cringed as he watched Marcus open another extra-large bottle of liquid, this time brown, and distributed it evenly over her shoes, watching them instantly change colour, some of them even steaming.

For what was about to come, Tatiana had to take three tokes of her spliff and an extra-large sip of her drink. Because this was the moment Marcus killed her.

She could hear him closing her car doors, still whistling, then striking the first match, which went out instantly with a passing breeze. Tatiana thought it was Mother Nature trying to save her shoes in her absence. But the biggest mother of them all couldn't stop him as he lit three matches together and put them back in the box. The resulting domino effect of fire lit up the screen as Marcus threw the burning box through the open back window and moved back quickly.

Still whistling.

The roar of fire lit up the screen and Quincy moved the phone back, with smoke sliding out of open mouth as the video ended.

'Wait, what he set fire to your car because of a PICTURE on your phone?'

'My car?! He set fire to my SHOES! See, this is why he's a wank face cunt hole.'

Mr Oh

Tatiana could feel a rant coming on as she stood up and faced Quincy. She wanted to see the same look of shock on his face that had been plastered on hers since she received the clip.

'If he wanted to just hurt me and burn my shoes, okay fine. I don't get why he would do that over a picture on my phone but whatever. But he didn't just do that did he? NOOOOO... he poured bleach on them first. Do you know what bleach does to a pair baby blue suede Jimmy Choo shoes? Or a pair of pink Kawaii scalloped lace up wedge sole boots WITH ribbons? HUH?! And THEN... what did he do? 'Cuz he wasn't done was he? NOOOOO! He fucking burned them. All of them. Just like that, poof!'

Tatiana noticed that she was shouting and waving her arms like Quincy had the answers.

He was cringing. 'That's VERY excessive.'

'YOU FUCKING THINK?!'

'Yeah, the least he could do was go out and have sex with someone else and even that would be a bit far.'

'Are you taking the piss right now strange suit man?' Tatiana turned serious.

'No, I'm just saying the shoes in the car thing, the bleach, it was a bit much.'

'I didn't think he could do that. And to me.'

'How long had you and...-'

The Tall Tales of Tatiana Blue

'You know what fuck him. Fuck my shoes that I spent over ten years collecting. Fuck my job that I've had to take time off from. Fuck my shoes. Fuck everything right now.'

'It's the shoes...'

'What else would it be? The car was insured, but the shoes were something else. I had Versace shoes suit man. VERSACE for fuck sake. I didn't even get to wear 'em.'

'I don't know 'bout Versace shoes but they sound important.'

Tatiana sighed. 'You men are something else. You want us to know everything about whatever football team you support but you can't...'

'HEEEEEEEEEY GUYS... what is it, smoker's corner out here?' Maya said, holding a cardigan closed across her chest.

'I've been getting to know your friend Tatiana. She's... interesting.'

'You could call her that.'

'I am interesting aren't I?' Tatiana added, taking her second to last draw. 'And you know what suit man, I don't give a fuck. I swear, I'm gonna get all my fucking shoes back, you watch!'

Quincy watched her as she took the last draw of her spliff and held her breath while closing her eyes. Exhaling and opening, there was evil in her stare. She held the burning butt between her thumb and middle finger and flicked it into the street.

Mr Oh

'What shoes?' Maya asked.

'I'll tell you later.'

'So you told a complete stranger before you told me? No offence Q.'

'She told me first cuz I'm a good listener.'

'Yeah and we all know why that is don't we Q?'

'Oi... Mia Maya? How many times, shhh...'

Tatiana could feel a wave of high washing over while her tipsy level stabilised as Quincy and Maya engaged in a play fight on the steps.

Wherever Marcus was, he was on her mind. She could see him lighting the three matches that lit the box up like a mini forest fire, lording over her shoes like a dictator.

'Anyway guys,' Tatiana said, realising she had been staring at the night sky, not taking any notice of the two friends chasing each other around cars. 'I'm gonna go.'

'Oh no, don't!' Maya groaned, running around a car to hold Tatiana's hand. 'There's more drink to drunk... I mean drink and, it's not even late.'

'Its 2am miss lady,' Tatiana replied.

'Is it? When did that happen?'

Quincy laughed. 'Yeah, it's almost time for me to be up for work.'

The Tall Tales of Tatiana Blue

Internally, Tatiana was torn. When she arrived, she didn't want to be there but now she'd had a drink or three, she was enjoying the feeling of being out. But the other side of her wanted to be at home, in her alcove of little decoration and no shoes, and just be alone. Tatiana wanted blood on her hands.

With the amount of shoes she collected over the years and the money she saved to own individually crafted moments of beauty in leather and suede, she felt like she didn't know how to go on. Since she started working as a security advisor for Fierce Designer Security Solutions, she got used to receiving huge discounts on the latest shoes from owners of shops that used her security services. From the sheer number of shoes, it was inconceivable that Marcus managed to get them all into the back of her car but, somehow, he did.

'I've got an early start tomorrow at work, so I gotta get some rest,' Tatiana lied.

'Awww... stupid work,' Maya said, alcohol from her breath filling the air between them. 'How you gonna get home?'

Tatiana knocked back her drink and could feel her annoyance rising as she looked down at her shoes, with Marcus filling her brain again.

'Night bus or Uber if i can get one. I'll be fine.'

'D'you want a lift Miss Blue? I need to go and see my weedman before he goes on holiday tomorrow.'

Maya put her arms around both of them. 'Yeah, give her a lift Q-Ball.'

Mr Oh

'Why you tryna make that sound dirty?' Tatiana chimed, her annoyance bubbling to the surface.

'It's okay, I don't mind, where do you live?'

'Stratford.'

'That's on my way. Alright, let's go.'

Tatiana handed her empty glass to Maya and they shared a hug as Quincy walked off to his car.

'Thank you for coming babe.'

'Thanks for inviting me, I needed a night out.'

'Yeah, I can tell... Who fucked you off? You look like someone really pissed in your champagne.'

Tatiana's anger boiled. 'I'm... I'm okay, I just need to sleep.'

Quincy pulled up with a screech, beeped the horn and this annoyed Tatiana even more.

'Get home safe okay?' Maya shouted drunkenly. 'And Q-Ball, drive carefully. Just cuz you have a high clearance level for...'

'SHUT UP!' Quincy yelled.

Tatiana got into Quincy's Nissan Juke and put her seatbelt on straight away, making sure not to scuff her shoes as she entered.

The Tall Tales of Tatiana Blue

'Thanks Maya. Go on and get back to your party. I'll talk to you tomorrow.'

He pulled away from the house with another screech of the wheels and an evil look from Tatiana as her head jerked backwards.

'Sorry 'bout that, I always like to fuck with one of Maya's neighbours. He hates when I wheel spin outside.'

'So you're a wind-up artist then?' Tatiana said, scenery watching.

Quincy gave her a quick glance. 'Marcus thinking?'

'Shoe reminiscing,' she said, gritting her teeth. 'I'm fucking telling you. I had so many shoes; some of them I had from when I was 18. And they're just gone. GONE! Worst thing is I don't even know where he left them burning. So my shoes and my car are out there somewhere. So no-one saw a burning car and decided to report it?'

He stopped at a pair of traffic lights and a silence fell over the inside of the car as Tatiana stayed lost in her thoughts. Quincy sported a puzzled look, playing *Red Balloon* by The Internet from a memory stick plugged into his radio.

'So, wait, if Marcus torched all your shoes, one, how come you haven't called the police and, two, how come you have those sexy shoes on right now?'

Tatiana took a moment; her thoughts melting in a solid blue flame like her shoes.

Mr Oh

'Police? REALLY? Anyway... me and police don't... we don't... get along so I'm waiting before I call the insurance... and these shoes... I stole them. Alright, I fucking stole them.' Tatiana said feeling judged.

'Really?' Quincy took his eyes off the road and looked her up and down.

'What you don't think a woman like me can steal? Don't think I'd be good at it? It was a fucking walk in the park... d'you know how easy it was? I didn't break in or anything... I just walked in and...'

Tatiana didn't realise she was yelling and pointing at Quincy, all her emotions over Marcus and her shoes coming to the forefront. With full-blown tipsy dramatics, she put a hand over her mouth and stopped talking.

'Yeah, you walked in?' Quincy chased her silence.

'Don't worry about it, let's just say it was easy. And it felt fucking good!'

For the rest of the journey, the conversation between Tatiana and Quincy was silent stares and missed eye contact. Her mind was sent into a trance by the passing scenery while Quincy watched her thinking.

The car came off the Bow flyover quickly and was speeding past a Holiday Inn as the atmosphere stayed tense and thick between them.

Quincy broke the silence first. 'Where'd you live?'

The Tall Tales of Tatiana Blue

'Go past the cinema and you can drop me off on the left near the church,' she replied, angry at the male voice that reminded her of who she wanted to forget.

Slowing to a stop and opening his window to exhume the tension, Quincy looked at Tatiana, who was staring at her shoes.

'We're here. Where do you live?'

'The downstairs flat over there,' she pointed at a random dark window.

'Oh, okay. Well, I don't know...'

'Look, let me cut you off there before you even start. I'm not one of those women who's gonna suck your dick just cuz you gave me a lift and no, you can't come in for coffee, which really means you wanna fuck. THAT, trust me, is not happening...'

'Listen Tatiana. I know you're still pissed off from what happened to you and you know what I would be too. But I'm not to blame for what he did. That's number one.'

She was mid-rant when Quincy cut her off with her finger in the air, pointed at him.

'Number two, what makes you think I wanna fuck you? I could be gay for all you know.'

Tatiana raised her eyebrows. 'ARE you gay?'

'Not since the last time I did my "are you gay" check. But you didn't know that, you just assumed I wanna fuck you cuz you're this beautiful,

Mr Oh

curvy, attitude of a woman, huh? Is that it? It's not all about trying to fuck Tatiana Blue ya know!?'

She sighed and rubbed her eyes vigorously. 'I'm sorry, I just...'

'Forget it... don't worry about it. And just FYI, in my head, it would be alright.'

'Just alright?' she replied, offended.

They sat in silence again as they both brooded over their own shit. Tatiana was glad she was almost home because then she could go back to her chair, naked, thinking about the bane of her life.

'Thank you for the lift.' Tatiana said, feeling too embarrassed to look at him as she opened the door and got out. 'And for listening.'

'Lemme ask you a question Miss Blue. How easy was it to get those shoes? Be honest.'

Tatiana looked down at her shoes and the corners of her mouth curled into a mischievous smile.

'It was...'

She chuckled, looking into his eyes before closing the car door and stepping back onto the pavement.

Quincy looked at her as he reversed, put the car in first gear and pulled away slowly, watching her become a mac-wearing shadow in his rear-view mirror.

The Tall Tales of Tatiana Blue

With the fresh air sobering her up, Tatiana waited for Quincy's car to disappear in the light flow of traffic before slow walking to her flat in the opposite direction.

With the friendly, yet mysterious, vibe of Quincy and the negative thoughts of Marcus lingering, Tatiana got home quickly and went straight to her room without turning on any lights. She wanted to enjoy the silence and the darkness of her life at that moment.

Taking her clothes off and tossing them on the floor instead of putting them straight in the wash basket, Tatiana just wanted to sleep. There was so much going on inside, she didn't know what to do with herself.

In nothing but her panties and her heels, Tatiana lifted the duvet behind her shoulders, wrapped it around herself like a cape and let her body fall on the bed. She rubbed her legs together and listened to the sounds of cars, buses and coaches on Great Eastern road, waiting for sleep to take over. Her last thoughts before sleep washed over her were of dead shoes with her hand between her thighs.

The leather of Ferragamo, the suede of Franco Sarto, the colours of her Kurt Geigers, the heels of her Manolos, the simplicity of her Robert Clergeri and the deliciousness of the Giuseppe Zanottis.

Her toes wiggled as she fell into a restless sleep.

Mr Oh

Okay, I'm sorry but, is this Oh guy serious? I can't sit back and watch this guy absolutely butcher the story of my life. He's not even telling the story right.

First of all, I didn't go to bed in my heels, that's just stupid. Who would do that? Why not just let a dog lick me in the mouth?

This Oh: all up in my Ribena, don't even know the flavour!

Right, well if you haven't guessed already who I am, my name is Tatiana Blue and I was asleep in my bed in nothing but my panties, no heels, having a quick sleep-inducing orgasm.

I didn't sleep in my heels but I did put them on my night stand under a lamp so I could see them. Trust me if you'd just lost over 200 pairs of shoes because of an absolute wank face, cunt-hole, you'd wanna keep your shoes as close as possible.

To you that might seem strange but I spent untold years buying those shoes and all of 'em just... gone.

Just like that!

Like they were never there for fuck sake!?

I MEAN HOW THE FUCK COULD HE...

You know what, let me breathe for a second because I always get angry as fuck when I...

The Tall Tales of Tatiana Blue

PHEEEEEEEW!

Okay, I'm back.

So, I was asleep... well it wasn't really sleep, more like conscious resting because I could hear everything. Orgasm didn't fully do what it was supposed to. The cars passing outside my flat, every second ticking away from the clock on my wall, the sound of someone walking in the corridor outside, Marcus whistling that fucking song from *Kill Bill*... I was all over the place but I still managed to sleep... even if it was only a light sleep.

I don't even know when I fell asleep properly but I must've slept because... well...

I don't even know what to say about what the fuck happened. But it happened. I know it did because I woke up there.

I went to bed, IN bed!

I know I did because I remember opening my front door, taking my clothes off, putting my shoes on the night stand and wrapping myself in my duvet, smelling the smells of my flat and enjoying the fact that Marcus wasn't there.

So, tell me why I went to bed in my flat and woke up on the floor of a changing room? Huh? Tell me that!

Mr Oh

I woke up feeling like something was wrong. You know that feeling? The sounds you hear in your sleep aren't the ones you expect to hear. I couldn't hear my clock on the wall, I couldn't hear the buses zooming past my window from Stratford bus station, I couldn't feel my duvet holding onto me like a hug from Deebo.

It was the cold that woke me up.

A fresh ice cold that nipped at my ankles and my mid-section which was equally weird because I remember going to bed in nothing but my panties.

My eyes popped open like I was late for work and I looked back at myself. And THAT was some scary shit.

I live alone for crying out loud, so I never expect to wake up looking at anyone, let alone myself.

I was on a floor. And I had clothes on, laying in front of a mirror. I blinked at myself once, then twice, then a third time before I woke up and thought, what THEEE fuck?

Far as I knew, I was in bed and there was no mirror near my bed so why was I suddenly looking at myself? I woke up quick, fast and in a hurry and jumped to my feet from a laying position; my eyes were still hazed from sleep, my body wasn't ready to be up so quick and there was a head rush as well as pins and needles running all through my body.

My knees buckled under me as I tried to look around and figure out just what the fuck was going on. More importantly where the fuck I was.

The Tall Tales of Tatiana Blue

I love my bed and I love my sleep so this was an absolute mind fuck to not be in it and not remember getting out of it. I actually thought I was dreaming. I pinched myself, listening to the buzz of a tube light above my head.

Everything was bright as my legs gave out and I fell to my knees facing a floor-length mirror. I was no longer in the panties I went to bed in. Instead, I was wearing black leggings, black Air Max 180s and a black spandex long sleeve.

I looked like *Colombiana* tuh rasssssss.

Moving closer to the mirror, I could see that even my make-up was done and my hair was pulled back in a neat dread ponytail.

'Whaaaat the hell is fucking going on?' I asked no one.

Confusion wasn't just an understatement. It was a lie!

I was completely and utterly confused.com/whatthefuck.co.uk

Sorry if I seem to be going on about it but it was so fucking weird. I mean, imagine you go to bed IN your bed and you wake up, like, in a train station and you have no idea how you got there. You didn't get out of bed and take yourself to a train station, you just woke up there. That's the level of confusion I was on.

In amongst being lost as hell, something caught my eye and I spun round to look behind, where I saw a mid-sized shoulder bag on the floor.

Mr Oh

I stared at it for a hot second, not sure whether to open it or kick it. In my mind it could've been a bomb so opening it was the last thing I wanted to do.

I made it back to my feet and decided to kick the bag then move back against the mirror, just in case. The way the bag scooted across the floor told me at least it wasn't a bomb. Still looking around, I reached for the bag slowly as it was the only thing in the room with me.

Then it vibrated and I swear on the memory of all my shoes, my skeleton damn near jumped out of my skin as I fell backwards onto the cold floor.

At that moment, I didn't know what time it was, what day it was or even where the fuck I was.

FYI – I swear a lot so if foul language offends, then you might wanna fuck off and go read a Mr Men book...

Where was I? Oh yeah, freaking the fuck out. I was physically shaking, that's how freaked out I was and the vibrating bag didn't make me feel any better.

I gave the bag another kick and I connected with something hard and small that I instantly recognised as a phone.

The Tall Tales of Tatiana Blue

Pulling the bag towards me, I spun it round to a small compartment, slowly unzipping it. With my feet, I flipped the bag upside down and watched an iPhone fall to the floor.

'What the FUCK?!' I said to myself, hearing an echo reverberate around the changing room.

Finding an iPhone 5 on any other day would be a serious Bruice bonus but, with me going to bed at home and waking up in, what looked like a changing room, I wasn't sure what I was feeling.

I left it vibrating on the floor for a few seconds before making it to my feet again.

The main screen had nothing on it. No folders, no apps, nothing, except for a single app called Tatiana.

I've never had an app named after me so I blinked at it a few times just to make sure it did in fact say my name.

On top of everything else I was calculating and trying to figure out, this was just another piece of shit in a maze of a mind fuck.

Worried beyond belief and feeling more uneasy with every passing moment, I pressed the app and the screen went black.

Suddenly, Quincy took the screen in the same grey suit, with a wickedly evil grin on his chops and a haze of smoke around him.

Then he started to speak...

'Hey miss Blue... and how are you? I imagine you're pretty confused as to what's going on right now but that's okay... I'll fill you in.'

Mr Oh

'What the flying fuck is...'

'Okay... I thought you'd...'

I screamed. 'Can you hear me!?!'

'Of course. I can see you too,' he said, then he waved at me.

The lines in my forehead were strong and deep in fresh confusion.

'Quincy, where am I?'

'Harrods.'

'WHAT?!?!'

'Shh...' Quincy said, leaning closer to the screen with a finger over his lips. 'I'd keep my voice down if I were you.'

'Harrods? Knightsbridge Harrods? Why the fuck am I in fucking Harrods? No, really, where am I?'

I could feel my lack of control over the situation grating on my nerves and my foul-mouth filter, which was already holding on by a thread, was about to finally fall. Like my mouth wasn't already foul enough.

'Miss Blue, with God as my witness, you ARE in Harrods. More specifically, you're in the Millinery on the first floor.'

At that point, he could've told me I was in a slaughterhouse for handbags, I still wouldn't have believed him.

I just kept saying to myself, 'but you went to bed though, so what the fuck?'

The Tall Tales of Tatiana Blue

Looking around, I could see that he wasn't lying. I definitely wasn't in my bedroom any more.

'Quincy?' I asked calmly, releasing the stress lines in my forehead and looking straight at the phone. 'Why in the fiery pits of hell did I wake up on the floor of a changing room in... Harrods you say? More specifically, the...'

'The Millinery.'

'That's it, the Millinery, yeah. Why am I here? No, hold on, we'll get to that in a minute. HOW did I wake up here?'

'Do you wanna know how you got here or do you wanna know WHAT is here?'

'Okay, first of all, you can't answer a question with a question. Secondly, what the FUCK AM I DOING HERE?'

I was losing my cool and I didn't like it. I was already mind fucked by all of this but what I didn't want to do was give him the satisfaction of seeing me in a state. Even though I was in a state.

'Tatiana... stop shouting. Loud noises are not the kind of thing you need right now.'

'What I NEED is...'

'Shoes right?'

I froze. He saw it.

Mr Oh

For a brief moment I forgot he could see me and realised my excited face must've been a picture.

My mind took a trip down memory lane of my shoes, looking so decadent and average squeezed into the back seat of a Mini Cooper. Why he would think to bring them up right now was beyond me.

'You wanna know why you're here Tatiana? Because I wanna see what you're made of. I wanna see if you really have the balls to be as bad as you think you are. Last night you said getting those shoes was easy right? Do you remember saying that? So I decided to see if you're able to back that chat.'

My mind was screaming out, who the fuck are you to challenge me?

The audacity of his ego was making my neck snake to the side and, weirdly, I started to calm down.

'Quincy... I don't know who the fuck you think you are...'

'What if I told you, you're currently in the general vicinity of about 18 different shoe designers right now and no one is around but you?'

'I'd say so fucking what?!'

'Last night when you told me about your shoes, I felt really bad. Not like I did it or anything but I just felt like that was a dickhead being a real dickhead. Real *Kill Bill* massacre at the wedding chapel kinda thing. Especially because he knew how much you loved your shoes. So, in my

The Tall Tales of Tatiana Blue

own weird, roundabout kinda way, I wanted to make it up to you. On behalf of Man.'

'By kidnapping me and leaving me in Harrods?'

'Kidnap? There's no ransom... you're free to go any time you want. Find a security guard and tell him you fell asleep in the changing room. I just thought, maybe you'd like to take the opportunity to get some shoes before you leave. You know, to start up your collection again.'

And that's when it all came heel clapping back to me. The last conversation I had with Quincy before he dropped me off and went on his merry way. Or at least I thought he did.

Apparently he didn't go home.

I couldn't help but giggle. I mean, who kidnaps someone and drops them off at Harrods in the middle of the night?

Really, my mind was still trying to wrap around how he pulled this off.

I'm Tatiana Blue for fuck sake. I'm not exactly a small girl in these streets or in heels. I'm extremely thick in the thighs too but don't think I'm not quick though.

Getting into my flat, moving me without waking me, transporting me and getting me into the changing room undetected couldn't have been easy. But how?

'What do you do Quincy?' I asked curiously. 'Like, for work?'

He smiled. 'I'm... a... contractor.'

Mr Oh

'A what?'

'Listen, you have about a little over an hour.'

'An hour for what?'

'There's 13 sections on this floor and you are in a shop called *The Shoe Salon*. Don't worry about cameras, they'll be taken care of.'

'Huh, what sections... fuck are you talking...'

'...there's Casadei just to the left of where you are right now, Zanotti's directly in front of you and the Louboutins are...'

'The what?'

The following few minutes went by like a flash and I felt like I missed it. Quincy broke down where I was, how long I had and where to go. According to him, I was in a changing room on the first floor in a shop called *The Shoe Salon*.

I had an hour before the night shift security swapped over with the morning shift security and there would be a 10 second window to get out of the building with the rest of the cleaners who were completing a floor-by-floor sweep.

In the bag by my feet was a map of Harrods, a lock picker, a taser, black bags, heat sensitive GPS, an Oyster card and a uniform. Each item was labelled clearly.

The Tall Tales of Tatiana Blue

If I seem rather calm about all of this, it's because what else could I do? I kept looking around, just to make sure I wasn't having a really realistic dream that I couldn't wake up from but I was awake.

Wide awake.

Quincy was just staring at me. The clarity of the screen had him in HD, analysing me as I squirmed, trying to figure out what the hell I was going to do.

'You now have 58 minutes Miss Blue, so what you gonna do?'

I honestly had no idea but I knew getting off the floor and gaining some equilibrium was job one.

Getting to my feet, a slight head rush hit me and I stumbled.

'That should've worn off by now,' Quincy said.

'WHAT should've worn off? What did you do to me?'

'We'll get to that later. Right now, you have two security guards doing an overlapping sweep of the section you're in right now. So whatever you're gonna do, now is the time to do it.'

Trust me, the pressure was unbelievable.

All I'd done was steal two pairs of shoes and bragged about it and here I was right in the middle of some next shit. The funny thing was, as much as I was thinking about how I was going to get out, I was also thinking about all the shoes that were a mere slick step away.

Mr Oh

'Tatiana, the more you think about it, the more you know you can do it.'

The way Quincy was looking at me; all smug and handsome was annoying me. I was thinking that whatever he did for a living, must've involved the analysis of body language. Watching me think and grin then frown, wondering if I could pull this off.

He knew I'd reached the point where I already knew I was doing this.

I sighed a heavy sigh, slung the bag over my shoulder and took slow steps to the changing room door.

On the phone, Quincy was grinning.

'You know this is fucked up right?' I said, with my whole body throbbing like a pulse.

'Miss Blue, you have two choices. Leave or get some shoes and leave... it's that simple.'

The stubborn in me didn't want to say it out loud, but we both knew what time it was.

'Well I DO like shoes!'

'You've got 55 minutes. See how many you can get. I'll bet you a £10 you can't get 10 pairs.'

The addition of a challenge made my eyes squint, my nipples hard and a serene calm wash over me that made Quincy's eyes widen.

'Have my money ready!'

The Tall Tales of Tatiana Blue

I hung up the phone and stood in the silence. My body was rocking back and forth as I closed my eyes. See where my mind would take me.

My first thought was, 'Harrods has a LOT of shoes.'

Yes they do.

If I was really in *The Shoe Salon*... I mean, have you even heard of *The Shoe Salon*?

There's no way in hell you can say you love shoes and not know about *The Shoe Salon*?!

I started to get excited. Adrenaline was beginning to pulse over my calm. The added pressure of the time constraint wasn't helping either.

I squatted down and put my ear to the door while searching the bag on my shoulder for the GPS.

The hand-held heat sensitive GPS looked like a Sky+ remote with a screen in the middle. Two red blips were on the left and right of the screen and continued moving outwards. The green blip, which I assumed was me, was motionless.

Now or never time.

'I'm gonna get me some Alexander McQueens...'

Turning the handle, I peeked through the door and heard nothing. I could see heels through the darkness, lit up by fancy display pieces and grand plinths of shoes. Keeping low, I moved out of the changing room and closed the door behind me without a sound.

Mr Oh

Scanning the room, staying in the shadows, I could see so many shoes, my thighs actually shook a little bit.

I could see a Rene Caovilla, a display of Brian Atwood, Stuart Weitzman, Alexander McQueen, Camilla Skovgaard, Balenciaga, Carvela, Chanel...

Staying in the shadows along a wall of shoes, I was in heaven. Just knowing I was the only one in the vicinity with all those shoes – a Jimmy Choo at two o'clock, a Kurt Geiger at four o'clock, a striking red Ferragamo heel at twelve o'clock – made me giggle to myself.

I didn't know where to start.

There were so many designer shoes passing my line of sight, I was overwhelmed by it all.

This was when I had one of those moments where I felt like I had no idea what to do and then the simplest idea came to me. I was creeping around a dark shop floor with delectable shoes all around me and I thought of one thing.

Stockroom.

Display shoes out front, full pairs in the back.

Where's the back?

My eyes darted to every corner of the shop, looking for cameras, as I moved along the wall, stopping at a delicious Georgina Goodman heel in black.

'Ooooooh... hello Mrs.'

The Tall Tales of Tatiana Blue

I reached out to touch the shoe and that was when my eyes caught a section of the wall next to me that had a line of light surrounding it.

'Stockroom,' I said to myself, feeling the wall, looking for a join or a hinge... something that would lead me to the... BINGO.

I ran my fingers over the wall until I felt a keyhole, all the while keeping an eye on the two security blips on the GPS.

Finding it quicker than I thought, I softly rifled through the bag for the lock picker. Not that I would know what to do with it though. It looked like something I'd seen before but I couldn't put my finger on where.

Call of Duty: Black Ops.

Don't think in mourning my shoes and being off work I just sat around doing fuck all? I got me a PlayStation 3 and I became a bad boy at *Call of Duty: Black Ops 2*. Online, I became a demon with a sniper rifle and queen of the drop shot and was regularly blocked from sessions because I was that damn good.

But it was that game that reminded me of where I'd seen the lock picker before. Resembling a glue gun with a bent wire, there was a nail file looking attachment underneath, probably meant for the lock mechanism. From what *Black Ops* taught me, you put the bent wire in the bottom part of the lock and the nail file in the top... squeeze the gun a few times, twist it and the top part of the lock should...

OPEN!

Mr Oh

If there was ever a time where I thanked God that computer games were based on real shit, it was this moment right here.

The lock slipped out and the door creaked open. I grabbed it to keep any noise to a minimum, holding the silence to make sure no one was within ear shot.

A few seconds holding the door in absolute quiet, I gave the GPS a quick check then moved into the stockroom ass first.

Closing the door in the same silence, I took a moment because my heart started to sprint when I was already on a steady jog. Not only because one of the blips on the screen started to move towards me, but I knew where I was. I'd seen this room before. I'd been here before. For work.

My company regularly worked with Harrods to ensure maximum protection for their designer products.

Quincy came back to my mind.

Granted, all I had to do was turn around and start picking shoes but I was wondering why would Quincy put me here? Did he know I'd done work here? If he did, how did he know? Who the hell is this guy?

'Sod it,' I said to myself. I wasn't gonna get any answers now.

But I was gonna get answers.

The Tall Tales of Tatiana Blue

With that to the back of my mind, I set my mind right and swivelled on my air bubbles with a smile. I clapped and held my hands over mouth to cover the shrill scream I let out as my eyes took in wooden mountains of shoes stacked high. Each mountain had A4 images of pictures of shoes and the designer's name and went left and right as far as the eye could see.

I stood up straight and marvelled with my mouth open, running my hands over my ponytail. I had no idea where to start.

This was it.

I was here.

Able to not only restart my collection again, I could actually improve on the shoes I had before.

I was in the presence of Elie Tahari, Joie and Michael Kors shoes for crying out loud.

Have you ever seen a Michael Kors shoe?

I've never had one... always wanted one. And that's the first shoe I went looking for.

Alphabetically stacked, I scoured the images of shoes looking for the name, keeping a low centre of gravity and moving on the balls of my feet.

If a boxset of Jason Bourne DVDs taught me anything, it was always stay on your feet and be ready to move.

Mr Oh

Quick steps through the stockroom and I was blurring past shoes, catching names I wanted to return to.

But first, I was on a mission for a Michael Kors.

Specifically a Michael Kors *Gideon Metallic-Trim pump*.

I'd seen it in last month's Vogue and I wanted to have an orgasm with them on. I had a similar Valentino pair before Marcus got to 'em but these were something else.

I found the aisle of Michael Kors and crouched lower, as the GPS started beeping. I froze, got low next to a shelf of Marc Jacobs shoes and checked the screen.

One of the blips was moving in my direction and nerves were coursing through me.

Getting caught in the changing room would be easy to explain off – narcoleptic tendencies would've been my preferred excuse – but in the stockroom, I couldn't have been there for anything else except for shoes. Plus the bag of assorted criminal accessories and the all-black get up wouldn't help.

Cue arrest, handcuffs, bail sheet, court, etc.

I watched the blip slow down. According to the GPS, the blip was almost on top of me, which meant the security guard was on the shop floor. I couldn't hear any movement but I stayed still.

Would he be one of those jobs-worth people who checked every crevice? Because if he was then he'd come in the stockroom.

The Tall Tales of Tatiana Blue

I listened as a tube light buzzed directly above my head.

Then the blip started moving, quicker than before in the opposite direction. Basically away from me, while the other blip stayed where it was.

Holding my chest, that real moment made me up my speed.

I stayed low and continued to scan until I found the Michael Kors section.

I ran my finger along the different types of shoes they had under the Kors section: sandals, slippers, wedges...

Heels were last in the row.

Beige shoe boxes were stacked high to the ceiling as fear started to push me on faster. In my head I knew I should've just found any pairs and started packing 'em away but my heart wanted those specific shoes.

I thought, fuck it, I'm here, why the fuck not?

Gideon metallic...

BINGO BANGO BONGO!

They were right in my line of sight, heaped on top of each other in columns of four, reaching eight rows across.

The undeniable and delicious *Gideon metallic-trim pump* in black.

Mr Oh

Found my size and pulled a box out of the row, making sure the remaining boxes stayed uniform in their columns.

I honestly felt like Gollum with the ring.

My legs folded under me and I sat on the floor with the box in my lap.

Yeah I knew I didn't have time, yeah I knew the blips would eventually do a thorough check and pop in the stockroom, yeah I knew all that. But I still held the box for a moment, enjoying the silence.

It was just me and the shoes.

At this moment, I was strangely aware of the fact that my leggings were hugging my crotch very snugly, my nipples were hard and I was suddenly a little horny.

Trying to blink through such a feeling, I reached for the box lid and slowly opened it. I was breathing heavily, my eyes were slipping to the GPS every few seconds and, after removing the mandatory paper, my eyes got real wide.

There they were.

The one thing equal to a tidy chocolate man with shoulder-length dreadlocks and no clothes on.

'Ooooooooooh, look at you!'

As I started to reach out and touch them, I pulled my hand back.

Out of nowhere a fit of laughter and bouncing up and down came over me and I hugged the box to my chest.

The Tall Tales of Tatiana Blue

Whatever Quincy was trying to achieve with all of this, he scored big by making it possible to hold a pair of brand new shoes in my hands.

Not forgetting that he'd apparently drugged, kidnapped me and moved my body to Harrods, he took points off his crazy score by putting a Kors *Gideon* heel in my hands. My fingers shook as I reached for one of the shoes, not sure which one to go for.

Yes I know I was killing a whole heap of time but this was emotional for me.

The one thing that I will never forget is watching my shoes burn and crackle and not be able to do a damn thing about it.

All because of a picture on a phone. An innocent one at that.

But all that meant sweet fuck all because I had a sweet black *Gideon* in a five and a half.

I held it up to the light like a diamond and licked my lips.

All black, suede, metallic trim, almond toe... oh yeah... Quincy definitely gets points off his crazy score for this one.

I held it to my nose and inhaled deeply, letting my fingers slide over the suede.

You know there's nothing like the smell of a brand new shoe. The heel brushed past my nipple and a shiver ran up my spine. I could feel my lips behind the cotton leggings getting thicker.

This was getting physically emotional.

Mr Oh

My wrist suddenly vibrated and I freaked the fuck out with a yelp like I just got electrocuted. I looked at my watch to ask what the hell that was. But I wasn't wearing my regular watch.

My wrist was wrapped in a thick black strap with a large digital display that flashed: 45 MINUTES.

Yet again, I got lost in a train of thought about just how slick Quincy was that I didn't even notice the thing on my wrist.

The time reminder snapped me out of my love-in with the shoes and I tried to return to my slick thinking mode, which was running in the back of my mind. And was working like a charm.

I jumped to my feet, reached into my shoulder bag for a black bag and looked around, trying to plan my next shoe stop. Better to have just shoes rather than the box is what I thought next and put them straight into the bag.

I had my first pair of shoes and I'll tell you now, it sure felt good. NO, it felt right! Wrong, but right. Didn't I love these shoes? Didn't I deserve these shoes? Weren't the shoe companies making so much money and were insured for such insane amounts that it wouldn't really harm their profits if they lost a few of 'em? I knew that last one was definitely true.

With the empty beige box back in its slot, I moved to the end of the aisle and looked left and right, staring at aisles of shoes.

'Harrods has Choo's, right?' I asked myself.

The Tall Tales of Tatiana Blue

And with that I was off, looking for the Jimmy Choo aisle of shoes.

With no cameras in the stockroom, I didn't need to crouch any more. I slung the black bag over my shoulder and did a sexy walk to the Choo section, enjoying just how easy this all was.

The way I know shoes – and if you haven't guessed already I KNOW shoes – and the names of designer shoes, I started remembering shoes I'd seen, shoes I'd heard of, mythical shoes even.

After picking up the beautifully colourful Jimmy Choo *Lira* pair, I was back to the top of the aisles, trailing designer names with my finger whistling the tune from *Kill Bill*. I caught myself and stopped instantly before switching to Floetry's *In Your Eyes* as more shoes came to mind and I went on the hunt.

Ferragamo *platform calfskin pumps with metal Vera* bow. Lanvin *Strass sandals blue* with glass pearls. Sergio Rossi *red Miladys* with the varnish finish and 5.9 inch heel. Nine West's *Cinched multicoloured court shoes* with peep-toe and platform heels. Dior *open-toe lagoon blue patent leather pump* with CD on the back of the heels. Givenchy *Gladiator platform sandals* in luxe Italian suede with shiny gold tone details. DVF *Zia 2* in gold metallic leather. Emilio Pucci *Satin sandals* with rhinestone detailing.

With the Michael Kors and the Jimmy Choo at the bottom of the bag, Quincy owed me a tenner. By the time the watch shocked me again, telling me I had 30 minutes left, I was comfortable in the stockroom. I

Mr Oh

was singing Jodeci's *Good Luv* low under my breath with a smile on my face, sliding down aisles of shoes on the ladder with wheels. By the time I stood at the door of the stockroom, looking back at the shoes I just ravaged, I had two black bags full of shoes.

With the blips on the GPS probably on a fag break, blinking on the outer rim of the screen, I calmed down, slung the bags over my shoulder and adopted a low crouch.

Turning the handle of the stockroom slowly, I pulled the door open a smidgen and looked through the sliver of darkness.

Once enough silence had passed, I slid the bags through the door first and followed, closing the door silently behind me.

There was no stopping once I made my way out and I was on the move back to the changing room, moving quicker than before. Listening to myself, I could hear that I was moving extremely quietly, even while carrying two bags of shoes and a shoulder bag of shit. Even getting back into the changing room, I was swift. I felt like a ninja the way I was moving and strangely enjoying it.

Putting the bags in a corner, I looked at my watch and then rifled through my shoulder bag.

I had 28 minutes and, according to the map and my memory of Harrods, there was one more place I just had to go. Like HAD to go.

The Shoe Boudoir.

The Tall Tales of Tatiana Blue

Sweet mercy with the suicide doors, *The Shoe Boudoir* is the absolute pinnacle of decadence draped around shoes in a mix of flowing black sheets and spotlights of deliciousness.

If you ever have a day off, go to Harrods and just sit in *The Shoe Boudoir* for five minutes and try on random shoes you probably can't afford.

You feel so damn sexy.

Of course I'd done it before. A day with nothing to do, no plans, down to Harrods for an afternoon of shoe slipping on and heavy breathing over leather stitching. Call me sad if you want, but I really love my shoes.

According to the map, I was standing in a changing room that shared a wall with *The Shoe Boudoir* which was on the other side.

'Quincy really did plan this shit out didn't he?'

By this point, with a sea of pumps, sandals and other assorted heels only a wall away, I was becoming less angry with him with every passing minute. The smile on my face and the renewed energy coursing through me was starting to feel worth everything he did to put me here. Even though I still didn't know what he did to put me here.

And his reason for doing it, though slightly egotistical in the beginning, was exactly what I needed.

I needed shoes. That was a given. But I wanted to prove something to myself. I wanted to prove to myself that I could actually do this. I'm not sure when Quincy's crusade to check my badness became my own but I was fully involved in making my point.

Mr Oh

My name was Tatiana Blue and I could do anything!

Oh, but don't think Quincy won't be dealt with.

Spinning on my heels, I turned and faced myself in a mirror.

I took a second to admire how sexy I looked in all black then it was back to business. It was at that split second that something caught my eye on the wall next to the mirror.

Moving in for a closer look, I saw someone had written on the wall in pencil.

OPEN ME

I looked at the words and said, 'Open what?'

Scanning the mirror and the wall up and down, I had no idea what I was supposed to open. Whatever part of the game this was, I had no idea how to play it.

Did it mean open the wall, open the door behind me because I'd done that already.

Holding my head to the wall next to the mirror, I ran my hand along the glass trying to figure out how the hell I was going to get from *The Shoe Salon* to *The Shoe Boudoir*.

The Tall Tales of Tatiana Blue

No doubt the front doors of both shops were closed and locked which meant no going through those.

I took my hand off the mirror to try and think what to do next when the glass moved away from the wall slightly.

I frowned and stared for a second, hoping I was meant to do that.

Was this what I was supposed to open?

My watch said I had 25 minutes left and this was when the pressure truly hit.

I wanted to open the glass but I was stuck to the spot.

What if it was a door that led to the security guard break room? There'd be me, head to toe in black, looking stuck like 'erm... sorry wrong room'.

My muscles were tense and I was willing myself to open the mirror and take a look but I was securely frozen.

'Move it Blue...'

Leading the mirror open – slowly – with a single finger, I carefully moved my head around the frame of the open doorway and that was when I completely forgave Quincy for everything.

With a mirror on both sides, I was able to catch my own look of shock as grandeur came into view.

Mr Oh

With the lights on, *The Shoe Boudoir* stared back at me.

Clear black marble floor with spot lights above and below, sheer black drapes and black box display cases of shoes. I had to put my hand over my mouth as I balanced myself and moved through the hole in the wall, catching surprised breaths with every shoe I saw. The spotlights made everything look untouchable like I was in the presence of royalty. And that was exactly where I was.

Moving through the hole as stealthy as possible, I felt the GPS slip from my hands and crash to the ground.

I froze again.

Dipping low, I listened for any signs that someone heard.

I counted ten seconds, with Mississippi's in-between. I reached for the GPS, closed the mirror and sat on the floor watching the walls for cameras.

None.

Which I found quite weird for somewhere like Harrods. I guess they believed in their security team.

I had to laugh to myself.

A memory of something Quincy said about the cameras tried to circle my mind but I couldn't remember what he said.

The Tall Tales of Tatiana Blue

The GPS showed no one rushing to my current location and I made it to my feet with a jump. Looking over the entire shop, I wished I had the time to sit down, try on shoes and just enjoy the decadence.

I knew I'd have all the time in the world once I got out of there and was in the comfort of my own space... but it all looked so sexy.

My slowly developing ninja mind kicked in and my watch said I had 19 minutes left before the shift change.

Sliding my shoulder bag to the front, I pulled out a plastic bag, started whistling Jordan Knight's *Give It to You* and went shopping like it was *Supermarket Sweep*.

Unlike *The Shoe Salon*, there was no stockroom. It took me a few minutes to realise the shoes were hidden under each display case. I broke out the lock picker, opened the first case of shoes and got to work.

I found a pair of Nicholas Kirkwood *Satin swirl* platform pumps in sky blue with the candy-coloured hues. Ahhhhh, a shoe to die for.

Had to pack two pairs of Giuseppe Zanotti *tobacco-coloured python print* court shoes. Those were damn near legendary in shoe forums. Sliding heels out of their boxes and throwing them in a black bag felt disrespectful to the shoes but I'd get 'em home and show them the love they deserved.

Shopping down six aisles of shoes, I was in such a happy zone, I didn't see the last aisle coming towards me.

Mr Oh

Christian Louboutin.

It was like Morpheus just taught me how to bend the rules of the Matrix the way everything slowed down around me. My eyes were as wide as clock faces and excitement was bubbling up from the soles of my feet. This was it... the shoes I'd always wanted but never owned.

The sexiest design of a shoe I'd ever seen.

Pump, heel, sandal and ankle boots.

However giddy I was in the stockroom paled in comparison to the shock that had me stuck to the spot. My head tilted to the side as two pillars of red bottom shoes stood before me, lit up by spotlights from both the floor and ceiling.

I exhaled my 'kiss my neck' sound and felt my shoulders relax. Feeling returned to my feet and I approached the display in awe.

I'd seen them in music videos and on the feet of celebrities and at work, but I'd never been in a situation where I could own a pair.

And that's what made me so nervous.

The first shoe that made me put a hand on my chest in awe was the *Louboutin Jenny Pump Bazin* in blue and pink. I slowly reached out for it and my fingers graced the material and I pulled my hand back like a child

The Tall Tales of Tatiana Blue

burning themselves. Shaking my hand, as if to remove a sticky substance, I smiled to myself.

'WoMAN up, you don't have time... Yeah, but they're Louboutins though... I can see what they are Tat but you don't have time... Yeah but, can't I just... Do all your justing at home, you've got...'

I checked my wrist and the digital display told me I had 14 minutes left.

'Let's go!'

Still enjoying the sentiment of the shoe, I put it back and went straight to the back of the display.

I was getting quicker with the lock picker. Seven seconds and VOILA, the black doors of the plinth opened and stacks of Louboutin boxes looked back at me.

I had to press my nipples in as they were poking through my top in over-excitement. A nice shiver down my spine followed.

The *Jenny Bazin* pumps were first into the bag, followed by the delectable leather *Fossile cut-out sandals* in caraibes and canari.

I didn't stop there.

Next was a multi-coloured suede *Pitou Python* heel, the stone-coloured *Diptic suede D'orsay* sandal and peep toe heel, the *Arnold Python* strap sandals in a rose Paris and flame colour, the *Zouzou Kid* pink corde pumps and, of course, the *Vampanodo* open toe sandal with the satin bow in blue.

Mr Oh

I bagged a pair of *Boubou Bazin* platform heels in tye-dye green, blue and white which sold for a vicious £925, a *Pick and Co* patent open sandal with the classic Louboutin spikes in black, a *Covered* ankle boot with the criss-cross laces in black and taupe and, with 11 minutes left, I found a *Highness Tatoo* pump in black. Not just your regular *Highness* though, these were the ones with the dragon tattoo. And those are hard to find too.

By the time I had the black bag slung over my shoulder, scanning the aisles for any signs of my presence, my watch shocked me.

10 minutes.

Weirdly I didn't want to leave.

There were so many shoes I was looking at that I didn't get. I needed more time.

In my heart and my mind and my soul, I knew I could get 'em all if I had enough time and a longer plan.

Not sure if I could get into Harrods but confidence was flowing through me and, with over £8,500 worth of shoes in bags ready to go, anything felt possible.

I started to take slow steps back to the hole in the wall then took one last look at the Louboutin display and logic went out of the window,

The Tall Tales of Tatiana Blue

linear thinking became curved and my ninja-like mind became an excited fat kid with a knife and fork in front of a Sunday roast.

You would think with all the shoes I'd seen and taken, there would be nothing else that could make me SWV.

That's weak in the knees, for those that don't know.

But you'd be wrong. I was wrong.

I didn't think they existed. Sure I'd heard rumours online and seen sketches but I didn't think Monsieur Louboutin would actually go as far as to make 'em.

As I just said, I was wrong.

Because behind the main Louboutin case was a tall glass plinth and inside it was something I'd give all these shoes away for.

No idea how I didn't see it before but I could see it now.

Ladies and gentlemen, in this glass case was a Christian Louboutin *Pigalle Botta Strass* black suede knee-high boot with multi-coloured crystals.

The price tag said £3,265 and my mouth hit the floor.

You need to see just how much of an absolutely ridiculous pair of boots they are. Online forums of shoe aficionados claimed they existed yet no one could provide a picture. Celebrities were hunting them down,

Mr Oh

trying to be the first person to be seen in 'em and one or two boutique owners heard of their existence but never managed to get hold of a pair.

And here I was, with minutes before the shift change, staring at the most beautiful pair of red bottomed boots ever created.

As another minute passed, my wrist vibrated.

Time was most definitely not on my side.

'Right, first things first – boots.'

I circled the plinth and opened the back panel to reveal boot boxes with only one pair of each size.

But only straight sizes, no halves.

'Fuck fuck and a third and fourth fuck...' I said to myself, wrestling with a dilemma. Since I'd never owned a pair of Louboutins, I didn't know if a five would be too small or a six would be too big. Really, I needed to try them on but, again, time was not on my...

Eight minutes.

My finger was flicking between both of them and I was mumbling under my breath as I checked the GPS quickly.

'Ip dip doo. Cat's got the flu, dog's got the measles so out goes you...'

I pointed to the five and chose again.

The Tall Tales of Tatiana Blue

'Ip dip, dog shit, fucking bastard, silly git, you are not it...'

I landed on the six, hoping this wouldn't happen.

Suddenly, my ninja voice screamed at me, 'TAKE 'EM BOTH AND LET'S GO!'

I didn't argue with logic and slid them into a new bag all to themselves. Letting go of the suede as they dropped into the bag, I sniffed my fingers and inhaled the fresh boot scent, which had a brilliant whiff of FREE attached.

Wasting no time on ceremony and with a sinister smile, I was back into the hole I came through, making sure to leave no finger prints on the mirror.

Closing it as much as I could, I put the two new bags with the two from *The Shoe Salon*.

Black bags had never looked so damn sexy.

I wasted a vital few seconds just smiling at the bags, knowing what was in 'em, covering my mouth to hide a wicked smile.

My reflection in the mirror looked at me and the pride on my face. God bless Quincy wherever he was.

With a sigh, I was on to my next mode of thinking.

How the hell I was gonna get out of there with four black bags full of shoes?

Mr Oh

That moment of thinking fell upon me like a giant rain cloud over a summer day in the park. My shoulders dropped, my smile sank into a frown of worry and my heart beat rumbled like thunder.

I needed answers and I had none.

'Think Tat think... Think about what? What am I gonna... relax and just think...'

In the far corner of the changing room, my eyes caught a pile of shoe boxes, loose papers and shop bags.

'There you go, put that stuff on top of the shoes so it looks like rubbish... yeah and then what? I've got rubbish... and you've got a uniform...'

OH YEAH!!!

In the shoulder bag.

I swung the bag and pulled out the uniform for the *Clean and Outstanding* cleaning company, flicking it to life. My reflection agreed that it was the right size and I wasted no time ripping open the buttons and climbing into it.

Quick with the buttons, I stuffed each bag of shoes with enough random rubbish to make them look believable. Making sure to surround the inside of the bags so no shoes imprinted on the plastic, I looked at my watch.

The Tall Tales of Tatiana Blue

Six minutes.

'We're going for a blend effect... you mean make it look like you're one of the cleaners... something like that I think, I dunno, I'm winging it right now... what'd you think I'm doing?'

I needed to stop talking to myself and start moving but the back and forth banter was helping to make decisions.

'So how are we actually gonna get out of here... doors are locked, don't see any more Quincy notes... maybe there's a vent or something or... let's see where people are first...'

I went to check the GPS and realised it wasn't in my hand any more.

'SHIT!' I frowned and spun around, looking at the floor, checking the uniform's pockets, and dropping to my knees to search the shoulder bag.

Nothing.

I looked at the black bags, hoping I didn't drop it in there.

'When did you last have it... you tell me, you had it in your hand... I know and the last time I checked it was... before the 'Ip dip doo'... so that means it's in... shiiiiiiiiit...'

I looked at my reflection, remembering where I left it.

Behind the fucking *Pigalle Botta Strass* stand.

Mr Oh

Patting myself down one last time, hoping and praying it'd turn up on my person, I looked at myself in the mirror fully annoyed.

'Well I guess we're going back then...' I said to myself and opened the mirror again.

Another buzz on my wrist told me I had five minutes left to get out... somehow. I mean, yeah I had a cleaner's uniform, but how was I gonna get out to slip in with the other cleaners?

The "how" was still a mystery and, I'm gonna be honest, I was shitting myself.

I know I'm making it seem like I was completely in control of my faculties and I was just strolling through Harrods like I had the keys but I was turtle-head bricking it in there.

Every noise made my head turn and my knees bend to keep a low centre of gravity.

Ever been so nervous that you can hear your own heartbeat? That was me as I hopped through the hole again, landing silently, squat-walking to the last aisle.

Trying to be as quick and swift as possible, I reached the plinth and ran my hands around the base, feeling the floor for the GPS.

'Come on... it's here I know it is... where the fuck are you...'

My little finger brushed past something and I reached blindly until I got a full hand on it, with one eye on the door.

I actually said phew, then laughed. Then frowned.

The Tall Tales of Tatiana Blue

Another buzz told me I had four minutes left and time was still ticking. I looked at the GPS, expecting to see the two blips still dancing around the edges of the screen.

And one of them was.

The other red blip was moving towards the centre of the screen. Right next to my green blip.

That was when I heard the keys in the door of *The Shoe Boudoir*.

Everything had been pin drop quiet up to now so the sound of keys jingling in the lock amplified around me. I looked through the glass plinth, past the colourful crystals attached to the Louboutin boots, and watched the door as a broad security guard walked through.

With his presence to the left of me and the hole directly in front of me, I danced with the idea of making a run for it.

'Either do it or you're screwed... no, he'll see you... this must be his final check before the shift switch... I got that but what are we gonna...'

Making a dash for the hole was out of the question as he closed the door without looking at it. He started to walk around the outside of the aisles. All he had to do was walk to the back of the aisles, turn right and he'd see the mirror that was no longer against the wall. Then he'd find the bags.

Then he'd find me.

That wasn't an option I was even contemplating.

Mr Oh

Dipping behind the plinth, I watched him walk towards the back of the shop.

My wrist buzzed. Three minutes.

I'm surprised he didn't see the mirror from where he was because I could see it. I was looking straight through.

'Why didn't you close the... 'cuz we were gonna be in and out... now what... you tell me...'

From a peeking position, I could see he was looking down towards the centre of the aisles. The way he was looking in my direction, it was like he could see me.

'Get his attention... with what... check ya pockets... you can't let him see the... I fucking know...'

At that precise moment, as he turned and saw the mirror away from the wall, the GPS slipped out of my hand and hit the floor.

'Are you fucking kidding me?' I mumbled then held my hand over my mouth. My eyes went straight to the security guard who was looking more intently in my direction.

Keeping one eye on the hole, he started to walk back the way he came while reaching for his radio.

'This is Osvaldo The Great to Russell The Reed at base, come in over?'

His radio kicked up static then a voice replied. 'Russell here, what's up foreign boy?'

The Tall Tales of Tatiana Blue

'I'm in the SB on my last walk-through and we haven't had any workmen scheduled to come in or anything have we?'

'Hold on, lemme check.'

My wrist buzzed again. Two minutes.

If I was bricking it before, I was full-blown about to shit myself now. He was slow-stepping towards the last aisle, craning his neck with his radio by his mouth.

With the GPS slowly sliding into my shoulder bag, I moved around so the plinth separated us, listening to his footsteps which were now approaching me. I could hear him breathing.

'Russell to Osvaldo, come in over?'

'Yeah, Russ, talk to me.'

'From what I can see in the diary, there's nothing scheduled for three months, why?'

'Because the...'

He didn't say anything else.

The radio dropped from his grip and his entire body shuddered then fell to the floor as I held the taser to his neck directly under his jaw.

Mr Oh

To be honest, I don't even remember reaching for the taser and touching it on his skin but I remember holding the thing on his wide neck all the way to the ground. He crumpled like a piece of paper and shook for what seemed like forever.

I'd returned to my low stance and watched him on the floor in front of me, still going through off-beat spasms.

'Nice one genius... what else was I supposed to... you know what? We don't have time for this... bags... yep, definitely time to go...'

The broad, caramel security guard was out cold. I'd never used a taser before so I didn't know what effect it would have on him or what was a sufficient amount of time to, ya know, zap someone.

He looked big so I wanted to make sure he stayed down.

'What was that Osvaldo?'

'Oh shit, the radio...'

Grabbing it from the floor, I started to move towards the hole, hopping through with no hands.

With one sweep of my hand, I picked up all four bags, jumped back into *The Shoe Boudoir* and closed the mirror behind me.

The bloody thing on my wrist buzzed again.

One minute.

The Tall Tales of Tatiana Blue

Osvaldo was still laying on the ground, motionless.

I had to stare at him for a second to make sure he was still breathing because he was so still. Maybe I zapped him for too long. Maybe I liked zapping him for too long.

Who knows?!

All I knew was that the door was open and I had to get the figgity fuck out of there. I clipped the radio on the inside of my front pocket and checked the map to find the nearest exit.

Rushing out into the walkways of Harrods, even dressed in overalls and a pair of Nikes, I felt special.

With my movements low and steady, the radio in my pocket crackled with white noise.

'Osvaldo... are you taking a shit again? Come on man, you can't do that and not tell anyone. Just meet me at the front doors when you're done. Remember fold, don't scrunch'

According to the map, I was near an escalator that would lead to an exit on Basil Street.

Dressed as a cleaner, I was thinking of the many ways I could lyrically spin my way out of the building. If I had to.

'What if there's security at the door... then there's security at the door... then what... you worry too much... you can't taser your way out of... why not... '

Mr Oh

Speed walking past shop fronts with grand displays, I found the escalator and let it carry me to the bottom. Being out in the open, where any security guard could see me was nerve-racking.

My wrist buzzed again and the digital display read...

'Time to go Miss Blue...'

With the bags of shoes slung over my shoulder, I was feet away from actually getting away with this.

As the escalator descended, I could see a set of double doors and single door come into view. And no one else in sight.

'Told you, you worry too much...'

I skipped off the escalator and ran to the doors, just hoping. Please be open.

The double doors and the single door were locked when I pushed them.

'This is why I worry... what for, lock picker remember?'

A quick reach into my shoulder bag and I pulled out the lock picker and was about to scan the lock when, from outside, a security guard and a doorman appeared, taking the last puffs on cigarettes.

The Tall Tales of Tatiana Blue

Instinct made my hand go up into the air and wave at them to get their attention. The security guard said something to the doorman and they both laughed as he unlocked the door with a large bunch of keys.

'I'm gonna figure out how to get out of this place one day,' I said as he looked me up and down.

'Ah, new girl with the cleaning crew huh? Don't worry, you'll get lost a few times in this place before you figure it out.'

I leaned against the open door, putting my body half way out. Standing in front of him, our bodies only inches apart, I looked in his eyes, hoping the locked contact would keep his eyes away from the bags.

'Yeah, first shift. Didn't realise this place was so big,' I added, confirming what he already thought.

As if on cue, the radio crackled in my pocket and drew his eyes to my breasts.

'Oh yeah, I forgot, I found this on the escalator upstairs. I dunno who it belongs to but...'

'Don't worry, this beat up radio can only belong to Osvaldo.'

He's not taking a shit, I thought.

In the distance, I could hear the rumble and clatter of a refuse collection truck.

The radio crackled again. 'Has anyone seen Osvaldo?'

Mr Oh

The guard excused himself and told me to give him a minute, meaning we weren't done.

Great.

I was inhaling fresh air with one foot outside and this guy wanted to chat me up.

'Yeah, this is Trent at the south side exit, one of the cleaners just found his radio... where?'

'On the third floor near the Toy Kingdom,' I lied.

'One of the prettiest cleaners I've ever seen said she found it near the Toy Kingdom.'

Oh for fucks sake, I thought, he's definitely trying to chat me up.

My wrist was continually vibrating, my heart was dancing to Busta Rhymes' *Gimme Some Mo'* and the black bags were slowly slipping through my moist hand over my shoulder. He kept his eyes locked on mine and gave me his best LL Cool J grin.

In the nervous state I was in, so close and yet so far, I played along.

'So what time are you meeting your girlfriend?' I threw at him, knowing he'd take the bait.

'I don't have a girlfriend,' he said, hiding his left hand.

Did guys still play this game? Apparently so.

'Oh... that's interesting...'

The Tall Tales of Tatiana Blue

'Is it?' he said, oozing hope and confidence.

'Yeah it is!' I said, making sure to add the right amount of Jill Scott sultry to my voice.

The one known as Russell interrupted us on his radio.

'Yeah, erm... Trent, did you just say a pretty cleaner? All of the cleaners are...'

'SO, I GOTTA GO!' I shouted over the radio, unsure of Russell's tone or what he was about to say.

It sounded like he was about to say something that would delay me further and I was enjoying enough fresh air to not want to hear it.

I grabbed Trent's hand and rubbed it with my fingers.

'Trent was it? Lemme go and give these to the bin men and I'll be right back.'

'Yeah,' he said dreamily. 'Right back?'

'Right back.'

Looking directly in his eyes, I gave him a tiny, yet effective, grin and eased past as he spoke into his radio.

'What was that last bit Russell over?'

'I said that all the cleaners here are men so which pretty cleaner have you just seen?'

'This beautiful looking...'

Mr Oh

Behind me, I could hear Trent describing me in a man's way – face, hair, backside – as I walked past a doorman who tipped his hat at me. I bowed from the waist in return then followed the sound of the bin truck, which was turning off Basil Street onto Hans Crescent.

Giving a light chase after the truck, I turned back to see Trent on his radio and another security guard coming out to join him, both looking and pointing in my direction.

'OI!'

That was the moment I took off running.

I went from a light jog to full sprint in a second and I was gone with the wind. With the pavements starting to fill with people, I ran in the middle of the road. The pavements, and the cars parked, became a blur as I caught a face of someone looking at me and put my head down as I could hear a security guard shouting into his radio.

'This is Russell, I'm in pursuit of a woman wearing a cleaner's uniform. Possible theft. Going onto Hans Crescent.'

The main security guy from the base office. He'd come down personally to take charge of the situation and was currently keeping good pace with me as I took a sharp left up Hans Crescent.

The Tall Tales of Tatiana Blue

Running alongside Harrods, trying to not let the bouncing bags affect my speed, I dodged morning commuters while still hearing Russell sprinting behind me.

'We need to get out of this uniform... we need to keep running is what we need to do, plus remember under this you look like a sexy cat burgular... he won't catch us... let's do it then...'

I took a deep breath, leaned forward and began to run on the tips of my toes. To Russell, it must've looked like I just turned on the afterburners. Trying to keep my top half as motionless as possible, letting my legs do all the work, I was quickly approaching the end of the path, which met a very busy Brompton Road.

'Left or right... right or left... choose for fucks sake...'

My afterburners took me to the right and as soon as I turned the corner, I stopped myself dead within a few steps, putting my back against a black standing advertising board for Zara. Turning quickly on my air bubble-supported feet, I brought my hand up in time to meet Russell, who came burning round the corner, kicking in his own afterburners.

Breathing heavily, I watched the shock of the taser hit him square in his breast plate and he went down quicker than Osvaldo did, yelping as he hit the ground.

His body did the Harlem Shake while his legs were doing the Electric Slide.

Observing my surroundings – on the main road – looking for anyone who was suddenly interested in the woman in the cleaner's boiler suit

Mr Oh

and the security guard on the ground, I watched him in wonder. A crowd began to surround us.

Then I acted, 'SOMEONE HELP...PLEASE...'

Looking around, I'd seen a portly man in a bad suit coming up the same path I'd just tore from and he approached.

'Is he okay?' he asked, smelling of coffee and piss.

'I don't know, he just collapsed. I think he's having a heart attack.'

A bit drastic to go with heart attack. I could've gone with spasm, seizure, allergic reaction even... but I was thinking on my feet and heart attack was the first thing that came to my head.

'Oh my god,' said the man. 'I'll call an ambulance.'

'You do that, I think I saw a policeman up the road, lemme go and get him.'

I looked down at Russell who was squinting at me.

God knows why I grinned at him but as I tightened my grip on the black bags on my shoulders, I winked and took off running again.

'You wait with him, I'll be right back.'

I was playing dodge the public and was moving down Brompton Road quick, fast and in a hurry. People were getting clipped on the shoulders as I kept it moving, with my free hand reaching in the shoulder bag for

The Tall Tales of Tatiana Blue

the Oyster card, which then made me think, what if there's no money on it?

A 74 bus was just about to pull away from a bus stop and I damn near ran in front of it, giving the driver my best puppy dog eyes. I sighed ridiculously loud when he opened the doors and let me on.

'Thank you so much, I'm sooo late for work.'

'Not a good idea to run in front of buses love.'

'I know, new job, first day. Wanna make a good impression.'

He waved me on and I beeped my Oyster card, the doors closed and the bus eased into the flow of traffic. I traversed the packed bus and went upstairs, scanning for a seat.

Feeling hot as hell, with my heart beating like crazy, I spotted a space in the back, next to a woman sleeping with her head against the window.

I walked down the aisle and swung the bags in front of me.

Before I sat down, I looked out of the window and saw quite a crowd had gathered around Russell, who was sitting up, supported by the rotund guy in the suit.

As the bus pulled away, I watched for as long as I could see.

Then I sat down.

And exhaled one hell of a breath.

Mr Oh

I'd done it.

I'd only gone and done it!

Looking around the packed top floor of the morning 74, guessing professions and destinations of the commuters, I smiled. Sat on my lap was close to £10,000 worth of shoes and here I was, looking like I'd spent my night cleaning toilets.

My smile widened. Then I chuckled. Then I full-out laughed to myself, drawing the attention of some of the bus folk.

'Sorry, everyone,' I said to no one particular. 'I told myself a joke.'

Wrapping my arm around the bags, I felt the long suede length of the Louboutin *Pigalle Botta* boots and I had to put my hand over my mouth to stifle my laughter. I must've looked like the craziest person in the world. And I didn't give a tiny rat's ass or a giant spider's bollocks.

I gave the bags the biggest hug and rested my head on my arms, grinning like a fool. Inside, I was drunk white girl dancing, throwing my arms in the air like I just didn't care. Every moment from the last hour played back in my head like IMAX.

The Shoe Salon stockroom, the shoes I missed...

Awwww, I saw so many absolutely nom nom shoes.

The Tall Tales of Tatiana Blue

I missed the Stella McCartney *Praline Nappa Bailey* knee high boot, the Miu Miu *Bicolor Patent* leather sling back pumps and, this one burned me now I think about it, the Givenchy *Zenaide suede Nautical Eyelet* heel in blue.

I couldn't remember everything I picked up, it was more of a snatch and grab, but I remembered I didn't pick up the Roberto Cavalli *jewelled snake sandal*, the Yves Saint Laurent *Ankle Cuff Paris Pump* or the darling Emilio Pucci *Dragon Resin and Calfskin Wedges*. All that was irrelevant as I looked up and realised this was my stop.

South Kensington station. One more step to increasing the distance between me and Harrods.

I shot up, darted down the stairs and squeezed through the closing doors with my bags behind me.

Counting them as the bus pulled off, I turned and ran into the station, holding my Oyster card in front of me.

Zipping past people with a turn off my shoulders, I pulled a dirty move and cut in front of a woman and her child, who was having a bitch of a tantrum.

I didn't care. I had to get as far away from here as possible and if this woman couldn't control her brat, why should that slow me down?

Yeah... me and kids ain't the best of friends to be honest.

Mr Oh

While he smacked and kicked her, I slid in front of them, beeped my Oyster card and was taking the escalator steps two at a time. I could hear a train pulling in but I had no idea where it was going, I just knew I wanted to be on it.

My tired legs buckled slightly as I rudely pushed past people without apologising. I got to the train and I stumbled through the doors. The announcement said I was on a District line train to Upminister. Get off at Mile End and get the Central line to Stratford.

With 15 stops until my next change, I took an empty booth of four seats, put the bags on the seat next to me and let my head fall back. I couldn't help but feel slightly more relaxed about actually getting away with it all as the train took off into the blackness of London's underground.

My thighs throbbed, not enjoying the morning run with no warm up. It was actually a surprise to myself how fast I could still run considering I hadn't been running since Marcus and I used to run together.

Wow.

Now there was someone I hadn't thought about for... an hour or so.

You can ask me when I fell asleep on the train but I didn't realise I did. My legs kicked out and I woke up as the train pulled into Mile End station. The first thing I did was check my bags, counting four. There was a train on the opposite platform as my train pulled in.

The Tall Tales of Tatiana Blue

'Come on come on come on come on…' I said, shaking off the nap and standing at the doors like a sprinter waiting for the gun.

The doors opened and I was the first one off, sprinting to the closing doors of the train on the opposite platform.

I took three large steps and managed to get half my body through the doors with a giant leap as they closed but my other half with the bags was stuck hanging out of the train.

Everyone looked at me – didn't help by the way – as I wiggled my leg in then forced the door open to get the bags in.

'FUCKING OPEN!' I shouted.

Catching myself, I covered my mouth and held my hand up to the people staring at me. The doors opened, I pulled the bags to my chest and held them closer than close.

Falling into a seat, I tried to catch my breath.

'That was close ladies, I almost lost you there.' I said to my shoes.

MY shoes.

They were mine.

Ferragamo *platform pumps*… MINE!

Dior *open-toe lagoon blue* patent leather pump with CD on the back of the heels… MINE!

Mr Oh

Giuseppe Zanotti *tobacco-coloured python print* court shoes... MINE!

Louboutin *Jenny Pump Bazin* in blue and pink... MINE!

Louboutin *Vampanodo* open toe sandal with the satin bow in blue... MINE!

Louboutin *Pigalle Botta boot*... Oh, there were two of those and they were both MINE!

I was one stop away from getting home and being able to fully relax. As much as I was enjoying remembering the shoes, I wasn't happy with the attention I'd drawn to myself by getting caught in the doors. If there were to be any repercussions from all of this, it'd be good to not be noticed on the way home on public transport.

I hate, and I mean deep down hate, the journey between Mile End and Stratford train station. It is like the longest fucking journey ever. The gap between most stations on the Central Line is like 30 seconds to a minute but the gap between Mile End and Stratford is like five damn minutes, I swear.

Yeah I know I'm exaggerating but, I needed to be home. I was yearning the protection of my own surroundings.

'Calm down... I just wanna get home that's all... we're almost there alright, just chill out... alright alright alright...'

My eyes closed, my hands wrapped around the bags in my lap and I listened to the train fly underneath Mile End road.

The Tall Tales of Tatiana Blue

Reaching for my inner Zen or some shit like that, I calmed my body down. Told the dancing inside to sit this one out and just relax. Rattling through the underground, it repeatedly dawned on me exactly what I'd done in the space of an hour.

In Harrods.

Mohammed Al-Fayed was gonna be pissed with me when he heard about this but, meh, what can he do? Does he even own Harrods anymore?

I was almost home as the train came out of the tunnel and a strong ray of sunshine blessed my face.

You have no idea how good that felt.

My chin raised and I let the sun glow over me as the train stopped and the doors opened. With a very long sigh, I got up and was on a quick walk to the stairs, taking them two at a time, swerving and moving quicker than those around me.

Anyone who lives in London, or any congested city, knows how to walk on a busy pavement, at speed, while avoiding other people. It's like an art. I was turning my shoulders to squeeze through gaps, swinging my bags to make gaps between walkers and talkers...

Oyster card in hand, I slid it across the reader and the final barrier between me and home opened and I couldn't control the butterflies in my stomach as I walked out of the station, looking at the ground.

Mr Oh

I passed the steps leading towards Westfield and began to jog around Great Eastern Road, the bags bouncing behind my shoulder as an uncomfortable reminder of my haul. Although my legs were burning, they wanted to kick in one last touch of the afterburner to get home quicker. But I didn't wanna be noticed as the woman someone saw running down the road with black bags in a cleaner's uniform.

So I jogged.

Four minutes exactly and I was at the front door to the block of expensive flats overlooking the Stratford Theatre.

'Where's my key?'

I ran my hand through the shoulder bag, hoping against hope that it was in there and I just didn't see it.

And it was.

'Niccccccce...'

Letting myself in, I greeted the rent-a-jobsworth at the reception and called a lift.

Quick ding, quick dong and I was at my front door, with my legs feeling like jelly.

The muscle of my arm which had been holding the bags most of the way home ached from gripping them so tight. But that was all Bisto because I was home.

The Tall Tales of Tatiana Blue

That's right.

My name is Tatiana Blue, I'd just stolen over 20 pairs of shoes from Harrods in an hour and, less than an hour later, I was home.

What have you done in the last hour?!

With the key in the lock, the door swung open and I tumbled in, closing the door with my entire body. For some reason, I was more nervous now I was home. It was like because I knew I could relax, I didn't want to because I'd been so tense for what felt like forever.

Leaning off the door, I opened my eyes and something inside me suddenly clicked and I became entranced with a new mission. Something I just had to do.

And I had to do it now!

I dropped to a squat, which made a fresh heat burn in my knees, and opened the first bag, removing all the shoe boxes and random crap I'd put in there.

I wanted them gone.

Away from my shoes.

One bag cleared, I made short work of the next three bags, throwing shit everywhere while planning to clean it later. Making old people

Mr Oh

noises as I got to my feet, I hobbled down the corridor and kicked open my bedroom door with purpose.

My thigh didn't like that and I could feel a massive cramp tightening my thigh muscle. But I'd almost completed my mission and I was going to see it through.

'Come on love... we're gonna make it...'

I got to the foot of my bed and turned all four bags of shoes upside and watched it rain heels over my duvet. I managed to watch each shoe fall beautifully on and off my bed before the cramp crippled me and I hit the ground, massaging my thigh, sucking air through my teeth and giggling. Sitting upright against my wardrobe, I could see that I wasn't dreaming, I wasn't in the middle of an intricate daydream, I wasn't playing a super advanced computer game or living a *Truman Show* existence.

This really happened.

I had shoes again.

Amazingly crafted, gorgeously inspired, stunningly fabulous, unbelievably delicious, creatively designed, internationally known – some not even supposed to exist – shoes.

And they were all fucking mine!

The Tall Tales of Tatiana Blue

Sitting on the floor with my back against my wardrobe and massaging my throbbing thigh, I looked at the mish mash of heels, straps, boots, colours, materials and designs on my bed. The cramp was totally worth it.

Well kind of worth it cuz it hurt like a bitch to be honest.

After a semi-pleasurable rub down - making me sound like Peter Griffin when he hurts himself - I checked the fluidity of the muscle before cautiously extending my thigh hoping it wouldn't cramp up again. More than anything, I just wanted to be close to my shoes. That's all.

Holding on to the door of my wardrobe, I struggled to my feet, keeping my thigh muscle straight and limped to the bed.

By the time I got to the foot of the bed, my wince transformed into a full grin.

'ALL MINE!' I shouted to my bed.

I remember reaching for random shoes, holding them up to the sunlight, enjoying the feel of the material between my fingers. Spinning them round to admire the colours from every angle, my body was behaving like one big nerve ending and an unknown substance was suddenly injected into me.

I know what that was... the elixir of shoes.

FREE SHOES!

Wrong or right, I felt happy.

Mr Oh

Reaching behind me, I stretched my arms, feeling tiredness begin to fuck with me. That was followed by a long yawn which made the joints in my jaw click. But not once did I take my eyes off my bed.

'I need a drink!'

Kicking the trainers off my feet, I shuffled to the kitchen and looked around, thinking with my ninja mind. Eyes on my bed all the way.

My rum was in one cupboard while my glasses were in the opposite cupboard. With one hand, I reached for the glass. With my foot – on my uncramped leg – I stretched to open the cupboard with the rum. Then I spun on my leg and circled until I was facing the bottle of rum I bought on a Caribbean cruise five years previously but never opened.

All done with the grace and poise of a ballerina.

A giggle and a pour and I was on my way back to my bedroom, remembering a spliff on my bedside table.

'It's not even 9am... So? Am I going to work? No, so what do I care... yeah but... but nothing, I just robbed Harrods... yeah that's true who cares about weed in the morning...'

The morning sun and the sound of increasing traffic blasted through my window as I shuffled back to my room. The first sip, while looking over my shoes, felt warm all over.

There was a Cheshire Cat grin that I couldn't hide as I ran my fingers over the leather of the Christian Dior *lagoon blue* pumps and trailed

The Tall Tales of Tatiana Blue

slowly and sensually over the satin of the bows on the Louboutin *Vampanodos*.

My eyes led to the spliff in the ashtray and I sat down on my shoe-shaped sofa in the corner of my room, my eyes still locked on my bed of shoes.

I know I keep talking about the fact that I kept looking at my shoes but put yourself in my... shoes. One hour, £10,500 worth of shoes, Harrods robbed. I was HYPE!

I screamed so loudly, I knew my neighbours probably thought I was getting a morning seeing to. To be honest, that would've been the perfect cherry on top of a very delicious cake.

And that's when Quincy came to my mind.

'Where is that guy?' I asked myself, with rum scalding my chest.

The way I was still vibrating, high off the running and the watching my back and the lock picker and the taser, I knew a little bit of good dick would've been the dollop of cream on my cheesecake.

And I like cheesecake and cream.

Reaching for the shoulder bag, which was still on my shoulder, I fished for the iPhone.

No phone call, no messages, no nothing! And my app had disappeared. How could he put me on some mad-ass mission and then leave me? He had questions to answer.

Mr Oh

No checking up on me to see if I'd been arrested or nothing... what a wanker!

I tried to call back the only number on the call list but it went straight to the voicemail of someone who did not sound like Quincy. Thinking I got the wrong number, while taking a long pull on my spliff, I tried again and got through to the same Dave who didn't sound like Quincy.

'Hmmm!'

All that was running through my mind was: fuck I've been set-up.

The longer I sat there on my bedroom sofa, drinking and smoking as the sun came up, the more I thought the police were on their way to my flat in a convoy to come and arrest me. I imagine Al Fayed would have a convoy of Jackson 5-0 at his beck and call.

'Pretty strange how you start being paranoid just as you start smoking... shut up...'

Exhaling to the ceiling, watching a haze of smoke groove in the sunlight, my eyes closed thinking about the possibility of being set-up. With my feet up on the bed, and a Louboutin *Jenny Bazin* heel tickling my foot, I knocked back the rest of the rum, quick smoked the rest of the spliff and just stared at my bed.

The same place where I fell asleep last night and, now, here was that same bed dripping in delicious shoes. My wrist vibrated and the watch I forgot about jolted my eyes open.

The Tall Tales of Tatiana Blue

I looked at the display.

'Time for a nap Miss Blue, you're tired!'

Well, how did the watch know I was thinking the same thing? That was my first question. My second was huh? My third was what the fuck as something pinched my wrist.

"OW! What the FUCK was tha..."

And then it happened again!

I don't know when or how I fell asleep but I woke up somewhere completely different. Again. This was getting stupid.

It honestly felt like I was developing narcolepsy.

Thankfully I woke up, not as far away from my bed as before. I opened my eyes laying on my queen-sized bed, looking straight up. My eyes darted from the left to the right, my senses took in all they could without moving with my arms still at my side.

Memories hazed through my confusion as to how I got into bed, considering the last thing I remember was that bloody watch pinching me.

My wrist was now bare.

Mr Oh

It was turning to dusk and the sun was going down beside the Stratford Picture House.

'Where's my shoes?!?!'

They were the last things I saw as my eyes closed so, if I was in bed then where were my shoes?

I sat up like the Undertaker, hopped off the bed and got low.

There was no illusion in my mind that it couldn't have been anyone else but Quincy who moved me, but where were my shoes? And where was he?

'Foot of the bed Miss Blue,' Quincy said from out of nowhere.

I spun around and lost my balance because, honestly, I thought it was God talking.

With one hand holding onto my bed, getting back to the balls of my feet, I looked every – fucking – where for the direction of the voice.

First things first, where were my shoes? Foot of the bed.

Leaning while holding the mattress, I could see my shoes laid out OCD neat, side-by-side and in an alphabetical designer order I noticed instantly.

'I DON'T KNOW WHY YOU LIKE TO KEEP DRUGGING ME BUT IT'S NOT THE COOL THING TO DO YA KNOW!' I shouted to my ceiling.

The Tall Tales of Tatiana Blue

'Why are you shouting, I'm only in the shower.'

My forehead screwed up.

Why was he in my shower?

I mean, when someone comes in your house for the first time, you'd feel a bit funny if they go into your fridge and take what they want. They have to come round a few times before they get their visitor status removed, right? Same thing. Sure he'd been the catalyst for me feeling more alive than I'd ever felt in my entire life and restarted my shoe collection with some of the world's most expensive shoes, but that didn't mean he could use my shower without asking. I only met him last night for fuck sake, now he is showering in my yard?

Maybe the least I could do was let him have a shower. Let him be clean before I drag him through the dirt and berate him to within an inch of his life.

Reaching for a corner lamp, I rose to my feet as the bathroom door opened and the light turned off. I didn't move from where I stood, slightly to the right of the bedroom door. I wanted to watch him come into my view.

Inside, I wasn't really sure how I'd feel seeing him again.

The last time I physically saw him, he asked me a question I didn't know how to answer.

How easy was it to get those shoes?

Mr Oh

I could hear his footsteps coming towards me and my inside suddenly warmed up. A lot happened since the last time I saw him in his very tidy three-piece with his healthy looking dreadlocks that my inner ninja wanted to pull. More than a little bit.

I'm not sure if the warmth in my belly was erotic or enraged. Seeing his face would answer that question.

Quincy walked into my bedroom at the same time as a fruity steam haze crept in waves. He was looking at my shoes with a black towel wrapped around his waist. I was looking at his towel – that I didn't own – around his nicely drawn in waist of chocolate.

First thing I did was smile. I couldn't help it. My cheeks bunched high on my face and I was beaming uncontrollably.

'I was guessing I was either gonna get a smile or a kick in the meat pies...'

'Just because you got a smile, doesn't mean you still can't get that Beckham to the misters.'

I wasn't sure if I wanted black towels or if I wanted the man in the towel. It was standing at 28% towels, 82% chiselled, chocolate, mysterious man with water dripping from the tips of his shoulder-length dreadlocks.

I followed and got lost in water droplets that splashed on his shoulders and ran down his arms.

The Tall Tales of Tatiana Blue

His eyes appeared to be reading me. He has those kind of eyes that seem to look at you and through you at the same time. Like he was reading a printout of my thoughts before I even spell-checked.

He was doing it over the phone when I woke up in Harrods.

He was doing it last night at Maya's.

And he was doing it now. Making my mid-section heat up nicely, may I add.

'First things first. I owe you £10.'

I gave him sarcasm. 'Yes you fucking do.'

He reached behind his back and gave me a folded note.

I unwrapped it and held it to the light.

'It's real, I'm not…'

'No,' I said, scrutinising the note. 'You're Nigerian and traditionally, you guys are into kidnapping, paper trail fraud, credit cards, drugging and subduing people and…'

'You make me sound like some *Criminal Minds* psycho.'

'Not far off. What you did isn't exactly normal is it?'

'If creating a moment for someone to be their true self is abnormal, then I don't wanna be normal.'

Mr Oh

'Huh?'

I was slightly confused because his body was distracting me. His hair was making my eyes green because they were long enough to reach his shoulders, which meant every time he turned his head, they flicked. That was my dream.

To have my own head of full grown thick dreadlocks like Lauryn Hill in her prime was what I aspired to. One or two individual dreads stretched to the middle of my neck but they weren't there yet.

'So, Miss Blue, how do you feel this morning?'

My neck snaked and it must've been that air of smugness about him that made me verbally unleash on him. 'Erm... HOW did you get in here last night? HOW did you get me out of my bed and into Harrods of all places? What gave you the right to do that? What if I got arrested? What if I got caught? What if I couldn't do this?'

I was loud and in his face as I stepped towards him pointing my finger.

'What if there were cameras I didn't see and I'm on CCTV? What about fingerprints? Why didn't you put gloves in the bag? How was I supposed to get out with just a uniform? You planned everything, right? You wanted me to get out with the cleaners? REALLY? Do you know what I had to do to get out of there in the end? And where were you? Huh? Sitting back, having a wank, playing with your suit? SAY SOMETHING FOR FUCK SAKE!'

Quincy's eyebrows were at the top of his forehead and he exhaled with his hands out in surrender. 'Okay, well that was a lot. From the top! I picked your lock last night, drugged you with a herbal mixture from

The Tall Tales of Tatiana Blue

work, transported you in a Range Rover, nothing gave me the right but what I thought would happen, happened... erm... what else did you ask? What if you got caught? You always had an out, which was a simple falling asleep in the changing room excuse and I knew you could do this, that's why I did it.'

He returned the answers before I was ready for them. And he kept going, stepping towards me with his yum of a body making me step backwards.

'The cameras that DID see you have mysteriously been erased, if you look on your fingers you'll notice a very thin plastic polymer to cover your fingerprints and yes I do know what you had to do. It wasn't what you were supposed to do, but you adapted and did your own thing anyway. And where was I? Didn't you see me on Basil Street when you left Harrods and ran right past me? I saw you. I was there the whole time!'

Rewinding the last hour in my mind, I played the moment I started to run in the middle of Basil Street. Running so fast, everything became a blur as I outran Russell, the handsome security guard who eventually got a taser to the chest. But there was one moment when I running and I saw one guy looking at me but I was moving so quickly, I saw him then he was gone in an instant.

I wanted to deal with that but Quincy was standing very close to me, having thrown back answers to each of my questions. Clear, concise, eloquent.

Mr Oh

The power of a man talking to me directly, strongly and honestly, while standing in front of me in a towel, had my nipples hard and my face fully flushed.

Over his shoulder, I could see my shoes all neatly lined, looking all beautiful and lovely and pretty and sexy and... yuuuuuum...

'How'd I do?' I asked curiously.

'Look at how you did.'

He turned to look at my shoes and his very strong back looked at me, all chocolate and defined and shit.

I know it's a cliché and contrived and the type of thing I never usually do but... I bit my thick lower lip.

I looked at his back and imagined digging my nails into it. Partly for pleasure, mainly for pain.

The pleasure was to say thank you for opening my eyes to the fact that what I thought were my limits were in fact nothing but stepping stones. The pain was for the fact that he violated my life by breaking in and making me his little lab monkey. At that moment, I didn't know what the future held for me. But I knew I wanted more shoes.

You know what I wanted more though?

Quincy taking that towel off and fucking the horse hell shit out of me!

Water sat in tiny puddles across his shoulders.

The Tall Tales of Tatiana Blue

He was oblivious to the sexually sadistic daydreams I was having while he was perusing my haul of shoes.

'Hey are those two pairs of...' Quincy said, turning around to face me and catching me mid-fantasy. 'Are you okay?'

'I'm cooler than a polar bear's toe nails thank you...' It was the only thing that came to mind.

Then we both shared a silence as his surprised eyes caught my slutty ones. I was in the middle of a fantasy of looking back at him as he pulled my dreads while straight pounding me, saying some outlandishly vulgar shit.

He started to read me. His eyes took in my whole face and I felt like he was touching me. My skin crawled pleasurably and I could feel his hands on my neck. But he wasn't touching me.

'Yeah, that would be nice.'

'What would?' I replied.

'From the back, pulling your hair, saying some nasty shit in your ear.'

This fucking guy!

So you're telling me he can read minds as well?

My face showed that he was right on the money and he grinned.

I played it cool. 'So... how did you do that?'

Mr Oh

'It's what I do.'

'What DO you do actually Mr Quincy, because all you've given me so far is that you're a... a what?'

'A contractor.'

'Yeah, whatever the fuck that is.'

Behind him, my duo of brand spanking new Louboutin boots – size five and six – stared at me, standing tall and so sweeeeeeeet lawd have mercy sexy.

I looked back at Quincy and that was it for me. I was on him so damn quick. He never saw me coming even though he was staring right at me.

He put his arms out to the side and that just allowed me to plant my lips on his. Once landed, I wrapped my arms around his shoulders and waited for his defined arms to wrap around me. I knew he'd touch me, I just had to kiss him.

Not to brag or anything but I'm a brilliant kisser. If you ever meet Quincy, ask him.

His arms drew around my body and... woooow... the way I was feeling looking at my boots then at Quincy, well...

Let's just say I wanted him inside me there and then.

It was a lion's roar of a feeling as I unwrapped the warm towel from his waist and threw it in the doorway. I could feel the warmth from his body and I was breathing like a fat person at a buffet. At the same time,

The Tall Tales of Tatiana Blue

something shot up towards me and rested against the groin of my leggings.

We both looked down, me more interested than he.

Of course since the moment I met Quincy, I wondered if he had a suitably-sized dick. Not that I was thinking of fucking him at the party last night, but I wondered same way.

Didn't need to wonder any more.

Quincy was facing his erection but he was looking up at me through his eyelashes, which were very long for a man. They were pretty. Never noticed them before.

As I was staring, he grabbed me by my arms and that made the breath suck right out of me. My eyes were wide with shock and eroticism, hoping he would find some way to get inside me. And fast. I was past the point of just wanting him... I needed him.

The buzz of my memories in *The Shoe Boudoir* were still rattling in my mind while my new shoes were looking at me, just waiting to be slipped into, buckled, tied and buttoned up.

Facing my shoes, I felt a strong breath on my neck and it was like a Lauryn Hill and D'Angelo moment: nothing really mattered. We were face-to-face. I could feel heat emanating off his chocolate and covering me. Every muscle in my neck relaxed and my head dropped forward onto his shoulder as he inhaled the back of my ear.

Mr Oh

Weirdly felt nice to be smelled. Not like I was a plate of food, more like I was a flower that was blossoming in his hands.

Though his hands were strong on my arms, the movement of his face on my neck was slow, leaving a trail of feeling wherever he went. Then he growled.

A real manly, jungle cat sounding, hungry growl that simply made me melt.

My tired legs buckled under me and I slipped out of his grasp, putting two hands on the bed.

Initially it was to get out of the feeling on my neck which was starting to feel a lot like foreplay. That's not what I wanted and/or needed.

I'd just stolen shoes from one of the most prestigious, elegant and expensive stores in the world and I'd gotten away with it. I was at a stage where I wanted the dick to punish me for what I'd done. Treat me like a thief and punish me accordingly.

Walking my hands back on the bed, leaving my rump within his reach, I looked back at him.

'You can't touch me until you take those off...'

I pointed at my leggings with my eyes and he followed.

He ran his hands up my legs, up to the sides of my stomach then down to my waistband.

My leggings slipped down past my cheeks and rolled to my knees as I held on to the bed, still looking back at him.

The Tall Tales of Tatiana Blue

'Naughty girl who lost her shoes...' Quincy said, pulling them all the way off and swinging my body round.

'Awoke in Harrods slightly confused...' He kneeled on the bed with his hands on my knees and disappeared from my line of sight.

'So shopping she went...' He parted my knees and pushed my legs back. Two fingers ran along the lips of my pussy, my back arched instantly and I whistled.

'With no money spent...' His fingers left my lips and I heard the rip of a condom pack.

'And now she has mythical Loubous...'

By the end of his impromptu rhyme – which by the way made me cheesy smile – the head of his dick slicked through my lips and my back arched again.

'Listen, now is NOT the time to...'

My voice was silenced mid-sentence, the sexiness of my back arch had fallen flat out and I felt my eyes roll in the back of my head as he slid inside me. Not fully... just past the tip. Yep, my eyes were rolling just past the tip.

He had his hands on my thighs and he was half-smiling at me. Watching him with water dripping down his chest, his stomach muscles tensing, a soft scent of shoe leather in the air... I was feeling good. And he was STILL sliding.

Mr Oh

The fucker almost made me cum there and then. A thick rush of blood to my head and everything I looked at was covered in a nice shade of blue. The white railing at the head of my bed got a strong grip as I could feel him sliding the rest of his length inside me. His seven and a half, possibly eight and three quarter, inches continued sliding inside me and I was slapping the frame like it owed me money, sucking air through my teeth and waiting for him to reach the end of my coco brick road. But he just kept sliding.

From out of the blue – hehe – he slid out to the tip and literally car crashed back inside me.

In my head I screamed, 'WHAT WAS THAT?'

My thick legs wrapped around him and pulled him on top of me and I held on for dear life as I clenched every muscle and froze for about 21 seconds. No multiplication needed to know I was done!

Then his hands slowly crept around my ass, even slower up my back and into my hair.

Into my HAIR ladies!

He was running his fingers between the roots of my dreadlocks against my scalp and I had absolutely nothing to say about it. I was Homer drooling in my mind. Marcus didn't even put his hands in my hair.

I just shut what they call the fuck up!

The Tall Tales of Tatiana Blue

Coming down off a shivering high, I rolled my head like a cat with its tummy scratched.

'Is this what you wanted? Huh?' Quincy asked, reaching one hand under my back. Holding himself inside me, he lifted me while turning us both around on his knees. He slipped out and flipped me over so I was facing my shoes.

'My shoes think you're not fucking me hard enough.'

'Oh really?'

I was hoping my innocent teasing would annoy him into pushing the boundaries of roughness and seeing how far I'd be willing to go. This was the stage I was at.

I was at the "call me a whore, spit on my pussy, stick a finger in my backdoor" stage. Anywhere beyond that was pushing it but I could be coerced. He could've pulled out a jar of coffee and a blowtorch and told me he was about to slow roast this pussy and I would've been like, suuuuuure, go right ahead. Long as my shoes were nearby, I was up for any down stroke.

Quincy ran his hands up my back and I purred. His fingers separated and spread over my scalp as he pulled my head back, used his knee to part my thighs. He slid in and my lips opened for him like they missed him.

Moment of silence for this excellent example of pussy slaying. And he'd barely done shit.

Mr Oh

One of his strong hands rested on my left cheek and my hips began to circle of their own accord. My G-Spot was rubbing against his circling head as I opened my eyes to see my shoes in front of me.

'Tatiana Blueee...' Quincy said playfully.

'Yeeeeeeees, that is me...' I groaned, my body bucking against him with no discernible rhythm. 'Say my name like that again.'

'Tat-iana Blueeeeeeee...'

The sound of my name rolled down my spine to where he was now pounding the right royal shit out of me. I was jerking forward with such ferocity, my bed was scooting across my hardwood floor. At this point, I was a mess.

Mentally and physically.

The feeling I wanted was currently opening me up with each hefty thrust and I stopped counting at the strike of the third orgasm. We were working a lovely tandem movement where I'd throw my ass back to him and he'd catch it with a nice, deep thrust that seemed to get deeper with every push.

I swore and cursed like my life depended on it.

'Fuck the shit out of me... I'm a shoe thief, stop being a prick and fuck me like one... get deep, deeper... look at my sexy fucking shoes... don't don't don't stop... oh you cunt...'

Then he stopped and pulled out of me. Cold.

The Tall Tales of Tatiana Blue

Whatever fantasy land of shoes and hard dick I floated in was suddenly pulled from under me and I turned my head back like *The Exorcist*.

'What the fuuuuck are you doing back there?! Didn't I tell you not to stop?!'

'Just wait five more seconds,' Quincy said breathlessly.

'You've got to be kidding me? My pussy's soaking wet, I'm cursing you the fuck out and you wanna play ga...'

Five seconds must've passed because he gave me one single, solo, numero uno thrust that filled me instantly. The shock of him withdrawing while I was enjoying him was one thing but then waiting five seconds then grinding uterus deep had me making a noise that was biblical.

All the clichés, I hit 'em one after the other.

While staying inside me, I slapped my bed frame to shit, moaned like an absolute dog, lost my equilibrium, called him a fucking bastard, played with my clit, grabbed the sheets, called him a bitch, pounded the bed with a fist, tried to look back at him, covered my face with my hair as I moaned and finally laid there as a new ripple of pleasure started over me.

Oh yes indeedy, apparently, I was needy for good dicky. And I say that proudly. The ting hit me nicely.

Mr Oh

While I squirmed on the bed, my whole body clenching every few seconds, I squinted back at him as he laid down next to me with an unbelievably smug grin on his face.

To be honest, the man had every right!

I was looking at him and still cumming so I had to put my hands up over my face. If I could move my arms.

His mouth looked like he wanted to say something but I was floating in and out of fantasy moments of suede open-toe pumps and dick.

He did that thing with his eyes where I felt like he was running his hands up my back and I shivered onto my side.

'How... do you do that?' I stuttered.

'What?'

'That thing where you look at me and it feels like you're touching me?'

'Not quite sure what you're talking about Miss Blue.'

I gave him a weak slap on the chest for such an answer.

That was when a heavier wave of ripples coursed through me. I rolled onto my back and a single wave of fresh leather brushed under my nose.

I managed to roll enough just so I could see my shoes.

My brand new shoes.

The Tall Tales of Tatiana Blue

All sexy and mine. And free.

I know I said before that I wasn't sure where this was gonna go but, think about it, just for a second.

Tell me you wouldn't if you were me?

All it takes is a bit of planning, the right equipment, a little bit of research... I could do this.

More importantly, I wanted to do this.

I wanted my shoes back.

Nothing could replace what Marcus took away from me but that didn't mean I couldn't start again. I'd pretty much decided I wasn't going back to work when I stole the Charlotte Olympia pumps for me and Maya.

'Let me know what you need and when you need it,' Quincy said, doing that mind reading shit again.

I took a long look at my shoes... geeeez Louise, you have no idea how good my sugars looked, standing all heel tall and just waiting to be slipped into.

My head turned to Quincy who was admiring my shoes with me. With waves of yummy still passing through me, I rolled onto my stomach and kicked my feet behind me.

'Shoe thief? Why not.'

Mr Oh

Footsoles and Pantyhoes

*T*atiana Blue she was.

Beautiful in flats, delectable and amazing in heels.

Oh, the heels.

Caramel topped with a chocolate honey glaze, thick deadlocks with a blue streak tickling her shoulders and draped in a shape-hugging skirt suit, she definitely looked the part.

Today was the day she was making a change.

No more gambling with her life, no more stealing, bye bye to the seedy leather underworld of which she was known as a queen.

Tatiana was no longer content with spending time forever on the hunt for the perfect shoe for her ever growing collection while giving hundreds of shoes away to those who couldn't afford them.

She wanted more. More from life.

She wanted quiet nights in arguing over the TV with a partner; she wanted a family, she even wanted white picket fences.

Deep down, she knew her need for change was rooted in her desire to have children. With her biological clock ticking and her soul finally craving and broody, Tatiana was changing for a future she despised for so long.

The Tall Tales of Tatiana Blue

Her heart longed for normality but, with as many shoes as she had in her possession, such an idea always felt like a pipe dream. Sort of like the nightmare her sex life had become.

Stolen moments with random guys scratched an itch but wasn't the cream she needed to heal. Rather than taking the time to go and meet someone who could be the yang to her crazy ying, she travelled the world. Stealing shoes.

She had flats, apartments and storage spaces rented out in different names which were perfect hiding places for stolen merchandise. Stocked floor-to-ceiling with shoes, the four storage rooms – all with different storage companies – became her home away from home. When she wasn't stealing shoes, she was in one of her lock-ups, trying on shoes she already stole.

Alphabetically, and in the order they were procured, Tatiana shelved her shoes in a neat, almost OCD fashion and only wore a select few out in public.

Italy, Spain, Bulgaria, Switzerland, West End, Colorado, Las Vegas, Paris, wherever designer shoes were made, she was there and made sure that she got what she wanted.

Louboutin suede buckle sandals from the factory with lax security in Paris, Marni satin bow slingbacks from the Prime Minister of Italy's wife with her open bedroom window, Roberto Cavalli lace up leather wedges from Roberto's 'secret' Switzerland getaway.

Mr Oh

DKNY, Jimmy Choo, Alaïa, Chloë, Emilio Pucci, Lanvin, Valentino, Charlotte Olympia, Alexander McQueen, Brian Stood, Bottega, Brian Atwood and Michael Kors were some of the names in her collection that made her the best designer shoe thief in the world.

Tatiana found it an adventure to pick the lock on a Reed Krakoff factory and have free reign over whatever shoes she wanted. There was an orgasm almost every time she turned on the lights in one of her storage spaces and boxes of shoes looked back at her.

With over 2,538 pairs of designer shoes in her collection, Tatiana was ready to give it all up in order to make a change.

That meant no more stealing, but she could keep what she already had. In her head, that was just good sense.

Standing across the road from the office of the Ebony Times, Tatiana could feel herself shaking. Nervous at the idea of getting the job and being called a fashion consultant.

It was a weird feeling for her considering, just last week, she balanced herself on the wooden beams of one of Jimmy Choo's China factories with no rope and security looking for her below.

A 'walk in the park!' she called it.

The Tall Tales of Tatiana Blue

Clip clopping with confidence in her Brian Atwood all black heels, Tatiana stopped at the crossing, looking both ways before skipping across the street.

She was ready.

She felt positive about her interview and her heart was pumping excitedly then she realised that, for the first time in a long time, she was tool-less. No lock picker disguised as her mascara, no safe breaker hidden in her blush compact, no taser and no retractable heels for quick movement.

For the excitement fiend that was Tatiana Blue, this was the first day of a new day. And the plan looked good and golden until...

Hold on, let ME tell the rest of this story because this Oh guy won't get it right. Who better than the man himself to break it down so it can forever be broken?

Hi, hello, what's up, wgwarn, what's good, what's crackalacking? My name is Russell Reed and, as you were about to find out, I'm the one that "apparently" fucked up Miss Blue's day.

Would I agree with that statement? No, no, hell fucking no.

She just happened to be in the right place at the right time for me. Doing what I do, it's all about right place, right time, quick moments, in out, no drama.

Mr Oh

Anyway, I'll tell you the situation then you tell me if I fucked up her day, deal?

Okay, so... oh yeah, she was crossing the road. And that was when I saw her. I was following one Greek PH and...

What's a PH I hear you ask?

How rude of me not to formally introduce myself.

My name is Russell Reed and I'm an upskirt addict.

I LOVE that shit.

I walk around with up to three, sometimes four, hidden cameras and I film up women's skirts. Nothing sexier than watching a woman's ass and thighs when she walks. But from beneath her skirt. Oooh, I'm telling you, the thought is making me hard right now...

A PH is a PantyHoe, that's what I call my ladies that I film. It's not calling the woman a hoe, it's just cuz it sounds like pantihose. And I do like pantihose. And pop socks and tights and knee high socks, suspenders, all that shit.

I mean, think about it, a woman's legs are sexy in themselves but, in motion, divine. Then there's the panties.

The best part. The thickness of lips pressed together.

The Tall Tales of Tatiana Blue

Upskirts work for me because of the panties. Especially on a nice ass, trust me, I'll be spitting on my hand and wanking out a 30 minute nut to that kinda clip on repeat. If she's going commando, 10 minutes.

Say what you want about upskirt clip makers, 'oh, it's illegal... it's disrespectful to women' or whatever but the way I've got the camera in my shoes and trainers, you'd never know. So why get offended if you don't know I'm doing it?

I'm probably filming up your skirt right now!? Like I said, I LOVE that shit. I've got over 4,000 DAYS worth of footage. Not hours.... DAYS...

24 hours in a day. 4,000 days. Do the numbers.

That's your skirt, your friend's skirt, your mum's skirt, your aunty's skirt, the pastor's wife's skirt, your cousin's skirt, your friend's skirt, THAT skirt...

So, anyway, where was I?

Oh yeah, I was in Chelsea, recording one thick-thighed Greek-looking PH who was giving me good footage on my trainer cam. I had another camera securely pointing up in a Primark bag I carried as my primary camera and that was when I saw Tatiana half-skipping across the road.

She was just... slippery.

Made me want to get naked and rub myself in vegetable oil in front of a slide-show of upskirts.

Mr Oh

Hands down, the sexiest upskirt I could ever wish to have. And I've had a lot.

I left the Greek and I was onto her so quick. Barging people, stepping on shoes, not giving a fuck. I just wanted to see what she had under that skirt.

The closer I got, the better she looked. From a distance her shape looked promising but from 30 yards, my dick woke up. That was always a sign of a good PH.

She stopped in front of a huge building and that was when I knew I could get her. A risky move but doable.

Filming up women's skirts isn't easy you know!?

I came from behind as she fiddled with her iPhone and it was as if I could see through her clothes the way her skin radiated. Caramac neck tattooed with something that started between her dreadlocks and disappeared beneath her shirt. Her skirt was fitted and formed tight to her thighs. Usually a problem for us upskirters because women tend to walk with less freedom in a tight skirt. More of a restrained sexy walk. But a woman in a flowing thigh length dress will walk free as a bird.

The thing with Tatiana, was the way she stood. She stood like someone was taking her picture. Her legs were looking all strong and thick, another excellent prospect for an upskirter. One leg was straight for support and the other was out to the right. And she had these shoes. These black, shiny, smooth high heels on. Her foot didn't look stressed in the shoe, it was just cool. I don't have a shoe fetish – just FYI – but I did

The Tall Tales of Tatiana Blue

like those shoes on her. They made her calves look good. That would make for a good lead up to her thighs and panties.

Quick check I was recording and I moved to within three feet of her back. She was lost in something on her phone because she didn't feel my presence behind her.

I checked my BlackBerry, which received a live feed from the bag cam. I positioned the bag between her thighs and swayed so the bag moved forward between her slightly parted legs.

Her inner thighs were stronger than the skirt showed. The backside was... well IS, just a feat of magic. Trust me, if you ever get a chance to fuck Tatiana Blue, take a moment to just marvel at her shape. It's a beautiful thing.

She had on what looked like boy shorts... but they were these black French knickers and they were sitting high on her cheeks.

I slid my foot cam forward for a second shot and that's when it all went downhill.

Out of the blue, she began the 'my phone is falling to floor, let me save it' dance. She did a two-step as her phone fell out of her hands.

I mean, come on, really? That happens JUST as I get a good shot?

She slapped her phone to one hand, passed it to the other and fumbled in between as she knocked it up into the air.

Mr Oh

I didn't see the phone coming my way, I was too busy following Tatiana as her thighs separated as she reached for the phone. Brilliant footage though.

It's like God knocked the phone out of her hand to help me out.

Before I knew it, my girl was facing me with her hands high in the air. It was like slow motion.

By the time I looked up, her phone fell straight into my bag at the same time I heard a loud crack. I didn't want it to be the camera, I prayed it wasn't as she knocked the wind out of me and pushed me to the floor.

In my whole history of doing this, never once has that happened. I mean what are the odds of that shit?

My phone goes flying, my bag cracks again as it hit the floor and Tatiana's weight forces me down fast and my head even faster. My head hit the ground so hard, I bit down on my tongue. The last thing I remember about that moment was lying on the pavement, tasting blood and looking at my camera sprawled out next to Tatiana's iPhone.

For some reason, the camera had gone from recording to playing.

Through my blurred vision, I could see the camera was playing footage of her. The walk up and the first peek between her thighs. The darkness of the unknown that lurks under every skirt or dress.

I'm telling you, I LOVE that shit.

The Tall Tales of Tatiana Blue

What I didn't love was the fact I could feel myself losing consciousness. My vision of the screen was deteriorating but, even worse, I could just about make out Tatiana's face as she made her way to her feet. I wish I could've lost consciousness before I saw her face when she picked up her phone then my camera.

I don't know if I said 'oh shit' before I fell asleep on the pavement but I thought it.

I could've sworn I was taken to a hospital because I DO remember hearing doctors talking and a constant beep from a machine. Like, right by my head. EKG, heart rate monitor or something.

For the life of me, I remember talking to a doctor, leaving the hospital and getting into a cab. God knows how the fuck I ended up back at home.

As I slowly found full consciousness, I could see I was sitting in the living room on my computer chair, which was weird because I had sofas so I never put that chair in the living room.

My blinds were drawn and the only light came from a small lamp on my book shelf. The back of my head was pounding, my eyes were watering and there was an acidic taste in the back of my throat. I went to massage my eyes, throat and head in that order but my arms weren't obeying orders. They stayed held together at the wrists by, what felt like, cruise ship rope.

Mr Oh

Looking down, there was rope everywhere; draped across my chest. My legs and arms were tied down and linked to the chair. Something in the back of my head, besides a big ass coco, made me think, 'where's the camera bag?'

This was the definition of a what the fuck moment because when I tried to stand up, my feet were also forced to disobey.

I was strapped the fuck down. And that was when I could hear something coming from my computer room. Sounds I knew all too well.

Wind blowing, constant rustling, random voices, car horns blowing. It was one of my videos.

From the sound of it, whoever strapped me to the chair was watching my work. A part of me hoped they were impressed with my sheer body of videos. In the state I was in, I was still proud. Wouldn't you be? If you'd pulled off some of the shots I had, you'd feel the same way. I managed to film women walking with their partners for crying out loud.

My pride wasn't fully erect because I was bucket ass nekkid and tied to my own chair like a terrorist in *24*.

Like, seriously, I DID start to panic. I mean, I didn't remember how I got home, which meant someone brought me home. Which meant this person had to be strong enough to carry me up my stairs.

Looking in the direction of my computer room, I listened for any sign of gender. A man's groan or a woman's whimper. Maybe even a ringtone. SOMETHING.

The Tall Tales of Tatiana Blue

Who the fuck brought me home? Not only home, but went on to further tie me to a fucking chair.

I was so pissed off, who the fuck ties people to chairs any more? And with rope as well?

By this point, I started to breathe heavily, looking around the room, trying to find something to give me a chance against whoever was currently scanning my collection. And if they found the collection, I prayed they wouldn't keep searching.

Shiiiiiit, the worst thing they could do was keep looking.

Particularly my external hard drive.

Suddenly, silence.

The sound of the video ending made me shush my own thoughts. Like the person could hear me thinking from the other room. That was also the moment I noticed that my hardwood floor was covered in a 10x10 clear plastic sheet.

I watched *Dexter* so I know what time it is when the plastic sheet comes out. Seeing it under the chair, my sofas pushed back, a nice little space, made me super fucking nervous.

Obviously, I was shitting myself by now.

I mean who else has such crease-less plastic sheeting like this except for workmen or crazy ass serial killers?

Mr Oh

My eyes were looking for anything I could grab and hide as a possible stabbing weapon unfortunately I wasn't going anywhere. But the sheet was hypnotic. It was like I could already see my blood spattered across it.

Another familiar sound drew my attention. Programs on my computer were shutting down. I could hear Skype closing and my base unit powering down. The giant of a man who brought me here to kill me was about to get busy on me.

'I'll be out in a minute,' a woman's voice said.

HUH?

My mind was screaming, NO FUCKING WAY.

I knew that voice.

I'd heard it before.

Once in the flesh but many times digitally. The inflections of her voice were sweeter than technology could translate.

The light in my computer room turned off and I stared at the door, honestly a little scared at what might come out. The closed door cracked open a little and a sliver of darkness stared back at me.

I knew she was there.

I could feel her watching me, reading what I was thinking, trying to plan an eventuality to whatever I was planning.

The Tall Tales of Tatiana Blue

Tatiana Blue stepped out of the room as graceful as a ballerina. All she did was walk out and close the door behind her but I was already dumbstruck.

I was going through a lot internally. 80% was fear, 19% was thinking how good her sex would be and 1% hoped she didn't find anything ELSE on my computer.

With just enough light to see her silhouette, Tatiana's heels clapped towards me.

A part of me was slightly more scared of her than if she had in fact been a tall Russian wrestling-sized dude with no neck.

She walked in and out of the darkness as her heels made me follow her path. She was obviously going for drama as she walked in and out of light beams from the lamp.

It was working because I was sweating like Janine Butcher in confession. The ropes around my nakedness were getting itchy and my dick was suffering the most. Fucking Tatiana was turning me on and all she was doing was walking around me.

She stepped onto the plastic sheet and the light hit her fully for the first time.

I tried to think about Boris Johnson's knees in the hope that my erection would instantly droop. But Tatiana grinned a pure cane sugar smile that monkey wrenched my train of thought. My dick betrayed me.

Mr Oh

'Russell Reed!' she said.

'Yes. And you are?' I asked back, not sure what was going on.

She laughed sweetly, 'You don't know me?'

I looked her up and down, my confusion probably being mistaken for arrogance. To be honest, I was confused. You'll figure out why.

Really, at that point, I just wanted to take her in. She wasn't wearing the business suit that she knocked me out in. She was sultry. And I don't say that word every day.

Skin fitted long sleeve, black.

Leggings, black.

Heels, a new pair of black with blue bows.

I looked back to her face, 'Should I know you?'

'You're the connect that fucked me over on that shipment of Choos... don't worry, I remember YOU.'

Believe me, you have no idea how happy I was to hear her say that. I don't know who this connect was but she thought I was him. Then my mind stopped. Connect? Connect for what? Choos?

'Connect? I'm sorry, I REALLY have no idea what you're talking about. What the hell are Choos?'

The Tall Tales of Tatiana Blue

I think I pulled sincere off. Her sweet but sinful smile dropped and she came closer to my face.

Standing on my left side, her thigh pressed against my shoulder, she pulled my head back and pointed her iPhone at me.

I flinched because I thought it was a gun.

Anyone would flinch, it was semi-dark, I just saw something silver coming towards me.

It made her laugh.

I felt like a bitch.

While she was scanning my face, I inhaled quietly, taking in the scent of shea butter and guava. Her dreadlocks with the blue streaks dropped over my face as the light from the phone passed over me.

I was thinking to myself, with my professional mind working, there's no way this can be her.

Now wouldn't that be a turn up for the books? Would've been the first time ever.

Tatiana tapped away and pulled some screens across her phone and a light shone in my eye. I squinted hard as she spun my head in a full circle, humming approvingly of my neck. I don't know what she was looking for but I know there was nothing there.

'Nothing there,' Tatiana said behind my ear.

Mr Oh

I froze.

Her hands showed no love as she checked behind both my ears then held my face into the phone light.

'What are you looking for?' I asked.

Then, she came over all confused, like she wasn't sure where she was.

She let my face go, dragging her nails across my cheeks and staring into my drowsy eyes.

'I think I've got the wrong person.' she said.

Fucking result.

She bought it.

Which meant she only found the videos and not the folders within folders with four passwords I spent hours setting up.

If she thought she had the wrong place, she'd leave.

My best chance of getting her out was to try and appeal to her better nature. If she had one.

But I'd seen her. That was enough.

'Please, I don't know who you think I am, but I'm not him, I swear. I just like to make videos.'

The Tall Tales of Tatiana Blue

'Oh yeah, I can see that... got yourself quite a collection there haven't you?'

I was staring her dead in the eye. In the dim light, I felt like the white boy with the burger in *Pulp Fiction*.

Her honeycomb eyes were scanning me, looking for a reaction. I was looking for the same, still thinking about the secrets hidden on my external hard drive.

Suddenly, she swirled in her heels, walked over to a long black trench coat and slipped it on.

This was another what the fuck moment for me.

Was she leaving?

Was she gonna untie me?

Was the plastic sheeting just to make me shit myself?

'I'm sorry Russell. I've got the wrong person. I am so so sorry.'

That voice again.

For the first and only time during our whole interaction, I saw remorse shine on her face. Her eyes softened and she bit her lower lip while looking me up and down. She looked really sorry.

And I felt bad for her. Even though I was the one still tied to a chair. Then she turned around and left.

Mr Oh

Just walked out the door. Closed it, click and everything. Didn't even say bye.

Relief was a fucking understatement.

My body started shaking at being so happy. I let my head drop and took a deep breath. I knew the next mission was to get out of the chair, but I just wanted to... you know... take a moment.

If the plastic sheet was there to scare me, it really did. From what I've seen on TV, you don't think to bring that type of something unless you plan to really fuck up someone's soul.

I didn't THINK she would kill me but, again, that plastic sheet fucked with me.

Leaning forward, trying to create some slack in the ropes, I looked for the closest table.

On my dark oak coffee table centrepiece, I saw an envelope with my name on it.

Large, Manila, A3 size.

I turned my head to try and see my name clearly and that was when my testicular intuition told me that someone was standing at my front

The Tall Tales of Tatiana Blue

door. You know that feeling when you know someone's about to knock on your door? It was that.

I stared, waiting for the knock. I hoped it was the cavalry. I was willing to take the stick for the roped up predicament I was in.

But if it was Tatiana returning to do some damage for whatever reason, she was locked out.

My front door automatically double locks.

The presence was still there though. I could feel them. I haven't got super powers but I could FEEL them.

The door knob rattled for a second then went silent.

Then I heard a little scratching noise at the door. Sounded like a mouse was scratching at the lock.

From my still bucket nekkid seat, dick scratching against the ropes around my waist, all I could do was watch.

As tense as that moment was, I couldn't tell you why I was getting hard. It was kind of uncomfortable because my dick managed to slip through a gap in the ropes. Felt like I was masturbating with sandpaper gloves and bleach lube.

I was annoyed but the scratching at the door made the lock click once and my attention was back on that.

Is someone picking my fucking lock?

Mr Oh

The door opened and Tatiana Blue walked back in with a bag on her shoulder and a smile on her face.

'I forgot an envelope. You haven't seen it have you?'

I was mouth open.

I paid good fucking money for that lock and she had it beaten in seconds.

She WAS as good as they said.

Her walk was more seductive this time than when she left. There was a glide in her slide.

In all black, with the long coat, she looked good.

She picked up the envelope and looked at me with a... I don't know WHAT kind of smile it was. It was somewhere between bi-polar and 'I just found a winning lottery ticket'.

'You know who I am don't you!?' she said with a straight face.

I looked up, telling a half truth. 'No.'

I still wasn't sure. I mean, if she was who I thought she was, this would be the most random of meetings... ever. I mean, the legendary ghost that was Tatiana Blue. With a face?

She squatted in front of me and turned her head to the side.

'Are you sure you don't know who I am Russell?'

The Tall Tales of Tatiana Blue

My eyes shot up from her open thighs, locked fingers, luscious looking lips, toned arms, dreadlocks and ended in my admiration of her full control of the situation.

'I know who you are. I didn't but I do now!'

'Nice to meet you Russell.'

'You too Tatiana Blue.'

That was it. The moment I said her name, it all made sense. But still didn't make any sense. What was Tatiana Blue doing in Chelsea?

'Wanna know what's in this here envelope?'

'Am I in any position to say no?'

She looked down at my dick and her smiled dropped.

Watching her flick the envelope between her fingers, I felt sweat drip down my side. She was enjoying watching me squirm.

'You SURE you wanna know? You're not gonna like it.' she said playfully.

'I haven't been too fond of where I woke up so just keep the bad news coming. What's in it?' Me and my big fat mouth.

'Good question. I was hoping you'd say that.'

Mr Oh

In my defence of what happens next, I'd like it to be known that I tried.

Her bag fell to the floor first, followed by her coat.

'Well, Mr Russell Adrian Reed, son of Marcia and Marvin Reed, in this envelope is something that, as I said, you're not gonna like.'

Did she just full name me? She knows mum and dad's names. OH SHIT... she found it.My fucking external hard drive. Because of what I do, I don't have my name and information out there for all and sundry. It's only in one particular place. Work.

Tatiana spoke while she reached into her bag. I watched her every movement, still confused as to why she left and came back. The plastic sheet looked back at me and I turned my head.

More mind fucked than ever.

'In this envelope is everything you've worked for. Your life's work. Dead. In a few simple pictures. I don't know how you found the time what with all your "other" work.'

Sweat was killing me and making the ropes an itchy bitch. My eyes were still scanning the room for something with a sharp edge. I didn't realise my sly eyes were being watched.

'Don't worry Russ, I've moved everything so we can have an uninterrupted conversation.'

'I'm not saying shit to you,' I said defiantly.

The Tall Tales of Tatiana Blue

If she was going to kill me, I wasn't going out like a bitch. No way Jose. But my defiance made her smile curl as she pulled out a bag from her bag.

She held the envelope and a drawstring JD Sports bag in both hands and shuffled on her high heels.

She was having the time of her life being able to tease me. Knowing what she knew probably made her want to fuck with me that little bit more. But I was trained, techniques in conflict resolution, avoidance, how to disarm using conversation, the basics.

The choice of the envelope or the bag was a tough one. My name instantly drew my attention but the introduction of the bag was a new choice.

'What's in the bag?' I asked, sweat running down my chocolate bald head.

'Another good question, Russ is two for two so far. Go for three and I just might let you see it.'

'See what?'

That sounded like the introduction of a second entity.

'Patience double R, all in good time.'

'Is this a game to you?' I asked. Honestly, I was starting to get pissed off. Who the fuck did she think she was?

'Yeah kinda. Not my usual kinda game but I am having fun. Don't worry, you'll be having fun soon.'

Mr Oh

The way she said that didn't make me feel good in my stomach.

The envelope slapped to the floor and she reached into the bag, her eyes locked on mine.

It all unravelled from here...

'Do you like music Russell? I loooove music. I'm a soul chick deep down. You like soul don't you Russ?'

My eyes were dead. Not giving her any satisfaction. It didn't matter, her smile told me she was up and away right now. Didn't bode well for me ultimately.

'Yeah, I prefer old...'

'...school, yeah, I saw on your Spotify, you have a lot of old music. Me, I like the new boys.'

Out of the bag came a folded white A-line skirt and a new pair of high heels in a large clear freezer bag.

'I don't care really...'

'Awwww, don't be like that... play with me at least.'

She smiled one Keri Hilson grin that disarmed me straight away.

I was hot, bothered, annoyed and I just wanted her to get on with it, whatever IT was.

The Tall Tales of Tatiana Blue

I couldn't get to my panic button or my phone... shit, I didn't even know where they were. Hadn't seen them since I licked up my head.

'Fuck you Blue,' I said. And I meant that shit.

'Oh you will, don't worry about that. One way or another you will.'

Stepping out of her heels, I was amazed at how tall she appeared to be, what pretty feet she had and how thick her legs were. Really, I needed to get out of the chair but she was very distracting in all black.

'Look, what do you want from me? Just hurry up with it and get the fuck out...'

'Oooooooo, a little touchy are we?'

'You already left, why come back?'

'Patience double R...'

Her calmness was working my first, second, third, last and reserved nerves. She smiled again. This time more sinister than the last.

'If you know my name, then you know who I am and you know there's gonna be consequences for what you're doing.'

'That's what the envelope is for... ooooh, I almost forgot my music...'

Her hands sat on her hips as she looked me up and down. Well, more down than up as she slid her iPhone between her leggings and her hip.

The elastic snap made me jump.

I couldn't tell you why I was so nervous.

Mr Oh

Well I could, that damn plastic on the floor.

'I think we need some Trey Songz...' she said. 'Set the mood.'

'Just let me go, you know they're gonna be here soon.'

'Oh I know exactly when THEY will get here... I've got all the time in the world.'

Out of her bag, Tatiana pulled out a speaker dock for her iPhone and placed it at my feet. I was thinking to myself, why are you watching her do this? Get the fuck out of this situation.

Did I? No. Could I, really? Probably not. Were the hairs on my testicles getting caught on the ropes and itching like Tyrone Biggums? Definitely.

But I didn't want her to watch me squirm. Whatever she was going to do, I wasn't giving her any joy from my pain.

'Are you gonna let me go?' I asked with every ounce of deadpan I could muster.

'Erm, no.'

'Tatiana BLUE? Are you gonna let me go?'

'I JUST said no, what makes you think I'm gonna change my mind just because you know my name? Try again double R.'

Some random generic R&B tune popped out of the speakers and filled the room. More annoyance on top of my pissed-off'ness. It was time to do something drastic, see how far she was willing to go.

The Tall Tales of Tatiana Blue

I took a deep breath while some whiny voiced yout' started singing about how HE invented sex. Arrogant prick.

'HELLLLLP!' I shouted at the top of my voice.

I didn't think anyone would hear and neither did she as she just... watched me. Didn't move towards me to stop my noise or anything like that. She just waited for me to run out of breath, which I did. But that was okay, I had plenty more where that came from.

Taking in another deep breath, I prepared an even louder shout.

Then she slapped me.

The bitch slapped me. With the back of her hand too.

That shocked me and made me super pissed at the same time.

'Get me out of this chair right now, do you fucking hear me?'

'How can I hear my music with you making all that fucking noise? Shut ya mouth.'

Tatiana looked down at me like I was crazy. She started the song again and stood in front of me, still holding the skirt and her freezer bag heels.

'Ready?' she asked me.

Was I ready to get out of the chair? Quick, fast and in a hurry.

'Are you gonna let me go?!'

Mr Oh

Tatiana kissed her teeth. 'You're ready...'

She did not mean ready to get out of the chair.

With the music and light creating an atmosphere I couldn't ignore, Tatiana swayed her hips to the music in a silent ting all her own. She was no longer looking me up and down, her eyes were closed. It wasn't like she had to watch me. I wasn't going anywhere.

'You know what Russell, I was not telling the truth before. I DID have the right man. I'm a little fibber.'

'If you are not going to let me go, then we have nothing more to say to each other. So like I said before, and because it had a nice ring to it, I'll say it again. Fuck you Blue.'

'Someone get a little slap and feel all emasculated?' she asked teasingly.

I don't know if she was trying to annoy me for a reason but she was good at it. Which annoyed me even more because I was supposed to be the one in charge.

'How 'bout we do it your way then? Or at least, the way you like to record it.'

Her hands slipped to her hips, fingers seductively massaging her skin as she looked me in my vex eyes.

Her thumbs hooked into the elastic of her leggings and pulled them down with the beat of the song.

The Tall Tales of Tatiana Blue

'You know what Russ, I've gotta give you props. You hid that stuff on your computer real REAL well...'

My eyes were, of course, stuck on two of the finest, thickest deep caramel legs I've ever seen. I actually started to think if I, somehow, got out of this, one of my first ports of call was the full upskirt video of Tatiana Blue.

She reached her ankles, bending from the hip, not the knees, like a good girl. Of course I was thinking of fucking her from the back. Look how she bent over, all flexible and shit.

Obviously for effect.

I didn't care. On the outside.

Inside, and down below, I was bubbling nicely.

The tail end of a six-pack snuck out from beneath her black top and sat over a pair of black lace French knickers with a picture of a high heel on the front. She stepped out of her leggings, looked down at her shoes then looked at me, getting right back to conversation.

'When I first looked on your computer, I didn't see it but I looked again and... oh, silly me, I forgot about the envelope... oh I'll do that in a minute.'

Honestly, so did I. It slapped to the floor what seemed like ages ago.

Mr Oh

She bent to pick it up, showing me my name.

'This, mate, is what they call insurance. See, after I found the... what did you call it? STUFF? I had to make sure that I covered my own back. So I went home, got some things and got to work.'

My face must've looked like I smelled shit and sardines because, again, she succeeded in messing with my head.

I didn't know what was going on. What had she done to me? Where had she done it? When even?

'Hey, randomly, do you like these Brian Atwood pumps?' she asked, holding up the shoes in the bag.

'Whoa, wait a minute...' I broke my unspoken vow of silence.

'When did you get to work?'

'You know these shoes go for £1,197? And you lot call ME the thief!?'

'What day is it today?'

Upright and lording over me, she smirked. 'Well, I brought you back Sunday, went home Tuesday...'

'What FUCKING day is it today?'

'Friday I think...'

The Tall Tales of Tatiana Blue

Now, this, was some real bullshit. How the fuck had she managed to KEEP me here and I couldn't remember it? And for a week, didn't anyone miss me?

'That's not the worst part,' she added. 'What'd you think I could've done to you in that time?'

Here's me in one big bitch of a predicament and she goes and puts that in my head?!

'See, when you saw me on Friday, I was on my way...'

'What the fuck? Are you a fucking kidnapper as well as a thief?'

She slapped me again, this time open palm forehand. Heavier and more forceful than before.

I REALLY couldn't tell you how pissed I was at that moment. Those slaps had some real venom in 'em and with my arms strapped by my side, I couldn't even defend myself or shake her the way I wanted to.

I had to watch the slap coming.

When my eyes eventually opened, keeping the anger under intense lock and key, she held a blue polished finger nail in my face.

'Stop interrupting me, its pissing me off!'

'You're the one slapping me and you think YOU'RE pissed off?'

Mr Oh

That was apparently the worst thing I could've said. The look on her face told me that something in my last sentence pressed the 'you know you fucked up' button.

'You know what, fuck the skirt bit. You've pissed me off now. I WAS gonna treat you a bit but you FUCKED it all up with your fucking talking.'

I really had set something off. Her calm demeanour during this whole exchange was light and breezy up until now.

The song changed at my feet and the same whiny prick from the last song came up, yodelling like an idiot.

In front of me, she was pulling her top over her head. The frantic anger she displayed as she threw her top onto the sofa did not make me feel any better.

She worked OUT that's for damn sure.

'Always like a fucking man to ruin a great, guaranteed thing by opening his fucking mouth. I know, all he had to do was shut the fuck up,' she mumbled to herself.

It was weird to see but she was full-blown talking to herself. I caught myself staring, her slender creamy dark caramelness was not bad to have to stare at while she went back and forth with herself.

Reaching back for her bra clasp, she paused to look at me.

'You don't deserve Lauryn and Aretha.'

The Tall Tales of Tatiana Blue

'Unusuaaaaal' whined the singer.

Tatiana closed her eyes and took in a deep breath. Raising her hands to her chest plate, she held it in. Whatever was going to happen was going down now and after all that slapping shit, she best do me something because I WOULD get out.

And God help her when I did.

Didn't have much time to think about getting out because she finally exhaled. And opened VERY evil eyes at me.

One look at her heels. She moved to them, slowly taking them out of the freezer bag.

Her left foot slipped in and the weirdest thing happened.

The heel disappeared and she was suddenly wearing a flat shoe. I thought it was fatigue fucking with me until she slipped her right foot in and the same thing happened.

Didn't know there was such thing as a collapsible high-heeled shoe. Then the funniest shit happened. Wasn't funny at the time, but in hindsight.

Looking up at me from her ankles, she pressed her thumb and forefinger on her left earring and, I swear to you, she grew.

No fucking joke, she grew.

I know my mouth was open because it's open now just thinking about it. Hydraulic heels.

Mr Oh

'Nice heels,' I said.

The legend of Tatiana Blue was apparently very true.

She went to over six foot three in her heels.

Standing well over me and grinning almost maniacally, Tatiana was breathing like it was her last breathe.

Then she calmed again.

The music at my feet changed to a song where the whiny voice sang about being successful.

Annoying because I could not see a successful way out of my current predicament.

'I know everything about you Russell. Everything. I know who you are, I know what you do.'

'So you know the best thing is to let me go don't you Blue?'

THIRD SLAP...

This time, to really humiliate me, she slapped me once with her forehand and followed the same path with an eye-opening back hand.

The Tall Tales of Tatiana Blue

Etiquette, old school training and my profession went out the window and I really wanted to fuck this woman up.

I'm tied to a chair and she gave me three clean connecting slaps. Of course I wanted to kill her.

'Early in the week, I thought about letting you go, but then I started investigating and that was when I found the STUFF on your computer. You really called the folder STUFF?'

I thought I was hallucinating because the angry Tatiana that looked like she was about to lose it was replaced by this swaying to the music, starting to smile again version. The back and forth of her demeanour was very unnerving.

'I don't know how you do it,' she said. 'It's like leading two, very opposite lives. I mean you technically have to arrest yourself. Anyway, after I found that stuff, I realised I was in a bit of fix because I could understand how SOME may class this as kidnapping, so I had to think outside the box.'

'Whatever.' I replied, indignant.

'Trust me, this is the bit you should be listening to. When you ran into me, or I ran into you, do you know where I was going? I was going to a job interview. That day was supposed to be the first day of my new life. But you and your fucking camera had to fuck it up. And now here we are. I mean how funny it is that we would run into each other like that? Well I'll tell you this; a fucking video camera is NOT gonna be the end of Tatiana Blue.'

She referred to herself in the third person. A sign of crazy or sexy?

Mr Oh

My head dropped and I spoke in a hushed tone. 'You can still fix this, just let me go.'

'No way Reedy, I've already done most of the work, you're only awake for the end of it. I would've explained all that but, being a man, you pissed me off by talking and lost the privilege, so now we're just gonna do this.'

'End of what? Do what?' I asked, sweating like Smokey in Deebo's pigeon coup.

Tatiana hooked her thumbs into her Frenchies and pulled them down to her special heels.

In my head I was thinking, so this is what we're doing?

'When I said I know everything, I meant everything. Good to see you passed your last STD test. That's the type of specimen I've been looking for.'

Now I don't know why the hell this happened. Even telling you now, I still don't know why my dick got hard when she said that. Maybe it was her tone and the way it felt like death was in the air. After the second slap, my erection shrunk with my growing anger and was nestled uncomfortably between gaps in the ropes. But he'd found his way up at the prospect of sex. He was stirring when she reached for her came off but he was uncomfortably awake now.

Traitor.

The Tall Tales of Tatiana Blue

'Bang me if you want but you know how this game is gonna end.'

'Not if I change the rules.'

She reached for my lap and I inhaled, watching her spreading the ropes, giving my dick space to grow. Her first contact with my dick was a soft one. Her warm hand encircled me and worked a slow deliberate rhythm.

'Tatiana... look...'

'That's the first time I've heard you say my name in the sexy way it deserves. Just for that...'

She opened her mouth and a long line of saliva landed on my helmet and disappeared between her busy fingers.

'Fucking me won't get you out of this?'

'Objection!'

Her slippery hand was starting to feel real positive but I tried to ignore the pleasure with random thoughts. What's gonna happen after I come? Why isn't she telling me anything?

I was feeling like pissing her off was a mistake.

'Tatiana Blue, that's your name isn't it?'

'Yes IT is!' she replied with a sinful sigh. 'You KNOW it is! Hmmm... Is your place bugged Russell?'

Mr Oh

Hearing her name was the key for her to open the door. She stepped out of her knickers that were bunched around her ankles and swung a leg over my thighs.

I gasped because she did it so swiftly. I wasn't ready for it.

We'd been so far apart for so long, I wasn't ready to be so close to her. My face was still burning from her slaps but, again, my dick was responding to her.

He's a slave to closeness.

I was breathing real heavy because I had no freaking idea what she was thinking. Maybe she wanted to say bye in a nice way. Who knows.

I certainly didn't.

Smelling of an intoxicating perfume and the odd taste I had in the back of my throat when I woke up, Tatiana held my face and looked into my eyes, with her hand down below making me wince in pleasure. Her skin pressed against me, I couldn't stop looking at her.

'Don't worry Russ, this isn't the first time I've done this. Although this is the first time you've been awake.'

'WHAT THE FU...'

Before I could get the expletive out, Tatiana spread the ropes so my dick could stand, raised herself up and sat down with no ceremony. It was a total pleasure shock to me but she took it the worst. Her locks were whipping about her face as her head and back arched.

The Tall Tales of Tatiana Blue

This was one of those moments when this whole situation didn't feel so bad. Watching Tatiana arch in my lap while her amazingly wet pussy slid tightly around my dick was one of the highlights. Her hips slid from left to right and her legs raised until there was nowhere for me to go but up and in.

We both sucked air through our teeth. I wanted to run my hands over her arched front; a soft hand between her breasts would've made the moment that little bit sweeter.

Only thing I could massage was rope and chair wood.

This was not how I saw this going.

Me fucking Tatiana Blue.

Tut tut tut.

But the pussy was worth it.

I don't know how pussy can be sweet but it was juicy fruit. All that slapping must've made her wet because she was dripping through the ropes across my thighs.

Back on an upright riding axis, Tatiana ran her nails across my bald head. Not a light sexy drag of soft nail tips on my scalp, oh no that shit hurt. She could see she was hurting me but, as I frowned, she dragged her nails deeper. Could've been her way of distracting me as her inner walls squeezed my dick. She lifted herself and came down slowly. I may have looked a picture of restraint but I was struggling.

Mr Oh

To have good pussy thrown on you is one thing but to not be able to touch, to feel, to rub a nipple... it was killing me. And by one of the most wanted people in the world?

'How lucky were you to run into me? Huh? Tell me Russell? You and everyone else in the world looking for me and you find me breaking the law?'

Her lips hovered so damn close to mine, I jerked forward, hungry for it. Nuzzling my face strong in her neck, she dropped her head and moaned. A progressive, climbing to a mountain top moan. I could tell she was going to come. Her walls were throbbing and she was breathing faster.

'You know this is rape don't you?' I said, trying to ruin her orgasm.

Breathlessly she replied, 'You've never once told me to stop!'

And then she came.

She held my face up in her hands and kept riding me on a wave of four orgasms, one after the other. Her hips were jerking with no sort of rhythm and she held my mouth open as if she was stealing my breath.

In her eyes was pure pleasure.

Being able to take what she wanted and forcing me to watch her do it was sweeting her up nicely.

Up and down stairs.

'Happy now?' I said sarcastically. I had to act like I didn't enjoy it.

The Tall Tales of Tatiana Blue

'Whew... AM I? Look at this face... can I kiss you Russell?'

I was quite shocked by the question. Considering what she was doing and her method of doing it, she had no problem doing whatever the fuck she wanted.

But to ask for a kiss, something quite personal.

Tatiana licked her lips just inches from my dry mouth.

She was waiting.

Her pussy was catching its own breath as she throbbed on me.

'You kidnap me, hold me hostage, do whatever weird shit you did to me THEN ask if you can kiss me? Knowing who I am, you don't think that's taking the piss a little bit?'

ANOTHER QUICK FOREHAND SLAP.

'STOP FUCKING HITTING ME!' I yelled.

'Stop reminding me of who you are!? How can I have a crush on you if you keep fucking reminding me?' she replied, grinding her hips with her question.

I had a reply, started with F and finished with K but her movement was too good a feeling.

Mr Oh

It was a good thing I couldn't touch her otherwise I would've rammed myself deep inside her with a kung-fu grip on her throat. Her slow, slick, grinding waist movement was driving me up the fucking wall. I wanted her to let go of my face but she wanted to see what she was doing to me.

'Fuck you Blue... this won't change anything.'

SLAP. BACKHAND.

'Yes it will... Oh God it will... this dick changes EVERYTHING...'

Oh... how I wished she didn't keep slapping me. They were some real face turning claps and my face was sizzling, not to mention I was already hot from being so fucking frustrated.

And she chose THAT moment to start riding me with expert precision.

'This... won't... change...' I tried to say.

She grabbed my face tighter and snarled at me as if she was transforming into something. Then she grinned in a way that worried me.

I was right to worry.

She licked my face.

Top to bottom, chin to forehead.

The Tall Tales of Tatiana Blue

'If I licked it, it's mine!' she said innocently.

'What?' I asked after a moment of shock and fresh arousal.

'Just one kiss. Please?'

Tatiana's hips were hovering on a medium heat as she awaited my answer. Smelling nothing but her minty saliva across my face, I was getting to an emotional point of exhaustion and a sexual point of orgasm.

'Stop! If I give you a kiss, will you let me go?'

She looked at her Mickey Mouse watch, 'If you kiss me, I won't have to.'

'Huh?' Her fucking cryptic answers were more than doing my head in.

Tatiana looked in my mouth. She was breathing normally and was feeling a new groove on the medium heat as her heels clopped on my floor, sounding like a stallion beginning to gallop.

Her lips were so close, we were breathing for each other.

I'd never had the urge to fuck and fight at the same time. Quite a mind fuck actually.

'Oh Russell... you could've been something special...'

Her lips were soft and cautious as she waited for my lips to respond before she grabbed my neck and kissed me hungrily.

'Oh fuck,' she muttered. 'Pete Becker.'

Mr Oh

She growled in the kiss.

The salt from her tears crept into our kiss. She sucked my lips as if it had been a long time since she'd felt such a feeling.

Tatiana had my face cupped in her hands, blocking out the world around us. She was flicking her waist good and hard, making my dick stab deep inside her.

'Don't do this... Tatiana...' I said, struggling to fight such beautiful movement.

'I have to. And I really want to...'

I would've given up my whole career just to be able to touch her face, feel the warmth of her back, tap her clit, something. Her nipples were in my line of sight, getting harder before my eyes under her bra.

'Wish you could touch me don't you?' Tatiana asked, breathlessly.

'I...'

My mind sent the sentence to my lips but the words never made it. I was physically being rained on, with drips of liquid splattering down my legs. One of her hands left my face and felt my heartbeat.

'You LIKE that don't you?'

'Shush...' I answered. Her sexy voice, after her moist lips left mine, was not helping my resolve.

'Don't you dare shush me, who the fuck do you think you are?'

The Tall Tales of Tatiana Blue

I couldn't hold it any more. My face must've looked ugly as fuck and I let out a deep, throaty groan. She sat down fully in my lap. The soft button I reached inside her was mushing my helmet and Tatiana's hard grinding hip movement made them kiss harder.

Her frowning face was a picture.

'Now you're gonna have to come,' she said.

'No, this... this is only gonna make... things worse.'

'After the orgasm I just had, there is no way this can get worse. Now, shush your mush and come inside me again.'

You KNOW that was the beginning of the end for me right?

With her hips looking like they were barely moving, but OH were they moving, she slipped her hand down to the moisture between our groins.

She dipped two fingers in, alongside my dick, then took her scented digits and rubbed them over my lips.

I tried to say no but her hand was quite tasty over my mouth and right under my nose.

'NOW you can come.'

Any guy, who can put himself in my situation, knows what happened next. The moment wasn't helped by her airy, voice in my ear.

Mr Oh

Every time I tried to speak, her taste slipped down my throat and made my hips jerk upwards. The succulent sensation of her walls getting wetter around me made me beg her to speed up.

But:

1) She had her hand over my mouth to stop me from talking.

2) The rhythm her hips were on was building up to an obviously orgasmic crescendo.

I wanted her hand off my mouth so I could moan free and proud. The pussy was THAT good. If things were different and this was a bedroom situation, I know damn sure I'd be hooting and hollering like I don't know what. Would I care?

Hell no.

'GOOD boy... Tatiana likes that dick where it is...keep... it... there...'

'Stop... please... I'm... gonna...' I mumbled under her hand.

'You're gonna what? Huh? You gonna come?'

Her goading was making the pussy sweeter and I was licking the back of her fingers, enjoying the flavour.

I nodded as my tongue tickled her hand and she giggled into a long moan.

She brought us nose-to-nose and her eyes searched mine as she winked. I felt my memory jerk back to someone winking at me like that a

The Tall Tales of Tatiana Blue

long time ago. My eyes closed and rolled around my sockets as my mind was fighting between the good sex that was about to be almost over and one of the biggest unanswered questions in my life.

Harrods.

Her pussy was sliding over my dick and I clenched my ass. I was trying to hold back but she was rolling herself all over me.

Boooooy, I can't lie, she dropped one sweet swirling stroke on me and I lost it. So deadly was the grind that I fell instantly silent. My eyes widened and I knew there was nothing I could do. Even my mind went silent.

Inside her, I was slick as grease and her walls were smooth as silk as each descent left a wet line of her travelling down my roped inner thigh. I was coming... and not even the Second Coming could stop me.

Tatiana, reading me, thumped her hips into my dick so hard, the computer chair rolled backwards.

'You've already done the big... biiiiiiig bit, finish the job.'

'Huh?' I mumbled.

'You can't... arrest me if... if... I'm pregnant with... your child can you? That would change things wouldn't it?'

Splash. Damn.

Mr Oh

She should've just slapped me again when she said that. My eyes were wider, I was trying to Incredible Hulk out of the ropes and, more than anything, I wanted her off me.

All her cryptic answers throughout this whole thing had been about this.

I know I didn't tell you I was police but, come on, you must've guessed. It's not information I just offer out when I talk to strangers. Not that you're a stranger but you know what I mean.

There's no specific task force assigned to her cases but there should be. If you added up all the reports of theft involving celebrities and their shoes over the world, you'd find a blue pattern. I'd been part of investigations where there was no evidence of a break in but shoes were missing. After a lucky break, we got a name, but that was it. No picture, no CCTV camera footage, nothing. We had this phantom stealing shoes all over the world and we had no idea what she looked like.

Anyway, as an officer of the law, fornicating with criminals is kind of frowned upon and probably lose you your job. Getting someone as sought after as Tatiana Blue pregnant, after mountains of legal red tape and paperwork, was definitely worthy of prison time, regardless of the circumstances. I mean, imagine trying to explain that Tatiana Blue kidnapped me and forced me to have sex with her?

She really chose her moment to drop that salient piece of information. When I was long on the road of no return. And this one started deep in my balls. Tatiana swirled her pussy in a circle and whatever fight I had shot deep into her.

The Tall Tales of Tatiana Blue

I came like two buses at once.

I was sweating and could feel myself spurting longer and longer streams of soldiers inside her.

'Who's a good boy?' she asked before closing her eyes and grabbing my jaw.

Tatiana shuddered then froze.

Shivered and froze.

Shook a little then froze.

Screamed, hushed herself then froze.

Her walls did the same.

I was a quivering, shrinking mess. She, on the other hand, was still vibrating in my lap. My men must've hit something right.

It was after that good feeling washed over me that I truly took in what she said. Because an orgasm like that needed a moment or two of thought.

'You... you...' I tried to speak as she uncovered my mouth.

'Me... you... Russell Reed and Tatiana Blue... it rhymes.'

'Are you fucking crazy?' I asked. 'You think sleeping with me will stop me from locking you up? You're a thief, you know we've been following your movements for...'

Mr Oh

'But I noticed you had no pictures of me in your STUFF files. See that's how I wanted it. You guys never thought about how come everywhere I visit, none of the cameras work?! So, that just leaves you. The only person who knows who I am and what I look like. And what my pussy tastes like. Well you and a few others but they all had "memory accidents" so you're special. You're my baby daddy unless we get married that is then...'

My eyes couldn't believe what my ears were hearing 'Are you seriously crazy?'

'Daytime policeman, night time upskirt voyeur huh? So you know how to keep a secret or two, don't you Russ? Just add this one to the stack.'

Standing up, she looked down at her thigh and the thick trail I was making to her knees. With both hands, she scooped and put them right back where they came from.

I couldn't believe what she was trying to do.

'Tell me being pregnant by you doesn't change things?'

'You know it does. But you're not dumb enough to think that this will get you pregnant.'

'No,' she scoffed. 'This was just to say bye. You got me pregnant earlier in the month.'

'Earlier in THE MONTH? HOW LONG HAVE I BEEN HERE BLUE?'

The Tall Tales of Tatiana Blue

Sucking a creamy finger she said, 'If you hadn't pissed me off, I would've told you everything but you and your fucking smart mouth. Don't worry, the envelope will explain the rest.'

THE ENVELOPE WITH MY NAME ON IT.

I forgot about that. Considering what just happened, it was understandable. My eyes shot to it as if it was the doorway to Narnia. What the hell was in that envelope that could explain the unexplainable?

My eyes swung back to Tatiana, who had just wiped herself with a towel, bagged her speaker dock and was checking her iPhone.

'Uh oh, time to go.'

'What? Where are you going?'

'Me?' she replied while slipping her bra straps over her shoulders and sliding into her knickers and leggings. 'I gotta go. No point being here besides the cavalry will be here soon to... help you.'

'Fuck no, who?'

I was frantic at this point. Who else was about to walk into this weird, coincidental, "I just had sex with Tatiana Blue" pantomime?

'Your cavalry.'

Mr Oh

Her bag was packed quick time and she was back in her original heels and trench coat. Crossing the plastic sheeting towards me, she checked her phone again.

'Russell baby, I've REALLY gotta go.'

'Don't you dare fucking leave me like this!'

Shushing me with a scented finger, Tatiana leaned in and kissed me while pushing the ropes back over my sloppy dick.

'See you in about nine months.'

'WHERE THE FUCK DO YOU THINK YOU'RE GOING? GET THE FUCK BACK HERE!'

Another slap. Both forehands.

'Stop shouting at me young man, who'd you think I am? Is that how you used to scream at Cheryl?'

My anger at those slaps would've made me go Super Sayian four if I was free but her last minute name check had me freshly confused.

How the hell did she know about Cheryl?

My ex-wife after seven years of marriage. Job killed the connection between us. But there was nothing in my file about her.

The Tall Tales of Tatiana Blue

'I told you, I know EVERYTHING...' she said, sensing my confusion. 'Good luck. I'll call ya... and make sure you get that promotion, we can't raise a child here so you're gonna have to move. Kisses and sexy slippers...'

She kissed her finger and placed it on my lips then turned on her heels and clopped to my front door.

I was sitting there, as I had been, watching her walk. It was more a sashay with a glide. Whatever it was, she was still sexy with it.

Tatiana opened the door as she sprayed her hands with anti-bacterial hand wipe. She ran a tissue over her hands and wiped the doorknob.

'Make sure you get to that envelope before SHE does.'

The way she said "SHE" told me that she really did know everything.

I was in a state of serious 'oh shit'. With our orgasms dripping down my thigh, I had to gather myself and think about:

1) What the hell was in that envelope?

2) If Tatiana really knew everything and SHE was coming, then I had to hide that envelope and come up with a good excuse as to what the hell I was doing like this.

'You know where I got those shoes from?' she said, looking back at her bag.

Mr Oh

'Tatiana, don't do this...'

'I got them from Brian's house. That man has so many shoes, he wouldn't miss a pair. Got them modified. Sexy ain't they?'

I struggled. 'You don't need a kidnapping charge Blue.'

'Please, how long have you lot been looking for me? You had to accidentally run into me.'

'This won't...'

'Everyone wins this way. You finally get the grandchildren your parents are harassing you for.'

'How do you know all this shit? You're a shoe thief on the run from police agencies on three continents, how do you win?'

'If you tell them what happened here, you know what will happen but if you don't, you get to keep your job and our baby gets to have both parents.'

'WHAT THE FUCK ARE YOU TALKING ABOUT? YOU'RE NOT PREGNANT, HOW CAN YOU BE? FUCKING UNTIE ME YOU BITCH!'

'A bitch ain't a hole for a man to fill, a bitch is a beauty in tremendously cute heels. Remember that! It's catchy ain't it?'

'Wait wait... one question, please?'

'Better be quicker than a lick,' she sighed

'Harrods!?'

The Tall Tales of Tatiana Blue

Her face went from confused to a huge smile that probably made me fall in love with her there and then. I KNEW it was her!

She turned her head sideways, blew a kiss and was gone in a whisper.

The door slammed and I was all alone.

Again.

After such a drama of a something, the silence of the room was unsettling. I even missed the whiny voiced singer she played at my feet. But I didn't have time to think about that.

My mind, thoughts and all my energy wanted to know what the hell was in that envelope.

My name stared back at me in thick black letters.

I didn't know what was in it but I wanted to see it on my own. Something in the way Tatiana spoke made me believe every word she put on it.

Teasing me because it was so close but I couldn't reach it.

'AAAAAAHAAAH, COME ON...' I screamed in frustration, trying to wiggle out of the ropes.

Then it all got that little bit more fucked up.

Mr Oh

My door buzzed which meant someone was downstairs trying to gain access to the building.

Of all the voices I could hear through the intercom, I was glad to hear my boy and fellow officer Jamal.

'Russell, it's me, Jamal... I'm here with Femi and... HER... look, I don't know what's going on but she said she was coming, so get your shit together cuz... BLOOD CLART, Femi, look at she in that black coat. Thank you darling... don't worry Russ, some sexy ting in all black just let us in...'

CLICK...

Tatiana actually let them in the building!?

For fuck sake.

I looked down at myself, a thin line of blood drawing from a cut on my face and sweat everywhere. Don't even know when I got cut.

In the chair, I started to rock, trying to tip myself in the direction of the envelope.

It wasn't the greatest idea and I had a feeling it would hurt going down but I had to do something.

Tatiana was right, it WAS gonna be hard to explain what I was doing tied to a chair, naked, with plastic sheeting under me.

The Tall Tales of Tatiana Blue

I'd get more sympathy if I was down on the ground so it looked as if my captor dumped me and fled.

Tip to the left, roll to the right, tip a bit more, rock a bit right, come on... you can do it...

With enough momentum, I slowly balanced on two wheels for what felt like ages and then toppled. I hit the ground and heard something crack in my wrist which made me cry out like a child. Anyone who has ever broken their wrist knows how much it hurts.

I landed with most of my weight on my shoulder which, added to my wrist injury, could be used for a good cover story.

Yeah, I was thinking about a cover story because, for some reason, I believed what Tatiana said. Which wasn't much.

I didn't even know what day it was. She said something about me getting her pregnant earlier in the month. But she said she'd been here a week.

You can see why I was on my side, in a next kind of pain, trying to scoot the envelope under my sofa before my door opened.

I must've looked like a right knob. I'd fallen and I couldn't get up. But how I'd fallen allowed me to get fingertips to the envelope.

If the three of my fellow officers took the lift then they should be at my door any...

Mr Oh

'Russell? You in there?'

'Yeah...' I shouted while fumbling with the envelope at the edges of my reach. I couldn't get enough grip on it to give it a good push. 'I'm down... I've been tied up...'

'We're coming in,' Tara shouted from behind the door. 'Jamal, kick the door in.'

Oh shit, come on... almost there... GOT IT.

I clamped two fingers on a corner and pulled it into my hand then tossed it with as much momentum as my injured wrist would allow.

I didn't see it but I heard it skip over the plastic just as my front door flew open.

Jamal and Femi were first through the door.

Femi saw me first and rushed to me with a smile.

'Fam, what happened to you? HE'S HERE.'

Jamal followed behind and worked with Femi to untie me. They wouldn't believe what happened here, but I had to work on my story because Tara walked through the door after them.

Strong and thick in her six foot one stature, Tara, my chocolate boss, strolled through my shattered door.

Her eyes expressed relief and she smiled at me as Jamal and Femi got me upright.

The Tall Tales of Tatiana Blue

I looked at the space where I hoped the envelope wasn't. And it wasn't. Result.

Making it to my feet, I used the rough ropes to give my dick a rough rub down. And yes that did hurt.

'We got the missed call from your phone. When we tried your house phone, it didn't ring and your mobile rang out. When did you get back?'

'Are you okay baby? What happened? How could you just take off like that?' Tara asked, breaking the rules of our private office relationship. I already told Femi and Jamal what was going on between us, they were my boys, but Tara didn't know they knew.

And her calling me baby in front of other officers was a new place for us.

I guess in the situation, all rules went out the window.

I looked at Tara in her tearful eyes and started my story.

What did I tell them?

What was in the envelope?

What happened to Tatiana Blue?

You wouldn't believe me if I told you...

Now, did I ruin her day?

Moody Blue

*H*er arms were aching, rain was pouring down on her and all she could see was shoddy brick work in front of her. The sound of traffic and the rain drown out the footsteps of the security guards she was hiding from as she held on with her contact surface gloves flat on the wall.

'Just another day in the life,' Tatiana said to herself, shaking her dreadlocks from her face, cursing the fact she didn't tie them up before she jumped out the window.

Not that she was scared of heights but she thought better than to look down as she dangled over twenty storeys up from the ledge of the Suchang Trade Company in Hong Kong.

And then it hit!

Shocked her and totally took her by surprise. It always did when it turned on.

Her contact lenses faded her vision to complete black and that meant only one thing. Russell.

Colour drained back into her right eye and she was back in front of the brick wall with rain drops falling over her eyes. Her left eye was seeing something else.

The Tall Tales of Tatiana Blue

Russell Reed was backing through his front door with a woman stuck to his face in a passionate kiss. He kicked the door closed as his hands ran up and down the back of the thick woman in a short dress.

'Who the fuck is this bitch?' Tatiana said, spitting rain water from her mouth.

Here she was thinking about and providing for their future and there he was, being a whore. Granted, she had yet to tell him that they had a future together but that still didn't mean he could whore around with any and every one.

'Especially some tramp with such terrible taste in weave.'

With her gloves holding fixed to the wall, Tatiana was forced to watch them in her left eye as they grabbed at each other's clothes, spinning through the hallway in a passionate kiss and there was nothing she could do about it.

She knew what she was feeling though. She was angry. More than angry, she was livid, which made her instantly calm.

'Oh Russell... trust me... I'm the only pussy you're getting!'

Russell and his companion were crashing against walls, discarding clothes and leaving a trail from the front door. From the hidden cameras she left around his flat, she was getting the best shots of a film she didn't want to see. Her arms were aching due to stretching for so long and she could feel the rain seeping through her clothes. Her Lyrca t-shirt and leggings were sticking to her skin and water droplets were constantly dripping into her eyes.

'The things I do for a fucking pair of Loubous,' she said, peeking into the window where two security guards were looking at the boxes she knocked over as she jumped out the window.

'CALL QUINCY!'

Tatiana heard her phone begin to dial in her earpiece as she was forced to watch Russell back into his bedroom and push the woman down on the bed with a smile.

'Hello?' Quincy answered with sleep in his voice.

'It's me.'

'You? D'you know what fucking time it is?'

'Yeah I do, why do you?'

'Always with the jokes Blue. What'd you want?'

'I need a fire alarm with sprinklers please.'

'Geez, what trouble are you in now?'

Tatiana focused on her left eye and could see that the mystery woman now had Russell on his back and was standing over him while pulling her dress over her head.

The Tall Tales of Tatiana Blue

She couldn't help the anger that was rolling through her; all she knew was that Russell was hers, she was coming back for him and there was no random woman in the world who would ruin that.

The sound of the window opening stole her attention and she began to walk her hands across the wall. The gloves were holding fine, though the rain was making her nervous as Quincy said the only problem they have is with water.

'I'm not IN to anything. I just need a fire alarm and a sprinkler malfunction,' she whispered.

'Where?'

Tatiana told him.

'Really Tat? Leave the dude alone.'

'When I want your opinion, I'll give it to you.'

'One day I'm gonna have a good retort for that.'

'Please?' Tatiana asked, spitting rain from her mouth.

'For crying out… Why are you whispering? Is that Cantonese I can hear?'

'Don't worry about what I'm doing, could you just do me this one favour?'

'ONE favour?!'

'One right now. The others don't count right now, just please.'

Mr Oh

Russell and his companion were both naked and laying on top of each other, sharing a passionate kiss and enjoying the feeling of each other's skin. With no audio coming through, Tatiana was forced to watch a silent version of events with the torrential rain distracting her senses and making it so that she couldn't concentrate.

She looked up at the window again. There was no one there.

Slowly, she scaled the wet brick wall and looked in through the window to find the security had left the room. She unlocked the window and began to climb in as Russell was slipping on a condom.

'Fuck that!' Tatiana said to herself as she lifted herself onto the window frame.

'You ready for it?' Quincy said in her ear.

'Do it NOW!'

With both legs swinging into the office, Tatiana crouched behind a desk and watched her left eye, waiting. The woman was bending over his bed and spreading her cheeks while he manoeuvred himself behind her.

The first splash of water dropped and it hit Russell in the middle of his forehead. He looked up just in time to see the rest of the water fall from the ceiling. The fire alarm followed.

'YES!' Tatiana screamed. 'GET YOUR OWN MAN BITCH!'

The Tall Tales of Tatiana Blue

She covered her own mouth and peeked above the desk, watching as the woman scrambled out of the room to avoid the cascading water which was falling throughout his flat. She was picking clothes off the floor as Russell was chasing behind her getting his own clothes on.

'Happy now?' Quincy asked.

'I'm out of the rain and my man is in the rain so I'm good.'

'Okay, good. I'm done. I'm going back to bed. You've got 23 seconds by the way.'

'Look at you, finding where I am. Don't worry,' Tatiana said, moving to the boxes of shoes she came for. Stuffing pairs of Christian Louboutin and Brian Atwood shoes into the bag she stashed under the desk. 'This is what I does.'

'Yeah but it's not just you is it? Just be careful.'

'Thanks DAD. Get some sleep. Say hi to Maya for me.'

'For the last time,' Quincy said, his voice waking up. 'I am not fuc...'

'Night Q-Ball.'

She pressed her ear and the call ended. In her left eye, Russell was throwing on a t-shirt and running out of his front door. She rubbed her stomach, enjoying the flutter of butterflies.

The lights went out as she swung her haul over her shoulder. She heard voices and quick footsteps coming towards her. Beams of torch light shone in her direction and she knew enough Cantonese to know they were coming her way.

Mr Oh

'You kicking already?' she said to her stomach.

Unwrapping a hair band from her wrist and tying her hair in a ponytail, Tatiana Blue jumped out of the window again.

The heal of heels

*T*atiana Blue I am.

And in case you don't know – which you should by now – I'm the sexiest bitch in this book!

Let's just get that out of the way.

It's a big truth, hard for some to take and there is no one that can tell me any different. After what you've read so far, you must at least have a little crush on me.

Even Mr Oh knows, which is why he let me tell this part of the story. Well, let is a strong word, let's say he was coerced violently. I'm telling it from start to finish and I'm gonna fill you in on all you wanna know.

So let's rewind for a second and flashback to the last time you saw me. That was Russell's place after leaving him tied naked to a chair after having given him some good, sweet extra loving. Actually, it was jumping out of a window in Hong Kong.

Well, first things first, yes I was pregnant, I wasn't joking about that. Yes I know it wasn't the best way to do it, but I'm not your every day, normal type of woman now am I?

I'm normal now though.

Normal ish.

I'm the proud normal mother of Charlotte Florence Blue, the most beautiful, amazing, tiniest, most chocolatey little girl I've ever seen. Hell yes I'm biased and I don't give a fuck. Ain't no baby prettier than my little Cha'Cha.

So you've been wondering where I've been and what I've been doing. Well I had a baby. But before that, I was a busy little bitch (that's beauty in tremendously cute heels if you remember correctly).

The Tall Tales of Tatiana Blue

After I left Russell's that day, I went on what people on road would call a "madness". I had to get busy, I had nine months to get as many shoes as possible before I couldn't see my own feet any more.

I was dangling from factory ceilings while trying not to vomit on security guards below, cramping while trying to climb out of a fourth floor window, experiencing false labour while being chased along a rooftop, back pain while holding Chloroform over a designer's face. I was picking *Gianvito Rossi Leather mesh* pumps and *Givenchy floral print leather* from Selfridges and *Zanotti snake stiletto* sandal and *Charlotte Olympia 'what's the scoop' satin* pumps from Harvey Nichols while my stomach got bigger and bigger.

I say nine months, it was more like seven before I well and truly gave up and couldn't lift my own body weight. I had my girl Maya help me when I got too heavy.

Oh, I've been training her. You remember my friend from the house warming? She's a good little thief now. Real quick, nimble, very clever, but she's part time though. I don't think she's ready to become a full-time lover of stealing shoes but she's a great help.

I hadn't done a mystery drop in a long time either and I missed those.

Oh, a mystery drop is when I take some of the shoes I've taken in random sizes and literally drop them in a different place in London. Somewhere hidden but reachable. Trust me, there's quite a few places like that in London. Then I'd let folk know on my twitter. First come, first served. Then delete the tweet. I'd usually watch the footage when I got home. Hidden camera.

Yeah, I get my Robin Hood on. 100% success rate too. There are some extra fabulous everyday women in London wearing some expensive ass stolen shoes.

Mr Oh

Anyway, by the time I had what I needed, I figured, steal some for myself, steal a few more in different sizes and colours I don't like and sell 'em on eBay.

And guess what? I'm doing alright. Well more than alright. I've got eBay on lock right now. I got shoes flying out the door from like five or six different eBay accounts and I'm making money foot over ankle. I think its six accounts... no, seven. Actually... wait... is it eight? Oh, I dunno.

Either way, I'm their highest seller at the moment. And if you're wondering how you can sell stolen shoes on eBay and not get arrested, well, why the fuck would I tell you that? Get your own hustle. Let's just say, I don't need to go back to a regular nine-to-five any time soon.

Yeah, I'm THAT good right now.

Well, at this current moment, I'm actually not doing too well but we'll get to that in a minute.

So, after I stopped stealing and took Maya's advice and just relaxed and sat at home watching my stomach grow and dealing with the morning sickness, stretch marks, loss of appetite and badly swollen feet, my Charlotte was born a month and a half early at Whipps Cross hospital in Leytonstone. Little madam came into the world peaceful and pristine as you'd like and she's been that way ever since. This was ideal considering where we live now but, again, I'll come back to that in a minute.

I'm a shoe thief on hiatus at the moment and now a mum who's loving it.

I'm elbow deep in nappies from a child that shits more than she eats, my place has become a mountain peak of vests, baby towels, bottles and formula tubs and my days of fabulous, free travelling, intricate heel lifting manoeuvres are a memory to me. I can't tell you the last time I

The Tall Tales of Tatiana Blue

went to one of my stash houses and just sat and looked at my shoes. I can tell you the last time I got shit on my hand changing a nappy though.

If I'm honest, I miss my babies like a man misses pussy in prison. All of 'em. My *Aquazzura Beverley Hills* sandals, my *Sophia Webster butterfly* pumps, my *Giuseppe Zanotti biker* boots. I miss the smell of my *Alexander McQueen cage* sandals, the way the heel looks on my *Birman python* sandals, the ruffles on my *Nicholas Kirkwood ruffled* pumps, the colour on my *Casadei monochrome leather*. My *Valentino Rockstud* heels, my *Zanotti snakeskin* boots, my *Saint Laurent Tribute* sandals. I miss them all. Do you know how many new pairs of Louboutins there are that I don't have? It's like sacrilege. I managed to hit the Louboutin store on Motcomb Street but the day I went to the Mount street store in Mayfair, a mother of a stomach cramp kicked in and that was the last time I went out to 'work'.

You know who I really miss? Maybe even more than my shoes? I miss Russell... that man has been the sugar in my dreams since I last saw him.

Ever since the arrival of our baby, yes OUR baby! Of course I put Russell on the birth certificate. He IS her father whether he knows it or not. But that's a chapter that is going to be opened and maintained today.

You see, today is nine months to the day that Charlotte was conceived and I'm actually nervous.

Me. Tatiana Blue. NERVOUS. Ha!

I haven't been this nervous since Harrods and that was years ago. Well there was this one time in Italy when I saw an Interpol car as I left a warehouse but this feeling is definitely worse. It's the feeling of knowing you're in trouble and you still have to go home and face the music.

Mr Oh

I told Russell I'd be back in nine months and I plan to keep my word. Of course he doesn't know that I'm already here and have been living above him since but hey, if a policeman can't find you and you live on the floor above him, maybe he should find another job.

We moved in, well we were moved in, about a month and a half ago. Due to the fact that my princess came early, I decided I wanted to be able to keep an eye on Russell and make sure he stayed ready for me, well us, to come back into his life.

I got the still very secretive about what he does Quincy to help move our stuff in with the help of some of his "friends". Real quiet men who didn't say much but looked like they'd possibly killed once or thrice before. I would've moved myself but Quincy pointed out that there was more chance of me running into Russell that way so he and his boys moved us right in. Feng sui'ed the place and everything.

Two spacious bedrooms, open plan kitchen, balcony with an excellent view of the Olympic park and literally on the other side of Great Eastern Road where I used to live. Always tickles to think that if Russell moved here a few years earlier, he would've found me without even realising he was looking for me.

So here I am. One floor above Russell Reed, the policeman with a fetish for illegal upskirt film making, the father of my child and the sexiest piece of chocolate this side of the Thames. And he has no idea I can see him.

Another bonus to having Quincy move me in was that he noticed the security cameras in the building which had been tampered with. A small but noticeable black box had been fitted to each camera and blinked a green light next to the camera's solid red. If you didn't know what you were looking at then you wouldn't think anything of it. But Quincy, as

The Tall Tales of Tatiana Blue

I've said before, does some very strange, clandestine work and he noticed it straight away.

The little black box gave someone direct access to the camera feeds, allowing them to watch the comings and goings of every resident in the art deco tower block called the Stratford Eye.

Could've only been Russell. He WAS thinking about me after all. He knew I'd come and he wanted to watch me when I arrived. So sweet. You know you're on a man's mind when he alters every security camera in a building to make sure you arrive safely.

When Quincy called me at Maya's, where I was staying, and told me, I thought it was so romantic. He went to all that trouble for little old me!?

I got Quincy to put a scrambler on his cameras so every time I came or went, the feed scrambled. Was a bit more trouble to get that fitted but worth it. Quincy had to actually break into Russell's flat to get that in place but he did it. Even slid in a multi-view camera behind his wall clock so I could watch him in his apartment from whenever I wanted.

With soundproof covering the wooden floors, me and Charlotte slipped in at night and woke up the next morning watching Russell sleeping next to his camera feeds, looking for me when I was already there.

And here we are! Charlotte is sleeping, Russell is home from work early and about to have a shower and Maya is on her way to...

My front door knocked, taking me away from one of my many many eBay accounts, which were all just anagrams of my name: Labia Tauten, A Butane Tail, Anal Tuba Tie, Bail Ate Tuna, A Beat Untila, Labia Tea Nut, Bait Ale Aunt, to name a few.

With Charlotte taking a nap, I shuffled to the door tying up my now all-blue dreadlocks, which had grown down to my lower back. I took a long

Mr Oh

stretch, giggling to myself that it could've been Russell at my front door. Peeking, just to make sure it wasn't him, I opened the door and yawned in Maya's face.

'Ewww... dragon breath,' Maya said with a hearty chuckle. 'You ready to do the do?'

'Of course not, I'm shitting myself. I'm usually all Slick Rick, but I've never done THIS before. Did you get my text?'

Maya slid past me grabbing Aretha, my left breast, while my arms were behind my head wrapping my hair.

'No, my phone is doing some madness at the moment. Where's my lil' Blue thang?'

'Shuuuuush with your loud self, she's sleeping...'

I paused. I had to because my eyes and ears were now drawn to Maya's feet. More to the *Brian Atwood suede* boots that she was about to clop on my floor.

'Ermmm... hello?' I said, pointing at her feet.

'Oh yeah, the "rules".'

'They're not rules, its one rule,' I replied kicking the door closed. 'No heels on the floor.'

Maya unzipped her boots and I tried to remember the last pair of boots I stole and, for the life of me, I couldn't even picture them in my head. I couldn't even remember the door number of one of my stash houses, let alone all four of them.

My fingers slowly caressed the suede of her left boot and jealousy washed over me from my head to my toes. I wanted them. I wanted the satisfaction of picking them up from a secure place without anyone knowing I was there.

'You like?'

'These are very yummy. Where'd you get 'em from?'

The Tall Tales of Tatiana Blue

'Brit Awards. Hilton Hotel. Katy Perry. She had a pair in red too which I got but I don't like 'em. Want 'em?'

'Well duh and say no more,' I laughed at the road colloquialism, trying to suck the green-eyed fever into the pit of my stomach.

'Nervous are we?' Maya whispered, walking on her tip-toes towards Charlotte's room.

'I am a little, I'm not gonna lie but it feels like this is gonna be the end of a big storm that's been raining over my head.'

'Yeah, yeah, yeah... fuck all that philosophical shit, this ain't Instagram. How are you feeling about seeing him again?'

'Who, Russell Reed, the father of my child, the policeman who has been working for years trying to arrest me, the upskirt fiend who became a father against his will? Yeah, I'm feeling upbeat, chipper and Kool and the gang.'

Maya poked her head in Charlotte's room before sliding on her socks across my floor and into the kitchen.

'For such an event, we need libation,' Maya said, finding a bottle of white rum in my cupboard.

'Fuck yeah,' I added, glad that my girl was here to help me numb the nerves that were making my hands shake.

The reason I was so nervous about seeing Russell again is, well, since the day I closed his door, I felt guilty. I didn't exactly give him a chance to do or say, well, anything. I didn't give him a chance to get to know me or find out anything about me. Then again, his nine-to-five consisted of trying to find and arrest me so the guilt wasn't pure. I felt kind of justified-ish. I mean I could've just taken him home, found out what he had on me and kept it moving. I didn't need to fuck him, technically rape him, and let him get me up the duff. I didn't need to take all those

Mr Oh

pictures and leave them in the envelope, even though that was fun. To be honest, I'm not as radical a thinker as I used to be.

Fiddling with my fingers, and flexing my toes on my padded hardwood floor, I didn't see Maya standing in front of me holding a glass of grey liquid and a rolled up spliff.

'To the balcony,' I chanted.

The sun was going down in the distance bathing the skyline in orange and purple while traffic provided the soundtrack to a perfect London evening. No breeze, nicely warm t-shirt weather, perfect.

'So, talk to me buttercup... you're about to see the love of your life for the first time in nine months, how you feeling?'

'Less questions, more lighting.'

I waited for her to light the spliff before snatching it out of her hand. The shock on her face and the playful kick she gave me said she knew she got caught slipping.

'So what're you gonna say to him?'

'I'll start with hello and freestyle from there I guess. To be honest I've just been watching the days tick away without thinking about what I would actually say to him. Just been watching him.'

This was my first taste of marijuana in a long time. After I got pregnant, I quit smoking altogether and I told Maya not to bring any weed around me until the day I planned to see Russell.

I'd only taken three tokes and I wished I didn't wait so long between spliffs because I could feel my entire body throbbing on a cloud of hazy goodness. The skyline fogged over right before my eyes and I had to rest my head on the balcony railing for a moment.

'What is this?' I asked, handing the roll up to Maya.

'What!'

The Tall Tales of Tatiana Blue

'This? What is it?'
'What!'
'THIS,' I pointed to the roll up. 'What is THIS?!'
'What! It's called What!'
'For fuck sake!' I laughed.
Numbness was throbbing through my lips and I sat down with my back against the glass railing.
'What time you going down there?'
'As soon as this drink is finished. Best to just do it and get it out of the way.'
'Yeah, I agree,' Maya said blowing smoke rings into the air. 'Just have it done and done. I know you're probably thinking about what his reaction will be... do you think he'll try and arrest you?'
'I wasn't thinking about that. I am now though! Thanks dipshit.'
Maya couldn't stop laughing. 'I am sooo sorry, I thought you would've realised that he could be SO pissed off that he actually arrests you. Imagine if he did. He'd arrest you for not only the shoes... and if they have a file on you as big as you say then that's a LOT of shoes, right?'
'Oh yeah...'
'Then there's the kidnapping, the torture, the...'
'Wait, I didn't torture him. I just drugged him and tied him up. That's not torture,' I reasoned while exhaling thick smoke above my head slowly.
'Well it's not a spa treatment. You know how the law works. They'll call it torture. So that's theft, no that's multiple theft, burglary, kidnapping, torture, assault, rape...'
'Is it REALLY rape? I mean he never once told me to stop. That's my defence. The whole time, from the moment I slipped him in to the time

Mr Oh

he came, he never once told me to stop. Alright, yeah he told me to untie him but he never said stop. I don't think.'

'That's your defence?' Maya laughed.

'And I'm sticking to it.'

We shared a high-five and a chuckle as the marijuana mixed with the rum/ginger beer in my glass and I felt good all over. I was starting to feel less nervous about seeing Russell and worrying more about being arrested. To me, that was a long shot. He'd have a lot to do if that was his plan and I don't think he'd do that. He better not.

Fuck that, Russell loves me. He wouldn't do that.

'So you really think he's gonna be like "oh hey, there you are, I've been looking for you?" And that's it?!'

The picture of such a simple reintroduction made me laugh while inhaling and I started coughing heavily. Maya slapped and rubbed my back while laughing at me with drool around the corners of my lips.

I caught my breath. 'You trying to fucking kill me?'

'I'm just tryna prepare you for every eventuality that could happen. This isn't just you coming home after a long day at work... he could actually punch you in the face.'

'He's a fiend for an upskirt but he's not stupid. Punch who and live where? This What is a lot!'

This was what I needed. My home slice, ride or die, been there since day one friend in my corner making sure I've got my shit right before going down there expecting happy families. Not that I hadn't thought about it myself. That Russell might not be so happy to see me and wanna do something stupid like take me in. I've taken steps for that eventuality, just FYI.

The Tall Tales of Tatiana Blue

You know the story so you know Maya's been around for years. She's become the voice of reason when I get ideas of grandeur like stealing from a Sultan with security in every room of his house or some shit like that. That one was definitely a challenge by the way.

I took the last puffs of the spliff and threw the burning end over the balcony, backed my drink and jumped to my feet.

'Starting to hear that Rocky music in your head huh?' Maya asked, slowly making it to her feet.

'Yep... the drink sweet me, the weed sweet me, I'm saccharine and ready to go.'

She rubbed my shoulders like a trainer motivating a heavyweight. I let my dreads loose and swung them free, ready to close a chapter and possibly open a new one. I felt immensely conscious of myself and my body and the way it had changed during pregnancy. Quincy and Maya said that I looked exactly the same but I felt different. I felt heavier in my core, my six-pack wasn't as visible as before, my thighs were more chunk than defined and Lauryn and Aretha, my breasts, had gone up two cup sizes.

'Let's go get 'em champ...'

We marched back into the flat humming *Eye of The Tiger.* Maya spun me by my shoulders and gave me a once over from my hair to my face – pulling random fluff from my cheeks – to my clothes, which were tracksuit bottom comfortable.

'No I'm not gonna change Maya!'

'Whaaaaaat? I didn't even say anything.'

'You didn't have to... I could see you were about to say suttin'.'

'You know maybe a dress or some tight trousers, show him what is truly standing at his front door.'

'I'm not going there to fuck him am I?'

Mr Oh

'But if he offered you some dick, you wouldn't take it? God knows he hasn't had any in a while, no thanks to you.'

'First of all,' I said pointing at Maya with a full comedic attitude.

'He doesn't know I've been sneaky enough to cock-block every piece of pussy he's tried to get since I left. Secondly, if Russell Reed offered me some dick, you best believe that dick is accepted, signed for and delivered on time, yessur!'

'Okay, well, on with the footwear and get yourself gone.'

I froze.

This was it. The moment I'd been building up to for the last nine months. I was about to be face-to-face with Russell Reed, the only man I wanted. He was my Pete Becker. The officer who was the man for me. I was so lost in my own thoughts that I didn't notice Maya sat me down and was putting my Adidas basketball boots on for me.

'You can do this... look at it this way. Get this done and we can start giving Charlotte to Russell while we "work".'

'Always a silver lining with you ain't it Maya?'

'Yep, usually a delicate silk lining.'

This woman was so stupidly funny and it was little lines like that one that made me glad I had her as a friend. Pretty much my only friend. As a shoe thief, you meet a lot of people, run from a lot more and get close to very few. I met and kept in contact with a few mums I met during my pregnancy but I don't keep in touch as much as I used to. Sucks but it's the life you choose right?

My arm was pulled and I jumped to my feet and was shuffled in front of a full length mirror next to my front door.

'You ready?' Maya asked, with her head peeking around my hair.

'I'm ready.' I wrapped a stretch of material around my dreads.

'You ready to go get your man?' Maya put my jacket on my shoulders.

The Tall Tales of Tatiana Blue

'He's already my man, he just needs confirmation!'
'Damn right!'
'Okay, let's g... hold on where's my phone?'
I spun on the balls of my feet, trying to remember where I was when I last saw my phone.
I called Maya to make sure she was still coming and sat... it's on the sofa.
As if on cue, my phone started to ring.
'Thanks babe, I know where it is.' I mumbled to Maya.
'That's not me calling you.'
'Oh, well then who the hell...'
Finding my phone nestled between the cushions, I checked the display and saw that Quincy was calling.
'What it is Mr Secretive? Off somewhere being secretive?'
'I found him!'
'You what love? You found who?'
'Him. I found HIM!'
'NO! No you fucking didn't!? Not now! Oh please say not now. Awwwww for fuck sake!'
I started to lose it. I was about to throw my phone against my front door when Maya slid in and took it from me, sensing my instantaneous anger.
'Who is this? Oh hey Quincy, wassup?'
He obviously told her because she turned to me with her mouth open and a hand on her chest. I stood in front of her with my hands on my hips not sure what the fuck to do.
'Ask him if he's sure. This isn't something to get wrong. Ask him!'
'It's him,' I heard Quincy say in Maya's ear.

Mr Oh

I watched Maya intently. I knew whatever her facial reaction or response, the truth was, Marcus had been found.

She looked at me with her hand still on her chest and nodded with her eyes closed.

This was not what I needed. I had just mentally prepared myself for a new beginning with a man who I'd already drugged and kidnapped and here comes that wank face cunt hole of the past who was definitely owed a drugging and a kidnapping. And a beating. And a castrating. And a water-boarding. And a Jack Bauer style interrogation and torture session.

Oh yeah, I was pissed!

You remember Marcus don't you?!

Lemme refresh your memory...

Marcus. Mr Marcus.

M and M. Motherfucking Marcus.

Marcus is the reason why I am the way I am. Technically.

Marcus is the bastard spawn I hate.

GOD... you have no idea how much I absolutely detest that man. I mean deep down loathing.

Every woman, and I mean every woman, has a man who has come through her life who they will hate FOREVER. Marcus is mine.

Years ago, me and Marcus used to go out. I was a working, earning, shoe addicted woman doing my thing. Working in insurance for high end boutiques and shoe stores. Things weren't great but we were together and semi-happy. Wasn't love yet but that's not to say it wouldn't have happened one day. Anyway, I took a picture of myself in a vest, pair of shoes and a skirt. Nothing sexy really, just wanted to see how my latest shoes looked with a skirt I'd just bought. Ladies, you've been there right?

The Tall Tales of Tatiana Blue

Well, he thought I took such a picture to send to someone else so he decided to burn my shoes. Not just some of my shoes, ALL of my shoes. Every single last pair of shoes I owned. Oh wait, no, he didn't just burn them, he poured bleach on them first and then he burned them. In my own car.

Just N*Sync. Gone.

And that is why I hate Marcus with the passion of the Christ. I'm not gonna go on about how much I loathe him and how much I really really loved my shoes because, by now you should already know. I was mad depressed for a while, then I met Maya and Quincy; Harrods happened and the rest is history.

By this point, I had to sit down because I could feel myself shaking. Moments ago, I was happy shaking because the thought of seeing Russell again made me physically nervous. Now, it was Marcus making me vibrate because I was getting more and more angry. I must've looked pissed because Maya tossed my phone and was stood by my side with her arms around my shoulders telling me to calm down. She'd seen me pissed over the years when I heard his name or something reminded me of him. I don't even watch porn with Mr Marcus any more because of him.

And Mr Marcus was one of my favourites.

'So what's the plan Stan? I know there's no point trying to even to talk you out of doing what I know you're gonna do,' Maya said with her curly afro resting against my dreads. It was like the physical connection of our skulls allowed our thoughts to travel into each other's mind. She knows me better than anyone. She knows when she can offer me reason and I'd accept it and when she should just shut the fuck up and make sure I know all the angles before I go and do something stupid.

Mr Oh

I know I hadn't been Tatiana Blue the elegant and calculating shoe thief in a while but boy did it turn on. My first thought was heels. Which shoes was I going to disgrace this fucker with and which stash house were they in.

I've got four places set up in London. One in Dalston, one in Finsbury Park, another in Hammersmith and a studio in Peckham. Two in Los Angeles, one in Greece, a two bedroom in Dubai and three in Japan.

What, you think all those shoes just sit up under my bed? Come on now. I've got THAT many shoes that I need THAT many places to put 'em. I've got people living in some of my stash houses – a la *Men in Black* – but most of them are closed off and inconspicuous.

Oh... and Maya got me another one in Mauritius as well.

Anyway, I wasn't thinking of flying out to get a pair of shoes, although my mind did seriously contemplate it for a minute.

'Where is he?' I asked, brushing my dreads out of my face.

'Huh?' Maya played stupid. Trying to delay the inevitable. As my friend, I appreciated the fact that she at least tried, but she knew I didn't wanna hear anything else except for where I could find Marcus so I could calculate how long it would take to get there.

I found my phone and called Quincy back. He answered first time.

'Where is he?' My voice was cold.

'Shepherd's Bush. Seems like he's celebrating a birthday.'

'His birthday isn't until...'

Quincy cut me off. 'It's not HIS birthday.'

'Oh reaaaaaally?'

Then I started to laugh. If I knew Marcus, he was probably dishing out some elaborate evening of this and that and ending in some dick, like penis is an appropriate birthday present. Like "hey, happy birthday, I got

The Tall Tales of Tatiana Blue

you some dick. The same dick I give you throughout the year. And many happy returns."

I hate men that do that shit. At least get me some heels and some dick.

My mind got back into business mode. Shepherd's Bush. From Stratford, that's clean across London. With night dropping, that might be a bit of traffic. I was cutting through London in my head, seeing myself passing London Bridge, up Embankment and on to...

And that's when I knew that I was a shoe thief for life, not just for Christmas. You know what I remembered is also up in that side of London? Mount Street. The last Christian Louboutin store on my list of shoe shops I was yet to steal from. With the tramp assistant who tried to treat me like a leper.

'Yeah, you see that smile there? I don't want no part of what thought is behind that evil grin,' Maya said, fluffing her hair.

'You know,' I couldn't even pretend. 'Mama's going to get her some REAL nice shoes before she goes to see that prick.'

'OOOOHHH THE BITCH IS BACK!' Maya shouted.

'Shuuuuuuuuuuuush, if you wake her, I swear...'

Maya covered her mouth. 'Sorry. Come on say it with me, it's been a long time since we've done it...'

'Okay, come we go...'

We stood in front of each other, grinning like school girls. Turning back-to-back, she grabbed my bum to let me know she was going first. We began to two-step away from each other while humming a random beat.

'Bitches ain't dogs or holes for men to feel...' she started.

'Bitches are beauties in tremendously cute heels!' I finished.

Mr Oh

We walked five steps away from each other and turned on the fifth step, striking a pose so fierce, both Mr and Miss Jay would've been proud.

Maya giggled before me and admitted defeat in the stare down before reaching for her drink.

'So, Mount Street huh?'

'Mount Street.'

Maya rolled her eyes. 'The last on your list.'

'I didn't tell you about the time I went down there when I was pregnant, like seven months. And I walked in to just look at the shoes. It was weird to be window shopping and know that I wasn't going to be back in the shop after closing taking what I wanted. But I just wanted to be in the presence of brand new Loubous, you know my fetish has never left.'

'You and those damn shoes. They're not even all that...'

I cut her off. 'Let's not do this again, alright? Leave my shoes alone.'

'So anyway...'

'As soon as I walked in, the woman in the shop looked at me like I was about to give birth on the floor. She was trying not to touch me and basically trying to usher me out. Properly gave me the "oh you can't afford to shop here honey" look.'

'And Lord knows you hate that!'

'Yessur I do...'

Even though I was planning a new caper and enjoying the science of stealing as calculations began, a thought of Russell tickled my spine. Marcus never left my mind though. To me, this last project was like killing two birds with one stone. Hit my last store and my last memory in

The Tall Tales of Tatiana Blue

one night. The sweet sweet feeling of weed and alcohol had me thinking clearly as I looked down at my phone.

'Oh shit, Quincy, are you still there?'

'You finished your little lesbifriends session? Or do you wanna know where he is?'

'Gimme.'

'I've already sent you the address. He's with a woman named Roz. It's her birthday and I've also sent the link to the feed for your viewing pleasure.'

I sighed. 'Thanks dude. I owe you one. I'll get Maya to suck your dick the next time she sees you.'

'Erm... how do you know I haven't already sucked his dick?' Maya jumped in.

'HAS she already sucked your dick Quincy?'

He groaned. 'Oh whatever you two. I'll get a shoe box ready, just call me when you need it, alright? Good luck... and have fun.'

'Will do.'

I hung up the phone, handing Maya my glass. She walked to the kitchen and I shuffled to Charlotte's room thinking of the perfect multi-functional outfit for the evening's festivities. As a shoe thief turned mother, all my spandex outfits and Lycra suits were replaced with comfortable tracksuit bottoms, Ugg boots and Air Max 180s. But I always kept a hooded spandex long sleeve and leggings close to hand. Force of habit.

I wanted to wear it for Russell. I imagined him wrestling it off me, bending me over a counter and fingering me. In the all-black outfit, that would've been purely sublime. Punish the naughty shoe thief kind of thing.

Mr Oh

Yeah I could've just said fuck it and left Marcus and Mount Street alone and just dealt with Russell but that wouldn't be very Blue of me now would it?

Opening my alternative wardrobe after checking on Charlotte, who was out like a light, I had to dig under blankets, bibs, unopened packs of vests and duvets before I found my old work bag.

'Well hello you,' I said to my tool bag carry case.

I got changed so quickly, I walked out and caught Maya by surprise. I checked my phone for the address and calculated a route from Mount Street to Roz's place in my head.

'Know where you're going?'

'Yep,' My mind was racing through London.

'Are you sure you wanna do this tonight, I mean...'

I brushed my finger over Maya's lips while she was talking making her words end with a 'lubber' at the end.

'You know there's no point, so don't even,' I said.

'Alright, well take my car. We'll be okay here, just go do what you have to do, come home, get ya man and by the morning you should have some police dick in your mouth.'

I frowned. 'Er, yeah thanks Maya.'

Then I thought about it. Didn't seem like a bad way to start tomorrow morning.

Bag on my shoulder, hair up with my phone in my bra and Maya's keys in my hand, I gave her a high five, a nipple flick and took the stairs, feeling alive all over again. That same nervousness I felt back in Harrods all those years ago was running through me. Marcus was on my mind that night too but the pain of his shit was fresh back then. I'm older now. Don't care as much. But he still has to recognise just how much he fucked up.

The Tall Tales of Tatiana Blue

I lifted the hood on my top and ran straight into the car park, straight to Maya's car and slid in with one swift movement and my bag on the passenger seat. Maya's Audi TT smelled like Black Love incense as I hooked up her GPS and put in my route.

The engine hummed excitedly and Tyler the Creator's *Blow My Load* played very loudly. Reverse, spin round and I was quickly dodging cars on the Bow flyover on my way to Aldgate. I'll admit, I wasn't driving safely at all but I didn't care. I was a confident, risk taking driver, didn't try audacious shit, but I could pull off a ninja move or two.

Braking suddenly for speed cameras and jumping yellow-into-red traffic lights, the HMS Belfast flew past me on the left and I was turning right on Embankment in under 10 minutes. From Stratford, that's 20-30 minutes on a good day but that's how fast I was driving.

All the while, Marcus was on my mind. As angry as I was, I hadn't thought about how I'd feel about seeing him again after so long. I mean, I am forever angry at that man and what he did, over fucking nothing. Okay, let's say I HAD taken that picture of myself to send to another guy, did the punishment fit the crime? FUCK arse no!

And if you agree then you might as well fuck off now because this story ain't for you boo boo.

Another seven minutes and I was passing Green Park and driving slowly past Mount Street, looking for somewhere to park. I forgot how opulent the shops were in this part of town as I past Marc Jacobs and found a spot 150 yards away from the Louboutin store. Not ideal I know but I drove around for ages looking for somewhere to park and this was the best I could find. Considering I was basically freestyling this job, I didn't have time to plan my getaway vehicle properly so this would have to do.

Mr Oh

My phone vibrated against my nipple and made my shoulders shimmy. I laughed to myself as I slid the car into the spot with one wheel whip to the left and one to the right.

I told you, I'm a ninja driver.

The engine died and I sat there for a minute. I didn't anticipate I'd be there so quickly so I wanted to take stock of what I was about to do.

I'd already done the homework on this place before Charlotte was born so I knew the layout and how I'd get in, I just prayed they hadn't refurbished the place and changed shit up.

I wanted to watch the silence of the area. Didn't want some random pacing policeman on patrol walking past and catching me hanging through a skylight.

My fingers caressed my bag on the passenger seat and I could feel my tools, ready to be used.

Excited was an understatement. I was hype. Like a missile waiting to be let off so I could fuck some shit up.

As you know, it'd been a long time since I'd been all up in the game again so I had to take a second to just, you know, savour the moment. Air sucked in through my nose and out through my lips. I slipped my ear piece in, just in case Quincy had something to say. Grabbing my bag, I got out of the car and moved swiftly but nonchalantly to the side of the building, hugging the wall with my back.

First things first. Security cameras.

I rifled through the side pockets of my bag and found my EMP disabler which was disguised as a blusher compact. One press of the button on top and all electrics in a 100-foot radius go night night.

I sighed. 'Here we go,' pressing the button once.

The Tall Tales of Tatiana Blue

The street lights in front of the building went out and I knew I was good to go. I left the wall and looked straight to the roof, which was my way in.

'Gloves' I said to myself.

Back in the bag and I found my contact gloves, which I always loved using.

Ever since I played *Call of Duty: Black Ops* and they used those gloves which stick to almost any surface, I was extremely giddy when Quincy hooked me up with a pair for free. Strong enough to hold my weight, but a little problematic in the rain, I put them on slowly, savouring more of the moment.

'Oooooooh... this is gonna be so fun.' My nipples rose against my bra as I approached the wall, guesstimating that it was about two storeys straight up.

'Let's see if you still got it... of course I still got it, who the fuck do you think I am...'

And there it was. My other voice. The one that pops out and talks back to me when I'm out working. She was as funny as me, always made me question everything and saved my backside on more occasions than I care to admit.

'Let's go then... after you...' I said to myself as I touched my first glove hand on the wall. The back of the fingers lit up with a green light on each finger as I came into the contact with the wall. My other hand did the same and I could feel my hands sticking. Rolling my hand off the wall from my palm and sticking again, I left the ground and began to climb the wall.

Spiderman makes it look a lot easier because, as a spider he has sticky shit on his feet. I was literally lifting myself up by my hands so it was a struggle to get halfway.

Mr Oh

My arms were burning because I hadn't kept up my gym routine and my legs were scrambling against the wall trying to give extra leverage to reach with.

I was sweating hard. Trying to catch my breath but not wanting to stop either. Nothing like stopping halfway then looking up and realising you still got half to go.

'Thought you said you still had it... oh fuck off...'

Hand by shaky hand, I kept going until I could see the top of the roof. My hand was close enough to reach it as I grabbed the ledge and held on, knowing I was a hand and a hoist away from being up the bloody wall.

I was seriously tired and out of shape. Maya would be giggling her ass off if she could see me now. Out of breath just from scaling a wall. Hard to practice parkour with a buggy these days.

When my heartbeat slowed to a normal pace, I inhaled deeply and lifted myself over the ledge with a 'hurumph' and a 'come the fuck on' to motivate me.

My dreads were longer than they were on my last time out so I had to carry extra weight and, honestly, I was already knackered. Baby weight was still holding onto my stomach, legs and face but I couldn't let that stop this train. Tonight, I was the dreadlock engine that could. And bloody well would.

I scooted low across the roof to the skylight that looked right down onto the shop floor of the Louboutin store. The moon above was peering straight through giving me a clear view of oh so many red-bottomed babies, just waiting to come home with me. My bottom lip was low and I was probably drooling at that moment.

A quick rifle through my bag and I found my trusty old lock picker. The same one I used in Harrods. Doing what I do, you go through a lot of

The Tall Tales of Tatiana Blue

tools but this one had sentimental value. I became attached to it and it's been with me ever since.

I touched around the circular dome for a lock and felt it move under my fingers.

'Oooooooo...' I said to myself as I tried to lift the dome which rose in my grip. 'Well ain't that something?!'

As I slowly lifted the glass, I looked around the inside of the dome lid for any silent contact alarms I might've tripped by mistake. None. I looked down for any cameras in the vicinity but the EMP would've taken them out. I gave another EMP burst just to be sure.

Back to the bag for my belt, which I wrapped around my waist. I hooked a thick wire from the belt and secured it to the base of the skylight.

'Always love this bit,' I said to myself as I calculated the drop, adjusted the greasy wire and stood over the open skylight.

I jumped into the air and fell feet first into the shop, hearing nothing but wind and wire running in my ears for a second. I was obviously still good at what I do because the belt grabbed me gently at the waist and my feet stopped so close to the floor I felt my toes poke the ground.

'Ricooooo suuuuuuave,' I giggled as I looked around, taking a mini torch from my pocket and putting it in my mouth. I spun around the wire for a second before unhooking myself and crouching next to a plinth of shoes. The glimmer of shiny red bottoms next to my corner eye instantly distracted me. My lips couldn't stop from rising into a dirty great big smile.

It felt good to be back doing the thing I loved more than anything in the world. Well, after Charlotte. It wasn't like a transformation into becoming a thief, more like a realisation. You know when you watch kung-fu films all your life and somehow think you can do kung-fu, it's

Mr Oh

kind of like that. Because I used to work with shoes back in the day, I just really thought if I ever stole a pair, I'd get away with it. So I did. Well, I do.

Scanning the room and taking my gloves off, my eyes were catching shoes, more shoes, the counter, more shoes, stockroom, more shoes...

BINGO... stockroom.

I moved low past so many shoes from my Louboutin's mental list that I kept stopping to stare.

'Ooo, the *Armurabottas*... OH shit the *Mado* boots... Fuck me, my walls are gonna love those *Azimut* boots, come to mama...'

And this is where I fucked up.

I touched a shoe.

Ever since having Charlotte, though I haven't been stealing shoes, I've still been making lists of shoes I want. Maya has been helping but there are some I've wanted to get for myself. Just to feel the pleasure of taking them for my very own. There were 10 pairs of Louboutin shoes and boots I wanted and every single one of them caught my eye.

My list consisted of the *Lady Spiked platform* pump in leopard print, *Taclou spiked* knee high boots, the *Python peep toe*, the *Armurabotta Pointy Thigh High* boot, *Snakeskin Daffodil* pump, *Spike Wars women's ankle bootie*, *Mado lace up leather over the knee* boot, *Azimut leather caged* boot, *Monicarina leather thigh high* boots and... The best of them all, the *Sexy Strass peep toe* heels – four inch pump with peep toe heel, covered in crystals.

Oh, those were coming home with me in multiple sizes.

And that's the shoe I touched.

I had to.

I reached out and picked it up from the display in awe. The second I did it, something felt wrong but I didn't hear anything.

The Tall Tales of Tatiana Blue

'You've tripped a silent alarm,' Quincy said in my ear out of fucking nowhere. I thought he was God the way he spoke so out of the blue. That used to happen all the time back when I first started and Quincy would be in my ear, silent until the last minute...and because his voice is deep...imagine James Earl Jones in your ear out of nowhere.

'Shiiiiiit... you had to fucking touch didn't you... erm, it was a *Sexy Strass*!? Of course I had to touch...'

'Oiiii, could you lot pull it together for a minute and focus, thanks,' Quincy yelled at me. At us.

'Stockroom. There's a door out of the building in the stockroom, if I remember correctly.' I was talking and moving at the same time. Past the counter, I didn't have time to be sneaky about it and kicked the stockroom door open first time. The door burst open as I heard a siren in the distance.

'Fuck, fuck, fuck, fuck,' I kept saying to myself. I mean what were the odds of my first day back in the game and I trip a silent alarm. What a piss take.

I took the torch out of my mouth and shone it in the stockroom of boxes of shoes in multiple sizes. I slung the bag off my shoulder and pulled a larger bag out, whipping it to life before laying it on the floor.

Then I got to work. Quick work.

The first shoe I found was the *Python peep toe* in my perfect five and a half. I took a six for eBay purposes. I did the same with the *Taclou, Mado* and *Azimut* boots but I took three sizes of the *Armurabotta*, the *Monicarina* and the *Lady spiked* platform pump because Aretha's nipple told me to. I couldn't find a five a half in the *Snakeskin Daffodil* or the *Spike Wars* ankle boot so I took a five and six while the single siren got closer.

Mr Oh

The last shoe on my list, the one that started all this quickness – the *Sexy Strass* – needed three five and a half sizes, two sixes and two fives. Just to cover my bases.

With my boxes stacked, I pulled the sides of the bag over them and zipped it up with a minor struggle. Covered and ready to go, I squatted low, swung the arm of the bag over my shoulder and lifted from my knees, testing the weight of the bag.

Another reminder I was out of shape as my legs and ankles cracked.

Considering I was carrying 28 pairs of shoes, I was able to move quite freely on my feet, even as the weight of the bag pulled me back off balance slightly.

I got to the door of the stockroom and realised the siren I previously heard in the distance stopped. Dropping the bag silently, I peeked around the stockroom door and saw two male plain clothes officers cupping their hands around their eyes on the store windows.

There was something familiar about them but I couldn't quite place them until one of them with a classical Nigerian face reminded me.

Femi and Jamal. Russell's police friends.

I couldn't fucking believe it. Of all the police in the world to send! I wonder if they were assigned to my cases as well?

The dudes I let into Russell's flat after I... well you know.

I could hear them arguing about whether or not to break into the shop to investigate.

'I can see a wire hanging from the skylight. I HAVE to break in,' Jamal, the bigger one of the pair said.

'You just wanna smash suttin' don't you? Been a while since you've, you know, smashed huh?' Femi said, looking in my direction through the window.

Thank God the darkness covered me. 'Shit...'

The Tall Tales of Tatiana Blue

'You know they're coming in don't you?' Quincy said out of nowhere.

'Yeah I know... Well, long as I've got one of my trusty tasers, I'll be alright.'

'I hope you kept up some training cuz here they come.'

Quincy went silent as the front door of the Louboutin store flew open in a crescendo of glass and metal.

'If anyone asks what happens, you did this yeah? I'm already on my second warning, I don't need the paperwork.' Femi said as Jamal moved slowly through the open door with a big ass torch shining from left to right.

I ducked down so the counter separated us and moved back into the stockroom, almost tripping over my bag of shoes.

'Don't fuck about,' I whispered to myself.

'Wire through a skylight, who else could it be?' Jamal said, treading carefully.

'No way! You really think "the legend" would trip a silent alarm?'

'She's been quiet for how long now... maybe she's been out of the loop for so long, she's a little rusty?'

'Who the fuck is rusty?' I asked myself. 'Oh lemme show you rusty.'

'You take the stockroom, I'll look for the master switch.'

'Why is it always me who gets sent into the dark places where people with weapons can hide? You're the one with no neck, why don't you go into the darkness for once?'

'Are we really gonna do this now?' Jamal said, shining his torch towards the stockroom. The beam of light shone over my head and onto empty spaces where boxes were missing. 'Grow a pair and check the stockroom.'

'Don't worry about my pair,' Femi said, shining his torch towards the stockroom. 'Leave that to your mum.'

Mr Oh

'JUST... go!'

I was still crouched by the door with my taser in my hand wondering to myself, would I have been caught by the silent alarm in my prime? It was a slick little thing. No sticker on the shoe or contact surface. To be honest, I couldn't even see it.

An update on security measures was in order. That was a thought to save for later. Meanwhile, Femi had his light on the door which I'd beautifully kicked open.

'Door's been kicked open,' he said.

'She's slipping,' Jamal shouted back.

'I swear, that guy and his fucking mouth.' I wanted to make sure I got my taser on that Jamal. He apparently didn't rate me or my legend at all.

I could see the beam from Femi's torch getting closer to the door and I got primed on the balls of my feet. Ready for him to appear around the corner and out of Jamal's line of sight. I sunk back deeper into the stockroom, sliding the bag slowly with me as I moved.

'You wanna add assaulting a police officer to your already massive list of shit?' Quincy said in my ear.

'STOP doing that,' I muffled. 'And they wouldn't be the first officers on my injured list would they?'

Femi appeared in the doorway of the stockroom with his torch in front of him, wielding it like a light-sabre. I'd tucked behind a wooden crate so the light missed me as he moved forward, right into a dark spot.

With the dark floor coming to light, getting closer to the crate, I held the taser by my foot and prepared myself.

I could hear him breathing heavily, his feet moving nervously towards me. As the light fell on the tip of my trainers, I flashed the taser once. By the time he swung the light towards me, I was already in his personal space, pushing the taser into his neck and holding it there. I covered his

The Tall Tales of Tatiana Blue

mouth as he tipped backwards and I held him on his way to the ground. As he lay down, his body convulsing, I replaced my hand with my crotch as I sat on his face. Kinda pointless really but useful in the sense that I was able to keep him quiet with my hands free and ready, just in case the Deebo-looking one followed behind.

'Shush,' I said looking down at Femi, whose eyes were staring straight up.

If you investigate me properly, you'll find out in police reports I have an affinity for shocking people with tasers and stun guns, particularly in the neck. I have a quite disturbing array of tasers, stun guns that look like phones, sniper tasers, shotgun tasers... You name it, I got it. I don't know what it is about electrocuting people like that but... hey what can I say? It makes my toes curl. And I'm not a killer, I just love shoes a lot.

As I was looking towards the stockroom door, Femi's leg kicked out and knocked over a stack of shoe boxes next to him. The noise freaked me out and I instinctively put the taser to his neck again and shocked him until his eyes closed and he started snoring.

'FEM? FEM... you alright in there? For fuck sake, and they still don't wanna give policeman guns,' Jamal mumbled to himself. He then got on his radio and sent a request for back-up, a possible officer injury and the gun cops as well.

'This is turning from bad to worse,' Quincy said all God-like.

'Who you telling?' I replied looking around for something, anything.

I was already at a disadvantage because I couldn't see where Jamal was in the store and I had no way to incapacitate him from where I was. The back door in the stockroom was blocked by a large stack of shoes boxes and I was running out of options.

Mr Oh

With Femi snoring against my crotch, tickling my clit, I leaned forward against the door frame and peeked around to see Jamal looking in my general direction.

'I know it's you Blue. Seems like your slipping in your old age.'

'Who's old?' I grumbled back to him. My ego made me respond. 'It's like riding a bike. Speaking of bikes, how is my baby Russell?'

'Pissed and looking to arrest your clart as soon as he sees you.'

I let my head rest against the door frame. 'Awww, I bet you a pair of Givenchy *Lia* leathers he doesn't.'

'Keep talking bitch, you ain't going anywhere right now so just sekkle yu'self. Your lift is on the way!'

'Snowball magic,' Quincy said in my ear.

'Really Q-Ball? Snowball magic is all you have to offer as a way out of this?'

'Trust me, it's your only shot right now. Make it a good one.'

'Yeah thanks,' I gave him my full sarcasm.

To the uninitiated, the snowball magic is the oldest trick in the snowball fight book and one kids still play today. The snowball magic is the classic trick to use against an opponent who may have you pinned down in a snowball fight. You need two snowballs for this distraction technique where you throw one into the air in order to distract your victim. The higher you throw it, the better the distraction, then hit 'em with the face smasher while they're still eyes to the sky.

Less snowballs, more shoes.

I ducked to the floor and found a *Lady spike* platform pump and an *Azimut* boot in odd sizes which I pulled close. I got back to my crouching position against the frame of the door.

'More police in six minutes, if you're gonna do it, do it now!'

The Tall Tales of Tatiana Blue

'Okay, geeez, don't rush me.'

Peering around the frame, I saw Jamal had abandoned his search for the main light switch and was slowly backing out of the store.

It was a classic now or never moment.

I mumbled to myself, 'Bitches ain't dogs or holes for men to feel, bitches are beauties in tremendously cute heels!'

Armed with the *Lady spike* in my left hand, I threw it with a hook and watched it toss high into the air, over the counter and towards Jamal who saw it too late. The darkness hid it's trajectory and it crossed most of the distance before he saw it. He raised his arms up to protect his face and was hit in the hand by one of the spikes. By the time he winced and began to check his hand, I had already thrown the *Azimut* boot, reached for a *Mado* boot close at hand and threw that too. He looked up in time to see both boots coming at him, square in the face one after the other. He tumbled backwards, tripped over the frame of the broken front door and began to fall.

'Good shot,' Quincy said in my ear.

I heard Jamal's head hit the ground and wasn't surprised to see him not moving. I sprung from the stockroom, hopped the counter and ran up on him with the taser and sat on his chest. His body vibrated as I shocked him twice but he didn't move. I checked his pulse which was pumping strongly, which meant he'd just knocked himself out. Big for nothing.

I put the taser to his groin and shocked him for five seconds, counting with full Mississippi in-between.

'Who's old and slipping? Bet your dick's gonna feel old when you wake up you Spongebob-shaped dipshit!'

'MOVE!' Quincy shouted in my ear.

Mr Oh

I was back in the stockroom, hoisting the bag over my shoulder and looking at Femi's silhouette in the darkness as he continued to snore. I held the bag close as so not to trip any other silent alarms, side-stepped past the counter, unhooked my zipwire and walked over Jamal's peaceful sleep.

'When you hear shit pop off, go in the opposite direction,' Quincy said in my ear.

'Huh?'

'Just get to the car, and when you hear shit, drive in the opposite direction and quickly.'

I jumped into my first step and took off running, pointing Maya's key at the car. The lid of the boot popped open and I slung the shoes in, slammed it shut and got in as sirens seemed to erupt from all angles. I started the engine as the intro to Elle Varner's *F It All* began.

My heart was beating so quickly I could hear it.

The sudden car crash that took place in my rear view mirror made me jump as my peripheral vision caught it. I turned around to look because it sounded like such a violent accident.

'Go, now!' Quincy said in my ear. 'Have a good night. Let me know when you want the shoe box.'

'Thanks Q-Ball,' I said, putting the car in first gear and tearing off down South Audley Street, taking back roads until I was up near Knightsbridge, checking my mirrors as I swerved around slow cars and jumped more yellow-into-red traffic lights while looking over my shoulder.

With a road of moderate traffic ahead of me, I slowed down and exhaled heavily, sliding my earpiece out and resting my head back. This was always the moment I liked to think about what shoes I picked up and how sexy they were going to look on my feet. Then the daydreams

The Tall Tales of Tatiana Blue

of my walls contracting while walking in said shoes would begin and my nipples would get hard. Lauryn first, then Aretha.

The further away I got from the scene of the crime the better. Not like I wasn't on my way to commit another crime but that's neither here nor there to be honest.

By the time I got up to the Olympia, I was nodding my head along to Jill Scott's *Beautiful Love* like I was on a night-time drive. I knew the best thing for me to do was to own my anger and not let it own me. If my anger took over, I knew I'd possibly kill Marcus and, for my list of crimes, I'd never killed anyone. Okay, I've assaulted, kidnapped, caused actual and grievous bodily harm, put someone in a coma once – that wasn't my fault – but I've never killed. That wasn't me. I didn't think anyone ever had to die for a pair of shoes.

Erykah Badu came through Maya's speakers with *Master Teacher part two* as I turned into Aynhoe road, giggling that Marcus was currently with a woman who lived on a road called Aynhoe. I couldn't help but see the words 'any hoe'. But my beef wasn't with her, if anything I was probably saving her.

I turned the engine off while the car was rolling down the street and steered it into a large space across the road from the address Quincy had given me.

In the dead silence of night, I sat with my neck craned, staring at a five-floor house with basement and attic. My blood began to boil because I knew Marcus was in there somewhere and I didn't like the fact that I couldn't watch his body vibrating due to severe electric shocks to the face, spine and groin. Not yet anyway.

Scanning all floors, trying to gain a clue as to where he could be, I looked at the third floor window and saw him stand with his hands on the curtains. He grinned into the night before drawing them closed.

Mr Oh

I actually punched a fist into my palm as I reached into my bag, pulled out my X3 multi-shot stun gun, two tasers, my lock picker and some lipstick flash bangs.

All that may seem excessive but I was going in there ready for some shit to pop off.

Getting out of the car quietly and closing the door with a bump from my hips, I slipped my tools between the waistline of my leggings, strapped the shotgun over my back and looked at the house.

I hadn't done any raw wall climbing in a long time but it was like dick, something you never forget how to climb. My earlier wall-climbing exploits proved I was out of shape but the skills were still there. Hand here, foot there, hand hold there, foot hold there. Bish bash bosh.

'Oh wait, let's do this properly.'

I unlocked the boot and looked in the bag off shoes for a pair of *Sexy Strass* heels and hooked them into the heel-holders attached to the back of my leggings. Both heels latched in and secure against the small of my back, I stretched, looked left and right and crossed the road, feeling my anger build.

The thought that kept running through my mind was that this wasn't what my life was about any more. I was over Marcus but I wasn't over what he did to me. I wasn't doing this for me, I was doing it for my shoes. The ones that never were. The ones that I never got to wear. The collectibles. The beautiful ones that always smashed the picture. Always every time.

I looked up at the window one more time and took one look around before hopping up six steps. I jumped over a small railing and onto a window frame, reached up for the ledge of a window box on the third floor and hung there for a moment. I had to wait to see if the ledge

The Tall Tales of Tatiana Blue

would hold my weight if I lifted myself up. Nothing like falling half-way because the ledge gives way.

I grunted silently, feeling the added weight of my body and hair as I pulled myself onto the crux of the window ledge. Thanks to a large tree in front of the house, I was shielded from nosy neighbours who may have been wondering about the dread head woman in all black climbing a window ledge in the dead of night.

With a lot more grunting, I made it up to the window frame. I nestled into it with my feet pressed against the wall. I sat still.

Why I didn't use my gloves, I don't know.

Finding a small gap in the curtains, I could see Marcus sitting on a bed with his clothes on, but it was the naked woman tied to the bed that was more distracting. Her face looked confused as she said something to Marcus and he replied calmly. I couldn't make out what they were saying.

Then a naked man stood in the doorway of the bedroom drying his hands. The woman on the bed, who I imagined was Roz, looked as confused as I did.

Marcus stood up and started to take his clothes off as the naked man walked closer to the bed. The woman began to struggle against her cuffed wrists and that was when I'd seen enough.

I had my lock picker working on the window, watching for any signs that I was being too loud. The one thing I could trust is that none of them would think that it was a shoe thief hitched against the window trying to pick the lock. Which was what was actually happening.

The lock was an easy one – early 90s, single glazed window – and I had to catch the window as it started to swing open. I held it before the hinges started to creak, listening for a sign that anyone in the room might've heard. The sounds of the room came to life and I could hear

Mr Oh

Marcus goading with his begging voice while Roz was demanding to be untied.

A lipstick flash bang rolled off my fingers as I found a gap in the curtains. Pressing the top of the lipstick before letting it go and watching it roll towards the bed, I counted to three and shielded my eyes with the curtains as it went off and a scream and two shouts went up.

The flash of light caught them all as I pushed the window open and moved low across the floor, making sure my feet made no sound. My hands were in my waistline looking for tasers while cutting through the light veil of smoke the flash bang threw up. I was crouching behind the naked man who was rubbing his eyes vigorously, had a taser in each hand and swung one up to his neck and one between his ass cheeks.

I've shocked a lot of people in my time but this was the first naked guy I'd lit up. And between the cheeks too.

Trust me, to watch him jump into the air, his legs go all spaghetti-like and his arms die at his side before he hit the ground was hilarious. He started foaming at the mouth before he face planted. Meanwhile, Marcus was still rubbing his eyes and Roz continued to scream, unable to rub her eyes.

'What the fuck was that?' Marcus said with an arm across his eyes. 'I can't see shit!'

'That's how I want you,' I said to him.

My first words to Marcus in over 11 years.

I swung the shotgun from my back and fired at Marcus' torso. 16 pincers attached to wires shot out and attached to his skin as he squinted in the direction of his fallen friend. The pain registered in his face, his whole body tensed and he fell backwards across the naked woman who was lightly wheezing on the bed.

The Tall Tales of Tatiana Blue

'FUCK meeeeeeeeeee...' Marcus said as he slipped onto the floor. I pressed the trigger then stopped. Pressed then stopped. Pressed and held then stopped.

The pleasure I received from watching his body jiggle on the bed was priceless. I wanted to keep shocking him but I didn't want to take all the pleasure away from making him suffer. Though a few hours of this would do.

'MARCUS WHAT THE FUCK IS GOING ON?!' Roz shouted with her eyes firmly shut.

'Trust me sugar, he has no idea what's going on. Nice boobs by the way,' I replied, reaching for her restraints and untying her.

Roz pushed Marcus's flailing arms and legs and rolled off the bed, trying to pull the sheet with her while squinting. I approached her with a dressing gown I found on the back of a chair with the pincers stretching from the shotgun.

'Here, put this on.'

'NO please don't...'

'As cute as you is, it's not you I'm here for, is it Mr Marcus?'

I looked back at him, in the foetal position. Roz put the dressing gown on as I walked to the bed still pressing the trigger of the stun gun. His body would relax then freak the fuck out. I wanted him nice and pliable so I could tie his arms to the same restraints.

'Up Marcus. Get up!' I shocked him again.

His yells gave me so much pleasure, you have no idea.

'Come on son, almost there you can do it.'

His arms stretched out and I hooked him up.

'QUICKER!' I said sternly.

Mr Oh

Watching him struggle on the bed, with Roz looking at me totally confused, was a powerful moment. I felt like the beauty in tremendously cute heels was back.

'There we go! That wasn't hard was it?' I asked him as I got his arms into the restraints. 'Nice and tight. Now we can talk!'

For five minutes, I paced the room, up and down, left and right. I was wrestling with what I wanted to say to Marcus when he woke up because he went to sleep. There was so much going through my mind at that moment. I wanted this for so long and it seems to have run up on me without being fully prepared lyrically. Not like I hadn't just assaulted two police officers and robbed one of the most high-end shoe shops in London so I was allowed to be a little distracted and unprepared.

Whatever I was going to say, I needed to say it now. I paced past the bed where Marcus was frowning in his slumber. With his naked buddy still face down with a taser between his cheeks, I played with the trigger of the stun gun I was still holding with the pincers stretched across Marcus' torso. Roz had moved from the floor to a chair in the corner of the room and was given explicit instructions not to try anything stupid or she'd dance like they did. That was all the threat I needed.

Marcus was greeted with two hefty slaps, back and forth across his face. He woke up instantly with his eyes as wide as moon pies. He took a second to focus before his eyes turned to me lording above him.

'Tatiana?! What the fuck are you doing here?'

'Hello Marcus,' I replied, calmly.

You, the reader, should know by now that the worst time to be around me is when I get very calm. It's like the more stressed and angry I get, the calmer I become. Remember Harrods? Remember Russell in the chair? Calm me is thinking me and thinking me is a bad woman.

The Tall Tales of Tatiana Blue

'What the FUCK?' he shouted at me.

I couldn't help the wide grin across my lips. 'What the fuck indeed? I bet you didn't think your evening would end in seeing me again, did you?'

'What the fuck are you doing here, how did you find me?'

'Oh, so you WERE hiding from me then!?' I turned to Roz. 'See he WAS hiding from me.'

She had no idea what I was talking about but just the fact a strange woman in all-black made the room go white then took out two full grown men with tasers and stun guns made her agreeable.

'Why is he hiding from you?' Roz said quietly with her knees pressed against her chest.

'Yeah Marcus, why don't you tell Roz why you were hiding from me?'

Marcus winced as he looked at the floor and saw the motionless, but still breathing, body of his friend.

'What the fuck did you do to Khane? Is he dead?'

'Does he look dead? I don't think he is anyway,' I played with him.

'Bitch, what the fuck are you doing here?'

'Do you know what a true bitch is Marcus? I've renamed it. A nice little slogan for what a bitch is, you wanna hear it?'

Marcus struggled against the restraints on his wrist and threw his body all over the bed, grunting and groaning. He didn't realise I went all scouts on the knots around his wrists so he wasn't going anywhere.

'A bitch to me is a beauty in tremendously cute heels. You like that? I do... I honestly felt really clever when I came up with that. What do you think Roz?'

'It's... clever.'

'What are you doing here Tatiana?' Marcus asked again.

Mr Oh

I turned back to him. 'Ah the ultimate question. What am I doing here!? What AM I doing here Marcus? Don't you think I might be here for the same reason you're hiding from me?'

'Why ARE you hiding from her Marcus?' Roz chimed in.

'Don't worry baby, I got this,' he replied.

I got down on my hands and knees and crawled up to Marcus on the bed until we were face-to-face.

'Erm...' I said quietly, turning to the visibly frightened woman on the chair. 'How EXACTLY have you got this? Does he look like he's got this Roz?'

'Nope.'

'That's what I thought. He doesn't look like he's about to GET a damn thing right now.'

'I swear to you Blue, I'm gonna...'

I slapped him with a swift and decisive backhand. 'You're gonna do what? Honestly, Marcus, what exactly could you do? See those things in your chest? They will literally have you shitting yo'self.'

'Are you out of your fucking mind? Shock me with those things again and see what happens to you.'

I was soooooooo hoping he would say that! I sat down with my legs crossed in front of him with the shotgun draped across my lap. My smile must've looked insane.

Inhaling happily with my eyes closed, I opened them while exhaling into his face. I stole one look at Roz before pressing the trigger, visually watching electricity travel through the wires into his body. His body grooved, random sounds escaped his lips and his eyes winced painfully.

'Marcus? MARCUS? Look at me!'

His droopy eyes opened and met my cold stare and clicking fingers.

The Tall Tales of Tatiana Blue

'Good. Now I have your attention. This IS happening, okay? There's nothing you can do about it so you're just gonna have to suck it up, okay? OKAY?! Good.'

'You fucking bitch! Watch!'

'Erm, didn't you just have our Roz here tied to a bed?' I ignored his outburst. 'Was our boy Marcus about to offer you some birthday dick? Hey, is Roz short for Rosalyn?' I got up, walked to where she was perched and sat cross-legged in front of her. I brought the shotgun with me for effect.

She looked up from her knees. 'Yeah it is.'

'Thought so. Love that name. Was he about to offer you some birthday dick?'

She shook her head, confused. 'Yeah, erm... I was blindfolded and then we had sex or at least I thought WE had sex and...'

She stopped.

'Yeah, I can figure out the rest. I was watching. Marcus pulled the old "Whodini" did he? Naughty boy... he asked me if I wanted to try that and I told him to fuck himself.'

'Really?' Rosalyn said, looking towards Marcus.

'Yep... introduced me to the guy and everything. He looked like... hold on...'

I jumped up and walked over to the sleeping black man on the floor with the taser between his cheeks.

I no longer own that taser by the way.

Crouching to his face, I recognised him as the same man Marcus introduced me to way back when.

'Well I'll be... same guy!'

Mr Oh

I was having fun now. I had control of the room; Marcus was under massive control and was shifting uncomfortably on the bed, Khane was still out cold and Rosalyn looked like she'd seen a ghost.

One swift hop up and I was sitting on the edge of the metal bed frame with my feet on the mattress while facing Marcus. A lot of energy was required to make that move look flawless by the way.

'Hey Marcus, you feeling good? Actually I don't care. It's nice to have you in front of me so I can say some things. Oh Rosalyn, sorry for having my feet on your bed. I won't be long.'

'Don't worry about it,' she said, visibly fed up.

'OI! Stop talking to her. My lady is nothing to do with you. Say whatever you want, I don't give a fuck. I'm gonna find you and your done, you hear me? You're dead.'

'Sorry to shrink your dick Marcus but you're not the first person to threaten to kill me. You're maybe the third man tonight who wants me dead though.'

Marcus tried to kick out at me but his foot didn't reach. We shared an awkward moment where he looked at me, trying to think of some other way to get to me. He tried another kick and failed.

'Really? Are you done?' I asked with my hand out like I was holding an invisible tray.

'Say what you want and run, ya get me?' Marcus sneered.

'Alright "blood", but, before I finish here and go HOME, I just have a few things I need to get off my chest.'

I dropped the shotgun by my feet, unlatched the heels from the back of my waist and began to unlace my trainers.

'Don't worry, these are fresh from the box okay Rosalyn?'

The Tall Tales of Tatiana Blue

Out of the corner of my eye, I could see Khane shivering in his sleep. It was fun to see Marcus look at his friend trembling on the floor then down at his chest.

'Don't worry about him, he's out. I've never tasered a guy in his ass before. In his cheeks, yeah, but never in his ass. Apparently it knocks you the fuck out. Maybe the neck helped too. Hope he doesn't shit himself. That would be awkward. Anyway... I'm not here to talk about your slimy friend. You know why I'm here Marcus.'

'You come all this way about your fucking car? After all this time?'

'My car?! I don't even remember what car it was. I'm here about my shoes Marcus.'

'Your shoes? Them worthless suttins?'

'And, see, this is why I...' My finger was quick on the trigger and I shocked the shit out of him. His hands clenched, body tensed and his toes curled as I watched the wires dance all the way to his chest with an electrical snap.

I felt the need to shake my dreads loose. My thick blue-tinged hair flicked about my face and I felt instantly alive.

'Fuck you Tatiana...'

'I would if I could but I can and I do. I'm actually quite good at it! Probably better than you were.'

'I swear...'

'Stop swearing and shut your mouth. Rosalyn, lemme' tell you what Marcus did...'

I sat there on the edge of her bed in the most bedazzling shoes and told Rosalyn everything. From the relationship to the picture to the bleach to the whole burning bullshit. I left no stone unturned and made sure she knew exactly how it happened. She watched me talk with my hands and describe, very calmly, how Marcus killed my life and

Mr Oh

everything in it. I went into the depression, the time off work, the alienation, my absolute not giving a fuck about anything, only stopping when the story got to Harrods.

'What do you think about all that Rosalyn? Does that seem fair to you?'

She winced. 'Nah, not really. That's a really fucked up thing to do. You set her car on fire?!'

Marcus looked towards Khane.

'Why does everyone keep talking about the car?' I asked no one in particular. 'What about my shoes? All my shoes.'

'Why are you sending pictures to a next...'

I cut him off. 'If you even think about saying that ghetto shit to me, I'm gonna slap you then I'm gonna shock you. For a long time.'

He stayed silent.

'I told you back then I only took that picture... you know what, I don't care about that any more. I'm just here to tell you... thank you.'

'Thank your mum, you bitch.'

'I am a bitch right now aren't I?' My feet kicked out and twirled towards him with a smile. 'I say thank you Marcus because, right now, I have more shoes than I know what to do with. I have so many shoes, I can't keep 'em in one place. And ultimately, I have you to thank for that. Without you, shit wouldn't have happened the way it was supposed to. So thank you Marcus. You're a wank face cunt hole but you made me so happy in the process.'

I shocked him as I continued talking.

'But don't get it twisted, you destroyed my shoes. My life. You poured bleach on 'em. And some other shit on 'em. In fact what was that shit? You know what don't worry. And you whistled that bullshit song you know I hate. And for WHAT?! Huh?!'

The Tall Tales of Tatiana Blue

Anger rose quickly and controlled my trigger finger. Marcus looked like he was transforming while receiving the Holy Ghost at the same time as doing the Funky Chicken. It was immensely fun to watch, just to see the spit fly out of his mouth.

The tip of my finger was turning white because I was holding the trigger with power and venom. I felt calm and collected as I slowly let go, watching the pincers rest in the middle of raised bumps on his chest.

I sighed heavily and let my head fall backwards. I turned to the left and caught Khane twitching. To my right, Rosalyn was frowning and wincing at Marcus.

'Right, my work here is done I think.'

Slipping back into my 180s and reattaching my *Strasses* to my shoe holders, I hopped off the bed.

'So now what?' Marcus groaned. 'You think you're just gonna walk away and disappear?'

'No, not really,' I said, handing Rosalyn the handle of the shotgun. 'I'm going home to be with my family. I've got bigger fish to fry than you right now Mr Marcus. Bigger dick shall I say.'

I put my earpiece in.

'Q-Ball, can I have my shoe box please?'

'Sure,' he said instantly. 'Shoe box delivered.'

'Thanks homie.'

My eyes drew to Marcus with a wicked smile. I knew the smile was wicked because Marcus looked at me with genuine fear in his eyes. Moving towards the window, I felt bad for Rosalyn as I stole a quick look at her in the chair. My eyes drew to her feet.

'Rosalyn, you're a five and half aren't you?'

She lifted her head from her knees and looked up like she'd seen me for the first time. 'Yeah, erm... How did you know?'

Mr Oh

I chuckled as I released the shoes from their holders and handed them to her. 'Happy birthday Rosalyn.'

I could see she didn't wanna take 'em. But I could also see there was a shoe lover in her. I watched her eyes focus on the red bottoms, analysing the beauty of embellished rhinestones. Slowly she reached out and took them from me with a smile that was confused all over.

'Don't think I forgot you Marcus, I got you something special. Something you're REALLY gonna love.'

It was super-duper fun watching Marcus trying to sit up, giving as much attitude as he could while Rosalyn was turning the shoes around in front of her, taking no notice of the shotgun on her lap.

'I got you a shoe box. It's not literal, it's metaphorical. You see, in this shoe box Marcus is a whole load of fuck up. Like the level of fuck up in this shoe box is so deep, I feel a little bad. Likkle ikkle though. Not enough that I'm not gonna do it. In fact it's already done.'

I opened the window and hopped onto the frame.

'In this metaphorical shoe box is the destruction of your credit score, the cancellation of your tenancy agreement, a fraud report sent to the Tax department about irregularities in your name, 12 points added to your driving licence, in effect cancelling your driving licence. Your bank accounts have been suspended, your car is being impounded as we speak and I wouldn't try and fly anywhere any time soon. You're on a watch list or three or twelve.'

With each consequence I ran off, Marcus' mouth fell lower and lower. He looked shocked, then surprised, then confused. His last facial expression was the realisation that I could either be talking shit or telling the truth.

'Whatever bitch,' were the last words he threw at me.

The Tall Tales of Tatiana Blue

'Your mum's a bitch! And her mum and her mum before that. Now is that the female dog or my sexy clever version? Have a nice night you guys. Rosalyn, sorry about ruining your birthday. Enjoy the shoes.'

I mouthed for her to close her eyes.

She didn't say anything back. I didn't wait to hear her speak as I was out of the window and scaling down the wall while throwing another lipstick flash bang behind me into the room.

Marcus screamed as Rosalyn jumped from the sudden explosion of light and sound. I imagine she squeezed the trigger of the shotgun at the same time.

Just the sound of Marcus screams made me chuckle as I slid down the frame of the ground level window, jumped down onto the steps and was back on the pavement. The feeling of "over" I was searching for coursed through me overwhelmingly. I got in the car, sitting in silence for a moment. My eyes drifted towards the window, just in case they came to look but that last flash bang would've kept them occupied.

I sucked in a large breath of air into my lungs and exhaled ever so slowly.

I'd finally found and dealt with Marcus. I could go on and feel like that wanker's cloud won't hang over me any more. You see the thing with Marcus was that I didn't hate him. We were good together back in the day. Good-ish. He was a good guy, I was happy. We weren't about to break up, put it that way. So the way things ended, I was kinda upset about it. For a second. The death of my shoes whitewashed that completely. I hadn't even thought of Marcus in that kinda light since this whole thing happened. But, how was I feeling at that moment? Like I was done. I mean I didn't steal shoes just to get back at Marcus but I wanted to be stronger because of him. And I was. I am.

Mr Oh

By the end of the breath, I started the engine and enjoyed the purr on my thighs which mirrored the noise I was making in my chest. I pulled off the longest wheel spin, making sure everyone heard me as I left.

Let me tell you, I felt good. Wicked, brilliant in fact. I felt like going home to deal with Russell was going to be a clean slate. A fresh break. Maybe a nice little family set up. I always wanted one of those, remember? Maybe this was about to be my chance to set that up.

I stopped at a set of traffic lights, remembering I hadn't checked my phone since it vibrated against my nipple earlier. I felt my boobs and found it nestled against Lauryn on the left.

Keeping one eye on the lights, I saw a number of missed calls and messages from Maya that made me sit up in my seat. I only felt one vibration yet I had all these missed calls and messages?

Opening the first message while putting the car in first gear, my eyes widened in fear:

'Come home NOW!'

That was it.

Nothing else, just 'come home now'. Every other message from Maya said the same thing. With the same capital letters.

Any parent knows how scared I got at that moment. When the person you leave your child with sends you that kind of message over and over and over again, you shit yourself.

My hype over Mount Street and Marcus disappeared and panic mode set in. I tried to call Maya back and her number just rang out.

I looked at the red light. Looked left, then right, slipped the car out of first and back in, then tore across the empty intersection with a million visions running through my head. I graced into second gear, revved then slipped into third burning through Knightsbridge, down Pall Mall in a blur

The Tall Tales of Tatiana Blue

and jumping a serious red with a handbrake turn at Embankment to fly past London Bridge.

You can imagine what I was thinking. I was worried that something happened to Charlotte. Maybe the police became slick overnight and found where I lay my 'locks. Of course I was thinking it could've been Russell finding me too. With all the set-up and the sneaking around and the breaking into his place and the no heels in the flat rule, it would piss me off if he simply came upstairs and found me.

I was doubting my decision to move so close to Russell as I pulled a slick move past a taxi at a changing light at Aldgate. I'd always been a fan of the rule "hiding in plain sight". I use it avidly and you wouldn't believe how easy it is to steal a pair of shoes by just doing it in front of someone. I try not to but sometimes needs must. In my head, the one place Russell wouldn't look for me was directly above him. Maybe he thought I'd pop by for a visit but not that I'd move in and live above him while watching his every move.

Then I had a random thought and wondered if Marcus was as slick as he threatened. Maybe he'd found my yard and done something to Maya. Not that quick though.

I tried her number again. Nothing.

It was the vagueness of the message that worried me the most. And why would you send the same message over and over again. No voice mail either.

My eyes caught the rear end of a turning police car as I pulled out past a bus at a red light and burned through, not checking the crossing for pedestrians. Fear and adrenaline took me through. Mile End station flew past me in a heartbeat as I leaned forward, pushing the car faster and faster, the engine being the only music I needed.

Mr Oh

I started rocking in my chair getting angrier with every car I passed. The not knowing was what was killing me the most. Maya was my good good friend so if something was really wrong, she'd find a way to let me know. We have so many ways of communicating you wouldn't believe it. But I didn't get anything except 'come home NOW'.

I felt like I was floating over the Bow flyover, swerving to compensate for a slight moment of flight. I was sweating, doing 70 and holding the wheel with my thighs while tying my hair up. Every speed camera from the city to the community could've flashed and I wouldn't have known.

Whatever was going on at home, I was going to be prepared.

'I swear if anyone has touched you Cha'Cha, they're gonna see a really angry fucking Blue... and they don't want that... calm the fuck down... I will not calm down...'

I took my foot off the pedal for the first time since Green Park as I curled around Great Eastern, looking up at the large block of luxury flats I live in. I slowed down to take the first left and slowed down further as I approached the second left that took me into the car park.

I didn't take any time to scope the place out or figure a way in that would give me an advantage. I buzzed my way into the building while sprinting and trying to call Maya back but she still wasn't answering.

Breezing past the lifts, I took the stairs climbing them three at a time. I was bouncing off the walls trying to get extra leverage that would carry me quicker to my place.

My hair escaped the knot I put it in and was wildly bouncing behind me as I reached for banisters to help pull me up the stairs while I kept trying Maya's phone. Her number was ringing but she didn't answer.

'Mayaaaaaaa...'

I climbed to my floor, turning down the corridor and almost slipped. One hand on the ground and I was back on my feet and flying the down

The Tall Tales of Tatiana Blue

corridor. I took four heavy steps to stop outside my front door because I was running so fast with my taser in my hand.

'Shit! Where's my keys?' I felt my body for the keys, not sure where I last saw them.

One hand slapped the door while the other was feeling Lauryn and Aretha to see if they were holding my keys.

'You left 'em in your fucking bag... shiiiit... I couldn't have... I bet you did...'

By the time I ran my hands over my lock, I was frantic. I couldn't hear the TV or anything from inside. With my ear pressed to the door, I slapped it lightly, hoping Maya would hear the soft rhythm and open the door.

In my head, there were about six men standing in different positions around my flat. Military types: crew cuts with no neck watching the perimeter, awaiting my mystical magical appearance.

My fantasy was broken as the door swung open while I was still feeling myself for my keys. Maya looked back at me with stoic eyes holding her arm across the door blocking my way in.

She didn't say anything, just looked at me, which freaked me out even more.

'Where's Charlotte? Is she okay?'

I didn't wait for an answer and pushed past her, feeling my dreads slap her in the face. As I raced through the living room, seeing everything still in place and no soldiers, I damn near tumbled through the door of Charlotte's room looking straight at her crib.

Empty.

'MAYA, WHERE THE HELL IS...'

'Stop shouting before you wake our daughter.'

Mr Oh

I heard that deep sexy voice from somewhere in the room and I instantly knew what was so wrong.

'Ain't you just a slick rick...' was the last thing I said before a piece of material came from over my head and smothered my mouth and nose. I tried not to breathe in as I wrestled the hand from my face. But whatever was on that handkerchief must've been odourless because I felt my legs go out from under me. My body began to drop as a strong arm hooked around my waist.

I lost consciousness as my body flopped on the bed and a figure walked past me holding Charlotte in his arms.

And this is where I've woken up.

My whole evening. Everything up 'til now and I get caught slipping with the old handkerchief trick. And so easily too.

I was offended.

My mouth was itchy, my nose was burning and my feet hurt.

Then my panic mode kicked in. I couldn't hear Charlotte or Maya or the TV or music. Just silence.

I stared at a spot on the ceiling and moved each of my limbs, feeling for any drowsy movement, just in case I had to hop out of the room on some gangster shit.

My stomach muscles contracted and I slowly rose, keeping my ears peeled for any sound.

The last moments before I lost consciousness waved through my mind in a haze and I could see bits and pieces. The one thing I remember hearing was the voice.

Russell's voice.

My legs slunk off the bed and I squatted to my alternative wardrobe while keeping an eye on the door. One hand rifled around until I found

The Tall Tales of Tatiana Blue

my X12 shotgun taser which was modified to look like a pink umbrella nestled under an industrial-sized pack of nappies. My hand wrapped around it and I instantly felt more positive.

Staying low, I slid to the door and turned the handle slowly, wincing at every creak. I peeked around the door and could see a low light coming from the lounge.

'Quincy, you there? What the FUCK is...' I felt my ear but my earpiece wasn't there. Didn't even realise it was gone. OR did I take it out after I left Mount Street? Wasn't sure, didn't care.

With the pink umbrella trailing behind my back, I started to move out of the bedroom and into the dark corridor.

'Could we, for once, just do things normally?' Russell said.

I didn't expect to hear his voice and I looked up. My head spun around wondering how the hell I could be seen when I was moving so ninja-like.

'Normal? Us? Nah!' I shouted back as I rose to my feet. An itch rippled through my scalp and I shook my head like Bob Marley feeling the rhythm.

I focussed on the light at the end of the corridor and walked slowly. Charlotte gurgled quietly and I was able to exhale a sigh of relief.

'You hungry honey? How was work today sweetie?' I joked.

'Don't you fucking dare!? This is not a joke!'

'OoOoOo serious Russell... I like this already.'

By the time I got to the end of the corridor and turned into the living room, my heart was all over the place. Butterflies in my stomach were fluttering like a fresh spring but my legs felt like they were on rum and Red Bull. Lauryn and Aretha felt like they were perking up and I ran my hand through my hair. I could see the back of Russell's head. He was sat on my sofa with his legs up and Charlotte nestled in a blanket in front of

Mr Oh

him. She was wide awake with her hands wrapped around his index fingers gurgling on one of her random freestyles.

I wanted to stroke his neck with one hand and shock him with the other. Over his shoulder I could see him playing with Charlotte and making faces at her. But I didn't want to see his face. Not yet.

'Where's Maya?' I asked, the grip on my weapon getting tighter.

'I sent her home. No point her being here as well. Least I know where to find her if I need her.'

'Find her?' My mind was racing.

'What, you don't think I know the set-up? Tut tut tut... silly Blue.'

There was something about the way Russell was acting. Very cool, calm and collected. Kind of like the way I was behaving when I last had him in my presence. Tied naked to a computer chair with plastic sheeting under him, for the look.

He was behaving like he knew something I didn't, which made me feel uncomfortable in my own space. You know I hate not being in control of things.

'Okay,' I started. 'So, what now?'

'We wait two minutes. And then we talk'

My eyebrows burrowed down across my eyes. I was stuck in a state of confusion because I expected the next time I saw Russell, he wouldn't be as calm as he was. He was staring at Charlotte, who was mesmerised by the outline of his face.

'Why two minutes?' I asked.

'Don't worry about that yet. Let's just say, one way or another this is gonna be done.'

I could feel Russell smiling to himself as I inhaled heavily and slowly walked around the sofa. Every part of him that came into view excited

The Tall Tales of Tatiana Blue

me with each step I took. By the time I reached the side of his face, I was dancing inside. His face was exactly as I remembered it.

And chocolate isn't the word.

Though both my parents are black, I've been blessed with a rather caramel-ish hue but Russell was the definition of chocolate. Like India.arie, Morris Chestnut, Ashley Walters, John Boyega good chocolate. With his trademark bald head and chin strap beard, Russell had his feet up on my coffee table with Charlotte in his lap and they were staring at each other.

The first time Russell lifted his eyes to look at me, I fell mute. I was running through my mental roladex for a quick retort or something that would break the ice but nothing was coming to mind. Such was his effect on my voice. All of them.

'Hey,' was all I could think of.

Geez, I forget how handsome he was in the flesh.

'What's up?' he replied.

This jovial interaction irritated me because he played along. He was riding the fact that he knew something I didn't.

Tapping the modified umbrella against my thigh, I balanced my weight on one leg and folded my arms. 'So, how have you been?'

The buzzer to my door went off and we both looked at my intercom system. I looked first because I wasn't expecting anyone, especially at stupid o'clock after the night I had. Russell slowly got up, whistling Pharrell's *Happy* as he walked to the door bouncing Charlotte in his arm.

I watched him like 'what the...' and rubbed my finger on the button of my umbrella.

He answered the intercom and told someone to come straight up.

Charlotte spit up and Russell wiped her mouth with a muslin square he had in his hand then looked at me. The smirk on his face was one I

Mr Oh

couldn't place. Was it anger? Hilarity? Was it the smile of a plan coming together?

We looked at each other for about 40 seconds. His eyes were all over me in my black outfit and my eyes were already under his clothes, running a mental hand under the waistband of his underwear. He was inhaling the scent of my neck and running his hands up and down my backside. My fingernails ran down his bald head and it hurt but he liked it. Then we shared our first imaginary kiss.

That's what happened in my head but in reality we were just standing across the room from each other saying nothing but thinking everything.

A strong hand knocked the door and broke our stare-a-thon. My hand gripped tighter as he turned around and opened the door, not far enough for me to see who was there.

He mumbled to the person, took an envelope, thanked them and closed the door.

My mind was planning shit. Hop over the sofa, two steps and I'm on him. Take Charlotte from him while shocking him in the ribs, find out what the hell is in that envelope and gain control of the situation.

It was a lot to watch him come towards me but not knowing what to do about it. Not just that but watching him holding OUR daughter in his arms made it look like he'd been doing it since the day she was born. He had Charlotte nestled so snugly, I didn't want to do anything that would endanger her. The way he held her told me he knew I wouldn't try anything. Clever monkey.

He sat on the sofa, put Charlotte back in his lap and began to open the envelope.

'What's that?' I asked, curiosity getting the better of me. I knew he was waiting for me to ask and I held off for as long as I could.

'An envelope. You know what they are DON'T you?'

The Tall Tales of Tatiana Blue

The first shot. It had to come somehow and Russell sent the first barb referring to the envelope I made for him. He was obviously still upset about that.

'Yessur I do. But I don't know what's in that one.' This was gonna be a long one. 'Cha, I need a drink.'

All this tension was killing me. I had no idea what was going on around me and for someone who's used to having so much control, this feeling was rancid. I had to try and gain some equilibrium as the umbrella felt like overkill in the situation.

As it stood, Russell had the upper hand and he was holding onto it. He found out where I was, apparently introduced himself to our daughter and had his feet on my furniture like he'd breezed past guest status and was allowed to do so.

I tossed the umbrella on the solo chair and shuffled to the kitchen, exhaling and taking my trainers off. Exhaustion was beginning to seep into my muscles. My thighs had been busy all night and were contracting of their own accord, my arms felt like jelly, the extra weight of my hair was taking its toll and I rubbed my eyes for what felt like the hundredth time.

'Drink?' I asked him.

'Not while I'm on duty, but thanks.'

The words 'on duty' made me pause on my way to the kitchen. My corner eye went directly to the X12, wishing I didn't put it down. Seemed like I may have a third policeman about to be put to sleep tonight.

Slowly and cautiously, I opened the cupboard and pulled out a pint glass, filled a quarter of it with white rum and the rest with cranberry juice.

I needed a strong drink.

'So, what'd you think is in this envelope Tatiana?'

Mr Oh

'Oh, so you wanna play that game do ya? Not tonight Russell, I'm tired.'

He looked at me, raising his eyebrows. 'Really? Like the last nine months have been a jog in the park for me as well right? What do you think is in this envelope?' He asked again.

I flopped into the seat next to my umbrella, my hair draping over my shoulders.

'Don't know, don't care. If it ain't the coordinates to my bed then I don't care.'

I really did care. It might've been an arrest warrant, pictures, could've been a bomb. Well, would've been a very sophisticated bomb if it was but my mind was all over the shop.

Russell, in a green Adidas tracksuit, reached into his pocket and pulled out Charlotte's bottle. He held her under his arm, slipped off the lid and dabbed some on his wrist before giving it a shake and slipping it into her mouth.

She took it without any fuss. Something I hadn't been able to do since she was born.

'You know what? I knew you were here. This whole time.'

'Liar,' I threw back.

'You think you can move in directly above me and I wouldn't know?'

'Yes and I think your actually kicking yourself that you probably had your boys looking for me all over the place but you didn't send them to the floor above yours. I KNOW you didn't know shit.'

'And how do you know that?' Russell said, pulling a piece of paper from the envelope.

'You're not the only one who can watch people on cameras ya know?!'

He chuckled. 'I thought something was wrong with the cameras. When did you do that?'

The Tall Tales of Tatiana Blue

I winked at him from behind my glass as I felt control swerving back in my direction. I had him lying to me already which means there was control up for grabs. 'Game recognise game, right?'

'Alright, one nil to you. This'll make it one all.'

He looked at the paper while I took a long sip, closing my eyes as the rum woke a fire in my belly.

'So she IS my baby?'

I raised an eyebrow. 'Is that what that is? Paternity test? Really Russell?! Do I look like one of your side dishes?'

'After everything you've done to me, you want me to answer that question?'

'Your safety may depend on it if you don't,' I fired back, feeling strength return to my body. It was definitely Dutch Courage but I rode it.

He chuckled again as Charlotte dozed off with the bottle in her mouth.

'I had to be sure. It's not like we did this conventionally.'

'Yeah... erm, about that, I'm sorry.'

I didn't hear the words until they came out of my mouth. I'd never, for once, taken the time out to think about what my games had to done Russell and his normal life. To me, it was all about what I wanted. Maybe he didn't want this in his life. Maybe he wanted to stay a swinging single bachelor law man who doubled as a perverted documentary maker. If you can call filming upskirts documentary making. Settling down was something I always saw as a dream for other people. I mean, criminals in general, never seem to make it to the end of the movie with their ill-gotten gains, a white picket fence around them and a family to love. I never saw myself as one of those people. I just liked shoes and felt like they were owed to me. I wasn't trying to get away from anything, I just wanted my shoes. But children and a man to come home to? That was a fairy tale. Happiness like that was something that stopped when hoes,

Mr Oh

side pieces and Olivia Pope became more acceptable than a stable relationship or marriage. Happiness was ruined when I watched my shoes go up in flames. I saw it as something I wanted but could never have. And as someone who always finds a way to get what she wants, that always burned me.

And then Russell came into my life. Well, perved into my life.

'What are you sorry for?'

'Everything. Drugging you, the borrowing...'

'You mean the kidnapping?'

'Yeah, that too.'

'The envelope, the slapping, Harrods, the tying me up, all of that too yeah?' Russell's voice was getting angry.

'Look, I'm apologising alright? Don't push it.'

'YOUR DAMN...' He looked down at Charlotte and whispered. '...damn right you should apologise. Not like it'll help but it's duly noted.'

'Oh yeah, the envelope...' I couldn't hold my instant laughter.

'What POSSESSED you to do that?'

I knew this question was coming.

'Alright look,' I sat up straight with fire burning throughout my entire body. 'I'm gonna do this once and once only so pay attention, alright?'

'Go head.'

One heavy sigh and I went in. 'Those pictures weren't about you. There were just insurance. You know what, in fact, let's go right back. Harrods. That WAS you wasn't it? That was you chasing me, wasn't it?'

'So you do remember?'

'I don't forget a handsome face.'

'Yeah, you hit me in the chest with a taser and left me there!'

I bent forward in laughter. 'Yeah, another something I'm sorry for. What a small world!'

The Tall Tales of Tatiana Blue

'Ain't it just?' He replied unimpressed. 'That shit hurt you know!?'

'Another thing I'm sorry for. Anyway, the pictures. I had to take 'em. What if you woke up and decided you wanted to arrest me? What if you found me? I'd have nothing.'

'Of course you'd have nothing. Don't you realise that you are a criminal? You're being looked for in countries I've never even heard of. It's like you don't even think of yourself as a criminal.'

'Yeah but who am I hurting? Do you know how much these shoe designing fuckers get paid in insurance pay-outs? They make more back if the shoes are stolen than the actual price of the shoes. No one loses out, I win every time. Done and done.'

'But...'

'I have never stolen from anyone who cannot easily afford to replace what they've lost. Mostly untalented too, members of royal families, Z-list celebrities, etc.'

Russell squinted at me. 'Okay, I don't need your CV.'

'Those pictures must've been funny when you saw them.'

'Do you know what happened because of those f-ing pictures? Didn't reach them in time. Played it off like I was sleeping with another woman.'

'Didn't you hide them?'

'No time, thanks to Femi and Jamal. They found it under the sofa and had it open before I could untie myself.'

'Those two... yeah,' I trailed off, wondering if they were still on the floor of the Louboutin store.

'They believed we were fucking! I was suspended for taking time off, I had to move, I changed stations, all because of you and your "insurance".'

'How did they feel about you being the father of my child?'

Mr Oh

'You think I told them that? I'm not stupid. That would've been a bigger investigation, more time off without pay. I didn't need the headache. I already had enough worrying about whether or not you were telling the truth. The one time I thanked God that no-one knew what you looked like. Like the way all the pictures hid your face by the way. You didn't have to sign each picture by the way.'

'Well VOILA!' I raised my glass, knocked the rest of my drink back and slunk into the chair flexing my toes and simmering on annoyance.

'So what now Russell? You're sitting there like you have all the answers and you know what's what, so what now?'

'We're not done talking yet.'

'But I'm tired and...'

'Busy night? Looks like the uniform of someone who didn't wanna be seen.'

'Look,' I started as I stood up, pointing my umbrella at him.

'I'm beat up right now. If you're gonna arrest me or call for back up, let me call Maya first so she can take Charlotte. Otherwise, close the door on your way out and let your head get small in the distance. Or, my room is this way. Peace and hair grease.'

The way I walked off, it was like I ripped my last rhymes of the evening, dropped the microphone and left the stage. It was perfect as I could feel his eyes watching me saunter off.

Yeah I sauntered.

I didn't walk quickly, just slow enough that he could watch my thighs sway and my cheeks bounce away in my leggings.

I wasn't sure what the fuck he was going to do but I knew that I'd given myself the power back by walking away from him. The instant he didn't call after me or threaten me with arrest, I knew he wasn't here for that. Watching him with Charlotte, the way he smiled at her and watched

The Tall Tales of Tatiana Blue

every nuance of her face, said that he was here for his chance to be a father.

I didn't know whether or not Russell wanted this for himself but I was answered when I watched him feed her. He had the correct amount measured in her bottle and was feeding her without any drama. Whenever it was me with Lauryn or the bottle, I was always greeted with the lips closed and the wailing.

'Night,' I said as I disappeared into the corridor.

'We're not done Miss Blue.'

'Then come finish me off then!'

I slammed my bedroom door and took a running jump onto my bed. I wasn't lying about being tired. I was absolutely bushwhacker knackered. It wasn't just a normal day of baby sitting and selling shoes. I was back in the swing and apparently I had some serious training to do to get my body back into shape. And research to do because that silent alarm thing must be new.

The sigh I sighed when my head hit the pillow was like an orgasm after an orgasm. I flopped around on my cold duvet for a few moments until I warmed up then wrapped myself, listening. Russell's heavy stomp could be heard as he walked up the corridor, deviating right to go into Charlotte's room.

I was probably next.

I mean, I'm sexy as fuck and dressed all in black. I've got an ass like Trina in her early days, my dreads come like a blue waterfall down my shoulders and my legs are Tina Turner in her prime and then some. Unless Russell became gay and I missed it then he was coming in here to fuck me.

To be honest, after the night I had, I needed it. Believe it or not, Russell was the last time I had sex.

Mr Oh

Yeah I know, THAT long ago. I've been CLOSE a few times like, don't get it twisted, I've done some stuff but no one has, ya know, "been up in the club" since Russell. Before him, I was scratching my itches regularly. I had pieces all over the place. Not like, north, south, east London. Like southern California, Dubai, Genoa, two in Mali, a Prince from Zimbabwe and some others scattered around. And as I said before, it scratched an itch but wasn't the healing cream I needed.

Russell was that cream sha-boogie bop!

I don't know what it is about that man that attracts me so much but I just wanna lay my head on his chest and watch random shit on TV. He makes me wanna live that life, even though I'm still partially buzzing thanks to all the shoes in the boot of Maya's car just waiting for me to touch 'em.

I want to live both lives to be honest and if I can't then one will have to go but when I want something, chances are I'm gonna get it. Nine times out of ten, I get it. Or I destroy it so no one else can have it.

Yeah, issues I know.

My bedroom door creaked open and Russell turned the light on and stood in the doorway.

'Come on, let's finish this,' he said.

'Russell, look. Here's the skinny right now cuz this isn't as fun any more.' I unwrapped myself from the duvet, sat up and put my hands in my lap with my back straight.

He looked uninterested.

'I am tired. I've had a long fucking day and an even longer night and I just want to lie down. That's all. You're here now and you know the truth. You know everything...'

'I don't know where you were tonight.'

The Tall Tales of Tatiana Blue

'Are you my man to be asking me that question?' I threw back at him, running my fingers through my dreads. 'Or are you asking as an officer of the law?'

'Where were you tonight?'

'Are you asking me as Russell the policeman, Russell the perv or Russell the potential love of my life?'

'Where were you tonight?'

I sighed. 'I went to see an old friend. I owed him something.'

'And what was that?'

'A goodbye.'

'You went to see a friend just to tell him goodbye!? Was it a handshake goodbye or a blowjob goodbye?'

'Sounds like Russell the potential love of my life right there!'

'And where does this friend live?'

'Now you're starting to sound like Russell the policeman and, if I remember correctly, you gained entry to my abode without my permission. So if you're not arresting me then I don't have shit to say.'

'Have you been with anyone else since you left?'

'Ah haaa, now THAT sounds like Russell the potential love of my life again. We can't have this flip-flopping you know. And the answer is no.'

'Why not?' he asked, moving to the end of my bed. He sat down with a glass of something in his hand and he took a long sip.

'You just want me to boost your ego don't you? Okay, fine. I haven't been with anyone else, mainly because I was pregnant. And that's gross. If I can't have the father of my child dancing in my club then I don't want no random ravers in there. For me sex is a plaster on a stab wound of a relationship and I was tired of stab wounds.'

He frowned. 'What club?'

Mr Oh

'Oh, okay. When I say up in my club, that's what I mean when I talk about sex. You know, UP in the club? Raw hardccore like Quick Draw McGraw?'

'For God sake Tatiana, you really are fucking nuts.'

'Why thank you.'

'Just because I'm being cool and calm with you right now, don't think I'm not still pissed with you for everything you did to me. I mean, seriously, who do you think you are?'

From running my fingers through to re-twisting my dreads, I looked at Russell with a confused face.

'Erm, I'm Tatiana Blue, the baddest bitch of them all! You know who I am Russell, that's why you fell in love with me. You see, I know why you're here. Stop me if I'm wrong.'

'Okay.'

Kicking my feet out of the duvet, patting the mattress next to me for him to come and sit closer, I took his drink from him and knocked it back. 'So, you found me, right? Now as a policeman, that puts you in a pretty precarious situation. Because if you know where I am then it is your duty as an officer to report my whereabouts and detain me until I can be taken in, right?'

He nodded.

'If I could guess, from the first missed call I had from Maya, you've been here for most of the night. I see no signs of you detaining me or any back-up being called. Which means you haven't reported my whereabouts have you?'

He half-nodded.

'Alrighty, but that's still bothering you right? But at the same time, on the flip side, there's Charlotte. You've met her, you can see how

The Tall Tales of Tatiana Blue

absolutely amazing she is and you want to see more of her don't you? Maybe more of me too?'

He didn't nod but instead looked at my bottom lip.

Told you he was going to fuck me.

'And now you don't know what to do. Call me in or live a life with one of the most hunted criminals in your office. Decisions decisions.'

I was weighing up my hands when, quick as a flash, Russell brought a hand up and latched one side of a pair of handcuffs on my wrist. By the time I knew what was going on, he was pulling me to the foot of my bed and latching the other side of the handcuff, which he'd looped quickly through a railing.

'Whoa whoa whoa... straight BDSM yeah?' was all I could say. In trying to pull my cuffed wrists out, a metal railing stopped me, in effect, detaining me on my own bed. 'Looks like someone's been practising. That was quick.'

'I've always been that fast, you just never got to find out cuz you tied me up the last time you met me. Not so nice now is it?'

I shook my head. 'It's alright. All depends on what you plan to do with me in this position though.'

'You think this is all a joke don't you? You think walking into someone's life and rearranging it for your own pleasure or for whatever you want is okay? Like you're THAT important. You can't just do what you want or take what you want in life. There's consequences.'

I was tipsy now as whatever he was drinking slammed against my senses.

'OoOoOo... that sounds promising.'

I watched him walk around and felt him kneel on the bed next to me.

'This isn't a joke Tatiana.'

'You know you still say my name in such a sexy way?'

Mr Oh

Then I heard a sound. I heard it before because I had a flick knife too so I knew the sound when the blade drew out. The excitement of a possible dicking disappeared and I started to fiddle with the handcuffs. I'd gotten myself out of tighter situations so I wasn't worried. With my legs free, I could bump him off the bed with my hips, onto my knees and, once the 'cuffs were off, whoop his ass.

Then fuck him.

There was no way this story is going to end without him being up in my club.

Before I could shunt him with my hips, he climbed on top of me and things suddenly seemed more promising, although the policeman with the flick knife did worry me a bit.

He let single dreads drip through his fingers before brushing them away. He grabbed the bottom of my top and cut slowly from the base of my spine, letting the knife glide through the material up to my neck.

'Tell me about the first pair of shoes you ever stole.'

'Is this foreplay?' I asked, turning my head to take attention away from the fiddling I was doing on the 'cuffs.

'Tell me,' he said with an airy tone. The wings of my top fell aside and I could feel his eyes on my back. His fingers ran down my spine where I could feel him staring at the 68 tattoos of shoes that ran from the nape of my neck to the crease of my buttocks. With space for one more.

The *Strass* would make a beautiful addition.

'It was way back when I used to work for Fierce Security Insurance. We used to have big clients like Harrods on our books, Harvey Nichols, Selfridges, the big boys. Anyway, something... happened to me and I had to take some time off.'

'What happened?' His hand reached around my neck.

The Tall Tales of Tatiana Blue

'Is this gonna be used against me in a court of law? Because I'd at least like to have a solicitor present during foreplay?'

'Information collected during foreplay doesn't count. It'd be inadmissible. Just tell me.'

'It's a VERY long story which ended tonight so, for now, let's just call it the unfortunate incident.'

Russell undid my bra and ran his fingers along the muscles in my back.

'One day, while I was off, I found I had the keys to one of the stores we were working with. I went to return them one day and I saw Ma... a woman trying to steal a pair of shoes. Proper rookie job. Standing in front of the security guard AND the camera. Pretty little thing. I didn't want to see her get arrested so I stopped her and told her to leave. Picked her purse from her bag and she was gone.

'I went out for a cocktail or six and came back to the shop but it was closed. So I took the keys I had and let myself in. I'd probably knocked back like every deadly cocktail on the menu because I was falling all over the place. The alarms weren't on because they were going through a refit of the entire store so I just walked in and sat there for a while. On the floor, just looking around at all the shoes. And I saw the pair that the woman tried to steal earlier and I literally said fuck it. I went in the back, got two pairs and was gone. That simple.'

'Is that why you are the way you are now?'

'How am I?' I asked turning around slightly offended.

'All fucked up and shit?'

Russell slid my leggings down to my ankles in one swift movement. The shock of the air touching my skin made me instantly raise my hips and he spanked me on my left cheek.

'First of all, yum but OW! Secondly, I'm not fucked up. Do you think it's easy doing what I do and staying one step ahead of you plonkers?

Mr Oh

Remember, you're not the only plonkers in the world looking for me. I couldn't run as many stash houses as I have, never have been arrested and be the best shoe thief in the world if I was so fucked up could I?'

I could feel myself getting angrier.

'FUCKED UP?! Did this prick... just call me fucked up? Baby, I've got more money than you. I make more money in a day than you do in two weeks.'

'Not anymore you don't.'

I lost it.

'Look Russell, I see what you're trying to do. Revenge for what I did to you. Revenge for the pictures I took. Revenge for the kidnapping. All of it. I get it. And you're going for dramatic with flick knife and the handcuffs but...'

My fingers undid the last latch and I quietly slid one side of the handcuffs off my wrist but kept my hands in place.

'Tatiana Blue, I am arresting you for...'

He didn't finish because I spun around, slamming my arms into his side and knocking him off the bed.

I'd had enough.

This fucking or arresting game had worn on my last nerve and I was out of fucks to give. My legs were out of my leggings and I discarded the shred of my top, tied my hair in itself and prepared for Russell to get back to his feet.

I wasn't sure where he was going with the sexy pantomime but I wasn't going to let him finish. I hopped off the bed to where he fell, stepping on his knife and hand at the same time. I slid that away, squatted next to him as he began to get up and put him in a headlock.

'Oh, what we gonna fight now?' he mumbled as I tightened my grip around his head.

The Tall Tales of Tatiana Blue

He pushed against my arm as we both got to our feet. I tried to lean back to put more pressure on the lock and he stopped halfway to a vertical base, leaning against the bed.

'I'm feeling froggy so I jumped,' I said in a strained voice.

Out of nowhere, his arms grabbed my waist and before I knew it, I felt myself being tossed over his head, back onto the bed and clean off the other side.

Landing on my naked ass, I gathered my senses and got straight to my feet. Russell did the same on the other side.

We were both huffing and puffing at each other, fighting for control of the situation with the bed in-between us. I watched him look up and down at me as my whole body throbbed with excitement and adrenaline. He looked at Lauryn then a long hard look at Aretha with my hair probably making me look like a wild animal.

'You need to take more clothes off if we're gonna do this.'

'I'm taking you in,' he said breathing heavily.

'Listen to you, sounding like you're about to have an asthma attack. You think you can take me Russ?'

That must've been his go sign because he scrambled across the bed at me. He planted his hands and hopped across just as I shuffled forward, grabbing his head in a reverse headlock and dropping my weight on his back. His body dropped on the bed and I squeezed his neck as tight as I could, spun around on top of him and got my arm back around his neck with my legs wrapping around his waist.

He was face down on the mattress. I couldn't hear what he was saying but they were strong words as he grunted once and made it to his hands and knees with me attached to his back like a dreadlocked, Velcro thick bar of toffee. Slowly, he backed off the bed and I pulled my other arm around his neck for better leverage and to hopefully bring him down but

Mr Oh

Russell was grunting like a man on a mission. He backed us off the bed and pressed me against the wall.

I hit first and the air knocked straight out of me. I tried to hold on to him but he was already turning around on me before I could get my grip back. A flash from my childhood kicked in and I grabbed his top from the bottom and pulled it over his head.

'Oh, come on Russell, not the old school ones,' I said, trying to shuffle out from under him. My knees managed to work up to his chest then my feet and I pushed him onto and over the bed. He looked like he was airborne for a moment before he hit the wall while still tangled in his green Adidas top.

That stopped him as his back slammed against the wall with a super loud bang and he sat on the floor, sliding onto his side with his arms still up in his top. His head slid down onto the legs of my dresser with a thud.

He huffed.

I puffed.

He lifted his top over his head and I could see on his face that he was done. His left eye was squinting while his right eye was wide open and his mouth was sucking in air like it was his last.

Erm, of course I felt proud. Not like I fight men regularly but I always felt like if it ever came down to it, I could take Russell in a one-on-one fight. I always kept myself fit doing what I do. It always required an extra level of fitness that included yoga, Pilates, spin classes, intensive swimming, I trained with an MMA fighter, Silat training with the C.L.I.T.S and I ran, like, everywhere. I ran from Greenwich Park to the Olympic park in 45 minutes. I don't think I have it like that anymore but I'm still sprightly. I may not be Ali in his prime but I'll Mayweather your ass. Well, I used to.... Tonight's strenuous work showed me that I needed to get back into the gym.

The Tall Tales of Tatiana Blue

If only Jamal could see me now, about slipping.

'Are you gonna eat my pussy now or you still going on with this arrest talk cuz I wanna get some sleep.' I found the flick knife on the floor and began to play with it.

'What do you want from me Tatiana?'

I leaned forward on my knees. 'To have you say my name like that ALL the time. Do you really think I would go to all this trouble just for some up in the club time?'

'What do you want? Huh? Do you want us to be together?'

'For God sake Russell, you're a policeman and you still can't figure it out. You've been chosen.'

'For what?' he asked, leaning against the wall to slide to his feet.

'To love me.'

'Is there a list?'

'Nope. Just you.'

'You know this is gonna be really difficult to maintain. The top brass at work REALLY want you. They seem to think you've gone underground and hope to catch you letting your guard down.'

'Well good luck to 'em. That's a bonus of being with you. You know what they'll do or say before they do.'

'We can't just be together,' Russell moaned. He made it up and he ooohed and aaahed back to his knees and dropped his head on my bed. The explosion of physicality woke me up some and I used the remaining energy to sit on the bed with my legs in front of him.

'Why the fuck not? If you can tell me you don't want me in any way shape or form, I'll disappear. And you know me Russell. You know I can disappear like a fart in the wind.'

Mr Oh

I had to put it all out there. From his appearance in my flat to his late night caller – at MY door – and the handcuffs and the fight, I wasn't sure what Russell wanted to do. It seems like he was fighting the conflict of keeping it professional and being 'the man' who brought in the legend that is Tatiana Blue or keeping it emotional and building a life with the legend that is Tatiana Blue.

I don't just say I'm a legend by the way, that's what they actually call me. If the shoe fits, you know I'm wearing it.

Russell climbed up my legs and looked like he was praying to me as I flicked the knife between my fingers.

'Look Tatiana, since you left me, there hasn't been anyone else in my life. It's been one disaster after the next. Like someone decided I had to save myself for you.'

'Oh, yeah, sorry about that.'

'So it's like... whoa whoa, why are you sorry?' He looked up.

'Don't worry.'

'It feels weird to say that I missed you when you left but I did. My relationship with Tara felt apart after you left. She bought the lie I made up. How did you make those pictures by the way?'

I scoffed. 'If you know how to make a woman think then you know how to make a man lay when he's unconscious in order to make a woman think.'

'Geezz, you're no joke are you?'

'Seems like you're only starting to figure that out. Are we any closer to fucking yet?'

'You know if we have sex that means it's gonna be me, you and Charlotte. Where did you get that name from? I like it.'

Russell was kneeling between my thighs and playing with the tips of my hair.

The Tall Tales of Tatiana Blue

'The first pair of shoes I took from the shop when I was drunk. They were Charlotte Olympia. Gorgeous things.'

'You couldn't name our child after a pair of shoes you bought? No... she had to steal 'em.'

'Yep. You're lucky I don't steal drinks otherwise she would've been called Baileys.' I said, passing the point of impatience and opening my thighs fully. 'So, erm... how 'bout erm...'

I whistled, pointed between my thighs and Russell chuckled.

'What makes you think I do that?'

'If you don't then you're gonna get cheated on a LOT in this relationship.'

'Touché,' he said as I ran my hands over the top of his bald head and led him to my lips, which were squelching in anticipation between my thighs.

The game was over.

I got my man!

It sure did take a hot minute and a scuffle but all that just made me want him that little bit more. It takes a strong man to deal with me so the fact that Russell even tried is a tick in his box. I was hot and sweaty, my dreads had fallen out of the knot I put them in and were tossed back as Russell's tongue parted my lips and found my clit.

The way I had to cover my mouth as an electric feeling rippled up the shoes on my spine. With my head towards the ceiling, my eyes rolled back in my head. Russell began slurping with my fingers rolling across his scalp and I sighed pleasurably. He rubbed my thighs while my hips were pushing to meet his mouth as if the more I gave him to eat, the hungrier he became. My hips had a groove all their own as he put an arm around my back and pulled me deeper into his face. I arched my back and let

Mr Oh

him pull me in, looking down to watch the splendour of a man, no MY MAN, getting my club all ready for his VIP entrance.

He licked something that made me sit up straight. My dreads dropped around us and created a private room where all I could hear was the sound of his lips against mine and the smell of my sex rising from his face.

'Are you sure you're ready to be Mr Blue? It won't be easy, especially being a pig in a blanket.'

Russell didn't respond. He stayed where he was, using his tongue in slow circular motions around my clit. I wanted him to enjoy me, especially as it was the first time he got to eat me.

My thighs hoisted into the air and Russell made me lay back as he stood up with my ankles in his strong hands. He looked Neanderthal in the face as he pushed my thighs back. I took them from him and watched him drop to his knees again and rub his face up and down my pussy, looking at me for approval.

My lips turned up. 'Hmmm, not bad. Not bad at all. I think we'll keep and train this one.'

Lifting his head every now and then to look at his wet mouth, I felt like a queen taking advantage. I was holding his face still and making my pussy glide into him by flexing my hips. He'd hum and stop then hum and stop every time my thighs blocked his mouth.

He started fucking my pussy with his tongue and I had to let go of his head before I squirted all over. It was our first official time together and I didn't wanna subject him to that just yet.

Unless he made me.

I slid my hands under his chin and pulled his face from my crotch and lifted him up for a very wet, tasty kiss.

The Tall Tales of Tatiana Blue

Our lips slid against each other and we both hummed and fought to get the rest of his clothes off.

Whatever indecision Russell was suffering before, he wasn't any more as he ran his hands all over me, making my body tingle. There was something about Marcus... I mean Russell's fingers... eeeek... that's embarrassing.

God forbid I ever make that mistake again.

Don't tell him I said that please?

I tasted exquisite from Russell's face and it made my kiss hungrier in his mouth. He stood up and I made sure my lips were stuck to his. My hands wrapped around the back of his head and held on as Russell dropped his tracksuit bottoms and his erection sprung up against my stomach.

We both looked down at his dick and, for the life of me, I couldn't remember Russell packing such a mammoth of a package before.

Lengthy and girthy enough to be just right, he was. And with a bit of a curve at the end just to set it all off and seek out those hard to reach places. I ran a hand over it and did a double take, as if Russell had grown over the last nine months.

'You sure this is what you want?' Russell asked.

'THEE worst question to ask at THEE worst possible moment.'

'I'm just checking.'

I grabbed his dick and, with our heads touching, we both watched me lead it between the lips of my low faded pussy, which slurped at his arrival. His head glazed through my lips and found my opening before I could adjust myself to receive him.

Mr Oh

My fingers dug into his shoulders and he cringed at the pleasure and the pain coursing through him. His back arched as I dragged my fingers from his shoulders to the middle of his back.

'Shiiiiiiiiiiiiiiiiiiiiiiiiiiiiiiiiiiiiit,' Russell trailed off into silence as he withdrew his hips and gave me an almighty first stroke.

Beneath my pelvis was a world of good feelings, eruptions and new beginnings as I instantly had an orgasm. I didn't see it coming, especially as I knew my cum number. I was expecting at least 17/18 of those strokes before I'd get off.

One stroke though? I definitely didn't see that coming. Lol, see what I did there?! (Didn't see the cum coming? No? Wow, tough room.)

My fingers dug into his scalp and my legs kicked into the air in celebration. I wanted to scream my fucking head off but so was the quickness of the orgasm, it got stuck in my throat. All I could do was open my mouth and stare at the ceiling as Russell froze to let me cum then continued stroking.

I let out one good, 'OH MY FUCKING GOD!'

Russell leaned back planted my feet on his chest. There was no pause in the stroke and he was back at it with his hands on my knees, swirling his hips in different directions.

I could feel his helmet dip against my walls and the feeling made me flash through the shoes I currently owned in Maya's boot. Each and every single one made my nipples more erect and Russell's stroke that little bit more electric. He had a hand reaching down to cup my buttocks, which lifted me closer to him. The way his dick slipped into the hilt of me made my legs extend and kick him off me as I felt another orgasm rippling from my scalp to my toes.

'What's wrong?'

The Tall Tales of Tatiana Blue

I didn't speak to him as my knees rolled into my chest and I draped my hair over my face so he couldn't see what he had done to me. Not that he needed to see my face. He knew. There was nothing I could do to stop the eruption and I didn't care how I looked, I was stuck.

Russell hooked my hair out of my face and looked down at me, screwing my face like I downed a cocktail of lemon, lime and baking soda. I was pulling my knees in tighter, trying to stop the goodness but I seemed to make it worse.

'For fuck... oh God... oh God oh God... ohGodohGodohGod!'

He was obviously not ready for me or what I was capable of as I squirted very hard. I heard the sound of something slapping Russell's skin as I arched my back off the bed. Squinting while squirting, I saw Russell hadn't moved and was running his hands through the liquid that dripped from his neck downwards.

My hips, waist and shoulders were vibrating on different rhythms and I went from my back to my front and onto my side, trying to get it to stop.

Suddenly, my body was spun onto my stomach, my cheeks were spanked and Russell slid inside me with no ceremony.

Just how I liked it.

'Oh no you don't. You trying to write me off?' I asked him, trying to wrestle out of the position.

'Yes I am," he replied, laying his weight on top of me and refusing to let up.

I collapsed flat and let him do what he was doing. I could hear a growl emanating from his chest and my thighs opened more for him. A slow stroke which grew into a speedy, deep, slamming pulse that had our skin clapping like a standing ovation had my mouth open. I had nowhere else to go but to take the slaying that was being dished out. Like I wanted to go anywhere.

Mr Oh

It was some of the best dick I'd had... ever! And I'd only felt two positions so far.

I was grabbing all about the bed, trying to slap or scratch him but he wrapped an arm around my neck and rode me deep. His face was buried in my hair and I could hear him inhaling deeply.

'Allllwaaaays... my... diiiiiick,' I shook out of my mouth as I tried to pull myself across the bed.

With the way Russell was giving me the concentrated, repetitive stroke from behind, I was having repetitive quick orgasms that kept my eyes shut. On one hand I wanted a moment to stop and enjoy the flurry of orgasms that were hitting me but on the other hand, I wanted more. I wanted dick for each and every one of my shoes. I wanted dick for the exit I pulled to get out of Mount Street, dick for the fact that Marcus was somewhere in London trying to pull stun gun pincers out of his skin. I wanted dick just because I hadn't had dick in so long. I wanted dick for each stash house. I wanted dick for my sexy dreadlocks. I wanted dick just for dick's sake. I wanted dick because I was Tatiana Blue and I deserved dick like this.

'I should've fucked you when you were awake,' I mumbled, squeezing my walls against him.

'You should've. You could've been cumming on me for ages,' Russell replied then twisted me on my side, curled my top leg and slid in from the side. Scissors style.

'Oh... you fucking fucker you...'

No words after that. As much as I had slept with Russell before, in a manner of speaking, I didn't remember him being so... much. From the side, he slid in my club so quick and deep, I actually tried to get away. Like, I was trying to crawl my way off the bed. I mean, lawd a'gawd, I was tapping the bed, trying to catch my breath. I wasn't rookie enough

The Tall Tales of Tatiana Blue

to fall in love just because of a good dicking, but this was making me fall in love with every stroke. I was imagining our future together, maybe one day showing Russell my stash house shoes, running in the park as a family, Timberlands for me, Russell and Charlotte. Summers in Victoria Park, outings to the Science Museum, dinner for two at Smollenskys on the Strand, hotel getaways to the Hilton, complaining about clothes being left on the floor, weekly shopping trips, greeting Russell with 'hey honey, welcome home' after he finishes work.

With my arm hooked under my bent leg, helping him reach deeper, I was pulling my own hair.

Flashes of my future stabbed into my mind with each of Russell's thrusts. 'You know I'm keeping the fuck out of you don't you?'

I was breathing fast but the strokes were faster. I didn't have anywhere to turn or anywhere to go and Russell had the meat of one of my cheeks in his hand and was lifting it to get in further.

'You fucking Versace *Olympia open toed* pumps you!'

Russell's dick had me talking about shoes that didn't exist while he's was breathing normally like this type of sex was a walk in the park.

I'd never been so unfocussed in my life.

'You gonna cum on your dick?' he asked, turning my head and making me look in his eyes.

I tell you, I didn't know what to fucking say to that. I mean I was seriously on cloud 27 'cuz I passed cloud nine like six orgasms ago with the last three sliding through on the back of others. I'd never had a dick before. Sure, I'd monopolised a few of 'em in my time but I never had one that I felt was mine all mine. Like, a dick I could call and say, 'Mama Blue needs to be seen to' and know that the dick is pleasure guaranteed. The idea of my own dick made my walls tighten around him as he was

Mr Oh

pumping me on the maximum speed setting. Drips of sweat fell onto my body and I reached back to slow him down but he batted my hand away.

'If this is your dick, then THIS is my pussy!' Russell said.

'Erm... dunno 'bout that. We'll see on that one.'

And then something ridiculously amazing happened and I well and truly realised fucking Russell was the one for me.

Another orgasm crept over me. Not like any of the others he'd given me, this one was ten times more powerful. My walls stopped throbbing and stayed gripped on his dick. I tried to tell him to stop moving but he wasn't listening.

'Oh God babe... wait... wai... just one minute so I... whoooa...'

My arms and legs punched and kicked until Russell slid out of me and that's when I truly began to enjoy the orgasm. With Russell leaving my walls to do their thing, my clitoris hummed and the feeling travelled from my groin all the way up to my mind. The headache was instant and everything went silent. I arched myself in the crab position and stayed there for about 20 seconds. My feet were sliding on the bed but whatever was attacking me had my mid-section in a state of shock.

And the feeling wouldn't stop.

Have you ever had one of those orgasms ladies? Those corrupt your soul orgasms? One of those ones that make all other orgasms seem like sneezes in comparison. Find you a man who can do that because GOOD GOD!!!

By the time my body came down from whatever lightning bolt it was riding, I was sweating like I spent a week in a hot box. My headache had graduated to full-on migraine, every muscle in my body felt like it had been exercised extensively and I couldn't feel Russell's presence as I rolled from side-to-side.

The Tall Tales of Tatiana Blue

He was sat at the head of the bed, watching me with a smug grin plastered across his face.

'Now who else can make Tatiana Blue cum like that?' He said.

'You like saying my name don't you?' I replied. I noticed that he always said my name like it wasn't real. And with an element of surprise in his voice.

'So? It's a sexy name.'

It took everything in me to push up off my stomach and make it to his chest. He opened his arms out to me and I snuggled in his personal space, enjoying his heartbeat pounding against my head. The weight of the sigh I let out took me and my voices by surprise and I closed my eyes.

'So is this us now Russell? No more trying to arrest me and all that shit?'

'I guess this is us.'

'You guess?' I tried to act offended but my insides were still tensing so my attempt must've appeared quite feeble.

He looked down at me. 'This is us. Me, you and Charlotte. No more stealing though, you hear me?'

I couldn't help the volume of the laugh that climbed out of me which hurt considering I was still cumming. I playfully slapped him with tears forming. 'You're funny Russell.'

'You can't just do whatever you want. You've got a family now.'

'My daughter is my family. You? Well we have to see if you're worthy.'

'I haven't once mentioned the fact that I haven't cum yet. That should count for something, especially as you just caught the Holy Ghost.'

'Okay,' I concurred. 'That's point scoring on a massive scale but, as far as family, we'll see.'

'Do you love me Tatiana?'

Mr Oh

Who the fuck said anything about love? I looked at him asking that same question with my screwed up face. There had never been any man who had been lucky enough to say he had Tatiana Blue's love. There was never anyone who had the correct mix of normal and abnormal that I required. Handsome with a touch of uncouth. Immaculate but a little messy. Honest but has the ability to toe the line when he needs to. Would allow me to get away with shit but then knows when and, more importantly, how to keep me in line.

Yeah, you can see why I never found anyone. I'm picky as fuck.

'I...I don't wanna taser you right now, does that count as love?'

'No. I want a straight answer.'

I sighed as he curled strands of my hair around his finger, making my toes tingle. 'I want you around me all the time. If that's love then yeah sure.'

In my head I was screaming, WHAT THE FUCK DID YOU SAY THAT FOR?

'Would you give up your shoes for me?'

I laughed louder. 'You REALLY are a silly aren't you Russell Reed?'

Charlotte's ear-piercing scream from the monitor on the night-stand broke the sensual moment and we both jumped off the bed on opposite sides, looking at each other naked.

'You go ahead,' I said, sitting back on the bed. 'Daddy.'

'I like the way you said that.'

'You perv. Go and check on your daughter.'

'No more stealing!' he said, pointing at me.

'And when did you make your last upskirt video?' I shot back.

He froze with a knowing look on his face.

Russell put his bottoms back on, went to the bathroom to wash his hands and face and went to check on Charlotte as I laid back on my bed

The Tall Tales of Tatiana Blue

and exhaled. My lower half had stopped throbbing but my stomach muscles would tense sporadically to remind me of what took place.

I could hear Russell talking to Charlotte and I couldn't help but smile. Was I really gonna become a housewife with two point four children and a network of mother friends and birthday parties and dinner on the table and supermarket shopping and all that normal shit? Why not?

Okay, well, maybe not exactly like that. Maybe the odd foray into the mix of robbing celebrities and designers, just to keep a taste in my mouth and some shoes on my feet. There were tons of celebrities with incredibly lax security who needed a visit. The Mileys, the Taylors, Kardashians, each and every single one of 'em.

Mother by day, shoe thief by night.

Another orgasm rumbled in my stomach as I tensed my entire body into the foetal position and the last thing I remember hearing was Charlotte gurgle. Russell was mumbling something about her family tree.

I don't know what a perfect life is but I fell asleep feeling like I finally had it.

Shoes, my man and my baby!

Hold on, you didn't think I'd actually give up stealing by the end of all this did you?

Well aren't you a silly rabbit?!

Blue views

*T*atiana wielded her Hitatchi wand massager like Darth Vader over Russell's bald head as she laid back, letting air out of her lungs at the same time as Flying Lotus' *Tea Leaf Dancers* played on Solar radio.

'What the fuck is that? Looks like a shower head!' Russell said, kneeling between Tatiana's open thighs. He adjusted the pillow under her lower back with sweat and her juice dripping down his forehead.

'Just like a man to not know about the most important sex toy since the vibrator. This is the... you know what, there's no point. Just keep doing what you were doing.'

'Yes Miss Blue.'

Tatiana purred. 'Keep saying my name like that and you'll have to call me Mrs Blue.'

Russell didn't respond. He grabbed the base of his slippery eight and three quarter inches and slid his tip inside her. She smiled as he inserted more and stopped.

'Lemme try something,' Russell said.

As hard as he could get, he squeezed his dick at the base to make sure he was at his maximum girth and he circled his hand. He could feel the head of his dick making circles inside her and so could she.

'Well that's different!'

The Tall Tales of Tatiana Blue

The more circles he made, the more she slid her back side-to-side across the bed. Her moans were lighter than the ones she had before their little break but more of those circles and she knew she'd be growling real soon. She brought the wand down to her clit as Russell leaned upright with the moonlight catching his body perfectly. Tatiana ran a hand up and down his chest before turning her massager on and softly dabbing it on her clit.

The first touch was sinful and her back arched off the bed. Russell took that time to fully slide inside her and she opened her mouth to scream but his hand covered her mouth.

'Shush your fucking mouth!' he said sternly while working his lower half. He could feel every muscle in his back moving as the vibration travelled through her clit and onto his dick.

'Gerret off,' Tatiana mumbled as she fought his hand away with her eyes crossed. 'You have NO idea how abso – fucking – lutely wicked this is!'

'Thanks,' Russell replied.

'Not you, the wand!'

After those words came out of her mouth, Tatiana closed her lips tight and screwed up her face with her dreadlocks loose and all over the place.

'Keep doing exaaaaactly that...' she trailed into silence as she ground the wand hard into her pussy.

Mr Oh

Russell had two hands on her waist and was bringing her into him, which intensified the stroke and her walls tightened around him. He was looking to the ceiling, riding the good wave with Tatiana's extremely toned thighs parting wider before him and her hips grinding.

Their skin was slapping, their rhythm was matching, her pussy was leaking and his dicking was reaching. Tatiana slapped the pillows next to her and threw them off the bed but she kept the wand in place.

'O... okay...'

Tatiana's stomach muscles clenched, her thighs tensed and her body froze as Russell continued his solid and smooth stroke. She moved the wand from the left of her clit to the right and that was it for her.

'OH YOU SWEET DICK FUCKER YOU!'

The pressure of the orgasm made her walls squeeze so hard that she forced Russell out mid-stroke. As he slipped out, she bucked her hips and began to squirt again. The first stream hit his groin but the more she moaned, the higher the cascades of liquid flew past Russell's shoulder.

He counted 12 individual squirts and smiled, extremely proud of himself. He'd made women squirt before but never on such a grand scale.

By the 13th dribble, the wand rolled out of her hand and lay next to her on the bed as she throbbed with a hand between her thighs.

'Oh yeah, I'm done. I. Am. Done!'

'Are you okay?'

The Tall Tales of Tatiana Blue

'I... see... its stu... stupid quess... oh fuck me...'

Something rippled through her and she straightened her back and stayed motionless before exhaling and taking a series of short breaths.

'Yeah, you're okay. I'm thirsty. You want a drink?'

Tatiana tried to reply but she could feel the shivers of the ripple coming back and she didn't want to move for fear of bringing it on again. She lifted an arm in the air and waved it like she just didn't care as the ripple started again.

'Oh sweeeeeeeeet *Strasss* heelss...'

Tatiana froze again while gritting her teeth. She rolled onto her stomach but that did nothing to stop the orgasm that was incapacitating her as she heard Russell's feet slap on her floor towards the kitchen.

She pounded the bed and laughed while still trying to catch her breath. 'So this is the sex I'm getting? Yay me!'

On the night stand, where she reached over and turned down her Bose speakers, her phone vibrated.

A message from Quincy told her to check her e-mail.

As quick as her shaky fingers could swipe, Tatiana read the message.

'Click the link. A little something for your viewing pleasure, Quincy.'

She scrolled down and saw a video attachment, clicking instantly.

Mr Oh

Her app loaded the video and she sat up against her remaining pillows, brushing her hair over her shoulders.

The video came to life in an explosion of colours. The film maker was using a hand held camera in a crowd of very loud women. The camera was pointed to the stage where a male stripper was dancing for a woman in a veil with a very manly jaw.

The camera person zoomed in on the stripper and Tatiana recoiled with a hand over her mouth.

'Marcus?'

The stripper went into his routine and the video stopped and an arrow pointed to the bride-to-be and said, 'man'. The camera changed from the hand-held view to a shot of the same room but from a security camera above the stage. Arrows pointed to every woman in the room and the word flashed again on the screen.

MAN.

'Oh Marcus... that hungry for money are we?' Tatiana said, laughing and snapping her fingers. 'Go 'head Marcus, shake what ya mama gave ya!'

Just then, Russell walked into the doorway of the bedroom with Charlotte in one arm, two cans of ginger beer and his phone held between his shoulder and his ear.

The Tall Tales of Tatiana Blue

'Yeah, okay, hold on one second. In fact let me call you back.' He hung up.

'Babe, you need to see this video. It's hilarious!'

'Erm, honey,' Russell said sarcastically. 'Did you taser Femi and knock out Jamal with a shoe this evening?'

Tatiana was looking and stayed looking down at her phone, trying to hide the smile that was growing on her face. She didn't mean to laugh but the memory of how she managed to get out of the Louboutin store and past Femi and Jamal the police officers tickled her.

'Wait a minute,' she jumped up on her knees. 'I didn't hit actually knock him out with the shoe, he did that to himself. Well actually, I did taser him but after, but he deserved it. D'you know what he said to me?'

'Is this our life now? You go out and do your shit and I have to pretend like I'm not a policeman?'

Tatiana's phone rang. 'Oh, look, my phone's ringing. Hold that thought and I'll be right with you.'

Russell scoffed as Charlotte gurgled in his arms and the sun came up over Westfield in the distance.

"Hello, Maya? Gurl..." Tatiana said, excited to tell her best friend how her night turned out.

'So you ARE okay then? Thanks for letting me know.'

'Oh shit, sorry. Yeah, I should've called you soon as. We're all okay. As you can imagine we had a lot to talk about.'

Mr Oh

'Oh did WE?' Maya said.

'I think it's we. We talked about it a little and I think we might be we.'

'How exactly is that gonna run?'

'Exactly how I say it runs. Don't you know who I am? I'm Tatiana Blue, the baddest bitch in heels. Miss "take your shoes without you even knowing". That's me.'

'Look. We've got a problem. Well, YOU have a problem.'

Tatiana put her phone on speaker and began to tie her hair up as Russell threw her a can of ginger beer and walked off mumbling to Charlotte. She caught the drink just before it reached her face.

'What problem? From where I'm sitting, everything is Bisto.'

'Tat, listen...'

'I got my man, my baby, some wicked dick...

'Tat, your...'

'I got...' She looked for Russell before whispering. 'I got a shit load of new shoes and I didn't pay for one of 'em... And Marcus is mad at me... AND I'm naked. What could possibly be a problem?'

'Tat... your stash houses have been robbed.'

'I'm living la... WHAT? WHAT THE FUCK DID YOU SAY?'

'Quincy wanted to tell you but he thought I should...'

The Tall Tales of Tatiana Blue

Tatiana froze. 'ARE YOU FUCKING SERIOUS? WHERE? WHICH ONES? HOW MANY SHOES?'

Maya went silent on the phone.

'DON'T FUCK ABOUT! HOW MANY?!'

'All of 'em!'

'WHAAAAAAAAAT?!?!'

Mr Oh

Different shade of Blue

*T*atiana Blue was livid.

You couldn't tell from the calmness that draped over her as she sat up in bed, twisting then pulling one of her long fraying dreadlocks. The grip she had on her phone was making the tips of her fingers turn white and her moistened throat was now dry as a bone.

'Say that again,' she said to Maya, who called her randomly in the middle of the night with the worst news she could ever expect to hear.

There was a low fire still burning between her thighs thanks to Russell tag teaming her with his dick and a Hitachi wand but that fire was instantly doused as her brain began to tick over.

'I don't know what happened.'

'How many of 'em?'

'All of 'em babe. All your shoes are gone babe!'

'You ALMOST had me there, anyway... lemme tell you about what I just did. Well what was done to...'

'Tat?! I'm not joking!'

Tatiana whipped her tablet in front of her and was already opening her app which connected to the CCTV cameras in each of her stash houses. Turning her Samsung Tab landscape, her eyes instantly locked to the two

The Tall Tales of Tatiana Blue

screens that were frozen while the others were switching between multiple cameras.

Los Angeles.

Greece.

She grinned manically to herself then frowned. Her mind was an M25 of thoughts and scenarios of who's, what's and where's as she folded her legs, staring at the still screens of her stash houses. Her London houses were flicking between each camera, placed in and around the neatly hidden flats, storage rooms and apartments. With her storage spaces, she had her shoes out and stacked wall-to-wall while her flats and apartments were furniture-less with hidden spaces and ply-wood walls made to look like the structure of the building, when really they were hiding stacks and stacks of stolen shoes.

Dubai was okay, according to the cameras still flicking, her three Japan spots were also flicking through cameras showing stacks of shoes neatly standing in alphabetical order and her other Los Angeles spot was looking back at her through a rotating camera.

She swiped away the active screens until she was left with two screens.

'Maya,' Tatiana said calmly. 'What the fuck is going on? Who did this? I can see...'

'Oh fuck, hold on, police are coming. Hold on.'

Suddenly, the phone went dead.

Mr Oh

'Hello? HELLO? For fuck sake...'

Still holding onto her calm demeanour, Tatiana looked at her phone as the call cut off. She dropped it on the bed and stared for a second, thinking that her worst nightmare had come true. Someone had been stupid enough to steal from her. Not just steal one or two pairs of shoes but all the shoes from two of her stashes.

Her phone rang again, this time with Quincy's name flashing across the screen.

'Q-Ball, what the fuck is..."

'I know Tat, I know. I'm looking at it now'

'How many of 'em have been touched?'

'Just Volos and San Dimas. The cameras went down but I got a screen shot off one of the cameras before they went down and...'

'And what?' Tatiana was now on her knees, putting her phone on speaker and tying her hair behind her.

'They've taken everything. All your shoes from both houses. I've just sent the pics to you. I don't know how they've done it but...'

'I'm gone!'

Tatiana hung up before Quincy could finish his sentence. She opened the message from him and looked at the two pictures of her apartments in Greece and Los Angeles, expecting to see floor-to-ceiling stacks of shoes looking back at her but all she saw was space.

The Tall Tales of Tatiana Blue

Empty, shoeless space.

Her eyebrows furrowed, looking at the wooden shelves she built to house her stolen wares, now naked and bare. Her mind was fully racing and, now she could see that it wasn't Maya playing a joke on her, Tatiana's mind went into instant code-red work mode.

Jumping out of bed, scooting over the wet patch she'd been proudly sitting in, Tatiana was thinking and moving.

Car, airport, flights leaving in the next hour, small bag, City airport, two days tops.

With her dreadlocks bouncing in a bun behind her, Tatiana opened her bedroom door and almost ran straight into Russell's chest with Charlotte sleeping in his arms. He'd put her down after her last bottle but he couldn't seem to leave her alone.

'Did I hear correctly?' Russell asked with a sly grin as she brushed past and ran into Charlotte's room.

'What do you think you heard?'

She didn't wait for him to answer as she disappeared into her daughter's room, leaving him standing in the doorway. She returned to the bedroom as he sat on the wet patch with Charlotte opening her eyes in his lap. Her eyes focussed on his and she burped.

Tatiana was pacing in different directions, not sure what to pack first with her phone glued between her shoulder and her ear.

'Come on Maya... answer your effin' phone.'

Mr Oh

'So it IS true then?' Russell sniggered.

Tatiana looked at him, her face a mixed picture of seriousness and restraint. Though she was suddenly in thief mode – for the second time in less than 24 hours – she wasn't in the mood to hear the sarcastic police tone of Russell and his self-righteous "crime doesn't pay" rhetoric.

'Russell, you know my "I'm not playing" face right? I know it's been a minute but you know what the fuck this face means right?'

'Yeah but,' he started while playing with Charlotte's hands. 'Come on... don't tell me I'm the only one who can see the irony. I mean, shoe thief gets robbed?! That's hilarious. I mean, that's like a barber getting a bad haircut or a rapper who can't...'

'Yeah I get the irony Russell, thanks,' Tatiana cut him off while looking through her black bag. She rifled through it, pushing things to the side and tossing items over her shoulder, replacing them with clothes from her nearby chest of drawers.

Fishing through different coloured vests, panties, sports bras and normal ones, socks and leggings, Tatiana picked out enough combinations of underwear, leggings, yoga bottoms and Sports bras to last her for four to five days but, in her plan, which she was still formulating, she would only be gone for two.

'So how does...'

'How much do you know about me Russell? I mean how much do you REALLY know about me? Do you know how many jobs I've been involved in? Do you know how many pairs of shoes I've stolen? How many I own, how many I've sold? Do you even know how I sell my shoes? Do you

The Tall Tales of Tatiana Blue

know how many stash houses I own? What DO you know about me Russell?'

She stared at him, looking for the answers in his face but he replied with a blank stare. Hearing the anger in her voice, Russell had the memory of that same voice stored in his brain where it played in his sleep and haunted his dreams. This wasn't a fact that Russell wanted to admit to himself, let alone to her, but Tatiana's angry voice made him hold his breath and take notice. The stern, controlled, stoic tone even made the thoughts in his mind quieten down so he could hear what she was going to say. The last time Tatiana's voice was that angry, she had kidnapped him.

Her straight, emotionless words left him with nothing to say. His only reply was a look away to his daughter who also looked away and stared at the tip of her mother's Hitachi wand which was poking out from under her pillow.

'Oh come, you gotta admit it. This is a little funny... I mean...'

Tatiana stopped folding a black long-sleeve top and turned to give Russell her full attention while her mind was already on the road to the airport, while searching for the next available flight to Nea Anchialos airport. He opened one of the drinks and took a long, thirst quenching sip. A chest rumbling burp followed from his stomach.

'Do you know how many pairs of shoes I've stolen Russell? Not how many shoes your ill-informed pig files have on me, but how many shoes I've actually stolen?'

Mr Oh

She walked up to him, playing with what looked like lipstick. He looked up.

'88,728 pairs of shoes!'

She watched his mouth fall open, followed by another burp which she fanned away as she got closer to him. 'Make that 93,218 actually. I sold 4,510.'

He looked like he was attempting the world's hardest maths problem the way his forehead wrinkled. His eyes were darting from side-to-side and he looked confused. 'How could you have...'

'997 jobs Russell. You do the maths. That's how good I am at what I do. This isn't some rookie just stealing a few shoes for fun, this is my job, this is my life, do you understand that?'

'There is no way...' he started, taking another sip.

'Believe it bacon butty,' Tatiana said proudly. 'But hold on, why can there be no way? Because I'm a woman?!'

Tatiana took the drink from him and knocked it back, following with a louder burp of her own. She kneeled down and touched her nose to Charlotte, who was bemused by her hair.

'I don't laugh when it comes to my shoes so this, right here, is not a laughing, joking, giggling, chuckling, sniggering matter.'

Russell remembered the anger in her eyes as she stroked his face. The fire in her glare as she was slapping the hell out of him in a former episode of their foreplay that felt like ages ago.

The Tall Tales of Tatiana Blue

'If this is what you want Russell,' she said, standing up and running a hand over her breasts. 'Then comedy about my shoes is not appreciated. At. All. Isn't that right Char Char?'

They both looked at Charlotte, who was playing with her hands and cooing.

'So, the next time you... wait a minute.'

Turning to continue packing, she stopped and her frown intensified. It was clear that something had just crossed her mind. A revelation that hadn't come to the forefront until now.

'Uh oh, what now?'

Her mind was running a thousand thoughts per second; driving to the airport, checking in her light hand luggage, napping on the flight. Everything stopped and Russell was the only thing she could think about.

She walked back to him, put her hands on his knees above Charlotte's head and stared into his eyes.

'Russell... I'm going to ask you a question and I'm only going to ask this once. Did you have anything to do with this?'

'With what?' he fired back.

'THIS! My shoes...'

'What the fuuu... How could I possibly have anything to do with this? Wasn't I inside you when this was probably going down?'

Mr Oh

'I don't know, it all seems a little too convenient that one minute everything is hunky dory and then...'

Russell stood up, made a pillow support and laid Charlotte down softly, well away from the mess they made. He stood in front of her, picked Tatiana up, making her legs wrap around his waist, strolled to the closest wall, slammed her back against it and knocked the air out of her.

Tatiana's eyes widened and she locked one hand on his throat and an arm around his neck, feeling strangely euphoric at the pain behind her.

'Who am I Tatiana? Am I a thief? Do I even have the capabilities of doing something like that? I don't even know what's happened yet somehow it's my fault. You don't think there's a phone call on its way from the boys at the top because of you? After that Mount Street shit, they may even pay me a visit. That's how badly they want you. Popping up out of the blue like this? They'll think you came to see me. There were always whispers that they never bought the story I gave them but it's not like they're wrong because here you are.'

'You ain't a thief. Voyeur for sure, pervert definitely but not a thief.'

'Exactly. So I'm going to have my own shit to deal with.'

She unwrapped her legs from his waist and pushed him back.

'I've got to pack. Where the fuck is Maya and why isn't she answering her phone. She can stay here while I...'

'Whoa... where you going?'

'Greece.'

The Tall Tales of Tatiana Blue

Russell looked perplexed. 'I don't understand.'

'Let's leave it that way.'

She went back to packing bras and panties, socks and comfortable footwear while her mind went back to a thousand thoughts per second.

She threw on a black fitted T-shirt, leggings and a workout pair of black Adidas. Looking around for her phone, she tried Maya again but her number just rang and went to voicemail.

'You can't just up and leave, what about Charlotte?'

'She has an aunty Maya who can look after her. I'll be back in two days, I just need to...'

'So what about me? Why can't I look after her, she is my daughter after all!?'

'You?!' she asked, looking up with a pair of white ankle socks in her hand and her neck snaking to the side. 'You?! Don't make me flare my nostrils.'

Diving into another drawer, she rifled through a number of different coloured passports until she found the one she was looking for and threw it on top of her handbag. 'I don't trust you ham sandwich!'

'That's rich coming from you. You disappeared after FORCING me to have...'

'Oh my God, are you still swinging that dead pair of Manolos? I didn't make you do anything you didn't want to do, I just put you in a position where you could do it AND do nothing about it.'

'You know what, we'll sort that one out later. This is my daughter too,' Russell added, turning to Charlotte who'd just spit up on her Minnie Mouse baby-gro. 'I've just found out she exists so, here's what you're going to do.'

She raised her eyebrows, laughing in her head at the fact that she was about to be told what to do.

'Oh really?'

'Yes,' he said deeply, grabbing her hair which had untied itself.

'You are going to go and do whatever it is you have to do, then you're gonna come back and we're gonna sort our lives out.'

'Oh WE are, are WE?!'

'Yes WE are! You're going to come back to me and Charlotte and, somehow, we're gonna make this work.'

'A thief and a policeman? No, a thief and the policeman who was meant to find the thief? Really Russell? You can't make this up I swear. How is that even gonna...'

He cupped her face and kissed her quickly, pressing his lips against hers while she was talking. Locking her hair in a ponytail, she submitted to his embrace, kissing him back.

A single shiver travelled up her spine, making her thoughts slow down to a traffic stop and her arms wrapped around his head while she hummed into his mouth.

The Tall Tales of Tatiana Blue

They separated and looked at each other in silence, their eyes saying everything their mouths weren't.

'Pack your shit, don't worry about Charlotte, just go and do your teefing thing then we'll talk.'

'About?'

'The future!'

Tatiana Blue never dreamed of a future with someone, anyone, especially Russell. In her mind, she would come back for him, there'd be some sort of altercation, he'd reject her and she'd disappear into the sunset, just her, Charlotte and her stash of shoes to keep them afloat. She wanted to believe that Russell would accept her but, in her world, that was equivalent to surviving in the Mafia and being able to walk away knowing where all the bodies were buried. A dream that would never come true. And here he was laying down what sounded like the first step in negotiations towards a future together.

Get the fuck outta here, said the voice in her mind.

She didn't know what to think. Was he serious? Was he playing her? Was this a set-up?

So many questions with no time to find the answers as her phone beeped and she checked it, hoping it was Maya.

Mr Oh

Instead, she received a picture from Quincy. For the next few hours, anything from Quincy would be opened immediately. His first image made her recoil in shock and absolute horror, though on the outside she was a picture of calm and serenity. The empty room she was looking at used to be full of nothing but floor to ceiling shoes, stacked alphabetically and as neat as a clean freak with OCD. A portion of her life's work. Gone.

Not that she didn't have four other stash houses in London alone, but, for her, it wasn't just about the shoes, it was the principle.

Who the fuck would rob Tatiana Blue, she asked herself. *Who would have the balls to do such a ridiculously, stupid thing?*

'Go woman, go! Whatever is going on, sounds like you need to get going.'

She ran her hand over her hair, looking to the ceiling while trying to piece together a running order of how she was going to do things.

With Russell and Charlotte laid out on her bed, playing with each other's faces, Tatiana picked up her side bag.

'Right, there are bottles of milk in the fridge. I expressed earlier today so she should be okay. But don't give her all the milk... throw in a bottle of Aptimil in the middle. I should be back by the time...'

'We'll be fine. I imagine you have everything here and whatever you don't have I'll go and get.'

Tatiana couldn't wrap her head around how okay Russell was being about all this and her inner voice told her to keep an eye on his

The Tall Tales of Tatiana Blue

responses. With two of her secret stash houses currently empty, trust for anyone was at an all-time low.

'Are you sure Russell?'

'I'm sure. If my people come round while you're gone, I'll just say she's my niece. We'll be fine. Just go so you can come back and we can have more sex fights. I like those.'

Slapping his head playfully, Tatiana bent down to pick up Charlotte, whose hands were reaching up to Russell.

'Okay sugar plum fairy, momma has to go and find out why someone silly is stealing from her. But I'll be back in two shakes of a lamb's tail okay baby?'

Charlotte grabbed one of Tatiana's loose dreads and tried to put it in her mouth.

'And look after your daddy, show him the ropes and how we do things round here. And make sure he doesn't touch anything he's not supposed to.'

She looked at him and he frowned. 'What?'

'Keep your hands to yourself. At least until I get back then you can put them hands on me.'

He grinned seductively, imagining the fire they could set in any bedroom, kitchen, balcony, bathroom, living room or wherever they decided to have sex.

Mr Oh

His daughter was placed in his arms as he stood up and walked behind Tatiana who was almost jogging to the door, looking over her shoulder to see if she forgot anything.

'Have you got money? Do you need any...'

She stopped walking and turned to him, holding in a giggle.

'YOU were gonna give ME money? I know I put it on you and my pussy does have some amazing powers but have you forgotten who I am? Silly billy.'

'How much money do you actually have? Something I've always wanted to know.'

Tatiana gave him another "really?" look. 'You're not ready to know the answer to that question.'

'Just go,' he replied exasperated. 'Say bye to mummy.'

She spun around worriedly and gave Russell another look he remembered when he was tied to his computer chair.

'What!?' he asked taken aback.

Tatiana squinted at him with her eyes taking him in from top to bottom. 'Nothing. I just... nothing.'

She secured her bag over her shoulder and gripped her other bag while walking to the door, staring at the first picture Quincy sent her.

The Tall Tales of Tatiana Blue

Okay, Volos first. City Airport rather than Heathrow... I swear to God, when I find out who did this, I'm gonna fucking kill 'em. How dare they? No, no, no. I'm not gonna kill 'em. That's too final. I'm gonna make 'em die slow. Scalpel slices and between-the-toe-paper cuts for weeks. Ouch, that sounds painful. Yeah more of that... I swear Russell, please don't have anything to do with this. Please please please... when's the next flight out?

With the front door open, Tatiana turned to face her new family, not ignoring the warm butterflies that fluttered in her stomach as she viewed her new beautiful handsome unit.

'Russell!?'

'Yep?' he said, looking at Charlotte's face with the grin of an excited father.

She rubbed her eyes in frustration, thinking about the nerve-wracking possibility of sitting down with Russell, between sessions of love making and angry groping, and sorting out the idea of a future together. Now she was dressed and on her way to the airport for two days, not truly having any idea what was going on around her and trying not to get caught up in the whirlwind of it all. Her bag was packed with clothes that were made to fit her perfectly but to also aid her in doing things she didn't want people to see her doing with perfect aerodynamics.

For now, Tatiana, Russell and Charlotte would have to wait.

Looking up at him, seeing two pairs of eyes looking back at her, Tatiana stroked his face and slapped it softly.

Mr Oh

'I swear to you,' she started. 'If I find out you had anything to do with this, I'll kill you. And I've never killed before but for you, I will make that exception. I will either love you or kill you. Okay honey? Take care of our baby and I'll see you in two days. Watch him Char Char.'

She caressed her baby's cheek, catching a quick glimpse of shock on Russell's face. She kissed them both before spinning in her black trainers and taking the stairs to Maya's car which she still had the keys for.

Picking up speed, taking two, then three steps at a time, Tatiana hit the ground floor running, bursting through the reception doors while thinking about all the things that were going on.

'Where the hell is Maya if I have her car?' she asked herself, using the key fob.

Sliding her bags onto the passenger seat, she started the engine, revved it once, reversed and pulled away from the Stratford Eye tower.

She set up her Bluetooth on her phone and called Maya again through the speaker system, jumping a red light and giving a driver the finger out of her open window.

'Your call has been forwarded to...'

'Fucking hell Maya... what the fuc...'

Tatiana tightened her grip on the steering wheel and fought to ignore the obvious feeling that kept coming back and pricking her conscience. She tried to throw out the negativity that had been flowing in her

The Tall Tales of Tatiana Blue

thoughts towards her best friend but the more she tried to ignore it, the more it made no sense.

Maya wasn't the only one on her mind in a negative way as she broke the speed limit on the A12. Her phone beeped and she tried to check it, while swerving between two cars that were occupying adjacent lanes.

Her phone suddenly rang and erupted over the speaker system, answering automatically.

'Can I speak to one Tatiana Blue please?'

'Well hello lover! Ooo that felt nice to say.'

'Where you going?'

'I told you already.'

'Where. Are. You. Going?'

'Who. Are. You. Talking. TO?' Tatiana replied, raising her eyebrows at the sound of his voice.

'Tatiana Blue, where are you going?'

She checked all mirrors before cutting across lanes to zoom past a crawling Nissan Micra, giving the driver the dirtiest of fleeting looks for going at a snail's pace in the fast lane.

'Listen Russell, the less you know the...'

'Which airport?' he demanded, with Charlotte giggling in the background. His stern tone made her restraint falter.

Mr Oh

'Closest airport to Volos, Greece.'

What the hell did you tell him that for? What if you get there he has a police escort waiting for you? Russell isn't stupid that's why. He sitting at home with your child... what did you leave Charlotte with him for... I had no choice. I can't get through to Maya...I don't like that either... you and me both...

A moment of silence passed with Charlotte's excited – and not sleeping – sounds the only proof he was still there.

'Why? Not setting me up are you Russell?'

'Not everyone thinks like you Miss Blue... ah here we go. Right... how far away are you from City Airport?'

She took a turn, linking neatly onto the A13. Coasting faster than she should've been, she felt the backend of the car swerve and adjusted the wheel accordingly while pushing forward.

'Russell,' she stamped on his question. 'I've got a lot of shit to do so tell me something or come off my...'

'Go to City Airport. There's a flight to Nea Anchialos National Airport leaving in 15 minutes so...'

'Are you helping me Russell? Because that's what it sounds like,' she teased, watching a small aircraft take off in the distance. 'I've checked their flights. There's nothing leaving tonight.'

The Tall Tales of Tatiana Blue

'Trust me, there is. Flight MB580 is leaving in 15 minutes. You're already booked on it as a UK dignitary for a self-defence conference that started yesterday. So get your hydraulic heels on.'

Glancing at the electric blue console of lights on the dashboard, Tatiana did the maths and took in what Russell was saying and what he had to do in order to get her onto a flight that wasn't on the public list of available flights.

The reference to her specially-designed heels with earring-controlled hydraulics, for quick movement but full fierceness, didn't slip past her either.

'I've still got those heels you know.'

'Show them to me when you get back.'

A warm shiver travelled down her spine and nestled between her thighs with a sinister grin crossing her lips.

'Russell?'

'How far are you from the airport?'

She took notice of his desire to know where she was and began thinking of alternative routes away from the airport. Just in case.

'Russell?'

'What?'

'Are you helping a criminal?'

Mr Oh

He chuckled. 'Don't worry about what I'm doing. Just go, be ninja woman and come back to some...'

'Ooh don't worry Russell, there'll be some cumming when I get back.'

The lights of the airport appeared in the distance with the O2 behind it as she drifted the car onto a roundabout with one hand on the wheel and the other holding onto the back of the passenger seat for leverage.

'Hurry home to us. We both miss you.'

'Us?' she yelled as she slammed on the brakes inches away from a Ford Focus. 'I SWEAR TO ALL THE GODS, NOT TODAY SATAN!'

A quick look at the clock and her 15 minutes was now down to nine and change.

Russell mumbled to grumbling Charlotte, who calmed down instantly on the phone. Tatiana slowed the car around the Focus with a rev of the engine, giving the driver the dirtiest look she could muster in the three second window before she turned into the airport's long term car park.

Fucking Maya...or fucking Russell... or fucking Quincy... this is too much right now... Russell said us... you've got seven or eight minutes Tat... what about the C.L.I.T.S? They wouldn't... of course they wouldn't. As many times as I've hooked them up... they wouldn't... move it...

'...or lose it. Okay, I've gotta go, I've just reached the...'

The Tall Tales of Tatiana Blue

'Go, do you...' he said.

'I'm saying this from now.... I want a house baby. Can we get a house?'

'We can talk about a house. Just make sure you bring me back a souvenir. And make sure you pay for it!'

'Kiss Char Char for me. And kiss yourself too. Good luck with the bosses.'

She hung up and giggled, knowing that Russell would spend his entire conversation with his superiors talking about her. What he'd be saying to them wasn't clear though she hadn't ruled him out as a suspect in the crime of the century that was currently under Blue investigation.

She hoped threatening to kill him would make his mind up about what he was going to say but she noticed that he was still sounding upbeat.

Taking a ticket while creeping for a parking space, Tatiana had another worrying light bulb turn on in her mind. 'Shit! The shoes.'

She remembered the 28 pairs of shoes she stole earlier on from the Mount Street Louboutin store which were still in the boot of the Maya's car. The same shoes that would have Russell's higher ups asking him if he'd seen or heard from the legend that was Tatiana Blue.

'Fuck...' she mumbled, slipping smoothly into a space between a Volvo and a Lexus, both gleaming in the night lights that illuminated the car park. Killing the engine, she looked behind her, picturing the shoes in the black bag, just waiting to be stared at, slipped on and admired.

Mr Oh

It's an airport... where else would you wanna keep something safe... keep them here in the car, what are you gonna do, take them with you? I could... no you couldn't... geez, aren't you at the airport to find out who STOLE your shoes. You wanna take more shoes with you? Come get 'em when you get back... Go find your other shoes first... fucking fuckers...

She picked up her bags, took one last look at the clock on the console and got out with a huge sigh. She had six minutes left and she still hadn't even found the check-in.

Slipping the car park ticket into her pocket, Tatiana took off running to the entrance.

With her hair bouncing, Tatiana felt her handbag for the outline of her passport and almost ran into a short, ginger-haired white lady with crow's feet around her eyes and a crackling radio in her hand.

'Stacey Blaine?!' the woman said.

Catching Tatiana off-guard, she pointed her radio with a frown on her face.

'Erm... yeah?!'

The name from her passport, which she hadn't shared with anyone other than Quincy and Maya, made her screw up her face at the woman.

Who the fuck is this ginger nut... and how does she know my fake name... what the hell... are the police already here? How the hell would

The Tall Tales of Tatiana Blue

they know to catch me here... Maya? Okay, taser lipstick in my pocket, one shot to her neck, back to the car and...

'We've been waiting for you. Come on. Have you got your passport ready?'

Still looking at the woman with curious eyes, Tatiana motioned to her bag. The woman grabbed her by the wrist and they both took off into the airport.

They breezed past the check-in, collected her boarding pass, ran through the airport and were at the security desk feeding her bags into an X-ray machine in minutes.

Holding her breath, like she did every time she was at an airport security checkpoint, Tatiana kept an eye on the security guard watching the monitor for any sudden changes in his demeanour. If he saw the tasers she had in her bag disguised as her make-up, he'd point at the screen or maybe call someone else over. But the lanky guard who gave off a scent of old clothes looked at her bag and fed it through.

She took off her ring, Ankh bracelet and anything else metallic and walked through the scanner, expecting the sound but getting none.

'Right, hurry up, plane's ready to go.'

The woman took off before Tatiana had her Adidas back on her feet and her Ankh on her wrist. Giving immediate chase, with her bags over her shoulder, Tatiana had never been given such dedicated, personal service and she liked it. She was used to first class and business class, but this was something different. Another addition to the whirlwind her night had become.

'Russell, Maya, Quincy, Marcus even... maybe the C.L.I.T.S?' she mumbled to herself with a frown in the direction of the twin-engine jet which she could hear on its last call announcement.

From the comfort of her home, Russell found her a flight, booked her on it and managed to get her fast-tracked through security with a name he could not have known. Before she left, she didn't show him any of her passports, nor did she tell him which one she would use so how could he have known?

'More fucking questions!' she said to herself, almost losing the red-head through a large group of suited men who were speaking Arabic.

'Come on Stacey,' the woman shouted with her radio crackling with random information.

They passed through a set of security doors and were galloping to a runway where a small plane was rumbling with headlights beaming.

'Yeah, we're here,' said the woman on her radio, pointing to the plane. 'Right, there you go. Enjoy your conference.'

'Thank you for getting me here,' she shouted back to the woman who was already on her way back to the airport.

Slowly up the steps, Tatiana handed her boarding pass to the stewardess who was waiting at the open door.

The Tall Tales of Tatiana Blue

'We've been waiting for you Miss Blaine, glad you made it,' she said taking Tatiana's ticket. 'You're seat is on the left aisle, down the front.'

'Thank you.'

Scanning seat numbers, she shuffled to her aisle seat while trying not to sweat. She squeezed her bag into an empty cabin over her head and sat down with her handbag next to a husky gentleman who was so lost in something on his phone that he didn't even look her way.

With her seatbelt locked in, a skeleton of a plan forming in her mind and time to kill, Tatiana ordered a glass of wine, thought twice and changed her order to a Courvoisier and coke, exhaling for the first time since she left.

Suddenly, a brand new rush of fear ran over her. 'Imagine if Russell set you up just to get Charlotte and you're about to be arrested... you've got nowhere to go. Who says this plane is going to Greece even?'

The captain's voice over the PA system broke her mumblings and she looked up.

'Welcome to our late flight to Nea Anchialos airport, Greece. Sorry for the delay, we had to wait for a last minute passenger who just about made it. This will be a four hour flight, maybe less. Seems like clear skies all the way, so strap in and we'll see if we can get in a little early.'

A stewardess appeared from nowhere while Tatiana was staring at the roof of the cabin, trying not to let her thoughts go from careful planning to violent revenge.

Mr Oh

'We'll be taking off in a moment. But I haven't forgotten your drink,' said the mixed race stewardess with the plunging neckline.

'Okay, can I also have a blanket please?' Tatiana mumbled, really needing the drink.

'No problem. We'll take off first then I'll bring it to you.'

She sighed, looking around the cabin for anyone who may resemble a police officer or anyone talking to themselves while holding their ear. There was so much going on inside her mind, she wished she was able to turn off the ideas and voices that were sounding like a congregation. Like the proverbial devil and angel on each shoulder, Tatiana's internal voices argued like siblings who hated each other. They never agreed on anything, always gave her positive and negative advice but also saved her from making silly or dangerous decisions that could have gotten her arrested or killed. They argued during her Harrods escapade, cursed her when she kidnapped Russell, saved her during her Mount Street rebirth and here they were again, running through the pros and cons of who could've had the balls to steal from her on a massive, almost impossible scale.

Russell! It's all too easy with him. I mean you kidnapped him... raped him... no we didn't rape anybody... come on, yes you did... he never said no... yeah but it was totally against his... every time you do this... I'm just thinking realistically. Imagine if he never let that go and he's been waiting for you to pop up like you said you would... so his best way to get me back is to steal my shoes? That's a stretch though. I mean he's still police. The one thing he wouldn't do is steal... yeah but he wouldn't take

The Tall Tales of Tatiana Blue

pictures up women's skirts but he did though, maybe he still does... there's no way Russell could pull this off, he's too small time and don't forget his ultimate plan is to arrest me. He's police... sexy though... well I know that... and he eats some wicked pus... FOCUS for fucks sake...

The plane crawled for a few minutes before making a small turn then stopping. The stewardess left the aisle and was strapped into her own seat. A scent from the chunky fellow next to her who smelt like he sweated Guinness had yet to buckle his own seatbelt around his stomach which was bulging through an off-white shirt with dried food stains. Tatiana was not happy being stuck to such an assault on her senses.

The plane began to tremble with the engines roaring as the jet prepared to pull off. Catching speed, Tatiana looked across the man's stomach out of the window to see London City Airport disappearing from view. Seconds later, the airport quickly became a row of houses which became darkness as the Beechjet 400A became airborne, leaving the ground and skimming east London as it rose in the sky.

Where the fuck is Maya though? The fact I can't get her on the phone doesn't make me very happy at all... me neither, I mean one minute she's calling telling us we've been robbed then the next... she's not answering any calls and no one can get through to her, I mean... what the fuck? Exactly... number one, she wouldn't fucking dare, two, she doesn't know where I keep all my spots so... so she wouldn't know where to go in the first place. She wouldn't go to Greece... and three, Maya is still part-time

Mr Oh

in this game so she isn't going to... but hold on, why not? Because she's Charlotte's godmother and your best friend? No fucking way... NO fucking way, Maya couldn't pull this off...

Tatiana could feel the plane climbing as a who's who of possible thieves began to run through her head. Turbulence rocked the plane from the left to the right and she exhaled again with her eyes closed.

But what about Quincy... what about... HE knows where all your stash houses are... in fact he helped you start them so he knows where they all are... yeah but Quincy isn't into shoes so... what does that have to do with stealing shoes... if he did, the shoes wouldn't be for him... maybe... maybe he's channelling his inner Bruce Jenner... nah, Quincy is loyal as fuck, he always has been... maybe that's why you wouldn't suspect him... maybe he stole them for Maya... because they're fucking... you still believe they're fuc... of course I do. I know Maya, so I know she's hitting that... anyway... yeah anyway, I don't think Quincy would do it... but he does have the resources though...

Her body could feel the plane levelling out as she opened her eyes and looked ahead but couldn't focus. Pros and cons of her nearest and dearest were making her feel miserable about her life. Barring Russell, these were people she loved and had been friends with for years so having to question their loyalty left a weird taste in her mouth. If only the crime didn't appear to be something any of them could do.

The Tall Tales of Tatiana Blue

With the seatbelt sign off, and passengers forming a queue for the toilet at the back, Tatiana unclipped her own seatbelt and stretched her legs with a massive yawn.

'So what's a hot piece of chicken doing in an expensive seat like this?'

The sudden question from beside her pulled her out of the 'which shoes were in the Volos stash house, I'll kill whoever did it, I need more Russell dick, imagine if we became a family' daydream so quickly, she felt whiplash in her thoughts.

The voice sounded groggy but it was the breath that slapped her out of her dream first. Her top lip turned higher up in disgust and she slowly turned to look at the mess of a business man sitting next to her. His pale skin appeared to be oily and he looked hot and damp like he attempted and failed a marathon in his suit.

Tatiana had yet to be offended about being called a piece of chicken and was still having her eyes disrespected by his appearance.

'What did you call me?' Tatiana asked, adjusting herself in her seat.

'Oh no babe, don't get pissed wiv' me. I was just saying... I like Nandos as well innit?'

'What the fuu...' Tatiana had to turn away from him as he managed to offend her again.

'Nah sweetheart, oh God, don't be one of those ones who get pissed at everything. I'm just saying... you're black and you like chicken right? And I KNOW you like Nandos right? How can you be black and not like...'

Mr Oh

'Oh my glob...'

She put a STOP hand up inches away from his face with a loud sigh of exasperation, reaching the end of her last nerve. Everything in her wanted to vent her frustration of her current position by putting this chunky, clammy man in an illegal choke hold until he stopped talking.

She took a breath. 'Hey is that the Eiffel Tower over there?'

Tatiana pointed to the window, making sure to draw her hand past his face. He followed her wiggling fingers which drew his attention to the window. Once he was fully committed, Tatiana pulled out her lipstick taser from her bag – which she had her hand on as soon as he started talking – gripped the lid with her index and middle finger and slipped it off.

It swivelled in her grip and she swung it low across to his oblivious neck. She put a hand on his mouth at the same time and pressed the shit out of it. His stomach wobbled in a wave of spasms and Tatiana leaned her elbow across it in order to minimise his movement while muffled grunts seeped from between her fingers. His body slumped, his arms fell limp and he did what Tatiana wanted. He stopped talking.

She quickly slipped the lipstick back into her bag while taking a look over her shoulder to see if anyone took notice. The whole thing had taken less than four seconds with a satisfied smile on her face.

The hand she had on his mouth reached over and slid his window shade down. His head fell to the side and his heavy breathing further sold the slumber.

The Tall Tales of Tatiana Blue

'That was wrong,' she said to herself, exhaling and resting her head back. 'Meh, whatever.'

At the moment her eyes closed, another stewardess touched her arm softly. 'Excuse me madam. Here's your drink and blanket.'

'Thank you. Oh and can you bring me another one please? I'm gonna need it.'

The stewardess looked twice at Tatiana, who looked back at her with a straight face while she used her teeth to open the plastic bag that contained her blanket. The strawberry blonde looked at the hunk of sweat who had his head against the closed window with his mouth.

'He talked himself right to sleep,' Tatiana added with a grin.

The stewardess flashed an awkward grin and moved to another passenger as Tatiana stretched out the blanket and draped it over Bernie, according to his Hilton Hotel chef's badge.

She made quick work of the first drink – adding minimal Coke and maximum Courvoisier – as her second reached her fold-down table.

'All my shoes. Just gone.'

Her stomach warmed with the second drink, she released her hair and let it fall down her shoulders and sighed heavily.

I need to get my tips done... Oh I'm getting my shoes back... yeah but how... first of all I don't even know who has them, let alone getting them back... I don't care, I'm getting all my shoes back and whoever took 'em

Mr Oh

is gonna... oh we already know what's gonna happen to them... Dexter, 24, Homeland style... and I've been waiting to practice my Huck techniques... oooh this is gonna be fun... another Tatiana Blue adventure... no but seriously though, I'm getting my fucking shoes back.

Tatiana took a long time to drift off to sleep.

The jolt of the wheels hitting the tarmac made Tatiana jump out of a dream where she was a blue high heeled shoe on her way to visit a shoemaker. Her eyes focussed straight ahead, flicked to the right then left then back again. She shook off the remnants of sleep and reached into Bernie's neck to feel for a pulse. He snorted at the same time and made her jump.

'Yeah, he's good.'

She stretched her arms high above her head before sliding her fingers between her dreadlocks, which were stuck behind her back. Wrapping them up into a tight bun, Tatiana's mind woke up, thinking about where she was and what she was there to do.

The plane pulled to a slow stop and everyone stood up at the same time, reaching for their bags and moving towards the exit. She stood up with another long stretch before sliding her handbag over her head and sliding her carry-on bag out of the overhead bin.

Slipping nicely into a moving line towards the exit, Tatiana gave the sleeping Bernie a sharp jab in the ribs. He reacted like someone shot at

The Tall Tales of Tatiana Blue

him, flailing his arms and sucking in air loudly. He looked around then grabbed his neck with a frown.

'We've landed Bernie. Time to go.'

'Oiii… what the… What did you do…'

Tatiana cut him off as the line moved on. 'We've landed.'

She could hear him groaning and cursing up a storm by the time she was giving a smiley grin to the stewardesses and walking off the plane and down the steps.

The heat hit her first and she puffed out her cheeks and flapped her top, hating herself for not checking the weather before she got dressed at home. The all-black everything look was not cooling as she felt sweat forming in the cups of her bra.

She followed the line of people into the airport where a check-point of uniformed soldier types were checking passports and tickets while holding automatic weapons.

'Who am I again? Stacey Blaine, that's it,' she smiled, almost forgetting her alias, something she had never done in all her years of travelling under various names.

Pulling out her passport and ticket, she handed it to a stone-faced, olive skinned man in a beret who looked like he hadn't smiled in a week or two. He flicked between the pages of her passport, scrutinising every stamp, then doing the same with her ticket.

Mr Oh

'Go,' he snorted while thrusting her ticket and passport at her. 'Go, go!'

Just leave it... nah but really though, is this guy drunk in the morning, who the fuck is he... you don't have time for this, my shoes are somewhere on this fucking continent, let's just go... yeah but you know though... yeah I know and he would deserve it too...

Tatiana snatched her passport with a grin and one eyebrow raised. She felt him watch her walk away and turned to find him looking right at her.

'Yeah I know. Watch me go... bitch!'

Quick walking past other passengers, recognising the airport, she looked up at the signs, looking for something like a bus or taxi sign. Sliding past people, thinking that any form of forward movement was one step closer to finding the fucker who stole from her, Tatiana moved fast.

Round a family on the left, between an undecided couple staring at the food court, around an elderly man shuffling, swerving with inches to spare past the pretty boy with the tight jeans, around another couple, almost bumping into a pair of security guards and following a sign for a taxi.

She spotted a battered blue and grey Toyota Prius with a triangle board advertising a calling card on top. Through the crowd of people

The Tall Tales of Tatiana Blue

outside the airport, she saw a quick way through straight to the back door. She slid in, taking the driver by surprise.

'Kaliméra sas,' he said in the rear-view mirror, greeting her with a frown over his moustached mouth. 'Pou' pa'te?'

'Can you take me to To Stefani tis Makrinas, and can you drive fast please? Fast as in now. Come on, go, go, go.'

He looked her up and down like he had just inhaled a foul smell, swung around in his seat and began to mutter to himself. 'Kariolis, mbixtis, xekoliara...'

Tatiana checked her bag for her apartment key as she listened to him call her a 'motherfucker', 'one who always fucks' and a 'girl with a torn asshole' one after the other in Greek. The curses raised a smile out of her as she stared at the pictures of her two empty stash houses on her phone.

'Are you a pisoglentis? No? Then shut the fuck up and drive,' she said, calling him 'someone who has fun with his ass'.

She could see his eyes in the rear-view mirror, looking back at her. His eyes screamed 'I didn't know you spoke Greek'.

Her grinning eyes sent back 'yeah dickhead, I speak the lingo'.

Pulling into slow moving traffic, he continuously looked back at her as she looked out of the window at rows of olive trees and a community awakening in the breeze-less heat. She could feel the edges of her head throbbing, realising she hadn't slept for long enough. The night before, she went on her first job in over a year – and was unfortunately rusty –

Mr Oh

then went on to find Marcus and make him pay for what he did, all before coming home for sit down talks with Russell that ended in the most physical, strenuous sex she'd ever had. It was okay that she was tired. There was a lot more sleep to come, but after she found her shoes and the prick who stole them.

The driver swerved from lane to lane until he was doing over 50 going past the Pelion Ski Centre and slow moving traffic, following signs towards Portaria village.

Tatiana was full blown sweating at this point and was fanning herself with a copy of Time magazine that she found on the back seat. Sweat was running down her temples, armpits and down her back. She felt a wet patch growing over her belly button, tickling her lower stomach and making her itch like crazy.

'Chill the fuck out,' she said herself.

Really she was talking to the voices and plans A, B and C that were constantly turning over in her head. So far, the road from the airport to her apartment looked the same as it always did. Local businesses, olive-skinned faces, Pinus Nigra trees on the banks off the Pagasetic Gulf, good sunshine, scents of food prepared in wood-burning ovens, good times and sexy shoes hidden behind the façade of a two-bedroom ground floor apartment.

'I'm putting them right back as well, watch!'

Two right turns and the driver was almost doing drift turns down a treacherous stony path that edged too close to the trees lining the road and made Tatiana feel like she could fall out of her door, down a cliff

The Tall Tales of Tatiana Blue

face and into the blue water of the Gulf that connected to the Euboic Sea.

One more left turn and Tatiana tapped him on the shoulder, making him brake suddenly. He stopped at the entrance to the village of To Stefani tis Makrinas.

Leaning forward, while enjoying the smell of Greek pancakes and smoked pork as it lingered over the horizon, she took a moment to just observe. Anyone who could find her stash and put their hands on it would probably have eyes on the surrounding streets, anticipating her arrival. The thin roads were relatively empty except for the street vendors who were setting up stalls and elderly couples taking morning walks.

'Efharisto,' she said, scanning the street for anyone who looked out of place. She handed the driver €100 and didn't look back because she was too busy scanning the rooftops and open and closed windows for anyone who may've been extra interested in her arrival.

As the driver pulled a sharp U-Turn – without offering Tatiana any change – she inhaled what she called 'the simple life air' and exhaled slowly. She used to enjoy coming to this particular stash house because of its idyllic views, the taste of salt rising from the Gulf, homemade Pasteli and Kourabiethes, free-strolling chickens, goats and Kalamata olives which were to die for. It was a perfect retirement spot. Tatiana would regularly think about buying a home there with a plot of land to grow fruit and vegetables while Charlotte picked lemons for her lemonade stand in front of their seafront villa.

Mr Oh

Her spandex black top was sticking to her torso with every movement and she was wiping sweat from her forehead with the back of her hand and puffing out her cheeks. Her hair was absorbing sweat, leaving cool trails on her neck.

Tatiana's was the third in a row of 12 stucco, plant-covered one floor apartments but she didn't walk directly to it, instead walking past trying to look for anything out of place. With her phone to her ear, making it look like she wasn't doing recon on her own place, Tatiana walked past two extra apartments before walking back for a second pass.

'Fuck this,' she said out loud, drawing the eyes of an elderly woman who was out watering her plants.

On her third pass, she walked up the path to her front door with her key in one hand and her lipstick taser flicking between her fingers. She leaned her bags against a wall and approached the door with quiet steps. She looked up at the door frame, searching for any sign that explained how anyone could've gotten in without any of her alarms going off.

'I don't get it. You would only look for an alarm if you knew one was here, which means someone...'

She quickly slid the key in the lock, turned it three times and pushed the door open with her lipstick held out in front of her, hoping to take someone by surprise.

Silence and emptiness greeted her as she held a fighting stance with her eyes looking around but everything looked normal, except for the missing beep of her alarm.

The Tall Tales of Tatiana Blue

Opening into a sparsely decorated living room, Tatiana took a careful step followed by another with her lipstick far out in front. She pointed it towards the kitchen and slowly walked in that direction, listening out for any changes in the room's acoustics.

Something, anything.

The silence was unnerving. All she wanted to do was check on her shoes to make sure this all wasn't some elaborate joke played on her by Quincy but her safety was most important so room checks were necessary.

With another taser masquerading as an iPhone 8 in her other hand, Tatiana swung out of the kitchen and into the bedroom and bathroom but there was no one to use her tools on, leaving her slightly disappointed.

She unclenched and looked around. A deep itch erupted between her dreadlocks and she slapped her scalp in annoyance and frustration. Picking her bags from the doorstep and bringing them inside, Tatiana exhaled.

'Let's do this!'

Slamming the front door with her foot and throwing her bags on a wooden-backed sofa with throw pillows, Tatiana took a moment. She stretched her back and ran he fingers through her hair, sliding sections of dreadlocks through her fingers. She lifted her top over her head, discarding it on the golden coffee table which sat in the middle of the room.

Mr Oh

Speed walking to the old television inside a wooden cabinet, Tatiana could feel her breathing getting faster and faster. She wanted this all to be a dream. A dream where she had just wasted a trip to Greece when really her shoes were still where she left them.

Tatiana pressed the power button on the television and stood back against the wall. Suddenly, the sofa, two arm chairs and the golden coffee table in the middle of the room began to vibrate softly. The floor separated with a mechanical sound of movement and began to slowly sink down into a large square of darkness. Ladder rungs appeared from the left side of the darkness and spotlights turned on as the lounge furniture continued to descend.

'Please let them be there, please let them be there!' Tatiana hoped as she put one foot on the first rung.

The first step was careful, the remaining steps were quick and hurried. As always, the heat below ground level was making the grooves between her hair itch that little bit more but before anything else, she had to see if it was true.

Sliding down the last six rungs of the ladder, Tatiana froze and took a moment. She stepped around the ladder and the coffee table with hopeful eyes but the picture Quincy sent her earlier on wasn't a lie.

All of her shoes were gone.

The racks and racks of alphabetically ordered shoes, along with Polaroid pictures with their name, date stolen and location and celebrity they were stolen from were gone. Tatiana could do nothing but stand there with one hand on her chest and one over her mouth.

The Tall Tales of Tatiana Blue

Her eyes flicked frantically from the left to the right, up and down. They went round and round and back again.

Having seen the picture, she expected to not be so shocked and yet, her heart was beating, her mouth was getting dry and she could feel sweat running down the back of her knees.

Designer shoes from some of her excursions were meant to be neatly stacked in their boxes between spotlights in the floor and along the walls, but whoever did this took everything. Every box, every picture, every shoe horn and shoe bag, everything.

'She even took my cleaning shit too,' she grumbled, looking for her tool kit of cleaning products she used on her stolen shoes. Not every celebrity treated their shoes well or had good hygiene so a collection of home made mixtures and solutions mixed with lemon juice, shoe polish and baking soda. She started to miss putting shoes through her rigorous cleaning routine before finding their way into storage.

Falling onto the sofa, Tatiana let out a huge puff of air while still looking around trying to figure it all out. Even the voices in her head were stunned into silence. She pulled out her phone and tried Maya again, failing to ignore the obvious signs that were running through her mind.

She wasn't answering her phone, she was nowhere to be found and even Quincy didn't know where she was, which meant only one thing. There had never been a time when Maya was unreachable. She loved being on her phone too much, whether it was playing Candy Crush, gushing over Mediatakeout.com or spending hours on Instagram for new shoes to steal. But not only was she unreachable, her phone was off.

'I swear to God! Maya...' Tatiana chuckled maniacally and hung up.

Maya was her best friend who she saved from a trip to a store manager's office when she watched her trying to steal a pair of Charlotte Olympia all-black heels. When Tatiana caught her and told her to leave, Maya thought that was the end of it until, the next day, the same shoes ended up on her doorstep with a note.

Tatiana and Maya grew closer and closer from then; going on jobs together, holding competitions to see who could get an impossible pair of shoes first, holidaying together and holding a great friendship that grew from a pair of stolen heels.

Suddenly, like a computer that had just been rebooted, Tatiana began to remember all the shoes that used to surround her. The Alexander McQueen shoes that used to be on the left, the Christian Louboutin stand from the job she pulled off in Paris, the Brian Atwood 12 which she managed to pull off in under 20 minutes from SAKS in New York during the Christmas sales.

I swear to God, I wanna cry right now... you better fucking not... why not... because you don't have one clue... I don't need clues, it's fucking obvious who did this... ahhhh man, my gold and black Walter Steigers were here... oh for fuck sake... small silver lining, at least your special Brian Atwoods aren't here... yeah but most of my Louboutin boots were

The Tall Tales of Tatiana Blue

here... oh shit, I forgot about those. I loved those boots... yes I fucking did.

Rubbing the sides of her temple with one hand and scratching her scalp with the other, Tatiana closed her eyes, tired of looking at the empty spaces her shoes used to occupy.

Her phone rang at the same time.

It was Russell.

'Hi,' was as upbeat as she could manage.

'So you landed then? Could've let me know you made it okay... would've been nice.'

Tatiana wrinkled her nose and held the phone away from her ear. This was not what she needed to hear at that moment.

'HELLO Russell,' she muttered miserably.

'Say hello mum,' Russell replied.

'Is that my Char Char Bear?'

'I taught her how to say hello.'

'Really Russell? She's not even a full three months old but you got her talking and I've only been gone a few hours?'

Tatiana kicked her trainers off and put her feet up on the sofa while playing with the ends of her hair. Every time she looked up, she saw her

Mr Oh

missing heels and shook her head. Internally she didn't know what to do. She was angry, confused, frustrated and stuck on what her next move should be. And no-one seemed to have any answers. Maya was M.I.A, Quincy would call if he found something out and there weren't any missed calls from him.

She leaned across to one of the lower empty shelves and pressed a solid panel of wood, which clicked and a drawer mechanically slid out. Empty.

'SHE TOOK MY FUCKING TASERS TOO?!?'

'You what?' Russell asked.

'Nothing... it's nothing. I just... Anyway...'

'Well apparently I got parenting skills that you don't.'

'Upskirt videos don't count as a skill you know," she spat back, scratching the back of her neck.

He paused. 'You sure?'

'So anyway,' she continued, ignoring him. 'How's my baby?'

'Wow, rude. Anyway, OUR baby is okay. She slept straight through, no problem. She only woke up like half an hour ago. We're just having breakfast.'

'DON'T give her...'

'I know, don't give her semi-skimmed. Or full-fat.'

'How did you know?'

The Tall Tales of Tatiana Blue

'Duh, I'm a father now. I did my research.'

Tatiana managed a smile through her pain. 'Okaaaaaaaay.'

'How is you?'

She sighed, took another look around and rubbed her head quickly in frustration.

'I'm just peachy.'

'Is that sarcasm Miss Blue?'

'Yep. I'm... I don't even know... I just...'

'As you said the less I know the better,' Russell added, cutting her off.

'Oh, by the way, if you look in the freezer, there's an envelope. It's got a spare key in it in case you need to get back in.'

'Why the fuck is your spare key in the freezer?'

'Is anyone gonna look for a spare key in the freezer?'

'Good point,' he laughed as Charlotte gurgled.

In all the excitement and the travelling, Tatiana didn't take the time to stop and think just how much she would miss Charlotte. Hearing her daughter having fun without her brought a lot of questions forward in her mind. Being that this was her first time away from her daughter since the day she was born, Tatiana suddenly felt like her left arm was missing. A sprinkle of guilt hit her thoughts that it took until she reached Greece for that feeling to arrive.

Mr Oh

On the one hand she was thinking in full legendary Tatiana Blue mode and would not allow the disrespect of her shoes being stolen to stand. But, on the other hand, she was thinking that only two of her stash houses had been hit. There were nine more spread throughout the globe that were still safe. Or as far as she knew, they were safe. She was contemplating going home and forgetting the whole thing, but her previous self wasn't letting her mentally rest and had her anger continually boiling.

She got her tablet out of her bag and powered it up.

'Has my house phone rung at all?'

'No, why?'

'No reason, just thought it might. If it does ring, don't answer it, just let me know.'

'Ma'am yes ma'am!'

'You silly.'

'Oh, didn't I tell you I'd be getting a visit from the bosses? Guess who has a meeting with his superiors at his flat in a few hours. Wanna guess what the topic of conversation is going to be?'

'Beautiful, sexy, talented me!?'

'Troublesome, difficult, ridiculous you, yes!'

She picked up a copy of Vogue from the coffee table, while listening to Russell mumbling to Charlotte. On the front of the magazine was a Post-

The Tall Tales of Tatiana Blue

It note Tatiana left herself more than 11 months ago when she was last there. There were three bullet points on the note.

- Buy some more batteries for tasers
- Start looking for another Europe stash house
- Remind Maya that she owes you for the 'Atwood heels in the hills' challenge

'Well tell them I said hi.'

'Yeah, I'll just do that! Hey superior officers, Tatiana Blue, the woman we're looking for says hello.'

Tatiana suddenly shot up from her seat and looked straight ahead as the proverbial light bulb turned on in her head.

'Holy shit… the challenge!'

'The what?'

'Russell, I gotta go. Take care of our baby and I'll see you soon. I'll call you when I can.'

'Okay…. Be careful. Say bye to mummy. Tell her to stop being a criminal and come home to us.'

Mr Oh

'Low blow McRib... I'll see you soon. Peace out.'

She didn't wait for him to say bye before she hung up the phone and was drawing her finger across her tablet screen, looking for her Tracker app.

Tatiana remembered the "Atwood heels in the hills" challenge like it was yesterday. One of the duo's many shoe-stealing challenges. The rules were simple: find one pair of shoes in the world and the first person to get the shoes and bring them back to a specific location was declared the winner. There was the "Loubou near the Louvre" challenge, the "Manolo from SJP" challenge, the "KKK Trip" challenge and the "Atwood heels in the hills" challenge, three of which were won by Tatiana. The last adventure, which was the first to fly to Los Angeles, steal a pair of Brian Atwood shoes, pose for a picture with Brian then back to Maya's apartment, was one of Tatiana's crowning achievements. Though they both got pictures with the bronzed, silver fox shoe designer, it was Tatiana's picture that had her lying in bed next to him while he was asleep and the chartered jet home that won it for her.

The memory of what she did during that challenge had her Tracker App zooming into an animation of the globe. A small tracker fitted on the back of Maya's battery in her phone.

'Please be wrong... please please please be wrong.'

On her screen, the globe was spinning to the Americas.

She watched the screen zoom into North America.

The Tall Tales of Tatiana Blue

West coast. Los Angeles. San Dimas.

'Maya you fucking bitch, I knew it... I swear to God I knew it!'

I fucking knew it... yeah we all knew it but we just didn't want to believe it... when did Maya grow a pair of ovaries... and step her game up too... don't fucking praise her, she didn't just steal one... I fucking knew it... Ooooh I fucking knew it...

Tatiana was back up on her feet and putting her top back on, even though she was still feeling the heat. At that moment, she didn't care about the sweat under her armpits or the numerous itches between her dreadlocks which she plaited into a ponytail. She had a new mission; her best friend.

She pressed the button on her television and, with the ladder rungs retreating back into the walls, she paced around the coffee table as the platform rose up back into the living room.

The smell of Katiki cheese was strong in the air as she took out her phone and tried Maya's number again, also checking to see if her GPS was on.

It wasn't on and the call went straight to voicemail.

'I really don't wanna have to fuck you up Maya but it's looking that way,' Tatiana said to herself.

Mr Oh

She tried Quincy but his phone rang out before going to voicemail.

The platform stopped, bringing the living room back to normal order and Tatiana called a cab to the airport.

I didn't wanna think it... yeah me neither but from the first time she didn't answer, something felt off... yeah I know and now we have to kill Maya... whoa whoa whoa, no we don't... we've gotta wound her. Like paper cuts between her toes, maybe scalpel to the back of her ankles so she can't walk in heels anymore... nah, this can't be it. She wouldn't do me like that... damn, that's fucked up. I like it but we can't do Maya like that... well she's obviously doing you like that so who gives a fuck... touché...

'Hmmm...' she said, suddenly having an idea. 'Did she...?'

Tatiana went to the kitchen while waiting for the cab. Feeling like she now had a purpose and some idea of what was going on, she could plan accordingly. Opening the cupboard underneath the sink, Tatiana bent down, looking for three boxes of Rice Krispies that she brought from London years ago. The cereal was finished but the boxes were useful spots to hide some of her tools.

Glass cutter disguised as lip gloss, locker picker set in a larger than usual compact which could fit in her pocket, night-vision glasses in a pair of regular Specsavers frames, battery-sized taser, flash grenade eyeliner, her favourite wristwatch grapple line and a number of tools she hadn't seen or touched in over a year.

The Tall Tales of Tatiana Blue

Tipping the boxes upside down on the kitchen counter while looking out the window, Tatiana ran her fingers over the tools and memories of their last adventures came flooding back with a smile.

'I cannot fucking believe her!' Tatiana groaned, running her fingers over her cache of stun guns and tasers, checking to see if they still worked. She swiped to her Tracker app and looked out of the window with a whiff of freshly made Trahana soup wafting by.

'Bedroom,' she remembered and took off to her bedroom with a kitchen knife in her hand. The room she was yet to sleep in was made up neatly with bright walls, rustic beams stretching across the ceiling and throw pillows cascaded over a queen-sized bed.

She opened the door and stale air rushed her senses, as she went straight for the side of the bed.

The simple village décor she kept for authenticity made her smile and think to herself, 'my bedroom at home needs to look like this'. A thought she had every time. She lifted the valence sheet and plunged the knife straight into the mattress, pulling the blade diagonally across. Ripping the material, Tatiana cut a large cross into the mattress and slipped her hand in, slowly feeling around the springs and stuffing for her bright pink umbrella, which was really an X12 shotgun which sprayed electric pellets that rendered the recipient unable to move. Just getting fingers on it reminded her of the last time she used it.

It was during a recon drive through the Hollywood hills. She was sitting low and reclined in a rental car on Blue Jay Way, watching Bentleys, Bugattis and other expensive cars pass her by. The air-con was filling the inside of her silver Ford Focus nicely and she was humming along to

Mr Oh

something by Janelle Monae keeping tabs on the comings and goings of Eva Longoria's home. Watching a gardening van coming through the gate, she didn't see the huge black Chrysler truck zooming past her and only noticed it when she heard the sound of metal scraping on metal. She was taking notes at the time and was jolted out of her train of thought as some trap-hop music blared and livened up the quiet street. The black truck with the fully tinted windows turned into a driveway opposite and stopped in front of large black iron gates. With her eyebrows screwed, her seatbelt whipping off and her door open, Tatiana got low and ran up quickly on the driver side window with her frown intensified and rapped her knuckle three times on the blacked-out glass.

The window slowly rolled down as the bass of the music exploded louder than she expected and made her recoil slightly.

'Are you blind as well as rich and stupid?' she asked as the window continued to roll.

'Bitch please. Here.'

'Khlo, no!' shouted someone who was sitting at the back.

A number of fresh American dollars came flying at Tatiana's face and she didn't have time to close her eyes. Watching the notes spread across her face, Tatiana frowned at the instant disrespect and had her X12 out of her bag and in her left hand before the money hit the floor. Swinging her arm in one swift movement, she rested it on the driver's open window and pressed the button. The dark inside of the truck was quickly illuminated as electrified mini pellets struck her face and upper body. Her shoulders went into instant spasms while a scream exploded from the back seat.

The Tall Tales of Tatiana Blue

'Shush...' Tatiana said. 'You people. SO rich and looked after. Never think it'll get real around here. Don't worry, she'll be fine. I'll be back for your shoes later.'

The female driver slumped sideways into the passenger seat while the back seat passenger was still screaming with her autumn brown hair whipping about her face. Tatiana gave her a dead-eye stare and she stopped her noise instantly.

'Have a nice day'

With the iron gates rolling open, Tatiana disconnected the wires, shoved her pink umbrella back into her bag and was sprinting back to her car. A massive wheel spin and a honk of the horn and she was gone.

'Yeah, good times,' she mumbled to herself.

A rusty-sounding horn beeped outside her kitchen window and she looked out to see a four-door Mercedes parked outside. Grabbing all the weapons that could pass regular travel security measures, she swiped them off the counter until they toppled into her handbag. She had no worries about customs thanks to the Quincy-provided lined hand bag and carry case she currently used. She tidied up the kitchen, putting the cereal boxes back and straightening up, before she waved at the driver to let him know she was coming.

She jogged back into the living room and looked around, making sure everything was back in place. Everything now made sense, even though she still had a lot of questions that were yet to be answered.

Mr Oh

The one person who could possibly find out where her stash houses were was the one person she was now chasing, even though there were still questions in the air, such as: why those particular spots, why would Maya steal from me and then call to tell me about it, who is helping her because she cannot do this on her own, the security pictures of my places, who took those?

'Fucking Maya. And fucking Quincy it seems. This the fucking thanks I get!?'

With her carry-on and her handbag, Tatiana opened the door and took one last look at her apartment. In her mind, she could picture Maya walking around, looking for her shoes, trying to find the entrance and failing. But, she didn't fail for long and that's where the daydream stopped.

But if Quincy helped her then she knew exactly where to go... what a pair of pricks... ankle cuts all round.

She slammed and locked the front door, walking slowly across chipped concrete steps to the back door of the cab, which opened by itself. The driver came round from his driver seat while Tatiana was on her phone waiting at the passenger side door.

'Airport please!'

There was no levity in Tatiana's voice as she spoke and dismissed his presence, slinking silently into the back seat. Her eyes were slanted,

The Tall Tales of Tatiana Blue

wishing she did more post-pregnancy exercise instead of watching Nollywood TV and Fresh Prince episodes on Netflix.

With her leg crossed, Tatiana stretched, trying to gauge just how supple she was and winced as her foot reached the roof.

'Shit,' she said to herself, hoping a physical confrontation with Maya was on the cards. 'Yoga when we get home!'

The driver pulled off a cheeky three-point turn in the middle of the small village road and was back on the road to the airport.

Scenery watching while lost in her thoughts, Tatiana was folding her hand into a fist and hugging her handbag. While she was envisioning the many ways she could put Maya in a submission hold, she was also thinking of what the hell was she doing with her shoes. Why those particular stash houses? How did she have the manpower to move the way she was?

She pulled out her phone and dialled Quincy again.

'He better have answers,' she mumbled to herself.

His number rang out and went dead. She tried him again and the same thing happened.

Tatiana frowned.

There was never a time where Quincy didn't answer his phone. As busy as he was doing whatever clandestine business he was involved in, he always answered the phone. He was the Al to Tatiana's Sam Beckett; whatever she needed, he could get without any problems. He provided

Mr Oh

all of her tasers, cattle prods, disguised tools and even her retractable heels, which he somehow improved for temporary levitation. If Tatiana needed the lights to go out in a shoe factory in southern Italy, then darkness would ensue. Schematics for Saks Fifth Avenue? Instant delivery. Current whereabouts of Brian Atwood? GPS coordinates sent post haste. There was never a shoe he couldn't locate, a designer he couldn't get real-time cameras on or a security system he couldn't beat. He was the voice of ultimate reason in her ear when she needed to hear it and he, somehow, had eyes everywhere.

Tatiana tried him a third time and got the same result.

'Fuck 'em both!' she said, looking at Maya's tracker blip probably moving around her San Dimas apartment.

Pulling her tablet out in frustration, she opened another app and entered Maya's latitude and longitude coordinates and a live feed of the nearest camera brushed across her screen. Though the screen was silent, Maya could be seen from a security camera across the street and this made Tatiana sigh heavily.

'Look at how she's disrespecting...' she shouted, getting uncomfortable in the back of the cab. 'Driver, could you hurry up please!?'

Surveying the scene, Tatiana did maths on the situation. She watched Maya stroking the suede of her Brian Atwood Maniac suede pumps in light blue before talking to a well-dressed, but obviously packing, buzz-cut beefcake of a man who was watching the perimeter around the building. She followed his stare and directed the camera to swerve to the corner of her street where another suited and booted man was standing with his hands crossed in front of his groin. She switched to a

The Tall Tales of Tatiana Blue

different camera from a Starbucks across the street and Tatiana got a better understanding on just how Maya may have moved her shoes.

Seven men were positioned around the snazzy apartment block which was surrounded by wild sedums plants which hid most of the art-deco building.

She twirled a loose strand of her hair around her finger, trying to watch and learn rather than plan and arrange. Unfortunately, the desire to see Maya's half-conscious, bloody face beneath her feet was blocking her clarity.

'Come the fuck on,' Tatiana shouted to the traffic that was growing on the road.

The driver looked back at her in his rear view mirror, cutting his eye and looking back at the road. She sneered and looked back at her tablet.

She watched one of the men lift up five fingers while she read his lips.

'Five more,' he said.

Tatiana closed the app and put her phone away while breathing heavier than before. She was thinking about her shoes being disrespected, touched, felt up and treated like a pair of JD Sports plimsoles. Then she started to think about Maya doing these things to her shoes and confusion set in. Maya was her friend so her reason for doing this was what she was struggling to get her head around. They both had shoes, they both stole from the wealthy 'because the poor need sexy too', they both had enough shoes to last them the rest of their lives and, even though Tatiana had more shoes because she stole full-time while Maya was part-time, they were both happy with their

Mr Oh

hauls. Tatiana could be halfway across a tightrope trying to escape building security and she'd go right back in to get Maya a pair in her size.

And now, here was her best friend, godmother to her daughter, all-round perfect comrade...

'Fuck this!' Tatiana gave the driver a handful of Euros and jumped out of the back seat, closing the door with her feet. She didn't stop to see how much the fare was, she just needed to be moving forward. She scooped her small bag and put her handbag over her shoulder and began a light jog with the airport only a short distance away.

Hunger was becoming an issue with her stomach giving puppy growls which would soon evolve into wolf howls. The heat was now stifling as it got closer to midday but, to her, everything was sort of okay because she had answers.

It was Maya who stole from her and it would be Maya who would pay for it, one way or another. Under the terms and conditions of their friendship, neither one was allowed to steal from the other. For any reason. Ever.

'Just one greedy bitch who's gonna get it...' Tatiana said to herself, carrying her bag over her head and cutting through the horn-blowing traffic.

With her body itching, Tatiana reached the airport and stopped for the first time since she jumped out of the cab. She wiped her hand across her forehead and bent down to catch her breath while leaning on her knees.

The Tall Tales of Tatiana Blue

She collected a leaflet from a man in a mobile phone costume and began to fan herself, letting the cool air chill her thoughts. The airport was busier than when she arrived less than an hour ago. The combined body heat of passengers departing and arriving made the stale stench of body odour warm up horribly in her nostrils.

Surveying through the crowd, looking for a recognisable airline, Tatiana rifled through her bag in search of her passport and a credit card but she stopped as she pulled out two burgundy European passports.

Opening her purse, while the tannoy made an announcement overhead, Tatiana opened one of the passports and frowned as a face that wasn't her own stared back at her.

'When the Horton Hears a Who did I steal Marcus' passport? Where the fuck did this come from?"

Staring back at her was a frowning Marcus with burrowing eyebrows and eyes burning through her with delicate intensity.

Flicking through the pages to see where he'd been to, Tatiana couldn't remember the moment she stole it. She ran through the events of the last 24-hours from Maya coming round with her first spliff in over a year, to Mount Street to Marcus to home and Russell. In between all that, she somehow picked up Marcus' passport, though she was struggling to remember when she obtained it.

'I haven't done it again have I?' she asked herself, sliding his passport into her bag and looking for her own.

She was referring to her phantom stealing which brought her multiple treats; gifts, shoes, jewellery, clothes and, on one occasion, a big bag full of money. But Tatiana could not remember stealing any of them. She couldn't remember planning the jobs, nor having the stolen goods on any of her lists of things she needed. And yet, there they were. Maya and Quincy used to find it funny when Tatiana would tell them stories about random stolen items that would turn up in her house but she had no idea where they came from. A mystery she was willing to ignore until she looked in the back of her wardrobe on one occasion and found three Hermes handbags which totalled more than £45,000 hidden in a black bag.

Her first port of call was finding the next available flight to Los Angeles airport. Second was checking the Tracker app to make sure Maya hadn't made any drastic movements out of the L.A. before she got there.

'Stay exactly where the FUCK you are!' Tatiana mumbled to herself while walking past a couple who thought she was talking to them. They turned their heads as they followed her instruction and stopped instantly.

With her luggage in tow, Tatiana looked up to the departures board scanning for flights to Los Angeles while fanning herself with a leaflet advertising currency exchange rates. Her dreadlocks bounced heavily behind her as she pulled out her credit card and froze.

'What th...'

She pulled out Marcus' credit card from her purse and stared at it from all angles. Perturbed and confused, she looked around to see if anyone

The Tall Tales of Tatiana Blue

could answer why her ex-boyfriend's current passport and credit card were in her possession.

The heaviest of sighs escaped her drying lips and she rolled her neck a few times, feeling the weight of the world baring down on her shoulders.

She was back in the game, her best friend had broken the cardinal rule in their theft-ship, Marcus was still around and Russell was at home playing daddy dad while probably telling his superiors where she was and what she was doing. Or so she thoughts continually said.

'Okay,' she said to herself coming up to a queue at the Virgin Airways counter. 'First things first, where did that fuck boy's shit come from?'

Tatiana looked up to the steel beams and high ceiling of the airport with a hand on her hip and her other hand unravelling her blue ponytail. She was trying to recollect the moment, during her visit to Marcus, when she stepped out of the bedroom and went in search of his credit card and passport. A memory she was struggling to recall.

'So I came in... flashbang boom... knock out one, shush the screamer...' she mumbled to herself. 'Tied up, talking, thanks and out with another boom.'

Her memories matched with her recollection of the event and she was as confused as ever because it still didn't explain how she had his passport and his credit card.

Another announcement on the tannoy woke her up again and put her back on her mission.

Mr Oh

In front of the counter was a queue that snaked around itself and disappeared towards the Emirates queue which was longer.

As if on cue, her forehead itched with a line of sweat running down her brow. She used Marcus' credit card to scratch her head and she smiled to herself. She walked to the self-service machine, continually grinning as she pulled up an app on her phone and held Marcus' card in front of the camera.

With the picture taken and the app loading, Tatiana searched the self-service ticket machine for the next available flight to Los Angeles and found there was one leaving in 20 minutes.

'Hurry up,' she muttered.

The app finished and a page of random numbers filled her screen, with only four of them highlighted. Memorising the numbers, she ordered a ticket and entered Marcus' card details into the machine. Taking another look at the app, three more numbers highlighted across the screen and Tatiana memorised them and entered them in when the machine requested her card's security code.

Her hunger had reached the point of rising irritation. Her lips were dry, she started to feel grimy having not had a bath or shower and Lauryn was starting to itch, which meant Charlotte was hungry.

'Cheers Marcus,' she said as her ticket began to print out.

She picked up her luggage and walked calmly to the departure gates, smiling and humming as she went.

The Tall Tales of Tatiana Blue

Walking to her gate, something calming crept into her thoughts. During her missions, Tatiana's calmness level would drop the angrier she got. Confusing for everyone else but completely normal for her as wild violent thoughts became calm plots of survival and escape. Maya never understood how her mind worked in that way, especially being able to see it for herself. It was during one of their joint jobs together that made Maya stop and amaze at the skill of Tatiana Blue and almost get arrested in the process. The job was to get a pair of Christian Louboutin Barbara suede bow-back pumps and a pair of Giuseppe Zanotti spotted calf hair lace-up pumps from two boutiques; one in France and the other in Italy. The first lady back with both shoes was the winner. Both Tatiana and Maya went to the Louboutin boutique on the rue de Grenelle in Paris first before flying over to the Italian Raspini store in Florence. The problem related to a jobsworth security guard in Florence who was adamant he'd caught and captured the legendary Tatiana Blue when really he'd managed to get his hands on Maya, who wasn't watching her back. The stocky security guard was shouting in Italian while saying something on a radio. Sitting high in the rafters was Tatiana, who was watching and wondering where and how she could help her friend. It was then that Maya looked up and saw Tatiana contemplating what to do as she perched on a wooden beam that stretched the length of the boutique. Maya lost sight of Tatiana as she tried her best to work her way out of the bear hug that had her completely in his custody. She raised her feet and kicked against a wall, making them both fall back with him breaking her fall. Neither of them stopped struggling as Tatiana floated slowly from the roof head first with two C2 tasers in her hands. Maya saw her first and leaned her body to one side, making space for her to strike. The guard didn't see Tatiana until the last second but he couldn't stop the tasers. And all of this was done with a big smile on her

Mr Oh

face and cool, calm thoughts running through her mind. This was the first time Maya witnessed Tatiana's crazy calm side and it worried her more than a little bit.

After a short walk through the airport towards her gate, Tatiana stopped at a café. She ordered diplo Turkish coffee and Kourambiethes biscuits and sat exhaling her calm anger while thinking about the little things that should've pointed to the fact that her friend was the shoe-teefing culprit.

The phone call at stupid o'clock, the fact that she said that all her stash houses had been robbed, the fact she hadn't been able to get her on the phone again since, to name but a few.

She reached for her phone and tried Quincy again. His number didn't ring like before and, instead, went straight to voicemail.

'And him too,' she mumbled while looking at her phone.

As much as Tatiana took all the risk and kept all her stolen goods for herself, she wasn't exactly alone in her exploits and considered Quincy and Maya to be the squad. Quincy was an expert in solving technical, logistical and security issues anywhere in the world with the click of a button. He was the man in the chair looking at six different screens, shutting down power grids and disabling security protocols without even breaking a sweat.

Maya was the platonic Mallory to Tatiana's Mickey. When they worked together, they were able to pull off the virtually impossible. Scaling tall, plush towers in Dubai, using electronic suction cups to hold onto pipe

The Tall Tales of Tatiana Blue

vents, safe breaking the strongest safes in the world and they did it all together.

'Used to,' she reminded herself, picking a piece of almond from her teeth.

Another bite into her biscuit and she checked her phone to see if there had been an activity from anyone. A message from Russell sat on the top of her screen and she opened it with a hop, skip and a jump in her stomach.

Looking back at her was Charlotte laying on her bed in a nappy and vest and Russell in his full police uniform laid next to her, both with smiles on their face.

Tatiana chuckled, seeing Russell in his full uniform in her house. She'd worked so hard to keep the police out of her life so to see one laying on her bed without wanting to arrest her was a big giggle for her.

'My family,' she mumbled to herself.

Finishing her coffee and looking at the time, she messaged Russell and said that she wanted 'to do him in and out of that uniform – it's going to be disrespectful'.

He instantly replied with a smiley face and a cheeky grin emoticon.

Still in all black, Tatiana cut through the airport swiftly turning her shoulders to avoid bumping into people and taking dipped steps in order to get around slow walkers without offending. She took no notice of the huge SALE posters in shop windows and the duty free symbols everywhere.

Mr Oh

Tatiana looked forward. Maya was currently in Los Angeles in the same area as one of her stash houses which was recently robbed. Business needed to be handled.

'BITCH GET UP!' screamed her phone in her left hand. The sudden explosion of sound in her first class seat made her jump out of her nap and look around very confused.

She wiped her mouth with the back of her hand, rubbed her eyes and yawned. A quick check on the screen on the back of the seat in front and she saw that they were not far from their destination. 20 minutes to be exact.

The cabin was sweltering and was winning against the cool air that was being pumped through. The stale air smelt of shoes and tired bodies as she stood up in her socks, picked up her washbag and made her way to the toilet. With the latch shut, she pulled out her phone and checked to see where Maya was on the planet, hoping she was still in the San Dimas area. She waited for her phone reception to attach to its American phone provider.

'Don't go too far baby... we need to talk!' Tatiana said to her friend who couldn't hear her.

Maya's blip appeared on screen in the same place and Tatiana exhaled.

She put her phone on the corner of the sink and reached for her toothbrush, toothpaste, flannel and a small bar of black soap. After a

The Tall Tales of Tatiana Blue

brisk wash of her important bits, Tatiana pulled up her leggings and shuffled to her seat just as the seatbelt sign turned on.

Excitement was the only thing coursing through her at the moment. With the element of surprise on her side, Tatiana would use her advantage and recon Maya and her movements before finding an opening to make a move. The idea of being back in the game with her tools by her side and action in her near future made her body come over all flushed with heat. Her nipples were hard and she was smiling uncontrollably.

Mount street shoes… freaking Jamal and Femi… Maya, that bitch… I'm so excited, I haven't shocked anyone in a few hours… seriously though Maya, why would you think you could get away with this… I really wanna fuck Russell in his uniform and get pussy juice on it… that's nasty… so… SO, what we gonna… oh yeah, then he can go to work sporting the juice of Blue… you are so freaking nasty you know? No chill whatsoever… so!?

The moment the wheels touched down, Tatiana was the first person up, gathering her bags together. A stewardess called for her to sit down, but Tatiana replied, 'Can't love. Got a date with an ass whoopin'.'

By the time the plane came to a stop and the other first class passengers began reaching for their bags, Tatiana was at the door, waiting for them to open. She was more nervous than she was in Greece. Her mind was completing the journey from the airport to her

Mr Oh

stash house, which was located on the posh side of San Dimas, Los Angeles.

Waiting for the doors, Tatiana checked her app and found that Maya was on the move, away from her stash house. Her eyes followed her best friend's constant movement, which meant Maya was in a vehicle. Looking at the map of roads, Tatiana tried to foresee any possible routes that Maya could take in order to escape.

'This is my town bitch, you don't know... oh, that's where you're going?' Tatiana said as she looked over the map and saw a dirt road leading to a private runway less than two miles from where she was. 'Perfect!'

The doors opened and Tatiana was the first person to catch the humid breeze that blew into her face, drying her eyes and lips instantly. She pinched and puffed out her top to try and create a small whirlwind of cool air but humid air replied.

'Fuck my back door!' Tatiana mumbled as she began to walk down the steps. By the time she got to the bottom of the steps, she could feel droplets of sweat sliding down her back. Her strong walk was tired and in need of a good night's sleep in a duck-feathered, supremely comfortable queen-sized bed with a 300 thread count. And a chocolate man in a police uniform to put the cherry on top.

'Soon,' she daydreamed, power walking through customs, flashing her fake passport and ticket with minimal fuss.

Holding her breath as she walked through the last set of doors before the arrivals hall, Tatiana could hear a hum of American accents around

The Tall Tales of Tatiana Blue

her and she exhaled. Usually, flying into LA/Ontario International Airport, Tatiana would start getting excited about the little things that made America a different type of home for her. The air was different, walking down the street was a journey where greeting strangers was expected and chicken and waffles was something that would distract her healthy eating kick. And the hundreds of celebrities who live in the area with lax security that made America her most successful continent to steal from.

With one eye on her phone, Tatiana walked quickly through the airport and out to the taxi rank where a long queue of tired people were standing looking exhausted and sun-beaten. The heat was slightly more bearable than it was in Greece but she could still feel spots between her dreadlocks start to itch.

Tatiana stopped moving suddenly. The blip on her tracker had stopped moving.

'What's wrong Maya, guilt lick you?' Tatiana said to herself.

She looked up to make sure no-one heard her when something caught her eye. A man in a suit was walking towards the car park holding a sign in his swinging hand.

On the A4 sign was the name Stacey Blaine.

With her head twisted to the side, Tatiana wrinkled her forehead, confused that her fake name would be written on anything.

A heavy couple whistled and yelled for a taxi behind her which started a shouting match between them and the people in the queue. With the noise stealing her attention, Tatiana looked back for the suited man

Mr Oh

who'd crossed the road and was about to disappear in the maze of a four-level car park of SUVs and large cars.

'MISS BLAINE?!' she shouted while jogging in his direction.

She held her phone tightly as the tanned, wrinkly man turned around. His eyes focused straight onto Tatiana's bouncing chest.

'You Miss Blaine?'

With the paranoia already swimming around her mind, Tatiana didn't know what to say. What if he was sent by L.A. police who were working in conjunction with Russell and his boys? What if he was sent to drive her into a police station where she'd be arrested on sight?

Tatiana had been on the wanted list of Hollywood's finest for over ten years and she was proud of that mantle. There were mass murderers, terrorists and gang leaders who'd been taken down from the list but she was still up there. She'd lost count of how many robberies she'd committed in and around the area but wherever celebrities slept, she was there. Singers, actors, their partners – who'd benefit from their wealthy partner's spoils – and their managers, CEOs and their partners, agents, directors, studio heads, designers, etc. Their faces were a blur but their shoes were real.

It'd been a few seconds and Tatiana still hadn't answered the man who was looking at her strangely, which only heightened her sense of danger.

'Who sent you?' she asked back, using her elbow to feel for where her taser was in her handbag.

The Tall Tales of Tatiana Blue

'My name is Tony and I work for Exclusive Entertainment Limousines,' he said flashing his badge. 'I've got a booking to pick up Miss Stacey Blaine.'

'And take me where?'

'Another part of the airport.'

Tatiana reached into her bag, felt for her iPhone taser and looked into his eyes, looking for the answers he wasn't giving.

'Why?'

'Listen lady, all I know is I've been paid to take you to a part of the airport. I've never been there before but it's in my GPS. That's all I know. I've got it punched in my GPS, so if you're ready to go. We've got a schedule to keep.'

Tatiana frowned more. 'Schedule for what?'

We don't need this... I know, we don't have time for this shit. Maya could be selling my shoes on street corners and we're here arguing with some handbag faced... just tase him and let's go... my God girl, the taser isn't the answer to everything... But it sure does stop the questions though...

He didn't answer the question. Instead, he took off towards a sky blue limousine nearby and opened the back door. Tatiana hadn't moved.

Mr Oh

She was running her mind through the list of people who knew where she was, then cross-referenced those names with those she knows in L.A. who would think it was funny to send a blue limo to pick her up. No one knew her as Blue on the American shores which added to the confusion. None of the names in any of her lists matched up which left her more confused than when she started.

Her sense of danger ran past tingling and went straight to throbbing. The grip she had on her taser was tight and ready for any kind of action. She looked at the driver standing next to the limo's back door.

'Miss Blaine, please. All I know is I'm supposed to pick you up and drop you off somewhere. I don't know anything else I swear to God.'

Reading his facial expressions, Tatiana's imagination decided that Tony was a former Mafia captain who was slumming it until his crew's next big score. His orange tan, leathery skin and slicked back ponytail said that he earned his stripes by silencing witnesses and providing for his Family. He had 16 nephews, all who were members and would kill for him if he asked.

'How far is the place?' she asked slow walking to the car, looking in every direction.

'It's just there,' he replied, making a gesture with his hand.

"Okay, let's go. Can't make us late can I?'

She watched him for a reaction but he gave none, making her even more paranoid.

The Tall Tales of Tatiana Blue

What if all the celebs you've teefed from got together and now the police are involved... please they wouldn't do something so professional as that... you never know... yes I do, that's why I just said it... Right now isn't the time for sarcasm... there's never a time for sarcasm... there is, just not here... OH MY GOD, this limo has blue leather seats!? Fuck the world, this is sexy. Oh, wait, this limo has comfy as fuck blue leather seats? This could be a set-up... I'd go down in comfort though... fix up and focus Tat, keep an eye on this guy. Something about him makes me nervous...

Her door slammed shut and she looked up as if to say, 'what the fuck dude'.

Taking in the décor, but not being hypnotised by the all blue interior, Tatiana's eyes were everywhere. Looking through any window she could find, Tatiana wasn't seated and, instead was turning on her knees, leaning across the sofas to get a better view.

Nothing untoward appeared as the engine hummed to life. She was trying to find a state of Zen in preparation for whatever she believed was about to go down.

Tatiana was expecting that, with her luck, she'd be walking into the biggest sting operation ever conceived and she'd be taken down forcibly and the press would just happen to be there to unveil the identity of the ever elusive Tatiana Blue. The limo turned out of the car park and followed a road around the airport. With her eyes watching the movement of every vehicle around her, Tatiana took a mint from a small jar in the side door.

Mr Oh

Poison... drugs... maybe they want you to go to sleep...

Tatiana spat the mint out and began to spit into a tissue, making sure none of the minty liquid trickled down her throat.

She opened and finished a half litre bottle of water in a matter of seconds just as the limo took another turn which lead further away from the airport.

Drugged water... shit...

'How much further driver?' she asked, looking at the bottle and clapping her lips together, searching her taste buds for a change in flavour.

'Almost there.'

Unlocking her phone and checking her Tracker app, she could see that Maya had gone back to the stash house and was on the move again.

'Shiiit...' she mumbled to herself. 'Shit, shit, shit, shit, shit!'

It was during the cursing storm that Tatiana saw the helicopter blades in the direction she was being driven. 'Erm...'

The Tall Tales of Tatiana Blue

The limo drove past rows of helicopters; some in states of repair, some being refuelled, one was stripped down to its engine but there was one at the end of the row which stood apart from the rest.

Keeping very cool on the outside but panicking on the inside, she felt the car begin to slow down. This made her look closely at the helicopter and its hangar to make sure no police cars would pull up out of nowhere and arrest her.

Slowing to a stop, the driver got out looking at his watch.

'Shit,' he mumbled before picking up the pace.

He quick-stepped to her door and opened it. 'Here you are Miss Blaine. We're here.'

'Where are we?' she asked, leaning her head out of the open door but not enough to catch a sniper bullet if there was one waiting.

'Helicopter hangar.'

'Who told you to bring me here?'

'Miss Blaine, I swear I don't know but there's a note here. Maybe that'll explain it all.'

'Where?'

Tony reached for the note – addressed to Miss Blaine – and handed it to her as she scrutinised it from all angles.

She handled the note carefully, dazed and confused as to who could arrange something like this without her knowledge. Or her permission.

Mr Oh

'Hakuna matata – signed a friend.' The note said.

Tatiana stepped out of the limo and took a full stretch with her arms to the heavens. She shook her hair and let it swing in the sunshine while stretching on her tip toes.

She flipped the note with nothing else on it.

'Who wrote this?' she asked angrily.

'I don't know.'

'WHO IS TRYING TO FUCK WITH ME?!'

Tatiana shouted at the top of her voice, losing her cool for the first time.

There was nothing in the world that could make Tatiana Blue lose her cool. It was a comment that was shared by almost all of her victims that the woman who robbed them was very cool, calm and calculated. Never raised her voice or made violent threats, never became physical unless it was with her taser and was always polite, unless the person being robbed was a dickhead in her eyes.

'Seems like someone has set up a helicopter for you to travel wherever you need to go. In my experience, that's someone with money and also foresight because L.A. traffic right now is beyond a joke.'

Tatiana's mind started to roll in thoughts of people she knew who had money and wanted to help her get her shoes back. Though one side of

The Tall Tales of Tatiana Blue

her mind thought she was being set up, the other side was now thinking someone was trying to help. But who?

Lemme try Quincy... still no fucking answer... I'm really not feeling this not answering my calls shit... I'm not even trying Maya... I'll see her in a minute though... what the fuck is goings ons?

She approached the helicopter slowly. Looking it up and down while circling, Tatiana was lost. Was she being helped or hindered here? Who was trying to help and why?

'Hakuna matata... I mean what the fucking fuck? WHERE ARE MY FUCKING SHOES?!'

Tony's neck jerked back as he watched the dreadlocked woman circling the helicopter go from 0% calm to 100% livid quicker than quick as she came back to the limo.

Her shade of chocolate caramel had taken a deeper hue, her neck muscles were taut and the sweetness in her voice had been replaced with a deep, strong gruff.

'Excuse me, erm, Miss Blaine...'

'Take my shit out and go,' she said looking at her phone.

'But what about my tip?'

Mr Oh

From looking at her phone, she then looked up to the sky exhaling strongly and sneering her lips. When her eyes finally made it to him, he could see that a tip might not be the best request. Instead of waiting for an answer, he unpacked her things, got into the limo and drove off.

Her hand went straight into her bag for her lock picker, which she planned to use on the pilot's door of the helicopter. According to her phone, and from the roads she was taking, Maya seemed to be going towards Brackett Field airport, which was only three miles away from her stash house and two from the airport. She'd flown into the smaller public airport for private flights many times and found it faster than coming in at LA/Ontario International.

Walking up with her lock picker in hand, Tatiana put it away as she saw the pilot approaching with his headphones on. Slender middle-aged white man who probably looked good in his 20s.

'Miss Blaine I presume?'

'Yeah,' she said dubiously. 'That's me.'

'Nice to meet you. Two things I love in this world. Dreadlocks and British accents and you have both.'

She was caught off-guard. 'What the...' she trailed off. 'Thanks.'

'Okay, my name is Terrance and I'll be your pilot. So, my instructions are to take you wherever you wanna go. So, where'd you wanna go?'

Tatiana was hit with a barrage of confusion. The gentlemanly compliment diluted part of her anger and the appreciation of her hair made her melt even more in the sunshine. But she returned to stoic

The Tall Tales of Tatiana Blue

anger when an old memory of her fun days in her San Dimas stash house slipped back. Driving down Crenshaw Boulevard to meet her weed connect in a rental then blowing smoke over her shoes while having impromptu runway sessions in front of her full-length mirrors.

'Take me to Brackett Field airport,' Tatiana demanded.

'That's not far. Okay, good job,' he replied with an air of unnecessary positivity. In her current mood of anger, frustration and irritation, the chirpy, upbeat tones of the Tom Selleck lookalike did nothing to cheer her up.

Clear blue skies above provided beautiful passage to Brackett Field airport as they got in and buckled up. Yet again, her sense of impending danger kicked in and she felt a pot of dread spill in her stomach. Another enclosed space where she could not escape and was ultimately a rat in a trap.

As the Brantly B-2B helicopter floated high above the city, giving her the best view, Tatiana opened her handbag and holdall on the empty seats next to her and began to pull out weapons.

'How long Mr Terrance?' she asked, putting her own headphones on and scrutinising his I.D. badge.

'Ooooooh gurl, I like the way you say my name. Should be about ten minutes.'

She frowned and went back to arranging and testing her weaponry while checking multiple tabs on the internet on her phone and tablet. On the seat next to her, she counted 19 tasers and stun guns. Some looked like actual tasers while others were disguised as everyday items. She had

Mr Oh

three C2 tasers which were disguised as lipstick, mascara and an empty bottle of perfume, two X3s both with multiple target range, eight stun guns in the shape of Samsung S4s, four Hotties, which were mini stun guns that fit in the palm of your hand. Her final weapons were the shotgun-looking X12, which was modified by Quincy to look like a pink umbrella and shot electric mini pellets and the X26 taser which was modified into a foldaway mini sniper rifle, hidden nicely in a violin case. The rest were other random tasers and stun guns.

Terrance was enjoying the clear flying skies when he stole a look over his shoulder and saw the arsenal of weapons she had spread out.

He couldn't help but do a double take. 'Holy shit...'

'Don't worry, these aren't for you, unless you stole from me too.'

'Oh no no no ma'am. I'm good, thanks.'

He turned back around and kept his eyes facing forward for the rest of the flight. Tatiana noticed the change in his demeanour and found it funny how he'd gone from Rico Suave to Mr 'I didn't see anything, I don't want any trouble' in an instant.

Tatiana went for her weapons belt and double shoulder holster and was clicking everything in place as she leaned forward to talk to the pilot. 'How long until we...'

'I'm beginning my descent now,' he replied nervously jumping as he turned and found her closer than he expected.

'Relax Terrance. They're just tasers and stun guns and, really, if I was here for you, I wouldn't come to your workplace. If it was you I wanted,

The Tall Tales of Tatiana Blue

I'd go to 650 E. Bonita Avenue, San Dimas, 91773 and hide in the bushes outside your ground floor apartment and catch you after a long day at work so you wouldn't even notice me. SO a couple of minutes you say?'

His shoulders became tense and he wanted to turn around and look but he didn't as he understood that Tatiana somehow found out where he lived in the space of minutes and just recited his address. Really, that took her seconds, but watching Maya's blip arrive at the same airport took longer.

Tatiana stared at the blip and looked below to see if she could spot her friend pulling into the private airport. As the helicopter slowly descended, Tatiana, who'd been bubbling on angry since she left Greece, was now full blown simmering.

Terrance passed her a bottle of cold water which she took without saying thank you and finished it in one massive sip.

'There!' she shouted to the window. 'I see you. But if that's you, who's driving the truck? Are my shoes in there?'

She pointed to the grey Mini Cooper which was being followed by a quick moving truck and watched them both turn into a hangar and disappear from sight.

Every weapon she attached to her belt, hoisted over her shoulder or slipped into her double holster was meant for Maya and she planned to use them all on her quite a few times.

'If it's Quincy driving, I swear to God, I might commit my first murder!' she said to herself.

Mr Oh

Terrance, who was already nervous, heard her mumbling to herself about murder and he started his own inaudible musings.

'Please let her just go...'

'OoOoOoOoOo bitch, I swear... come on Terrance, land this thing.'

He lowered the helicopter closer to the tarmac, four hangars away from where Maya's car disappeared.

Tatiana had the door open and was out of the helicopter before Terrance could land. She threw her bags out first and landed shakily after them. The leap to the ground was further than she thought and she braced for the landing, crouching to absorb the force while her hair was blowing every which way. Looking up to the hangar, she gave Terrance a thumbs up over her shoulder and was on her way with her bags.

The wind from the rising helicopter almost pushed her off-balance. Her hair was now free and blowing wildly as she dipped her head. She walked slowly, trying to get a feel for the hangar from a distance, looking around for security guards or any of the men in suits who were previously watching Maya's perimeter. Coming up on the first of the four hangars, Tatiana crouched and slow walked against the closed doors.

A trio of industrial bins stood between her and the second hangar and she stopped and crouched down for a moment to check she was ready.

One last check of her phone to make sure Maya was in the vicinity and she put her phone and tablet in her handbag and slid both bags between the large bins.

The Tall Tales of Tatiana Blue

Through the sounds of planes taking off, Tatiana could hear what sounded like another vehicle and she poked her head around the bins. Another truck had arrived and stopped at the open hangar doors.

Maya walked out and shook hands with the driver and they both disappeared into the hangar.

'She really thinks she's running shit doesn't she? Huh? Running shit with MY FUCKING SHOES?!'

A sudden fit of rage came over her and she punched the closest bin three times, leaving a small but visible dent. The pain didn't register in her hand.

You know that's gonna hurt soon right... I don't care, I'm livid... calm do... FUCK CALM... you know what happens when you don't calm do... STOP TELLING ME TO CALM DOWN... you got this far being calm so just... FUCK SHIT UP IN THERE? OKAY THEN!

In her bag, she rifled around and found a large black hair-band which she put on her wrist. She reached behind her head and pulled her deadlocks together then folded the length up to the middle and tied it with the elastic band. Tatiana rocked her head from side-to-side to see if the band would hold before she sneered, spat on the floor and checked her weapons.

'C2 good, Hotties ready to burn, X3 on, X12 on my hip and X26 on my back.'

Mr Oh

Everything suddenly stopped and Tatiana closed her eyes, trying to imagine talking to Maya in between body shots and UFC-style kicks to the back of her thighs.

'At least stretch a little... what for?'

Her nerves were shredded and her mouth bone dry as she tried to lick her lips. She had a mobile phone taser in one hand and an X23 in the other as she crept around the bins and ran low past the second hangar to the side of the third hangar with her back against the wall.

Without any recon on the hangar, she would be walking in blind and that was what kept her stuck.

'Fuck this, I'm GETTING my shoes back!'

Tatiana Blue inhaled deeply, closed her eyes and lifted her head to the sky.

'This is for you Loubous.'

She pivoted around the corner and began to walk strongly past the third hangar without looking in to see if anyone would see the chocolate dread woman dressed in all black, armed with enough stun guns and tasers to neutralize a small town. Her face was blank and the heat was making her palms sweaty but she kept moving. The weapons on her shoulders clinked with each step but Tatiana didn't care as she rolled her neck, unsure how many people Maya had with her.

Reaching the edge of the fourth hangar, Tatiana switched to a dipped low strut as a strong faced, buzz cut soldier type walked out of the hangar trying to light a cigarette. His attention was on the sky which was a perfect shade of blue with no breeze. He didn't see Tatiana approaching in the distance from his left as she swung her silenced X26 sniper stun gun from her back, locked it in the pit of her shoulder, looked through the sight, armed and took one shot. The match he struck for his cigarette hit the ground before he shook his body down to the ground.

'One down…' she said to herself, swinging the gun to her back while still moving.

Tatiana stepped over his motionless body, putting a finger to his neck to make sure he was okay. The second truck moved slowly into the hangar and disappeared from her line of sight. Stopping at the edge of the hangar doors, she used the reflection of her phone taser as a mirror to see into the hangar. Many men, all with matching buzz cuts and chiselled faces were carrying boxes from the trucks to the back of a Lockhead L-100 Hercules medium-sized cargo plane.

Though the hangar looked dark in the reflection, Tatiana counted 16 men carrying boxes into the back of the plane. Turning the phone to see the rest of the hangar, she found more men standing around engaged in conversation.

'Gonna need a bit more than a phone,' she said to herself, replacing her phone with the X12 which was swinging from a strap on her shoulder.

She cocked back once and held the barrel close to her lips, remembering where she saw people before she swung the corner with her multi-shot taser held out in front of her.

Mr Oh

With her heart in her chest, she crept low to the back of the second truck. Her eyes were everywhere, trying to find a position where she wouldn't be snuck up on but still be able to see everyone she needed to.

'I'll take this truck and dump it up the street and then we'll...'

Tatiana heard the American voice before she saw anyone and she got as low as she could. Sliding her feet out from behind her and sliding onto her stomach, she shuffled under the truck.

The owner of the voice came round the end of the truck and closed the back doors with Tatiana watching with her finger on the trigger. She watched his feet walk around and disappear into the cabin of the vehicle. She rolled out just as the engine turned over and jumped to her feet while crouching behind a stack of boxes.

Suddenly, two more voices began to approach her hiding spot and Tatiana started looking for another spot but she was stuck. Any movement in any direction would give away her position and make her lose the element of surprise that she was trying to hold on to.

'Fuck, fuck, fuck,' she whispered to herself. 'Fuckity fucking fucker with no fucks left.'

'How can one person have so many shoes? I mean shit, we need a fucking cargo plane just to move 'em all.'

'That's women for ya.'

Tatiana waited until they were close enough, using the sound of their voices as a marker. She popped up from behind the boxes so quickly, the men jumped back with their hands in front of their faces. The distraction

The Tall Tales of Tatiana Blue

gave her enough time to aim her X3 in between them and, as she pulled the trigger, two pincers shot out and hit them both; one in the cheek and one in the neck. The volts passed through the wires and they screamed out loudly, just as the truck pulled away.

'No, THAT'S women for ya!' Tatiana said as she walked past the writhing bodies on the ground. 'Three down.'

There goes the element of surprise... I don't give a fuck, I want my shoes back and this softly softly shit ain't working for me... go on then, get yourself killed, see if I care... fuck you.

In the back of the plane, three men came barrelling down the gangway in her direction and she smiled. She dropped the stun gun next to the two soldiers and reached for her sniper rifle, aiming, pausing and shooting in one swift movement. As one of the men took a shot straight in his groin and went down, the other two seemed to run faster towards her. She tried to get another shot off but they separated and came at her from different directions.

She swung the gun behind her and had a Hottie in each hand. Coming around the boxes, trying to get closer to one before the other got to her, Tatiana kept her hands down trying to anticipate their movement.

'COME ON THEN!' she shouted in her best cockney.

'Wait Miss Bl...'

Mr Oh

Tatiana cut him off by rushing into his space and holding both Hotties to his abdomen. He dropped instantly and yelled out on the way down. She turned on the balls of her feet and dipped low, expecting the third man to be behind her. She held her arm out as he ran into the Hottie which was crackling in her hand and his body shook as he dropped to his knees.

'SHE'S HERE...' he started to shout but Tatiana shocked him in his throat and he gurgled into silence.

'Six,' she counted.

Looking up, after making sure he was down, Tatiana saw four more men running towards her with black batons in their hands.

'MUMMY'S HOME AND SHE WANTS HER SHOES BACK!' she shouted as she dropped the Hotties and pulled out her lipstick and mascara tasers.

The men separated and surrounded her but Tatiana saw it coming and moved out of the circle before it could form. Running up to one of the men, she kicked him behind his knee and he buckled then received a shot from her lipstick in his neck. No time to watch him go down as she half turned into a black man in a tight t-shirt and jeans shorts. She had no time to hit him as his muscular arms wrapped around her from the back. He locked his fingers in front and leaned back, trying to lift her off her feet. She countered by locking her leg around his, adjusting her grip on her mascara and reaching down to his groin. His arms opened straight away and she lifted her foot behind her which connected with his testicles while shaking off the residual feeling of electricity that passed from him to her.

The Tall Tales of Tatiana Blue

I felt my foot separate his balls… shit, you didn't have to stun him AND kick him… fuck that, you see the size of hi… WATCH OUT…

The third man didn't wait as long as the others and rushed her from the side. She took a few unsteady steps before she planted her foot down, swerved on the ball of her foot and let his momentum swing him round. For a brief second, she had enough space to get her lipstick right under his chin and she shocked him quickly while elbowing him on the top of his head. Her bun of hair swung around as she looked for the fourth man.

'Nine down, seven to…'

Tatiana didn't finish her sentence as Maya crept up on her from the back and quickly plunged a syringe into her neck. She swung around as her friend jumped out of her personal space.

'You?! You absolute stink-faced, dry foot biiiiiiiii…'

Tatiana Blue trailed off as she tried to fight whatever substance was coursing its way through her. Left knee buckled first and she dropped to her right, all the while keeping her eyes on Maya, who was making hands gestures towards the plane.

'I got this… she'll be out in a minute.'

'What the fuck Maya?'

Mr Oh

She was losing her grip on her pocket tasers and could taste almonds in the back of her throat. She was becoming hotter with every passing moment and her eyes blurred over as more footsteps ran towards her.

Tatiana was down to both knees and had her hands on the ground, trying to catch her breath.

'Shit, what the hell was in that?'

'Oh, this,' Maya said looking at the empty syringe. 'A lil' something something Quincy made for me.'

Tatiana could hear the footsteps slowing down behind her but she didn't have the energy to look at them.

'I can't believe you two did me like this,' she said coughing. 'What the fuck?'

Maya walked up to Tatiana and dropped to one knee in front of her. 'I know this won't make any sense to you right now but we did all this for you. All of us.'

Laying on her side on the hot ground, Tatiana's heavy head drifted off while she asked herself, 'All... of... who?!'

She wasn't sure if it was Maya or God whispering in her ear because whatever was flowing through her blood stream had her off with the shoe fairies. But she felt like she could see the airy words of the voice floating alongside her.

'A bitch isn't a hole for a man to fill, a bitch is a beauty in tremendously cute heels...'

The Tall Tales of Tatiana Blue

Okay, this is where I, Tatiana Blue, take over and tell you the rest of the story because it's about to get sooo juicy.

I woke up tasting lead and almonds in the back of my throat. My eyes were as dry as foot bottom and I could smell what I thought was 'badussy' (that's booty, dick and pussy for the uneducated).

My head was pounding, I felt like I'd been punched in the head by Floyd Mayweather without a head-guard and, if I was starving before, I was eat-a-horse ravenous now. But my hunger would have to wait.

I didn't know where I was or where I was going, all I had was my wits and what I could hear, which wasn't much thanks to the noise-cancelling headphones I had on and the blindfold over my eyes. It was hard to focus on anything with Beyoncé's *Blow* playing in my ears. That's my jam!

My hands were handcuffed behind my back with another set of handcuffs holding my locked wrists against a cold metal surface. With my fingers feeling along the corrugated metal, I could feel vibrations which told me that I was moving, though I hadn't determined what I was moving in.

Mr Oh

There was a presence to my right wearing either Impulse or Lynx deodorant and I could feel that I was being watched by more than one pair of eyes. Whenever I moved, I felt eyes on me.

My muscles ached as I tried to roll my shoulders but I had been secured from above as well as behind.

I laughed at such secure restraints. 'Damn Mya... you really know me don't you?'

I could feel footsteps moving towards me on a metal surface.

'What? One set of handcuffs behind your back to hold the great Tatiana Blue? Hell no!' Maya said lifting one ear of my headphones.

In that brief moment of having the padded headphones off my ear, I could hear plane engines and mixed male voices. From the movement and the sound of the engine, I figured that we were on the cargo plane that I just tried to stop. And if that was true then that meant that my shoes were nearby.

'Hey MyMy, remember that time when...' I started to say.

'Noooo, no thank you,' Maya cut me off and let the headphones snap back on my head.

I knew if I could just get Maya talking, I could find a way to hook her in, get myself out and begin to formulate a way to get out of here and get my shoes back.

Maya probably knew that too which was why she locked me off.

The Tall Tales of Tatiana Blue

To be honest, I wasn't feeling confident at this point. My shoes had been successfully stolen – by my best friend no less – and here I was a kidnap victim of the fothermuckers who'd taken my shit. And there was nothing I could do about it.

It didn't help that the fuckers in question just happened to be the same people who watched and helped me become the legendary Tatiana Blue.

They'd trained with me, worked with me, helped me get some of the most excellent and useful tools and weapons ever made and now I was at their mercy as they had me and my shoes in a precarious position.

I knew it was just Maya who did this to me but it seemed that Bonnie and Clyde effort with Quincy providing the manpower to assist.

'There is no fucking way I'm gonna let you live after this, you know that right?' I shouted to no one particular. 'You know who I am Maya, you know what I do and you know what I'm capable of.'

The headphones were ripped off my head.

'You know what...' Maya started.

The blindfold came off and a searing white light shone straight into my eyes, causing me to wince.

I squinted like my life depended on it, trying to swallow with no liquid in my throat. My head thrashed from side-to-side, more in trying to find out how close anyone was to me. Information that may serve me well when it comes to an escape.

Mr Oh

I tried blinking once. Then twice but nothing broke through the white light. Another try and I could see a large metal container in front of me. Another set of blinks and I could see another container.

'20 minutes Maya,' said an electronic voice.

'Thanks,' she mumbled.

My vision was clearing and, as it did, so did the reality of my situation.

Right before my blinking eyes were over 40 large boxes stacked to the ceiling. The boxes were aligned neatly and I could tell from the way the boxes bulged that, inside them, were my shoes.

Thankfully not all of them. Lord knows they would've needed a bigger plane. But my entire San Dimas stash. And that's a lot of shoes by itself.

Further down the gangway some of the men were constructing a metal container panel by panel around the smaller boxes and I watched, transfixed.

With the rest of my sight returning slowly, I could see booted-feet all around me.

After a few more blinks, my eyes were fully open and I could see just how Maya may have pulled this all off.

Seated and belted up around the boxes were 30, steel toe boot wearing, buzz cut rocking, non-smiling beefcakes who all sat with their backs straight and their eyes forward. Most of them I recognised from previous Quincy memories. They all looked menacing as they were armed with shoulder holsters and ammo belts but no weapons. That

The Tall Tales of Tatiana Blue

part made me frown. I was wearing the same kind of holster and I had weapons in mine…

My eyes dropped to my arms and I felt that my weapons were gone. I tried to grind my back against the seat but there was no weapon stopping me from doing so. Which meant Maya had my weapons. MORE of my weapons.

'Where is she?' I rattled in a low raspy voice. 'Tell her she really needs to bring her fuck face of a…'

'Why I have to be a fuck face?' Maya replied, walking along the gangway towards me. 'What did I do to deserve that?'

I couldn't keep my eyebrows from rising. Did she really just ask me that?

'You don't even know how much I wanna fuck you up.'

'Yeah,' my old friend said casually. 'I do. I'd wanna fuck me up too. Like, if I was you right now, I'd wanna kill a bitch, you know?'

'Reading my mind are ya?'

Maya came and sat in the empty seat next to me, giving one of the beefcakes a piece of paper that he instantly took and walked away with.

She turned to me with one arm reaching behind me on the headrest. 'Look Tat, I know…'

'What do you know? What the fuck do you know?'

Mr Oh

Her face was close enough to me that if I could lunge forward, I could get my teeth around her cheek and not let go. My anger had me reaching for my baser animal instincts at this point.

Maya frowned while looking at my mouth and moving back.

'Listen, first of all, stop talking to me like I've done you something, alright? In the position you're in, I can see how it looks. The only thing I...'

I couldn't help the scoffing sound I made in the back of my throat as I looked around the cabin of the plane, making sure Maya could understand what I was trying to say with my eyes.

'The position I'm in?' I looked around to someone, anyone who could make me understand just what the flying fuck she was talking about.

So according to her, she was stealing MY shoes to help ME? What the fuck kinda logic is that? And she thinks that'll stop me from hitting her repeatedly in the face with my forearm?

Even though I've always got something to say, I was literally speechless. Looking into Maya's eyes while my kidnapped shoes were still being boxed next to us, how could she be acting like she hadn't crossed a line here? Maybe she wasn't used to the L.A. sun and was slightly delirious because from where I was sitting, she'd done the Electric Slide, the Moonwalk and the Nae Nae over the line.

A super loud crackle above my head broke the tension and I looked up.

'Landing in ten minutes. Wheels down in ten.'

The Tall Tales of Tatiana Blue

Maya stood up, brushing close enough past me that I could've bitten her. I didn't think she'd walk that close so I wasn't ready with my teeth.

'Sorry Tat, gotta go and talk to the boys. Be right back.'

'Sure, take your time babe,' I replied sarcastically. Wasn't like I was going to open a bottle of wine and enjoy an in-flight movie. I didn't even know where we were landing, let alone having any idea what Maya wanted to talk to the boys about.

She walked away with her curly hair bouncing behind her, somehow looking like she'd been working out. Her grey cat-suit with a black bomber jacket looked good on her. Was a weird feeling that I still thought my girlfriend looked good while wanting to fuck her up.

'BRING IT IN FELLAS!' Maya shouted.

The men sitting around me got up and walked to the back of the plane where Maya had gone. Some walked while others limped and frowned at me as they passed. They must've been the few I took down before I got caught slipping.

See, I told you not to be all kamikaze about it, now look at you... is this really the time for I told you so... but I did tell you... you know sometimes you can let some of them go ya know... I put in work on some of 'em though, did you see... alright alright, so how are we getting out of this one... I honestly don't know... neither do I...

Mr Oh

Talking to myself wasn't paying off the way it usually did because none of my voices had any bright ideas for me. All I had was the hope that I could hear what Maya was telling the guys and use that to get me the hell out of here and somewhere so I could start to make sense of it all.

I craned my neck as they gathered around Maya as the last container was built around my shoes.

'Almost... just need to... gather at... find your own... gloves at... making the call... took longer than I thought she would...'

'YOU TALKING ABOUT ME OVER THERE?' I shouted at the huddle but I didn't break the pep talk as they all laughed in unison without turning around.

My eyes drifted away from the itty bits I was picking up because none of them added up to anything in my head. My attention was on seeking a solution to my tied up predicament. That was the moment my eyes fell onto the metal container the men constructed in front of me. More importantly, the tiny silver square stuck to the side that beeped a constant red light.

'Maya's tracker!'

My eyebrows dropped and the muscles in my arms strained as I tried to reach for it. Duh.

How did... well she obviously found it... and she stuck it to my shoes... exactly... yeah but why would she fucking do that... it's like she wanted

The Tall Tales of Tatiana Blue

you to...well this doesn't make any sense... what kind of thief wants to be found...

Maya and her boys looked like a sexy, in-sync army as they broke from their huddle and walked towards me. She led them past me and winked. Her eyes lead to the tracker and she looked back to me.

'I know we look sexy don't we? Figured it out yet?' she asked me.

'Only thing I've figured out is which hand to slap you with first.'

'Oh babe, I can't wait to see the look on your face when...'

A low vibration rumbled in her pocket and she pulled out an iPhone, looked at the display and made sure I saw the smirk on her face as she turned around.

'We're coming in now... yeah, she's here... yeah not a good idea right now. Okay. See you soon... yeah I know, I'm shitting myself too.'

'Who you talking to? Is it that fuckboy Quincy? I GOT SOME HANDS FOR YOU TO CATCH TO Q-BALL, JUST WAIT!'

Maya covered the phone with her hands. 'Would you mind shutting the fuck up?'

I opened my eyes wide and tilted my head to the side. My look was screaming, 'has this crazy heifer lost her curly-haired mind?'

I'd never had a fight with Maya. Sure we trained together, although my sessions were more intense, but we never went one-on-one. We'd

Mr Oh

thrown jabs and blows but we never got, ya know Tyson-Holyfield with it. Soon as I got myself out of this maze of restraints, that was going to change. She had me under control, she'd successfully stolen from me – TWICE – and she had me transporting MY stolen shoes to where the fuck ever. The teacher was being schooled by the student.

With soldiers walking and limping to their seats around me, fastening seatbelts and nudging each other excitedly, Maya walked to the end of the long gangway. My stomach felt the plane descend drastically and I inhaled deeply.

'WE'RE ALMOST DONE BOYS... LET'S GET THIS FINAL PIECE DONE AND WE'LL BE HAVING BBQ BY EASTENDERS O'CLOCK!'

The men cheered and banged the fuselage of the plane as Maya's eyes met mine. Without speaking, I was asking her why. Her eyes replied with sorrow and her mouth a wry smile.

I was seriously missing something, I just hadn't figured out what.

She slammed a red button and the back of the plane rumbled with a loud siren and the gangway slowly opened. A thick, suffocating rush of air knocked me back against my seat. Squinting while my dreadlocks broke free and began to flow all over my face, I could barely see Maya, who was holding on to a metal pipe while looking out to the ground below.

'DROP NOW NOW NOW...' a voice said over the PA system.

The Tall Tales of Tatiana Blue

My attention followed the voice then switched to Maya who pressed another button. Before I could connect anything with anything, the metal boxes of my shoes slid quickly down the gangway and out of the plane. There were no ropes, chains or anything attached to them, they just fell the fuck out of the plane. I felt tears instantly well up in my eyes as the second large container slid off the gangway and disappeared out of my line of sight.

'MY FUCKING SHO... OH MY SHIT...' I looked straight to Maya with fire burning in my eyes.

My friend looked at me with her index finger over her lips.

At that moment right there, I calmed down.

Watching my shoes go flying out the back of a plane was the final straw and I had no more anger to expel. It all sucked internally and my frown turned to a normal stare as I sat up straight and looked ahead of me.

I cut my eyes to Maya, who was watching me intently, then cut back to the pencil-neck in the Primark t-shirt who was sitting in front of me. We locked eyes as the gangway began to close and he looked away as my stare bored through him.

Taking another deep descent that tickled my ovaries, I heard what sounded like the wheels rolling out and braced for landing. While holding a face of serenity, my insides were yelling, 'where are we landing, how can we be landing already, where have my shoes gone, why steal my shoes just to drop 'em out of a fucking plane over wherever'.

Mr Oh

Maya found a seat near the door and strapped herself in while my face was as calm as morning ocean waves but inside, oooooooh, I was screaming and kicking shit all over my happy place. Something in my friend's face said she knew what was going on inside me as she refused to make any more eye contact with me.

Best thing really.

We hit the ground suddenly with a massive jolt. The plane must've hit the tarmac and become airborne again as we all bounced twice before shaking along as the engines kicked in and we began to slow down.

Some people applauded but most began unbuckling their belts and collecting bags, clothes and hand radios.

I sat there looking up at 'em all like, fuck all of you! So fucking happy that they stole from an independent, motivated black woman who was doing her thing and minding her own business.

But that was all okay. I had been memorising faces since I hit the fourth hangar so I'd already made it my mission to find every single one of these fuckers and burn their lives to the ground.

The plane came to a sharp halt and the gangway began to open. The men walked off the plane in conversation into bright sunlight as if nothing insane just happened. I expected them to be ducking for cover under a hail of falling Louboutin and Brian Atwood heels but they all walked calmly.

I wanted to frown because, NOTHING WAS MAKING FUCKING SENSE.

The Tall Tales of Tatiana Blue

WHERE WERE MY SHOES? YOU CAN'T JUST DROP SHOES OUT OF A FUCKING PLANE AND THEY JUST DISAPPEAR!?

'Come on you,' Maya said walking towards me. I didn't notice the keys jingling in her hand because I was lost in a daydream of dislocating my own shoulder and using the extra leverage to rip out her throat with my teeth.

She stood on a seat more than two spaces away from me and unlocked something and I instantly felt slack on my wrists.

'There's one,' Maya mumbled.

She carefully shuffled under my seat and unlocked something that created more slack.

'There's two,' she said. 'I'll let you do three.'

Standing up and walking away, she threw the keys over her shoulder and didn't look back as they skidded close to my feet.

My arms came from around my back and I was free. Except for the chain that was secured around my waist which I didn't see until just now. Totally screwed my plan of jumping up from the seat and rushing Maya with a spear to the mid-section.

'I'll be here when you're ready.'

Grabbing the keys and looking up, I felt my hips for the lock then sourced the key with the process of elimination. I was trying not to get frustrated as every key seemed to be wrong while I was so close to two things; one, getting some answers and two, getting my hands around Maya's trachea.

It felt like I tried every key twice with no luck. In trying to remain calm, I was getting more flustered with the keys.

A low, concentrated grunt erupted from the pit of my stomach.

'Key with the pink on it,' Maya shouted. Very calmly for someone who was about to need surgery.

Locating the right key, you have no idea how I exhaled when the lock clicked open and the chain fell away from me. I rubbed my wrists, rolled my arms, massaged my shoulders and circled my neck while straightening my back. Pins and needles tingled to my fingertips and I flicked and rolled my wrists.

I let out the biggest sigh. It was like I didn't realise how constrained I was until I was free from the restraints. I'll give Maya her props: she tied me up nicely. I taught her well.

See, how can I be proud of her and about to fuck her up at the same time?

My hands rested on my knees and I slowly rose to feet. My legs were dead and needed a bit of stripper shaking all about to bring them back to life.

'One sec, I'll be right there, okay? Don't move!' I said without looking at anything but my thick thighs.

The Tall Tales of Tatiana Blue

'I'm here!'

For my final stretch, I raised my arms above my head and stretched as high as I could. I lifted off the heels of my feet and stood on my toes as I counted to ten before releasing and smiling.

'There you go… yummy,' I mumbled to myself.

One quarter pivot and I was walking down the gangway towards Maya who had a rucksack on her back and was looking to the sky with her hands over her eyes.

She took no notice of me as I calmly huffed and puffed and was about to blow her clart down.

'Isn't technology a beautiful thing? I mean, we're old school so we remember four channels and teletext but the things people can do today, it's amazing.'

I was cracking my knuckles while she was having a wonder of the times moment. Whatever the fuck she was looking at was of no importance to me. What did matter was probably scattered along the ground of wherever the fuck we…

'Where are we?!' I demanded with my footsteps getting heavier as I got closer.

'Biggins Hill,' Maya said, still looking up over the plane into the sky.

'LONDON? We're home?'

Mr Oh

As if things weren't already confusing. How did we get back here so quickly? Far as I remember, I went kamikaze then woke up chained up In San Dimas.

Hold on, how long was I out for?

'Yes ma'am. Home sweet home.'

'Good. Not too far from home.'

Those were the last words I said before walking to within striking distance of Maya's face. My left/right two-piece swung at her but she leaned backwards and watched as my fists past in front of her face. I caught myself quickly as so not to stumble but Maya was still looking up.

'At least look before we do this,' Maya pointed, letting her rucksack slide off her back to the ground.

'Fine, I can wait to... what the flying...?'

'Technology sugar.'

My eyes had seen some weird and wonderful things in their time but this was something I thought I'd only see in a Marvel film. The two metal containers that went flying out of the plane were hovering slowly in a row. I could see small puffs of gas pump out of the containers from the top and the bottom as they got lower and further into the distance.

'How is that... what did you... who the fuck is doi...'

'Fight first, talk after?'

The Tall Tales of Tatiana Blue

I wasn't sure where Maya had picked up this sudden burst of energy and command but it threw me. The Maya I knew was willing to go to war for a shoe but wasn't willing to lead the charge into battle. Being a part-time version of me, Maya wanted the shoes but she didn't have the same taste for satisfaction that I always felt when someone richer and stupider than me had such amazing shoes and probably didn't appreciate them the way I would. More importantly, how the shoes deserved to be appreciated. But that's for another story. Basically, Maya learned how to do what she does from me, thus she is beneath me so her current demeanour was offending me and I had to whup her for the disrespect. In a nutshell.

I put my hands up, palms open and began to circle my best friend as she did the same. Her eyes weren't as angry as mine but she still owned a steely stare that told me she wouldn't just let me pummel her and get away with it.

'Thought we were bitches, huh? What happened to that?' I asked, making her flinch by flicking my wrists.

'We are babe. Always have been and always will be,' Maya replied staying on the tips of her toes. 'Beauties in tremendously cute heels for life.'

Yeah keep her talking… so we can hold her attention… then we'll… yeah we'll come in with the distraction slap.

'There's nothing beautiful about what you did to me.'

Mr Oh

'Still haven't figured it out have you Tat?'

Thinking she would be strictly on defence, I was almost caught by a neat jab, jab, right cross from Maya as she slid out of my space and back to her arm's length distance. My neck was on Ali status as I dipped to the left and the right.

A part of me became strongly offended that Maya would even throw any sort of punch when she was the one who...

'FIGURED OUT WHAT?' I shouted.

Frustration was coursing through me because I had Maya in front of me and she still wasn't bleeding. I still hadn't put a hand on her and she wasn't wincing from a wealth of strategically placed body shots that were designed to hurt hours later.

Where the fuck are my shoes flying to... that Quincy sure does have some toys...

I lead in with a straight kick followed by a swinging arm which missed her by inches as I felt my hand separate her hair. I stopped in motion and switched my momentum, catching her going back the way she came. My hand caught her shoulder but she was quick to bring her arm in and swing it in a circle, turning my potential arm grab into a reach for her clothes. Again, she was out of my body space at a safe distance looking at me with resignation.

The Tall Tales of Tatiana Blue

'Why I stole your shoes. Still haven't figured it out. Out of all your stash houses, you don't think about why those particular two?'

'Don't care. All I know is that the shoes that I individually put in there were last seen flying somewhere over Bromley.'

In the distance, I could hear the thunderous roar of the cargo plane beginning to take off while we were still circling each other on the runway. One or two soldiers were on the outskirts of the private airport with their fingers locked to the railings watching two of the fittest, sexiest shoes thieves go at it.

'Use your number six Tat.'

I hated when Maya told me to use my number six. Usually I'd laugh it off as I never took offence to it but today, at this particular moment, it pissed me the fuck off. I mean, your brain isn't a sense so how is it your sixth sense? Asks the woman who talks to herself.

In her direction, I took a half skip and inhaled before throwing a mad combination of punches at her. I mixed from jabs and crosses to forehand and backhanders and leg kicks while screaming my rage out. My mind was busy at the same time. Why did Maya hit those particular stash houses though? She knows I've got four in London, hell she spends more time there than me trying on shoes and sitting amongst them with pride. Things I used to enjoy doing when I had the time.

I can't see them any more... where are they going... I can't tell, it looks like they're going towards the city... I need to hit this woman for fuck sake...

Mr Oh

Such was my fury of my hands, I didn't know if I was even hitting her. My thinking was 'throw 'em at her and see what hits'. I could hear her grunting while she was defending but, with her arms crossed in front of her face and torso (very Dragonball Z like) I had no more energy left.

I know this makes me seem like all the talk about Tatiana Blue being this bad boy fighter is bollocks but you have to allow me. I hadn't trained properly in months, I'm still carrying a LOT of baby weight and I'm not as tight in places as I used to. And Mount Street. And Marcus. And the madness at the hangar. I've been doing the most out here.

Still tight in the important place though.

'Are you through?' Maya asked as she came out of her defence stance.

'Soon as I... catch my...' There was no way I was catching my breath anytime soon.

I'd been more ninja when taking on the soldier-types she had with her but now I felt lethargic, drained, like I was fighting with weights on.

'You ready for the story morning glory?'

I looked at Maya, still confused as to why she was still so chipper and upbeat about everything. With the level of foul she reached with her actions, how was she still in a rhyming words space?

'Where are my shoes?' I asked tiredly, wishing I was still in bed.

'Bromley Common by now.'

The Tall Tales of Tatiana Blue

I swung with my left, countered with my right and went low for a body shot which she wasn't ready for and she stumbled backwards with pain on her face. 'Wrong answer. Where are my shoes?'

She chuckled, coughed and bent over. 'Wow, nice shot. Okay, are we done now? Cuz we have somewhere to be.'

The balls of this woman! Disrespected me beyond all belief, had me chasing her across the world and she was laughing. Was I missing the joke? Obviously because I was becoming calmer with each passing second.

My shoes just floated off into London for crying out loud!

I set my feet. One foot in front of the other in order to get a good push off so I could rush her to the ground before going Rhonda Rousey on her.

'BEFORE... you do that,' Maya said stepping back further with a hand out. 'Listen to this first.'

She pulled out her phone and held it in front of my face like it was supposed to calm me down. I must've been foaming at the mouth the way she looked at me but I didn't care.

A voice on the phone said hello.

I was in a sprinter's stance with my left fist cocked and ready to pop but I took the phone with my right and held it to my ear without taking my eyes off Maya who was still looking mighty smug.

Mr Oh

'Do YOU know where my shoes are?' I asked, not caring who I was talking to.

'Hey lover!'

The voice made my fist soften and my eyebrow raise up.

'Russell? No fuc... RUSSELL?!'

'Look, before you go apeshi...'

I instantly found it funny. At first a giggle then a chuckle which grew into a laugh which transformed into full blown evil genius realising his fool-proof plan cackle.

'Russell, Russell, Russell!'

That devious fuck! Here I was SUPPOSED to spend the rest of my high-heeled days with this guy and he... I knew it. I fucking knew it. Didn't I know it? Didn't I say it was him?

Something in my body language must've changed because Maya was no longer so far away from me and my fist was no longer balled.

'I think the best thing will be to...'

'Whoa, hold the fuck on... where is my daughter?'

'She's here, don't worry, say hi to mummy.'

Charlotte gurgled softly and I exhaled. Not that I thought she may be in danger but, with my whole entire world seemingly turning on me, I needed to know.

The Tall Tales of Tatiana Blue

'I'm coming for you Russell.'

'Yeah yeah yeah, I know. Just tell Maya if she wants to see it, she's gonna have to kick speed right now.'

Suddenly, a black Audi A4 pulled up to a wheel spinning halt. With the phone on my ear, I watched a man in green overalls jump out, throw the keys to Maya and take off running towards the hangars he came from.

'I told you from the start that if I found out...'

'I know baby but once you know what is...'

'No baby here double R, I'm going to find you, cuz I know where you live and...'

'I won't be hard to find, Maya is bringing you to me right now.'

My old friend, who was holding her ribs and sucking air through her teeth, opened the driver door and leaned on the roof of the car.

'Let's go... I don't wanna miss it. She's got a neat head start too.'

I had no fucking idea what was going on around me, which is weird because I'm Tatiana Blue. I'm calculated, observant, ridiculously skilled, nimble, and as sexy as Jill Scott's voice and the best shoe thief to ever walk this earth but I was stuck for answers. Nothing made sense. Again. Maya kept telling me to think about it but I couldn't find any answers among the heel clicks of confused information I was trying to calculate in my brain.

So, as far as I could tell, Russell, Quincy, Maya and a whole bunch of soldier-types were involved in this whole cacadoody idea to steal from

Mr Oh

ME!? I mean, really, am I not just the wrong bitch to think you could do that to and get away with it?

'Your shit is in the car already, let's go!'

My anger was slowly abating. The tenseness I'd built up ready to rush Maya was throbbing away and the livid in me was being taken over by perplexity.

I'd broken another hairband as my dreads draped around me like a cloak while I was looking at the phone. Russell just hung up on me, like that wasn't salt on the insult.

'Get in, come on Tat.'

What, were we friends again? Did she not just steal my shoes or was I losing my mind?

My face was still a mix of vexation and confusion as I got in, tossed Maya's phone into her lap and quickly grabbed her ear, pulling her towards me. Her whole head followed and I twisted for extra emphasis.

'Are YOU REALLY PULLING MY EAR?' she asked in pain.

'Where are my shoes?'

'Currently being driven to London Bridge... look could you... owwwwww...'

'Why London Bridge?'

'Because that's where it's gonna... owwwww for fuck sake, get off...'

I saw her hands coming and locked them down with one hand.

The Tall Tales of Tatiana Blue

'Where's what gonna?'

'OWW... owwwwww... shiiiiiiit... where you're gonna die!'

My hand released her ear lobe before I even sent the command. She was rubbing her ear and giving me dirty looks while I was lost in another realm of confusion.

There's a lot of confusion going on here folks, believe me.

'Lemme rephrase that,' Maya said turning over the key and revving the engine. 'It's where they THINK you're gonna die!'

She pulled off from the runway so quickly, my passenger door closed by itself. She whipped onto a side road, pulled up to the security barrier, showed a pass and was flying down the A233 towards Bromley Common before I could even manage anything that resembled words.

Kill who... kill you... I wish a bitch would try and kill me... that's what I'm saying...

'Are you lot for real?' I turned in my seat. 'Start from the top of the beginning of this fucked up story.'

Maya sighed, giving my hands a quick glance before looking at the road ahead.

'You know what started all this?'

Mr Oh

My head turned towards her but there was nothing in my face that said I was ready to play 20 questions. I was still bathing in a lot of energy that was leaning towards punching her in the face.

'Mount Street.'

'Louboutin store?' I frowned, unsure how last night's last shoe tryst, which happened to be my first in nearly a year, had anything to do with my shoes being stolen and my death being arranged.

'Yeppers, that's the one,' Maya said, taking a quick look over her shoulder before taking an illegal turn on a roundabout, leaving horns honking behind us.

'I don't have any of my tasers to hand Maya but I swear, all it takes is one pinch and you're...'

'They're in the boot. Okay, okay. Remember Jamal and Femi, the two police officers...'

Answers weren't coming quick enough for me as I cut Maya off.

'Yeah, Russell's friends. I told him about those two... well, he told me... anyway, yeah so?'

'Okay... you have to promise you won't be mad at me.'

I hadn't even heard what she was going to say and I was already boiling back up to my fist clenched anger level. That's like someone starting a sentence with, "I'm not racist but..."

'Maya, look, you are skating on white girl booty thin ice right now so I suggest you tell me everything!'

The Tall Tales of Tatiana Blue

She hunched her shoulders and looked at me from the corner of her eyes.

I had no idea what she had to tell me but the delay told me that whatever it was could have the potential to royally piss me off. Like I wasn't already pissed off.

Two flights, a helicopter ride, blue limousine, stolen shoes, some one-on-one with some dudes, tasered a fat dude on a plane, too much bloody heat, itchy as fuck, best friend turned snake turned possible friend again. And all of this in the last 24 hours!?

I was tired and I just wanted to go home, let my dreads loose and have Russell lay on my back with his weight keeping me pinned to the bed.

'Whose idea was it?' I threw in before Maya could talk again.

'Huh?'

'Who had the idea to do this? Who had the VERY first idea?'

'Hold on, before I tell you that, you have to hear what led up to...'

I had to turn away from looking at Maya as we sped through Croydon. It was the best thing to do as my nerves were way past shredded and on their way back from the dead.

'Maya... SUGAR... there's still a bit of love in here for you,' I said tapping my chest. 'But... SOMEONE NEEDS TO TELL ME WHAT THE FUCK IS GOING ON!'

As I shouted, I slammed the dashboard with both my hands and Maya swerved the car. She corrected her over-turning and pulled over to the

Mr Oh

side of the road. We both sat there for a little in silence. Not looking at each other, just breathing.

See, when I say we are best friends, I mean that truly. Why do you think she got to write the first chapter in this book? Cuz she's my girl. Well was, I don't know any more. All I do know is Maya was looking at me like she was thought I was going to gut her like salmon and sell her organs on the black market.

Wasn't a bad idea but I hadn't been on the black market for a while so, too much hassle.

Maya reached into her bomber jacket and pulled out a pair of black thick-rimmed glasses. She looked at them, blew the lenses and held them out to me.

'Put those on.'

'I don't wear gla... Maya, I'm starting to get really...'

'PUT THEM ON!' Maya demanded. 'You want answers, put them on.'

I snatched the glasses.

'Really, snatching?' Maya said, pulling away from the pavement and back into the light traffic.

'Stealing shoes from me, really?'

'Touché, but mine was justified.'

'HOW THE...'

'Put. Them. ON!' Maya cut me off.

The Tall Tales of Tatiana Blue

For a quick moment, we shared a smile together but as quick as it arrived, the moment was gone.

'What am I supposed to do with these?'

'PUT. THEM. ON. FOR. FUCK'S. SAKE!'

'Why? Are they gonna give me a *Men in Black* flash or something?'

Maya stuck her arm out of her window and gave someone a very stern finger, followed by some mumbled words about the driver's mother.

'You want answers. There they are.'

For the way the last few hours went, I wasn't in a trusting mood. But I was also tired as fuck so I didn't think anything else could go THAT wrong from where I was sitting.

I stared at the glasses, feeling the car going faster than the local speed limit.

'Camera,' I said pointing at the yellow box we were about to pass.

'Not my car,' she replied and picked up speed.

The speed camera flashed but Maya didn't flinch, she just kept driving at the same speed, overtaking on both sides of the road and jumping lights.

She looked at me. 'Come on. What can you see?'

Mr Oh

Her excitement was making me more nervous but it was also making me more intrigued. I couldn't see any holes in the frame that could hide a secret syringe or gas outlet that could poison or knock me out.

I slid them slowly over my eyes, waiting for something to click so I could take them off again. But nothing happened. The lenses weren't prescription and everything looked the same.

Right before my eyes, the world in front of me faded to black and was replaced with a view that was no longer my own.

'HOLY GLOB!'

'What can you see?' Maya asked.

'Shiiiit… what am I looking at?'

'Can you see…?'

'It's like I can see through someone else's eyes. Where is this? Who is this?'

'Tatiana… meet Aries.'

Suddenly a hand, that wasn't my own, appeared before my eyes and held a single thumb up. I swear, I had to move my own thumbs just a little bit to make sure it wasn't me.

'Who?'

'Sorry, I should've said it properly. Tatiana Blue, meet Tatiana Blue.'

That made me choke on the little saliva I had in my throat.

The Tall Tales of Tatiana Blue

'I beg your fucking pardon?!'

'She is you.'

'Erm, no the fuck she's not!'

Maya did a sudden turn down a side road. 'Fucking traffic. Look, I tried to tell you before you got all loud and Connor McGregor. We're doing an Aunt Viv' with your shoes.'

My head was turning, trying to look around the cabin of the vehicle but I remembered that it wasn't my view I was seeing. The one called Aries or the other Tatiana Blue was driving something big on a relatively empty road somewhere. No houses or cars, just gravel.

'An Aunt Vi... but how can you do an... OHHHH!!!'

Suddenly, the entire escapade made sense.

For those of you not hip, me and Maya have code names for the different types of scams, operations and jobs we have to pull in order to get shoes. It's not all stealing from the stockroom of shops. Sometimes we had to pull off elaborate-style slick shit moves in order to get some of our shoes. We'd have to deal with celebrities and designers stepping up their security, moving their design workshops, etc. Plus it's easier to say 'let's do a Porkpie' or 'let's do a Lupalinda'.

So, an Aunt Viv' is a classic switcheroo. Simple and easy. Pull a switch with a random patsy who has no idea what's going on and have the authorities chase THEM while I get away sweetly and scot-freely. Obviously, with different situations, the Aunt Viv' changes but that's basically it.

Mr Oh

My confusion lay in how they were going to pull off the switch and then it hit me. There is no switch.

Maya said before that we were going somewhere where 'they thought' I was going to die.

Who thinks I'm gonna die... I don't know I'm watching it like you... who's gonna care if I die or not... I'm confused... me too, I bet Quincy hooked up the glasses though... you KNOW he did. This is right up his alley... no but for real though, what the glob is going on?

Her phone rang through the car and I lifted the glasses.

'Yeah?'

'She's ready. I'm ready. Are you ready?' Russell said.

The sound of his voice annoyed me and aroused me at the same time. There was a certain authority in his voice which was missing before which had me listening to his every word.

Maya looked at me. 'You ready?"'

'Anyone wanna tell me where my shoes are yet?'

'Put the glasses back on. We're ready. Probably about five minutes behind her. Call it.'

'Keep your eyes open. Okay, see you soon.'

The Tall Tales of Tatiana Blue

He hung up and Maya gripped the wheel stronger than before and drove with solid purpose. Her eyes were watching the road carefully and she paid me no attention as I lowered the glasses back onto my face.

My sight was now taken by Aries who was driving a truck with ease. She was looking in her mirrors a lot more and I noticed a sign directing her to London Bridge.

A loud cackle of sound exploded in the car and I jumped. Before I could take the glasses off, I could hear the monotone drawl of a police officer.

'Officer to control, we have a reported sighting of Tatiana Blue. Repeat Tatiana Blue has been spotted...'

'Where OVER...' another voice asked.

'Heading towards London Bridge sarge... get EVERYONE on this NOW...'

In all the commotion that was going on and the abuse my senses were taking, I was still trying to piece together what was going on, what part everyone played and how this was going to play out. There was so much happening, I didn't know where to put my attention.

Hearing my name over the radio, through the speakers, was throwing me off as I could see the hands and arms of someone else who began to respond to the wail of sirens that rang out in the distance.

I could hear the sirens. There were a lot of them and I couldn't even tell you where they were coming from. A low, distant rumble said that a helicopter had also been deployed.

Mr Oh

In my sight, Aries was still looking through all her mirrors as she passed Monument station.

The radio was going crazy. A report from the helicopter pilot came in to say he was airborne, another helicopter pilot chimed in to say he was in the area, Waltham Forest, Lewisham, Islington and City police all said they were sending cars and someone with an authoritative voice yelled to get Russell on the phone.

Aries pulled the truck out of the line of cars she was in, drove on the other side of the road and ran a red light making cars swerve behind her. Crossing a junction, she looked left as a police car came zooming towards her.

Above, I could hear the low helicopter passing as we were still speeding on the approach to Borough train station. The car slowed down but Aries was pushing the truck hard. I could see from her strong gears changes and quick turns that she was moving at speed. It was a wonder she hadn't hit anyone.

'We've spotted her sarge... just pulled up behind the truck, she's not stopping, repeat she is not stopping. She's turning right on Upper Thames Street... DON'T YOU FUCKING LOSE HER...'

Sirens blared from every which way. I lifted the glasses a few times to watch six police cars and four full vans fly past us and, to be honest, I felt mighty proud. I mean, look at the turnout for me. Little old steal a couple thousand pairs of shoes me.

The Tall Tales of Tatiana Blue

People on the street were watching the cars and vans with their sirens blaring, all rushing together. Coupled with the helicopters above, I sure did have London's attention.

'Reed here, what's going on?'

Russell's voice rumbled low through the speakers and I lifted the glasses to look at Maya who was already looking at me.

My eyebrows screwed down.

Maya's eyebrows raised. 'D'you get it now?'

I tuned my ears into the multiple conversations going on over the police scannner about me.

'We're in pursuit… of Tatiana Blue. She slipped up, but we've got her. She's driving a truck around London Bridge. We've got visual confirmation of shoes, possibly stolen, in her possession and since you're the only one who's seen… does she have dreadlocks?'

I leaned closer to the radio, hanging on the suspense of Russell's question.

Sliding the glasses onto my forehead again, I watched Aries lean out of the window and look up towards the helicopter above before putting her attention back on the road.

'Pilot confirms dreadlocks…'

'It's her!' Russell said, his voice full of menace and pride.

'Oh shit…' I slipped out.

Mr Oh

Aries made a strong turn that forced her to lean with the truck as it held the road onto Southwark Bridge.

Maya was pressing forward, forcing the car to swerve around other vehicles, cutting into the empty bus lane during operations hours and barely missing pedestrians who cursed as she pulled off.

Aries had run out of road according to the plastic barriers that blocked both ends of the bridge. But she didn't stop and, instead, picked up more speed. Watching her change gears, check her mirrors and pick up even more speed made me real nervous for someone I didn't even know. But seeing what she was seeing made the ride all the more exciting. Sizing up her decision making and all that.

'Look,' Maya said, turning down the crackling radio that was lively with reports of people claiming to have seen me. The car stopped and I lifted the glasses and got out with Maya. Pedestrians and other drivers were running to the wall of London Bridge as they listened and watched police car after police van follow the truck which was barrelling down the bridge with no signs of stopping.

Glasses down, I couldn't see Aries' hands on the steering wheel but I could see out of the windscreen and according to how fast she was going, she did not plan to stop.

Then all I could see was sky.

Maya nudged me sharply, I lifted the glasses again and looked up to see the truck in the distance take to the air over the side of the bridge.

I inhaled a second after everyone else and slid the glasses off my head.

The Tall Tales of Tatiana Blue

My eyes were horror movie wide open and recoiled like someone kicked a ball at me.

The truck seemed to hover in the air for what seemed like forever. Whatever propelled the eight-wheeled truck had given it an arch of height that literally made it point up before dropping towards the water.

'Keep watching, this is the money shot,' Maya said, leaning towards my ear.

Nothing was registering with me at that moment. All I could think about was what's gonna happen to…

And then came the money shot. Out of fucking nowhere, the truck's back doors blew open and shoes shot out as the water cascaded in a huge wave. The truck sounded like a deep plop in the water but the splash that followed was massive.

Forget all that though. Ask me what my face looked like watching all my fothermucking shoes drowning in the River Thames!? Ask me how hard I was gripping Maya's arm as over 3,000 pairs of shoes began to bob in the dirty, nasty ass Thames water. Ask me!?

I dare you!?!

I don't 'ucking believe it… is that my Sergio Matrix, oh God, there's my D'Orsay metallic pumps… yes I saw… I wanna cry. Look at my Weitzman mule sandals, my Zanotti booties… yes I see… how can they jus… oh God my Choo Kayden sandals, I'm done…

Mr Oh

Then it hit me, hard and comically. 'Oh... shiiiiiiiiiiiit!'

When I tell you the laughter that came out of me at that moment was disgusting. Full on Sid James, Frank Butcher vulgar type laughter. Then I was just... stuck. I didn't know what to do or say or think or who should I be tasering first. With every ball of anger that would begin to roll inside me, a fresh layer of understanding would come in and unravel. Every train of thought started with violence but ended in a sane, yet still confused, understanding.

Maya was looking around at the crowd, who were now staring at me hunched over in my filthy laughter.

'SHIT! What about Aries?' I asked no-one in particular then turned back to the wall of the bridge to see the end of the truck submerge and shoes bubble up to the brown, murky, icky surface.

'Let's go... NOW!'

Sensing the tone, I put my head down and quickly got back in the car where Maya turned up the radio again.

'Yeah she's gone over Southwark bridge... did you say gone OVER the bridge... get me some water boys out there as soon as possible... block off the bridge from both ends and keep the press... the press are already at the scene sarge... then cordon off all surrounding streets, if she's dead I wanna see her body... sarge, from up here, I haven't seen anyone come up...'

The Tall Tales of Tatiana Blue

Pulling an illegal U-turn, making the car bounce and bop as she forced the wheels over a median, Maya changed to second gear and was driving back the way we came.

I literally felt like I'd just watched a film and the heavy set-piece action scene was over. I was breathless.

'Now what?' I said, still not knowing what to say while unanswered questions were rising in my mind.

'Now, we eat!'

Maya turned the radio down and was driving with a smile.

'Okay, so I'm getting it that stealing my shoes wasn't supposed to be you just stealing my shoes, I think!?'

'Don't worry your dreadlock rasta clart. You'll get all the answers from YA MAN.'

Russell... that lying... caring... oh don't give me that. I'm trying not to hate him... and I'm thinking about fucking him... see, this is why we don't get anything done... go my way and at least one thing will be done... you are too nasty... tell me I'm lying though... yeah, could use some stress relief... answers first...

Hearing Russell in full-on police mode, his voice deeper and sterner, turned me on just that little lot of a bit. But there was the other side of

Mr Oh

me that was thinking about the logistics of the wild goose chase they sent me on. And why? And how? Like how did...

'I know you have lots of questions you wanna ask and I would, but, it's such a long story and I'm absolutely marvin' right now. Like, I feel weak. And you know I can't concentrate when I'm weak.'

She's right, she can't. Maya can be a bit of scatter brain at the best of times but when she's hungry, just make sure you have a Snickers nearby because she'll start to sound and move like Eeyore. And she'll become slightly deaf. Weird to see but strangely fascinating too.

I didn't answer. I was too far gone in plotting my entire journey up to this point but trying to think of it from a planning perspective. From where I was sitting, a lot of what happened was down to me making a choice and seeing it through. So how could they have planned for me to make random choices and still manage to end up where it all finished?

My face must've looked like I was doing Joey maths (I'm a huge *Friends* head so Joey maths is the confused look you have on your face when you try and divide 232 by 13.)

'Here we go,' Maya said loudly. Her excited voice pulled me out of my trance just at the same time she pulled the handbrake to turn off the main road. She spun the wheel with one hand into a railway arch and floated sideways through thick grey plastic curtains that bounced over the car.

I flinched slightly. To be honest, it looked like a wall to me so my hands came up to protect my face. Like that would do anything.

'Shut up!' I said to Maya without looking. I know she was smiling.

The Tall Tales of Tatiana Blue

'Whaaaaaaaaatt?' she said with a chuckle. 'Oh, there's the wheelbarrow.'

She began counting railway arch doors. 'One, two, three, four, four and a... AH HAAA.'

I wished my hands were in front of my face as she stepped on the brake quicker than I was ready for. My body swung forward and my forehead hit the dash before swinging roughly to my seat.

'Seatbelt,' she said, reminiscent of the game we'd play on jobs together. 'We're here.'

I had to punch her three times in the same spot for that. I shot forward so fast, my hair cascaded around my face.

'Where?' I said holding my forehead.

Don't know if you've ever been to the viaducts under London Bridge but, they're kinda manky. Old bricks that look like they will give at any second, mice, grime, probably asbestos floating around here somewhere too.

A train rumbled overhead and sounded like a jet engine as I opened the door, looking around cautiously. Things still weren't 100% making sense so I was still on my guard.

Thinking about my tasers in the boot, I wanted to reach for one and hold it in the palm of my hand. Just in case. I always feel better with a taser in my hand. Or in my bag, or tucked into my hair.

'Let's go... I'm starting to go deaf.'

Mr Oh

What'd I tell ya? She's at the last stage of hunger.

Standing in front of a brick work arch with blue awnings and a brown door, I wasn't sure what was supposed to happen next. I sure as hell couldn't smell any food and Maya was looking weary on her feet. She approached the door while taking a set of keys out of her pocket. Watching her shaky hand search for the key, I thought I heard a voice.

My hair flicked and caught me in the face.

'What?' Maya said looking at me from over her shoulder.

'I heard a voice.'

'That's your voice'

'No dip shit, a male voice.'

The door opened and Maya walked through the door into complete darkness without hesitating. I stood back and watched. All I could see was black. No glimmer of light or reflection, nothing. I wasn't even sure if there was a floor in there.

'Come onnn...' Maya echoed from inside.

'Can't you turn a light on...' I worked myself up.

My first step went through the door, my second took me into pitch black. The door closed behind me as a crescendo of sirens drove past and I jumped in the darkness. I know I didn't close it because I was thinking leave it in open just in case I need to get the hell out of there.

The Tall Tales of Tatiana Blue

Instinct told me to crouch low and feel the room. No point standing straight up hoping to walk into something.

'Where the fuck is the light in here? Maya?'

Silence replied.

I had my hands out in front of me scanning the darkness for something that would give me a picture of what type of room I'd just walked into.

'SURPRISE!!!'

A big ass shiny bright light came from out of nowhere to accompany the extremely loud eight letter word that made me jump clean into the air with my legs going in a difference of opinion. Though I couldn't see clearly, I could make out bodies all around me.

Shielding my eyes from the light, I squinted enough to make out lots of t-shirts, shorts and thick thighs.

'Hey honey, welcome back! How was your trip?'

Russell Reed had his arms out and was walking towards me holding two short glasses of a something pink and sparkly.

The room erupted in applause as he careful put his arms around me and hugged me with all the muscles in his body, while making sure not to spill anything on me. My eyes, which finally adjusted to the light, locked onto what looked like a buffet of food, another table of drinks and a very big screen TV that was showing the news, which had gone into a 'NEWS JUST IN' report.

'This is for you... everyone, go eat. Me and the missus need to have words.'

I took the drink from him, knocked it back in three large sips, gave him the glass and looked at him with scathing eyes.

'Oh, you THINK?!'

Whatever was in that glass tasted like heaven and fruit and warm alcoholy goodness and was definitely something I needed another two of. I took the other drink from him and knocked it back the same way.

'Same again. Chop chop.'

Russell gave me a dirty look before disappearing into the throng of people I started to recognise from the cargo plane. I scanned the crowd and found the nine lucky gents who had the pleasure of thinking I wasn't living that violent life.

'Hey,' Maya whispered behind me.

Turning around quickly, I heard Charlotte giggle before I saw her face and I broke down. Don't ask me why I started crying but the tears streamed uncontrollably.

I'm not one of those over emotionally dramatic people but for some reason, after the night/day/night and day again that I had, seeing my baby again was just too much.

The Tall Tales of Tatiana Blue

I scooped my beautiful chocolate wonder miracle from Maya's arms as she jogged off towards a long table of food. There was a LONG pause as I could see Russell had my child in a 'My daddy's a policeman' baby-grow. I had to laugh.

'Hello you. Hello beautiful you! Did you miss your Mummy? Yeah I missed you too. Did Daddy do a good job looking after you? Am I possibly gonna have to kill Daddy? Maybe tase him on his nipples? Hope not, we quite like him don't we? Yes we do...'

Russell appeared holding two drinks and was leading me towards a door that led off from the main room.

He walked first through the door, turned on the light and held the door open for us. 'After you mama and baby.'

'No, no, no... you don't get to do that!'

'Do what?'

Look at him, all innocent and handsome and shit... focus, its answer time... I'm focusing on that mouth though, you mean to tell me after going to Greece AND L.A. for NOTHING, you don't wanna fuck the shit out of his face... that... yeah and squirt in his eyes... is neither here nor there...

I nestled Charlotte close to my chest and covered her ear.

Mr Oh

'You don't get to say sweet shit, romantic shit or any type of Joe, Barry White, Jodeci shit, okay? All I need to hear from you is what the fuck?'

We'd walked into what looked like an abandoned office equipped with metal desk, dusty filing cabinets, grimy sofa and what looked like blood stains on the floor.

Russell had two clean chairs which didn't fit this room and he unfolded them and put them in front of each other while Charlotte's drowsy eyes blinked at me.

I slowly sat down. 'Daddy's been a naughty prick hasn't he? Yes he has!'

'Daddy played mummy!'

My neck snaked. 'Why don't you start at the part where someone said to someone, "hey, let's steal shoes from Tatiana Blue".'

'Well if Tatiana Blue wants the truth...'

'Careful, you know I like it when you say my name,' I said quickly and angrily.

'It's your fault all this happened in the first place!'

'Maya said that same shit to me. Mount street right?'

'Before you left, I told you that the boys upstairs were probably going to come and talk to me about you. And they did.'

'What did they say?'

The Tall Tales of Tatiana Blue

'They wanted to know if I'd seen you or heard from you or had any form of contact with the criminal mastermind called Tatiana Blue. Their words, not mine.'

'Wait, did they actually call me a criminal mastermind?! And what did you say?'

'Yeah they did and I said we just had sex and I can't wait to see you again. Of COURSE I said I hadn't seen you. But I did say I know where you would be.'

'Good boy.'

I caught myself staring at his face and having fantasies about waking him by squatting over his face.

'I knew about Mount Street before you got home.'

'How?' I frowned.

'Your two best friends in the whole world, Jamal and Femi.'

'Of course it was.'

'Soon as you left, they called me and told me you were back. Then I found Maya and...'

'Erm, yeah, how did you do THAT? Let's talk about how the fuck you ACTUALLY found me.'

Russell sipped his drink in a very sexy manner that agreed with me. 'One story at a time. So, I found Maya and we sat down and we talked and I made her an offer she couldn't refuse.'

Mr Oh

'Couldn't?'

'Wouldn't refuse. Because she saw the magic.'

'Magic?'

'Think about it Blue. You went off the grid. Having Charlotte meant that you fell off the radar and everyone started to think you had retired. I mean, it'd been long enough so we thought you'd just given it all in. And then, what happened?'

'Mount Street,' I sighed.

'Didn't help that there aren't too many black female shoe thieves out there who could actually pull off a Mount street job. Wasn't rocket science to figure out it was. What is it with you and those shoes?'

'They're a part of the holy trinity: Charlotte Olympia, Brian Atwood, Christian Louboutin.'

'Anyway, I came to Maya with an idea. What if the boys couldn't find you? What if they couldn't find you because you were dead? Then they'd have no reason to be looking for you, correct?'

Russell's mouth was turning me on something rotten. 'I smell you. Keep talking.'

'So I spoke to Maya and I told her what my idea was and she thought about it and why I was doing it and she saw the logic.'

'And all this before I'd even made it home with the shoe?' I laughed. 'Quincy?'

The Tall Tales of Tatiana Blue

'Maya spoke to him. Soon as she told him the plan, he was on-board. Said it would be a lot of fun. Hey, random question, what does he do?'

'I've known the dude for years and I still got nothing on that one.'

'He's got access to some weird shit.'

'I know, right?'

'Anyway, I got Quincy to do the prep work, Maya to do the thief work and you did the rest sweetie.'

I had no other expression for him except confusion. He'd made the last 12 – was it 14 – hours seem like an episode of *Breaking Bad*.

As he was talking, things were making sense in my head. If Russell knew about Mount Street before I came home to him then that would explain why Maya was gone soon as I got home and why I couldn't get her on the phone. She was too busy stealing my shit.

'But why those particular stash houses? Why not any of my London spots?'

'That was Maya and Quincy. He knew you had the least shoes in those spots, plus Maya thought it'd be better to leave the London spots untouched. Where are they by the way?'

'Yeah yeah,' I laughed. 'Whatever Jackson 5-0.'

Russell took another sip and I caught myself staring at his neck, watching his Adam's Apple bounce with each gulp.

'What about my shoes in the Thames?'

Mr Oh

'Casualties of war!'

My eyes widened. 'Really?! Did you just call suede Charlotte Olympia peep toe heels casualties of war? Who are you? I don't even know who you are.'

'You'll get over it. It's not like you don't still have how many other pairs of shoes.'

His attempt to deviate from the story while Charlotte hummed in my arms did not go unnoticed. 'What about the tracker? Was I meant to find it?'

'No, but Maya found it and activated it once we knew you were in Greece.'

'How did you know when I was in... Oh, your phone call.'

'Yep. Simple phone call talking about other things. You had no idea.'

'We were talking about Charlotte. Did you use my baby to distract and rob me Russell?'

'Well when you put it like that, yeah a little. And I feel bad about it. Ish.'

'Well good. You should.'

I kissed my sleeping daughter on the forehead and shared a knowing smile with Russell as a loud cheer went up from the other room.

'Any more questions?' Russell said, finishing his drink and standing up.

The Tall Tales of Tatiana Blue

'Hundreds of 'em but I'm hungry and I'm tired and, I really really could do with some dick.'

'And I could really REALLY do with giving you some. Just need to gimme a minute. I imagine there's gonna be a lot to...'

Russell's pocket began to vibrate and he pulled out his phone.

'Yellow!?'

'Your bird bit the dust mate,' a voice said as Russell put the phone on loudspeaker.

'Have they recovered a body yet?'

'They should have one before the end of the night. They've called in a lot of officers. Air, land, sea, they got the dogs out. It's like a terrorist attack the way London is lit up right now. Where are you?'

'I'm going back to the airport, see if there's something I can find there.'

'Listen, this is a shit show out here, all to find that dead bitch!'

'Who the fuck is...'

Russell muted the call, held the phone to his chest and looked at me with angry eyes. 'Shut up dead woman!'

I whispered. 'Oh yeah... sorry.'

'Sorry 'bout that boys, TV was too loud. How's it looking out there?'

'Like every policeman in London is here looking for her. It feels like we wanna find her just so we can see her face.'

Mr Oh

'But you two have seen her. Didn't she hit you with a shoe...'

'Alright, alright....'

I wasn't sure which one was talking. To be honest, they were both talking and I couldn't tell the difference. Although the last 'alright' sounded like Jamal, the cheeky one of the pair who tried to say I was slipping in my old age during the Mount Street job.

I didn't care cuz I was probably never gonna see them again. But I did hit him with a snowball so meh.

'We don't think she's dead!'

I was glaring at the contours of my baby's face and my eyes looked up to meet Russell's.

'What?!' he said hiding a laugh.

'It seems a little too easy. One night she comes out of retirement – out of fucking nowhere – then she's spotted twice and suddenly she can't drive a truck and crashes over a fucking bridge? With her shoes too? We've never been able to catch her with a shoe and then this?'

'I don't know. I didn't think of it like that. Maybe she needed to come out of... I mean did she retire?'

I closed my eyes, shook my head and mouthed the word no.

'Exactly... where did she go during all that...'

Russell didn't see me reaching for his phone as I took it from him, ended the call and handed it back to him while slowly rising to my feet.

The Tall Tales of Tatiana Blue

'Can we eat please? Mama needs to eat. Oh and keep an eye on those two. If they already don't think I'm dead then they'll be nosy in the future.'

Charlotte was peacefully hiding under her hands in my arms and I didn't care about whatever look he was giving me. I could feel his eyes on me. There were more important things at hand. I could smell chicken and curry goat and that was more important than the two policemen who were going to be a potential problem in the later days.

My man opened the door for me and the group all raised their glasses in my direction. I was standing there, still in my all-black outfit, feeling majorly topsy turvy and smelling a little bit funky. Topsy turvy from the day and the drink but mainly because my shoes were gone and I wasn't sure how I felt about it. I recognised one of the guys from the hangar who I hit in the neck with my Hotties and remembered how angry I was and how determined I was to get my shoes back. Hours later and I wasn't sure if I was happy they were gone or sad they were 'casualties of war', according to Russell.

'Here, lemme take her, I got a travel cot set up over there.'

He carefully slid Charlotte out of my arms and walked hunched over to a corner with a low light hanging high over a travel cot. I could hear him whispering little high-pitched mutterings to her and I found his back so damn attractive.

Walking through the door, my eyes were drawn straight to the big ass TV on the wall which was replaying the moment the truck went up and over the side of Southwark bridge and landed in the Thames. The news

Mr Oh

report showed the crash from different angles as the public sent in videos of their view.

'Whoa,' I stopped Russell as he walked back towards me.

'What about Aries? What's happened to her?'

He scanned the room with a new drink in his hand. 'She's erm... oh... hold on...'

His next few steps were quick ones in the direction of a man in a R.I.P Uncle Phil cap turned to the back with a chicken thigh hanging out of the side of his mouth. They exchanged a few words and the man pulled out a device that looked like a phone but had an extra-long antenna; satellite phone probably.

'She's here!' Maya shouted, opening the door of the aqueduct and walking in with a woman under her arm.

Everyone in the room turned and raised their glass before rushing towards the one I assumed was Aries. She was hi-fiving people and smiling and then she saw me.

Excusing herself from conversations and sliding a drink out of Russell's hand as she passed, she stopped right in front of me.

She was smaller than me by about three inches and the first thing I noticed was her bright smile. Her skin tone was the same shade of melanin with a touch of caramel as mine and she had box braids with blue tips instead of my trademark dreadlocks but, if you didn't know the difference, they'd look familiar. Body not far from mine in my prime,

The Tall Tales of Tatiana Blue

looked like she could handle herself and, most important, she was cute. As an impersonation of me, they did pretty damn good.

'Hello,' she said as I was taking her all in. 'My name is Aries and it is an honour and an absolute pleasure to meet you.'

With her hand held out, I smiled at her. Something about her was exciting me. There was an air of 'getting shit done' about her, plus she had a glimmer in her eye that said she'd been forced to make a life or death decision once or twice. Her hello said she knew my work and she held my hand longer than social norms dictate. She rubbed the back of my hand with her thumb and her smile went from sweet to seductive. I think Aries wanted to fuck.

This woman just drove off a bridge all in the name of saving my life. Well technically, ending it but I couldn't not appreciate her for it. Maybe Russell could be persuaded to bring her in once or twice.

'Aries, you are officially and automatically one of the bad bitches.'

Aries frowned. 'Thanks... I think."

'A bitch ain't a hole for a man to fill...' I started.

'...a bitch is a beauty in tremendously cute heels...' Maya shouted from across the room.

I scanned the crowd for her voice and saluted her. 'I don't know how many ways I can thank you for what you did.'

'No Biggie Smalls. It was a pleasure. Being chased by the police, driving off a bridge, faking your death. Where was I not having fun?'

Mr Oh

There it was. The something about her I felt click in me before any words were exchanged. She liked what she did. The excitement, the pleasure of fulfilling a task, the adrenalin pumping, I could see myself in her so much. We both laughed and I hugged the shit out of her.

I felt her hand caress my lower back.

'You hungry?'

'Starving. I had to float quarter of the way down the Thames before I could get out so I am fully Hank right now.'

She had to float down the Thames? Fuck me.

'Oh, and while we're on the subject, I just have to say it. You have or HAD one of the sexiest shoe collections I've ever seen. When we were taking them, I, God's honest truth, felt bad. They were too sexy to be stolen.'

'Too sexy to be stolen? And you say that to a shoe thief?'

We both laughed, gave each other a hi-five and another hug and I sent her to go and get something to eat.

There was a lot to compute and some of it still wasn't making any sense. But that wasn't a problem, I'd just ask Russell when I got on top of him and made my hips do the swirly jerk. That'll get all the answers I need.

Accepting congratulations from some, shaking hands of some more and discussing taser fighting techniques with some of my earlier victims, I was ready for food.

The Tall Tales of Tatiana Blue

Listen, let me tell you about the plate of food I made. It was epic. Legendary. Flavours on mouth-watering flavours.

I hit that table of food like a woman possessed. Macaroni and cheese, as standard, rice and peas, jollof rice with no peas or carrots, curry goat, stew peas, chicken (BBQ and roasted) and there was potato salad, avocados and green leaf salad on whatever space I had left on my plate.

With my war plate ready, I left the line and almost walked into Maya, who was laughing raucously with one of the guys who met my taser earlier on.

'SO!?' she said, hooking her arm with mine.

'So...' I replied.

'Are we good babe?'

I took a quick look around the room and laughed. 'You lot went IN, just for me. And you? You know what just hit me? Your first phone call.'

'What about it?'

'I asked you how many of my spots got hit and you said all of 'em.'

Maya grabbed my shoulders and laughed. 'Didn't that scare the shit out of you? Bet you hopped off the dick for that.'

'Listen, I was getting the sweetest, you know what, you're a cow for that but it DID work. I was on the phone to Quincy like THAT!'

'Are we good babe? You punched the shit out of me before.'

Mr Oh

'You're all good with me sugar pop. This food is about to have a problem though.'

'Yaaaaaay,' Maya screamed in my ear. 'Good, good, because I was speaking to one of the boys you put to sleep. Did you really shoot him in the groin with a...'

'For the self-preservation of my shoes, yes I bloody well did.' I said proudly.

'Wanna talk about how we're gonna replace those shoes?'

I sat down and began to map out how I was going to get through the big plate of food I had before me.

'See, that's why this is gonna get you a pass. Already coming up with ways to make it up to me. You ARE a good friend.'

'Damn right I am.'

'Where's Q-Ball?' I asked, planning to give him a dead leg when I saw him.

'Right here,' said a voice from behind me and I swivelled on my heels in surprise. 'Q-BALL!?!?!'

Standing before me in a t-shirt and jeans, Quincy smiled with his back-length dreadlocks tucked under a baseball cap.

MY BOY WAS HERE!

The Tall Tales of Tatiana Blue

'Dude, what the fuck are you doing here?' I said followed by a combination of punches to his arm and stomach. 'I should've known you wouldn't stay away from my death party.'

'And get the opportunity to pour a lil' alcohol out for those who didn't make it? Of course I had to come out.'

We laughed while I protectively held on to my piece of chicken. My first instinct was to look for Russell in the crowd but I could already feel his eyes on me. By the time I turned to find him, he was already standing behind me with a hand on my shoulder. Full 'she's mine' mode.

'So THIS is Quincy?' said Russell, holding a fajita wrapped in kitchen towel.

'Russell...' Quincy returned dryly. 'I'm glad you took my advice and went through with all this.'

Russell scoffed while Tatiana moved out of their space and watched from the sidelines, enjoying the testosterone that battled silently between them.

'I saw what was best for her and said why not,' Russell scoffed.

'But thank you Quincy. Thank you for everything you did.'

Watching them shake hands and share a smile did wonders for my ego and the warmth between my thighs was quite the sweet experience. Watching two of my sexual conquests standing in front of each other, looking like they wanted to throw down but professional respect was keeping them locked in a staring contest where neither of them smiled. Maya tapped me on the shoulder repeatedly while whispering in my ear.

Mr Oh

'Looooook at 'em...'

'I know... It's like I can see the threesome. I wonder...'

Russell broke the stare down. 'Let's get you some food.'

He led Quincy towards the food table while me and Maya watched them walk away with our mouths open, wondering what they'd talk about.

I turned to Maya and from the look in my eye, she knew what I was going to say.

'You want your shoes back don't you? I know, I know...'

'You know!' I said in her ear, still taking everything in around me.

'What you girls talking about?' Russell said, appearing between us out of nowhere.

'Replacing all my shoes that are currently floating down the Thames.'

'Can we talk about fucking first?' Russell said without skipping a beat.

Maya opened her eyes wide and raised her eyebrows before moving towards the food table. 'Wow,' she mouthed from a distance.

'Listen, I know you lot were probably talking about another job but you've gotta stop now Blue. You have a child now and a man who is in lo... a man who is happy that every day he will get to wake up next to you...'

'Whoa, whoa, whoa! Don't try and gloss over that like you didn't just choke on saying you love me for the first time.'

The Tall Tales of Tatiana Blue

My plate slipped out of my hand and I didn't care. Well I did a little but I could get more.

He looked sheepishly at the floor and blushed. I swear I wanted to fuck him right there.

I mean come on, big black policeman in charge looking shy and saying he's in love with me after just risking his career and his freedom to fake my death? He was so gonna get some after all this.

'Wait, helicopter and limo. Who set those up?'

'Maya. She knew you'd... '

'Do you love me Russell?'

He dropped dead silent. His eyes swung from the left to the right and he fiddled with his fingers.

'I might. Something about a woman steam rolling into your life and turning it upside down made me fall in love with you. Fucking criminal.'

I covered my mouth in fake horror. 'Now you're one too.'

'Yeah but they don't know that.'

Russell's phone went off with a message and I snatched it from him. It was a picture of a warehouse full of shoes. From the looks of the CCTV picture, they looked like Louboutins and Brian Atwood shoes but I'd need a closer look.

I deleted the message and gave him his phone back. I looked for Maya in the crowd and she spotted me and winked once.

Mr Oh

'I love you Tatiana Blue!' Russell said officially.

'And you should, I'm cut from a cloth of loveable, huggable sexiness.'

'Aren't you gonna say it back?'

I gave him a look. 'Who said I love you though. I'll tell you this. If you got me another plate of food, I know I'd feel more love TOWARDS you. It's your fault I dropped my food in the first place.'

'Kiss me you dead lunatic.'

Russell ran his fingers through my hair and I purred instantly. He brushed single 'locs from my face, licked his very LL-like lips and kissed me.

My neck, nipples, pussy, toes and every inch of skin on my body responded.

And yes, of course I was in love with Russell Reed. This is the man that risked everything for me and he did it with ease. Any man willing to go to those lengths was worthy of Blue love. He didn't need to know that though.

I'll tell him one day.

Our kiss ended. He picked up my dropped plate – food and all – and went straight to the food table where he began making another plate. For me.

I slipped his phone out of his pocket without him knowing.

Yep, my policeman was getting ME food.

The Tall Tales of Tatiana Blue

I replied to Maya's message, asking for the details, schematics of the building, security information, and the usual. She replied that she had them already and was ready and waiting for me.

I deleted the message with a smile.

That would have to wait though. There was a man who just declared his love for me who needed to be eating and showing me that he's serious about our future.

Then something hit me. A batch of 'I'll never be able to' came flooding into the front of my thoughts. I'll never be able to try on the Pierre Hardy Metallic Booties I got from Kylie, the Louboutin mesh sandals from Khloe and the Zanottis from Kim Kardashian, the Fendi zig zags from SAKS, the... Geez Louise, I lost a lot of shoes.

With a new plate in my hand, I cut a section of macaroni and cheese and took the room in. All these people were here to help me and, being much of a loner, it felt weird knowing all these people knew who I was and what I did.

'Shush,' someone said loudly in the room. 'They found a body.'

Everyone turned to the TV but I was first to stand in front of the screen. The reporter was standing on the banks of the Thames where I could see a Birman cage sandal washing up on the stone shore.

According to the unconfirmed report, divers found a body but that was all they were willing to say.

Russell slid up behind me. 'That's not us.'

Mr Oh

'So whose body is that?'

Russell shrugged.

To be honest, that was nothing to do with me. Hopefully, I'd be dead to the police and the media and all those other enforcement and security agencies that were looking for me. Dead to them all.

I had a very unconventional future ahead where me and Maya would keep stealing shoes and Russell would keep telling me to stop and I'd ignore him then give him some sweet, some nasty, some gushy stuff until the next time he asked.

Me, Russell and Charlotte. Living together, sleeping in the same bed and being happy. It was the straightforward albeit disjointed future I wanted.

'Kiss me criminal,' I said to Russell as he leaned over my shoulder. He nestled his face in my hair inhaling deeply and wrapping his hands around my waist.

'Anytime dead woman.'

'Love you co-conspirator.'

'Love you too thieving toerag.'

And that's me.

That's my story. Everything that happened to me and now I'm done.

The Tall Tales of Tatiana Blue

Don't miss me too much, I'll be around. Whenever you see a celebrity in amazing shoes looking fabulous, know I probably have those shoes now. Whenever you see a new shoe coming out, know that I've already been to the warehouse and picked a few for myself.

This is my life.

I am Tatiana Blue and I am STILL a beauty in tremendously cute heels.

Mr Oh

Enjoy a snippet from the my next book, a novella called

The League of Chocolate Gentlemen.

The Tall Tales of Tatiana Blue

Mr Oh

VALERIE   -   15th February, 21:48pm

A spreading echo of instruments against the tiled bathroom walls made Aretha Franklin's *Bridge Over Troubled Water* sound live as Valerie McKenzie pulled back her shower curtain. With a large towel wrapped on her head and another sliding back and forth across her back, she stepped onto a black bath mat, enjoying the feeling of Egyptian cotton between her toes.

Looking at herself in the mirror, she rested her hands on the sink and sighed, scrutinising the crow's feet in the corner of her eyes and skin slackening on her neck. Running her fingers over her marble sink, she finished drying herself and looked into her own eyes, preparing herself for the night she had arranged.

Hot air sucked through the vents, clearing the mirrors and bringing clear reality to her view.

'Miss Parker! You just don't know!' she said to herself.

Her chocolate hands rounded her breasts, down her hips and across her cheeks. She looked over her shoulder at her bum with cellulite and deep stretch stripes.

She sprayed Elizabeth Arden's Red Door on her neck and greased herself down with Astral, humming to the old school playlist that was playing *Close The Door* by Teddy Pendergrass. Her toes were tapping and she started swaying while brushing her teeth. Looking at her neatly arranged creams, perfumes, combs and brushes, Valerie exhaled deeply, ignoring a pain in her midsection and began to dance. Her electric toothbrush was doing the work while she was bouncing her breasts to the beat.

Her grin was genuine on her face as she used two cotton buds.

Smiling as she model walked from her en-suite bathroom, Valerie pushed open folders of houses and flats to the floor and sat down with a huff. She sprayed deodorant, second guessing her outfit which was hanging on the door of her walk-in wardrobe. A part of her wanted to change the shoes for something more delicious but she was advised by a

The Tall Tales of Tatiana Blue

blue-haired friend that they were the perfect heels for the occasion. She then thought the hair piece she'd chosen was wrong but she remembered what she was told by about the seductive combination.

'A bitch is never wrong!' Valerie mumbled to herself, stealing a quick look at the time which was beamed via laser onto one of the walls.

Blinds were drawn down over full-length windows which were blocking beautiful views of the London skyline. Her minimalist style was evident in her room with only a queen-sized bed, side table and full length mirror present.

Time gave her a pep in her step and she moved quicker. She looked in the mirror, putting on her hair, silk blue dressing gown and Stuart Weitzman black leg wrap leather sandals. She opened her dressing gown, ran her hands on her naked hips and laughed at her curves. Covering her mouth, she admired the draw-in of her waist, the fullness of her hips and the fact that she could see her behind from the front.

Her intercom interrupted the music as she closed her dressing gown and sashayed to the door, spanking herself as she walked with intention.

Mr Oh

QUÉ - 15th February, 21:51pm

Standing completely bald and fully bearded at the gate of Valerie's complex, Qué rang the intercom and waited. It wasn't the usual Valerie phone call he was used to receiving. Usually Valerie would call on a particular day and always featured a driver who would pick him up and drop him at Valerie's before dropping him home afterwards. Such was the way Valerie did things.

But on this occasion, Qué made his own way to the extravagant gated community that was currently cutting him off from his long-term friend with experienced benefits.

The intercom buzzed and the gate creaked open for him to enter. The silence of the night was slightly unnerving as the empty roads and pavements began to unnerve him. He felt like he was in the wrong place at the right time. Usually the driver passed through the gates and dropped him off at her door. He walked down Valerie's path with blue star creeper, beach strawberry and hazelnut shell plants leading the way to her door.

He was still wearing his work clothes, which consisted of a grey t-shirt, black cardigan, trousers and shoes. He had come straight from marking books when the idea of taking Valerie from behind pulled him out of his red pen zone.

He rang the doorbell, keeping his eyes on the surrounding apartments, enjoying a cool breeze that nipped at his ankles. He could feel the usual signs of nerves and adrenaline begin to flow through him.

With his head turned to the door, he could hear Valerie clipping and clopping on the other side.

'She's got heels on. It's about to be a dirty night methinks,' Qué mumbled to himself.

The lock began to shackle from the top of her door to the bottom and Qué followed with his eyes as the door opened. Bathed in red light,

The Tall Tales of Tatiana Blue

Valerie's heeled foot came into view followed by the rest her leg.
'Hey you,' she said, peeking around the door.
'Good evening,' he replied. 'You okay?'
'I'm fine thanks, you coming in or you waiting for a hand-job on the doorstep?'
He walked through the front door, taking her perfume in as he passed. From the corner of his eye, he could see a wealth of skin through her open dressing gown and the skin on his balls tightened. Valerie adventures were always that: adventures.
The art on her walls looked bathed in orange as he took his shoes off, shuffled in his socks and sat down. Valerie followed behind him, putting a Desperado Guarana with lime on a coaster on the table in front of him.
'Be right back,' she said and disappeared out of the room.
'Take your time,' Qué said, running a hand over his bald head.
A streaking guitar began as Chaka Khan's *Tell Me Something Good* started throughout the house and he couldn't help but nod his head.
He took a deep swig and almost choked as Valerie's intercom rang again.

Mr Oh

REECE   -   15th February, 21:53pm

Trains, buses and a long walk had Reece feeling hot and extremely bothered as he pressed the intercom for Valerie's home. Leaves danced behind the gated community as a subtle breeze rushed past his ankles. He fanned himself with his t-shirt, kicking his legs in his jeans trying to cool down.

The sound of the gate unlocking made him jump as it creaked open in front of him. He watched the neatly kept front gardens of Valerie's neighbours, admiring the colours and variations of the plants. He didn't know what type of plants they were but they caught his eye.

'Hmmm, maybe I should pick a few for V,' he giggled to himself.

He didn't make it up the path before Valerie's door opened and she leaned her head around the door. Her open dressing gown flowed in the breeze and her leg wrapped around the door.

'Coming in?'

Reece smiled brightly. 'Yeah I'm in there.'

Lifting his t-shirt, he ran his hand over his stomach showing the bottom of his six-pack. He watched her eyes light up as he slid through the door, taking a playful pat on his backside as he kicked his shoes off

'Easy baby, you know I got enough long diiii...' he trailed off. The other man sitting on the sofa drinking his favourite drink made him pause.

'Reece, this is Qué. Qué, this is Reece.'

From the moment his eyes locked onto him, Reece sized him up. They were near enough the same height, same build, he was bald and chocolate where Reece was more caramel infused with lighter tones thanks to his father's Trini roots. Valerie ran a hand up his back - a spot

The Tall Tales of Tatiana Blue

she knew very well - and walked past him with her dressing gown flowing around her, revealing slivers of skin. He couldn't help feeling torn.

Qué stood up and offered a hand out while Reece was expecting a fist-to-fist. He shook his hand and muttered something that sounded like a greeting.

'Yeah don't worry, I'm as lost as you are,' Qué said, noticing Reece's uncomfortable disposition.

He nodded back, looked him up and down then away to the walls. Valerie always had her rooms lit up in different colours but tonight, the colours were melting together slowly with some very smooth soul he didn't recognise.

From behind, Valerie ran another hand on his back and appeared in front of him with a Desperado.

Valerie waved a hand and the music muted. With a colourful drink of her own, she took Reece by the hand and sat him next to Qué before standing in front of them with one hand on her hip, demanding their attention.

'Right boys. Let's not act like we don't know what this is. If you don't think you can do it, no problem. I'll get a driver to take you home. If not, you know where the playroom is.'

Valerie flowed out of the room waving her hand on the way to the stairs.

Mr Oh

Printed in Great Britain
by Amazon